Emma Donoghue is an award-winning writer. Born in Dublin in 1969, she now lives in Canada with her family. Her novels are the international bestseller Room, which was a finalist for the 2010 Man Booker Prize, *The Sealed Letter*, *Life Mask*, *Slammerkin*, *Hood* and *Stir-fry*. Her short-story collections are Astray, *Three and a Half Deaths*, *Touchy Subjects*, *The Woman Who Gave Birth to Rabbits* and *Kissing the Witch*, and her works of literary history include *Inseparable*, *We Are Michael Field* and *Passions Between Women*. In a career that has bridged lesbian and mainstream literature, she is widely acknowledged for having made lesbian themes accessible to a much wider audience

D1150784

79 661 362 5

Love Alters

Lesbian Stories

Edited by Emma Donoghue

ROBINSON

Constable & Robinson Ltd
55–56 Russell Square
London WC1B 4HP
www.constablerobinson.com

First published in the UK as *The Mammoth Book of Lesbian Short Stories*
by Robinson Publishing Ltd, 1999

This edition published by Robinson
an imprint of Constable & Robinson Ltd., 2013

A copy of the British Library Cataloguing in
Publication data is available from the British Library

ISBN: 978-1-47210-985-9 (paperback)
ISBN: 978-1-47210-986-6 (ebook)

Printed and bound in the UK

1 3 5 7 9 10 8 6 4 2

Contents

Acknowledgments

I would like to thank those who suggested or recommended stories, lent an ear or a book: Ailbhe Smith, Alison Hennegen, A. S. Byatt, Carole Nelson, Deborah Ballard, Debra Westgate, Gillian Spraggs, Joyce Chester, Margaret Monod, Maria Walsh, and Paulina Palmer.

The editor and publisher are grateful to the following for permissions granted:

Dorothy Allison, for "River of Names", from *Trash* (Firebrand Books, Ithaca, New York 14850, US, 1988), copyright © Dorothy Allison, 1981

Rebecca Brown, for "The Dark House", from *The Terrible Girls*, copyright © Rebecca Brown, 1990

Anne Cameron and Harbour Publishing, for "Did'ja Ever Hear of a Goolieguy?", from *Women, Kids & Huckleberry Wine* (Harbour Publishing, 1989), copyright © Anne Cameron, 1989

Christine Crow, for "If Pigs Could Fly", copyright © Christine Crow, 1999

Jane DeLynn, for "Puerto Rico", from *Don Juan in the Village*, copyright © Jane DeLynn, 1990

Elise D'Haene, for "Self-Deliverance", copyright © Elise D'Haene, 1995

Emma Donoghue, for "The Tale of the Kiss", from *Kissing the Witch* (London: Hamish Hamilton and New York: Joanna Cotler Books), copyright © Emma Donoghue, 1997, used by permission of HarperCollins Publishers and Penguin

Mary Dorcey, for "A Country Dance", from *A Noise from the Woodshed* (London: Onlywomen), copyright © Mary Dorcey, 1985

Marion Douglas, for "Magic Eight Ball", copyright © Marion Doulas, 1999

Patricia Duncker, for "Aria Nova", from *Monsieur Shoushana's Lemon Trees* (London: Serpent's Tail, 1997), copyright © Patricia Duncker, 1997

Dale Gunthorp, for "Kermit's Room", copyright © Dale Gunthorp, 1999

Susan Hampton, for "The Lobster Queen", from *Surly Girls* (HarperCollins, 1990), copyright © Susan Hampton, 1990

Jane Harris, for "Monopoly", first published in *The Crazy Jig* (Edinburgh: Polygon, 1992), copyright © Jane Harris, 1992

Annamarie Jagose, for "Milk and Money", copyright © Annamarie Jagose, 1990

Aileen La Tourette, for "A Triangular Eye: 1, 2, 3", from *Weddings and Funerals*, by Aileen La Tourette and Sara Maitland (Brilliance Books, 1984), copyright © Aileen La Tourette, 1984

Tanith Lee, for "Love Alters", copyright © Tanith Lee, 1983

Jenifer Levin, for "La Bruja", from *Love and Death & Other Disasters: Stories 1977–1995* (Firebrand Books, Ithaca, NY 14850, U.S.), copyright © Jenifer Levin, 1996

Anna Livia, for "Pamelump", copyright © Anna Livia, 1984

Elizabeth A. Lynn, for "The Woman Who Loved the Moon", from *Amazons!* (DAW Books), copyright © Elizabeth A. Lynn, 1979

Ingrid MacDonald and Women's Press (Canada), for "The Catherine Trilogy", from *Catherine, Catherine* (Toronto: Women's Press), copyright © Ingrid MacDonald, 1991

Sara Maitland, for "The Burning Times", from *Telling Tales* (London and West Nyack, NY: The Journeyman Press), copyright © Sara Maitland, 1983

Shani Mootoo, for "Out on Main Street", from *Out on Main Street* (Vancouver: Press Gang Publishers), copyright © Shani Mootoo, 1993

Jane Rule (in Canada) and George Borchardt, Inc. on behalf of the author (in the world excluding Canada) for "Middle Children" from *Theme for Diverse Instruments* (Vancouver: Talonbooks, 1975), copyright © Jane Rule, 1975

Ali Smith, for "Free Love", from *Free Love* (London: Virago), copyright © Ali Smith, 1995

Michelene Wandor, for "Some of My Best Friends", copyright © Michelene Wandor, 1986

Marnie Woodrow, for "In the Spice House", from *In the Spice House* (Minerva Canada), copyright © Marnie Woodrow, 1996

Shay Youngblood, for "Funny Women", from *The Big Mama Stories* (Firebrand Books, Ithaca, New York 14850, US), copyright © Shay Youngblood, 1989

For the women of Vic Road,
past, present and future.

Introduction

The custom is to start anthologies of lesbian short stories with a
good two pages of hand-wringing. Given that short stories
neither wear T-shirts with slogans on them nor go to bed with
each other (except between the covers of anthologies), in what
sense do they have sexual identities?

There are two basic approaches to this issue: the biographical
and the thematic. Recent years have seen a number of excellent
anthologies of short fiction by self-defined lesbians writing
about anything they like. But these have tended to produce a
focus on North American authors writing within and to their
lesbian communities. What I wanted for this anthology was a
broader gathering of writers and a more international range (in
style as well as subject matter) to the stories.

The twenty-nine authors showcased in the *Mammoth Book of
Lesbian Short Stories* have little in common, then, but the fact
that they have at one time or another written on lesbian themes.
Coming from all over the world – England, Ireland, Scotland,
Wales, South Africa, the US, Canada, Jamaica, Trinidad,
Australia and New Zealand – they are women of all persuasions,
whose erotic lives and labels (if they agree to wear any at all) are
not at issue here.

Lesbian-themed short stories have been written since the
second half of the nineteenth century, but the literature shows a
clear watershed around 1970. New York's Stonewall Riots of
June 1969, the subsequent movements of Gay Liberation and,
perhaps even more importantly, Women's Liberation, left an
indelible mark on lesbian fiction. Jane Rule's work often explores

both sides of this line; for instance, in her early story from *The Ladder* magazine, "Middle Children", we watch a lesbian couple move from a discreetly closeted partnership at college towards a quietly radical experiment in communal living. Similarly, Michelene Wandor's narrator (in "Some of My Best Friends") reminisces about the time before words were put to things – "i didn't know about the word lesbian then, id just got on with it and not known what it was called" – and the time afterwards, when labels were firmly glued on.

This anthology explores the modern side of that watershed. Before 1970, the important works of lesbian literature tended to be isolated novels but, in the last three decades, the short story seems to have become the favourite genre. Anthologies – with their multiplicity of voices, their relatively egalitarian and collective vision – have become enormously popular, and have created an encouraging atmosphere in which new writers, in particular, find themselves able to publish work on themes still considered off-puttingly controversial elsewhere. At the end of the 1990s, the only difficulty in compiling a collection of three decades of superb lesbian stories is that there are so many to choose from.

But this is not a "Best of", or a round-up of familiar classics of the genre. Well-known authors are represented here, but not by their best-known work; I am particularly grateful to Marion Douglas, Christine Crow and Dale Gunthorp for giving me brand-new unpublished stories. Many others, especially US authors who are widely anthologized, have been left out to make room for less familiar names. Stories by writers of more than fifty books sit alongside new fiction by women who have not yet published one, and both kinds, I think, profit by the juxtaposition.

Parts of the mainstream media still cling to a clichéd perception of lesbian culture as stuck in a timewarp circa 1970; witticisms about leg hair, man-hating, tofu and political correctness continue to do the rounds. As a contrast, I have decided to emphasize the contemporary; the majority of these stories come from the 1990s. But Jane DeLynn's narrator in "Puerto Rico" reminds us not to generalize about decades and their prevailing moods. This is a 1990s story set in the 1970s; it cuts across the grain of the kind of fiction in which the discovery of a same-sex orientation is experienced as a profound homecoming. As DeLynn's narrator remarks about gays and lesbians in the age of disco:

> Disillusionment had already begun to set in, a disillusionment similar to that in love when you realise that the two who thought they were one are really two after all.

Some of my biases will be obvious. For this collection I wanted to gather stories that read, and satisfied, like stories; I excluded "short shorts", prose poetry, and excerpts from novels. The one novella included is an outstanding triangle of interlocking fictions, Ingrid MacDonald's "The Catherine Trilogy".

Though a huge proportion of lesbian fictions still concentrates on the rites of passage of coming out and getting (and losing) the girl, and the naturalistic "two dykes in a flat" premise continues to thrive, that is not the whole story by any means. Something that surprised me in researching this anthology was the number of explorations of a formerly taboo topic, the sexuality of young girls. Part One, "Child's Play", groups stories in which a child or teenager becomes aware either of her own nascent lesbian feelings or those of the adults round her. Moving from the confusions of pre-puberty to the first claiming of adult autonomy, these contrasting stories stake out a new territory in lesbian fiction.

"Present Tense" brings together a variety of short fictions about contemporary adult life which share a (literally tense) preoccupation with sex and romance. The object of desire is frequently elusive: unnamed, unknowable, out of reach, or dead.

In the third section, "Family Values", a phrase co-opted by right-wing fundamentalists is reclaimed as an umbrella term for stories with very different angles on domestic life. Lesbians are seen in relationship to the families that raised them, their ethnic communities, and the children they give birth to or are startled to find themselves co-parenting. The final story by Elise D'Haene, a superb example of a sub-genre that grew up in the 1990s, is about the profoundly familial alliances sometimes formed between lesbians and gay men.

"Past Times" brings together two fairytales set in imagined pre-modern eras, and a historical story and a trilogy which make art out of real historical moments of unbearable pain. Lesbian historical fiction is a growing genre; this reflects, I think, a new cultural confidence, and a consequent ability to write ourselves into the past in different ways.

Finally, a very eclectic section called "Possibilities" emphasizes the new tendencies in lesbian fiction of the last fifteen or so years to explore outside the boundaries of naturalism. Some of these stories are subtly surreal, while others incorporate folklore images into everyday life, and one is set in a future society where same-sex relationships are the conservative norm.

Lesbian literature has always had certain gifts from the fairy godmother. Its strengths include a disregard for taboos, and an ability to question traditional structures and values (literary as well as social). The best of lesbian fiction is enlivened by a sense of wonder and vision, as well as a certain ethical urgency: a conviction that how we live our personal lives has an impact on the wider world. And increasingly, the freshness of this genre's themes and preoccupations is being matched by a daring originality of style.

I hope the varied pleasures offered by this harvest of fiction will amount to a better definition of the modern lesbian short story than any I could invent.

CHILD'S PLAY

Child's Play

In many countries, there is no "age of consent" for lesbian relationships; legislatively, they don't exist. In others, the legal age is set at the same age as for heterosexual relationships, or a few years later. But what the stories gathered in this section explore – all but one of them being written in the first person, significantly – are the secretive, captive years before adulthood, in which a girl's life is not yet her own. To name the feelings described in these stories as lesbian is to acknowledge that children have their own sexuality, which is not to say that it is the same as that of the adults around them.

Lesbian coming-of-age novels sometimes make the mistake of presenting identity as crystal clear, the crossword puzzle that needs only to be filled in. (*I always knew I was different, because I hated skirts and liked softball; now I know I'm gay, and that explains everything.*) What unites the stories I have chosen for this section is a much greater complexity, a recreation of the polymorphous perversity of the young. In Jane Harris's punchy study of "Monopoly" – a wholesome euphemism for a game that must be played on a big bed – there is no word for what these girls are to each other, nor are they searching for one. Instead, the narrator offers us the most vivid, concrete, colloquial words for what the two of them do together, and what she feels about it. Their explorations take place in the context of the traditional childhood games of doctors and nurses, prisoner and guard. Harris's story raises one of the most common themes of this genre: the parting of the ways. Why does the intense female bonding of girlhood last for some and not for others? The girls in

"Monopoly" are starting to pull apart; the friend has started "sucking up to boys recently", whereas the tough-minded narrator is clinging to a game that is almost over, "deciding my next move".

In Anna Livia's highly controversial story of a friendship and its mixed motives, the eleven-year-old narrator and her friend are divided from the start by the disabilities that keep Pamela – a girl of extraordinary abilities who defiantly names herself "Pamelump" – in a wheelchair. But the two children forge a shaky alliance against the cruelties of a South Africa riven by race and class, and create a world of play which shuts out adults and their qualms:

> They're always turning grey, or green, or shakey, and you have to go on as if you hadn't noticed. How they feel is their problem and you have to keep it that way.

Livia adopts a light and naturalistic style for this account of an appalling choice that will mark the narrator forever. Her story raises painful questions, such as, how responsible is a child? Is it an individual's right to decide whether her life is worth living? And how much can be demanded in the name of love?

"Don't judge a book by looking at its cover", warns one of the characters in Shay Youngblood's story about how a child-hood passion can shape a whole life. The disarmingly homey opening gives way to a startling story of poverty and emotional loss. The slow retelling of the lives of various "Funny Women" to the young narrator is just as important as what gets told; the old woman can only reveal her childhood secrets to a child. The stories of Miss Tom, Miss Juliette, Miss Ruth and Miss Lily all intertwine; love takes on different faces but never fades. What holds their narratives together is a strange Southern landscape where women can pass as men, black people as white, and incest can be the worst betrayal or the sweetest romance.

The two girls in Marion Douglas's drily funny story of small-town Canadian life in the sixties, "Magic Eight Ball", invent a microcosmic world inhabited by the McCrackens, a tiny doll family. Mrs McCracken, her blue plastic skirt whittled off with a knife, becomes a surreal and contrary oracle. Sexuality is only one of the many enigmas that puzzle the young narrator of this story, whose yen for both a girl and a boy leads her to conclude that "Love is an expanded and slightly shameful feeling, like stretched out elastic bands from old underpants."

Accusations of abuse of trust often overshadow narratives about desire between teenagers and adults; this is "dodgy territry", as Jane Harris's narrator would spell it. In Susan Hampton's "The Lobster Queen", it is the fourteen-year-old girl who begs the thirty-year-old wife and mother to "kiss me properly", but that does nothing to simplify the ethics of what lies between them. This haunting story captures the pervasive feeling of "waiting" in adolescence, the "frozen zones". The woman teaches the girl to fish, to seek out the point of balance between greed and patience.

> Later the girl will write the letter and hide it, unable to post it in case the opening of questions closes everything that has happened.

The eighteen-year-old narrator in Ali Smith's "Free Love" is on the threshold of adulthood as she briefly escapes her Scottish town for a weekend in Amsterdam. This peculiarly moving story manages to handle the rarely mentioned subject of lesbian prostitution alongside that of exuberant teenage love. Finally, the "sordid" intervenes, bringing betrayal and loss, but the vision at the heart of this story lingers: "It's free, she said, the first time should always be free."

Monopoly

Jane Harris

These your wee milk bottles? says Campbell. This where the milk comes out?

Uh-huh.

Can I get the milk? says Campbell. Does it come out for me?

Uh-huh.

We're supposed to be playing Monopoly by the way. Least that's what we told Campbell's mum.

We're needing the big bed in your room so's we can spread the board out, alright Mrs Campbell? I said. Oh aye. It's always Monopoly we say we're playing. Sometimes we do play it, just for show right. Personally I hate the game.

Campbell puts her mouth to one of the pink lumps on my chest. I can feel her nipples, the fold of her breasts. See sometimes I hate my stupid stuntit efforts. Campbell sucks. I'm like that, out of breath; it's a dead weird feeling, pure exciting.

See if my mum knew.

Of course no milk comes out. I hope not anyhow. I've not had a baby yet anyway. Campbell says she can have weans soon if she wants to. I asked mum about that and she said that was right what Campbell said. If that's what she's wanting, my mum said.

Mum's not that keen on Campbell. See Campbell's mum and dad used to stay up the Drum and my mum thinks she's a bad inflence.

Course, to have weans you need boys. Campbell's been pure sucking up to boys recently by the way. Last week we were hanging about up the road as usual waiting for the van and this Smitty comes stoating along with his mates. First of all right she

just ignored them right, just normal. Then she keeps asking us if
they're looking over. So I says naw. Because they weren't. Then
she starts shouting at them like a pure headcase, slagging them.
So I says shut it but she wouldn't shut it so right then pure
brassneck; they come over and she was like that, ending herself.
Like a big daft lassie.

That Smitty's nearly seventeen. Fancies his barra. Campbell
was like that, talking to him right, just ignoring me. I could of
been emdy.

She gives me a thorough examination. When she's the
doctor she always says: I'm going to give you a really thorough
examination, Miss Ferguson. Not like me. I get bored real
quick with arms and legs and stuff. I'm like that, just examin-
ing the interesting bits. This is just one of the games we've got
by the way. We've got all kinds. My favrite is "captured". That's
when one of us is prisner right and the other one's the capturer.
And the capturer gets to do whatever they want to the prisner.
That's pure brilliant. Campbell likes it too. She likes being the
capturer.

Sumdy's comin up the stair.

That's the ball up on the slates.

If we'd of went in Campbell's room we'd of been left in peace.
In here the place'll be going like a ferr cozits her mum and dad's
room. I told her that the smornin stupid cow.

I'm like that, pulling my T-shirt down and tucking masel in.
Panickstations. Monopoly pieces all over the shop man, in the
covers, spilt across the board. I'm staring at them, kidding on
I'm deciding my next move. But inside I'm thinking, emdy that
knew enthin about Monoply'd be onty us: the wee dug and the
racer in the middle of the board right, and there's a coupla hotels
in the jail by the way.

It's Campbell's dad.

He says it's the two of us he's after and in he comes.

Me and Campbell look up from concentrating on our game,
the both of us pure astonisht that it could be us he's looking for.
Mr Campbell says he's been out the back and it's come to his
attention that his gnome's got no head left. Been knocked right
aff, he says.

He settles down on the bed like he's preparing hissel for a long wait at the bus-stop. He pushes his eyebrows up at us. I look over to Campbell, right, wondering if it's OK to laugh. It's not. Campbell's frowning away good style like she's trying to imagine what in heaven's name could of happened to the poor gnome's head. Which is intresting since it was her that threw the brick at it.

Mr Campbell's waiting. He makes a face like he's got all the time in the world. He's no bothered about the Monopoly. Obviously not an affishonado. He's tall, Campbell's dad. Old-fashioned looking.

Puts brillcream in his herr.

He looks right like one of they dads in the rcading books we got in Primary school, the dads that were always in the garage sorting the car with the boy. Not like my dad, he's modren. My dad makes cakes for my mum when she's out at work. And we've no got a car.

My dad says that's because of the ozone layer.

It was me Mr Campbell, I say. I broke it.

Oh, says Campbell's dad. Right. He looks down at his shoes. He bends over and starts rubbing away at his toecaps, trying to get more of a shine on them.

Jacquie was away round the front, I say. We were playing, a . . . a game. I banged intit. It was a accident. Campbell's staring at me as if I'm pure mental by the way. But she'd get skelped see, if he knew it was her. I'll get nothing.

Oh, says Campbell's dad again. He straightens up. He's got a big riddy from bending over. Well, Elspeth, he says. Just you be more careful.

Yes Mr Campbell.

Anyway, he says. Time yous two were getting interested in boys, not playing boys' games out the back eh. He pats Campbell on the leg. Aye, Jacqueline? he says.

Yes dad, says Campbell. She'll not look at me. She knows this is dodgy territry.

Where do yous stay? she said to that Smitty last week.

You know fine where they stay, I said. They're Drum boys. And she's like that, kicking us. So they said they stayed up

Kinfauns and then she says that's where she used to stay before her mum and dad flitted. And that Smitty says who's this? pointing in my direction and Campbell looks at me and you'd swear she didn't know the answer by the way. Ventually she says: Just one of the lassies from Stonedyke, she says. Just one of the lassies. Then Smitty says, Oh aye, a snob, and Campbell doesn't say nothing, just blows a stoater with her hubbabubba. I'm not chewing mines but.

I'm just standing there with my mouth open.

Bealing.

Not that she'd of noticed, she was already up the road with Smitty and that. See you later, she shouts back. Chomping away at her hubba, making it go crack, crack. I'm telling you that's cruelty to bubblegum by the way.

Just as well she was away up the road but or I'd of punched her lamps out.

So she's not looking at me the now, because she knows what she'll get later. She's lucky I'm still speaking to her. I told her how it was going to be, she could have me and nobody else. Not Smitty, not any boy. And if I so much as saw her looking sidieways at emdy, that'd be it. Jotters. I'd not come round any more and she'd always have to be on her tod. See, she's not got any other friends right, there's nobdy ages with her round here and all the one's my age don't like her cos she's weird.

So I just reminded her about that and I tellt her how it'd be.

See our Jacqueline's wearing a bra now Elspeth, says Campbell's dad. He says that every time I'm here. Every time. He's taking the mick right because I've not got one. He pings the strap.

Leave dad, just leave, says Campbell. Her face is all went pink.

Soon be shaving her armpits, he says. Me and her mother'll not be able to get into the bathroom. She'll be in there, shaving anything that moves. He laughs. He thinks this is a great joke. Funny thing when he laughs Mr Campbell, there's not much noise. He just sort of wheezes a bit and rocks backn forwars.

Look dad, just forget it, says Campbell. Okay? She's near enough bubbling. She comes round my side of the bed and starts picking oose off the covers.

Are you wanting money for your gnome, Mr Campbell?

Aye hen, he says. A hundred quid. He lifts a hundred pound note out of the bank and folds it into his pocket. Then he starts laughing again. Hee haw pure bloody hilarious Mr Campbell. Just don't let it happen again, he says, in between gasping. Okay? He's more weirder than Campbell is.

Okay, I say. He winks at the both of us then off he goes wheezing. Me and Campbell wait till he's down the stair then we start picknup the pieces of the game and putting them back in the box.

He'll not be back now, I say.

Campbell's saying nothing. She keeps shuffling the Chance cards.

Haw deafie, I say. What if we do "captured"? C'mon, you can be the capturer and we can be, Americins, Americin spies. She likes that, specially, when we're Americins. We can do the ones she like more often then she'll not be bothered with that Smitty character.

She's still not saying nothing but. Taken the hump.

Sometimes I really like her by the way, then other times I'm like that, can't be bothered. She thinks she's brilliant know what I mean, just cos she's got a new bra and a couple herrs on her fanny.

Pamelump

Anna Livia

When Pamela's mum heard me calling her daughter "Pamelump", she went all grey and quiet. Not grown-up type serious, like when they catch you telling a dirty joke, or saying a rude word, but really grey, like after someone's been sick. I thought she was going to burst into tears, if she didn't hit me first. Pamelump noticed everything: her mum going grey, me being scared I'd get the belt, then scared I'd hurt her mother. Pamelump always noticed. She had to. We went right on playing, though. First, because it wasn't fair to strain Pamelump's memory by making her keep too much for too long. Seeing as she couldn't just note things down like I could. Second, because you have to. They're always turning grey, or green, or shakey, and you have to go on as though you hadn't noticed. How they feel is their problem and you have to keep it that way. All they want is to pass it on to you.

Actually, the rules were more complicated than that because, whatever you do, and however much you go on playing, they have said it, and you have heard it. They were Pamelump's rules. She said sometimes it was much worse when everyone pretended, because then she couldn't be offended, or angry, or anything.

When we were younger and the driver took us into town, I wheeled Pamelump places to look at windows and shops or to play with water. I had to steer her over the smoothest ground, and make sure to check beforehand that her tyres were full but not hard, otherwise she got jolted down in the chair and couldn't see anything but sky. All the kids would crowd round.

"Why's she in a chair? She's older than my boetje and he walks by himself."

"Can I push? My mum lets me push our baby."

"Where's your legs? Why've you got no legs?"

"Never grew in my mum's tummy." Her most generous explanation.

"Forgot to bring them, didn't I?" When she was feeling sarky.

"Same place as my arms." That's when she was angry and wanted to shock. It's such a small town, Luanshya; most of the kids knew her. But there were always some. A cousin from Ndola or a new family fresh out from Scotland. They said that no one had warned them, but I think some kids are naturally spiteful. Then they'd want to see what she looked like under the shawl, even the ones who'd looked before. They wanted to see how a shoulder goes when it doesn't have an arm on it. I know what they wanted because I was like that when my mum first told me. Now that I've washed her and dressed her, shaken her with fury and patted her so often, I know what she looks like. Just exactly the way you would expect a girl to look who doesn't have arms or legs. Where you or me go on, she stops. That's all.

Her mother had the African dressmaker cut Pamelump trousers with long legs, long-sleeved shirts, to pretend she might have arms and legs to fill them. But Pamelump complained she couldn't use her stumps with all that cloth flapping around. If people didn't like the look of her, they could look elsewhere. Well, the kids looked and the grown-ups looked away. I couldn't tell which hurt Pamelump worse. She made excuses why we couldn't go places: the shops had too many steps, it was too hot to sit under a shawl. Then we stopped going anywhere except the bush and the farm where we wouldn't meet anyone who didn't belong to Pamelump.

Pamelump didn't really need to go anywhere. Her teachers came to her and she sent things away to England for correcting. Mostly her books returned marked "excellent". Pamelump was more proud of that than anything because the English teachers didn't know about her and couldn't have been marking her up. She worked out everything in her head then typed it with her chin, or checked it on her computer, though she had to program the computer. Her mother asked if I'd like to have my lessons with Pamelump, too. I would've, very much, even though Pamelump was a year older and much quicker. But my mum said, "I do draw the line at that. I'm afraid I really do draw the line at that. We said you could befriend her, and with your father away the money comes in handy, Lord knows, but really! If you spend any more time with that poor little lump, you'll forget what normal is."

Pamelump was my best friend, but I did have other friends. Girls at school I could run, skip and play British bulldog with, so I wasn't in any danger. Besides, with the radio and the papers, and the way people acted, Pamelump knew what normal was and she wasn't even it.

"My mum says it's really kind of you to go and sit with that poor little Pamela."

"My mum says she'll die soon and that's a kindness to all. They don't live past puberty."

"What's puberty?"

Pamelump used to ask me what my friends said. She already knew about puberty. She was watching out for it. And she knew all my friends' names. Her mother invited them to her birthday parties and some of them would come, on their best behaviour. But they could really only play British bulldog and skipping, so they weren't much fun for Pamelump.

"We going on the trampolines, Wendy, you coming with?"

"Ner. Pamelump's driver's coming for me."

"You play there every arvo. They should get a black to sit with her." I didn't like having to tell Pamelump what the other girls said. I didn't like the way she called them "your friends", as though I agreed with them. It wasn't as though she didn't know. I already said about her noticing everything.

"You only come because my mother pays you. You're just like all the other shoppers."

"Shoppers" is what she called people paid for friendship. She was like that about the servants too. They were always kind to her, but she said it was because they were Africans and had no choice. She wanted them to love her just because. I said it was true we were poor, and my mum needed the money with my dad away, but I came to see her because she was my friend. She ignored that and asked: "Where's your dad, then?"

"Away."

"Away where?"

"He'll be home soon."

"I know where your dad is."

"Where is he, then?"

"He's in prison."

"No, he's not."

"He is."

"How do you know anyway?"

"Cos I read the papers not Teddy Bear Annual."

I didn't know what to say. "He never did it. He's an innocent man."

"Never did what?"

"What they say."

Pamelump looked at me. "He sold tickets on the trains. But sometimes he didn't give any ticket. He kept the money instead."

"No, he never. My mum says he never. And they're going to prove it and then they'll have to let him out and apologise in front of everyone."

Pamelump sneered at me, "So my only friend is a liar and her father's a thief."

If it would of been anyone else, I would of slapped her. Instead I sneered right back, "And my only friend has no arms, no legs and no brain."

"Your dad's cape coloured."

"And your mum lets her daughter play with one cos no one else would do it."

"See, see!" yelled Pamelump, "I was right all along. You only come cos you're paid to. You shopper. Shopper. Shopper. Tickey hopper."

"I won't be your friend any more."

"Then what will your mum do? Have to get a job instead of sending you out."

"She's got a job." And then I remembered and started to cry and couldn't stop. Usually Pamelump's good about crying, but after what she said I didn't want to be anywhere near her anymore. I ran out into the bush and hid in the mealies.

"So you're a coward as well as a liar," Pamelump stormed at me from her chair. I should have heard it bumping over the ground. "You can just run off and leave me."

"And you can get Benjamin to wheel you after." Benjamin turned away to examine the mealies. We got used to having our rows in front of people.

"Well," said Pamelump, as if she was beginning to be nice again, "what are you so upset about?"

"My mum," I told her, "she fainted at work. They sent her home. Now she's scared they won't take her back cos of my dad. They keep telling her to stay home and rest and it must be a very difficult time for her."

"Why did she faint?"

"Cos she didn't eat anything. I never noticed. She always said she ate breakfast after me and my brothers went to school. But it wasn't true. She didn't eat anything."

"Why though?" asked Pamelump, "Why didn't she eat? Was it because she was upset?"

"No! There wasn't anything to eat. She gave it all to us."

"It's alright, Wendy. It's not your fault. You just thought you were being good and eating your breakfast not to worry your mother."

"Yes," I sniffed, "I didn't know."

"And my mum will give your mum some money. Till your dad gets out."

"No," I said, "my mum wouldn't take it."

Pamelump looked at me. A funny little look, like making a child confess she's fibbing.

"No, honestly. She hates taking your mum's money."

"Then my mum must ring up the shop where she works and tell them they can't sack her."

"You can't tell your mum anything," I said. "My mum says the fewer know the better."

"Mum's alright about most things," said Pamelump. "It's only me she's funny with."

I don't know what Pamelump told her mother, but they let my mum go back to work and she had her meals in the canteen like salaried staff. After they'd eaten. All alone in the great big kitchen.

Pamelump did all sorts of things no one else did. I don't just mean thinking up strings to pull with her teeth, levers she could press with her tongue, but the games we played. She stored it in her memory to save herself the trouble of moving things around. She would think through whole crossword puzzles or chess games, just gazing at the empty pattern, and she was always right the times she asked me to write it down for her. That's how she played our games, but she made up no-arms-no-legs-games that were much more exciting. She said if you thought who got paid how much for doing what, it was obvious that all work consisted of was moving things around in the world. The further you were from the actual moving, the more you got paid. So we played moving games, where you touch nothing and remember everything.

"I give up, Pamelump, I don't know how Vincenza The Invincible is going to escape Brute Beit. You've got her hanging upside down on a meat hook, and it's Cecil Rhodes' Birthday so even if she gets away, no one will be around to give her tickey for a phone call."

That's when Pamela's mother turned grey.

"Wendy, dear, I'm afraid it's time for you to go now. I'll drive you. No need to wait for Benjamin."

But you remember it all, don't you, Pamelump? Because it's you I'm talking to. There isn't anyone else. There simply isn't. I wonder if you knew what it would be like afterwards? I tell the story to myself often, to keep it alive, and it sounds strange now. Written down. I have never spoken of it to anyone. Never. To anyone. Do you know what that means? I try to keep it in order, in time at least, and it comes out like the children we were. I shall continue, I think, as if to a stranger. I feel a great need, after all this time, to make it separate from me. To say, "Yes, I did do that, and that, but look: there was all this time before, all this time after. Here it is on these pieces of paper. You can pick them up, you can take them away. They are not me. I am over here; far, far away; over here."

Maybe if there'd been a trial. But there was no trial. Only silence. Everyone was advised not to mention your name to me. Not even your name.

Pamelump's dad was very rich. Almost a millionaire. When his baby got born without arms or legs, he set up a trust fund for her so she could have everything she needed, or at least everything money can buy, which is not the same thing. She got all the gadgets, the attendants, the electronics but, after a while, she started to say no, because it was against her Philosophy. Lot of people offering her the stuff didn't think no-arms-no-legs people had a right to their very own Philosophy and should be grateful for all that hardware which was going to make their pitifully amputated lives that much more bearable.

"When I say I'm Pamelump, they say that's a wicked joke, calling attention to my poor affliction, 'stead of showing what a keen mind I have. Maybe being limbless has sharpened my wits, had I thought of that? I don't see them sawing the arms off their own daughters; rather go down on their knees and thank the Lord. If they won't call me Pamelump, they only think of me as the poor afflicted."

"Wendy," Pamelump's mother began on the drive home, "do you like coming to see Pamela?"

"Yes," I said. I tried to remember not to chatter. When I chattered to my mother about Pamelump, she said it wasn't natural, and then I'd have to play more British bulldog till she got over it.

"You don't have to come. I hope your mother doesn't make you?"

"Oh no, Mrs Geldenhuys. She thinks I come a bit too often."

"And what do you think, Wendy? Sometimes when I'm writing letters I hear the two of you laughing and I think how nice that you're friends."

She didn't say: "How wonderful", as if neither of us deserved friends. And she didn't say "How nice for Pamela", as if her daughter shouldn't aim so high.

"Mrs Geldenhuys," I said, my heart beating almost in my throat, "Pamelump is my best friend. My Very Best."

The charcoal burners' smoke drifted across the road so she couldn't turn to look at me.

"I'm glad," she said. "I wondered if I ought to let her go. You know, there's a special school in Jo'burg."

"She'd miss me," I said.

"Yes," said Mrs Geldenhuys, "I think she would. We did visit the school, but I don't think she liked it."

"No," I said passionately, "Pamelump's better than them."

I didn't mean "a better person". When Pamelump came back, she told me she had worse handicaps, but could do more, than anyone else there. They sort of flopped and let themselves be afflicted because all the helpers thought, "yes, that's how the afflicted should be."

"Is 'Pamelump' a nickname you have for her?"

"Yes."

"Doesn't sound very kind."

"No."

"For a very best friend, it sounds distinctly cruel. What does Pamela say about it?"

"Why don't you ask her, Mrs Geldenhuys?"

"I'm asking you, Wendy."

"She told me to call her 'Pamelump', and if I think a lump's a bad thing, I shouldn't play with her."

Next day I went to Pamelump's straight after school. We were going swimming. I didn't tell my mum because she wouldn't think Pamelump could; and if she knew, she wouldn't think Pamelump should. Miss Mbata came with us; she stayed on the side to make sure nothing happened to Pamelump. The pool on the Geldenhuys farm is behind a mulberry grove, which means you get mulberries floating in it. It also means you're completely hidden from the house. Pamelump wears a life jacket for swimming, though she has to stay on her back. She says she just loves being out of doors with no clothes on, floating up and down the little ripples of the pool, watching the trees sway and the berries drop. She moved about quite easily; her back was very strong. She sort of rocked. I was proud of the swimming because it was my idea. I dived underneath her and she had to guess where I'd turn up; she rocked over to where she thought the next mulberry would fall and tried to catch it on her life jacket.

She let me pull her round the pool by her arm stump. When she suggested it, I felt so strange, like I wanted to cry. Or burst. She hated the other kids staring at her, always wanting to prod, feel how the skin tucked in; and now here she was, asking me. I knew it was just a game in a swimming pool, but I felt like doing ten somersaults.

"What you looking at?" she asked.

"You," I said, "your mouth's all red with berries, like kissing."

She turned sideways on the life jacket, picked up a berry and blew it at me. It got me on the cheek and splattered. We laughed and I took hold of her stump and we started to whirl off across the pool, making the water rush up over the edge. We charged round and round till we were taking the water with us and it made a tide that carried us on even after I'd stopped running. I looked down at Pamelump to see if she was still laughing. She looked adorable with the mulberry stain and I bent down towards her, not knowing yet what I was going to do. I still held her stump in my hand, and she seemed so trusting and happy that I kissed her, right there where her arm ended.

I felt all her muscles go hard. What a terrible liberty. She hated being mauled or slobbered over. She'd think it was pity and never let me near her again.

"You kissed me," she said.

"Yes," I said.

"Why?"

"I wanted to," I said, "I just wanted to."

Pamelump was quiet, weighing things up. She had to plan more than me. I waited. Then I looked round to Miss Mbata, but she waved so I don't think she'd seen.

"I'm glad," said Pamelump finally.

I beamed. I hadn't expected as much as that.

The water was still moving lazily along in the swirl I'd made. We let it float us around, both on our backs, hand to stump.

"Wendy! Pamela!" It was Mrs Geldenhuys. Pamelump looked furious when her own name was called second.

"What are you two doing? Wendy, I expect this was your idea."

"No," said Pamelump, "I suggested it this time. We asked Miss Mbata to watch us and ..."

"I'm appalled," said Mrs Geldenhuys, "absolutely appalled.

Don't you know how dangerous it is? What if Pam fell onto her face before Miss Mbata could reach her? What would you do, Wendy? Would you know what to do?"

"What makes you think I'm crazy as well as a cripple?" Pamelump screamed. "I can swim, you know, just because you don't let me ..."

By now Miss Mbata had come round our side of the pool.

"I'm very sorry, Mrs Geldenhuys," she said. "It'll never happen again. It was such a hot day and I thought there'd be no harm if she wore the life jacket and I was watching."

"You should have asked, Miss Mbata. I do not pay my servants to decide my daughter's welfare behind my back. We will speak of this later."

"She didn't decide," Pamelump spluttered. "Why won't you listen? I begged her."

Mrs Geldenhuys looked half terrified, half proud. She wheeled her daughter back into the house. "Now listen, you two: that was a dangerous, stupid trick to play. It might be safe enough for you, Wendy, but Pamela has to take more precautions. In future, if you want to go in the pool, Miss Mbata will go in the water with you, and you'll ask Benjamin to watch from the side. Have you got that?"

We nodded.

"And Pamelump, I don't want to see you taking advantage of the goodwill of the servants."

When Mrs Geldenhuys had gone, I turned to Pamelump. "She's going to let us swim."

"And she called me 'Pamelump'!"

Next time I went to Pamelump's, she told me we weren't going to play anything. She had to talk to me. I settled down on the front stoep, next to her chair. She liked sitting there on her own, watching the bougainvillea.

"I want to die," she said.

"Why?"

"Because I'm getting older."

"That's no reason."

"People like me don't live past puberty."

"Then why do it yourself? Anyway you might ..."

"I don't want to be an exception. It's only going to get worse. I'll have to hire nurses to do everything for me when I'm grown up."

"I like doing things with you."

"But you'll get tired, Wendy. You can't hang around me the rest of your life. Lifting me in and out of swimming pools, feeding me, washing me."

"If you were someone else, you wouldn't think like you do. Anyone can dive and play British bulldog."

"Except me."

"It's nothing special."

"Unless you can't do it."

She paused.

"Do you only like me cos I can't move?"

"I like you because I have more fun with you than with anyone else."

"Well it's not enough. For me, it's not enough, You're the only friend I have, Wendy. I'm surprised I wasn't smothered at birth."

"Don't be silly."

"It's not silly. I have nothing to live for."

"Mulberry trees," I said, "and bougainvillea and the water lapping under you."

"I can't get to them."

"And me, Pamelump, you like me."

Pamelump was so quiet she scared me.

"It's not enough."

"I'm not enough?"

"No."

Another silence.

"You'll leave me, Wendy."

"No, never . . ."

"Already."

"What do you mean?"

"My mother called you first. You're the normal one, so it must be your idea."

"But that time it was."

"You said 'let's go swimming', as if it was that simple for me. I had to do the planning."

"You always do the planning."

"So it doesn't count."

"Pamelump, I have arms so, when I'm with you, I do the things you can't. I don't know what it's like not to have arms; you have to plan it."

"Well, I can't die unless you help me. Will you help?"

"That's a terrible thing to ask."

"Probably. But will you help me?"

"No."

"Wendy, every other human thing makes one choice. Whether to go on living. I can't choose, because I can't kill myself."

"How would you do it?"

"Sleepers. You must give me some of my mother's sleeping pills while no one is with us."

"What about the servants? And Miss Mbata?"

"Afternoon off Wednesday."

"Your nurse?"

"For Christ's sake, can't I even die without worrying what everyone will feel about my poor, afflicted body?"

I didn't believe her. I didn't want her to die because then I ought to die too, and I wasn't finished living yet. The sun on my back and ripe mangoes in the grass, it was enough. Why wasn't it enough for her? Because we were different. Because she could not ignore her mother's orders and sneak off to the pool by herself. Whatever we did, I had two arms and two legs and she had none. But when I kissed her, I thought it might be alright. That she might let me do things for her, agree to go on living. It wasn't such a bad world. I was furious. What made her think she could go off and leave me? Why wasn't I enough?

"Will you help me?" she asked again.

I nodded. "I'll get the pills, but I'm not feeding you. It's murder."

I was eleven years old and I was very clear about murder. But that wasn't the reason. I didn't want her to die, why the hell should I have wanted to kill her?

– Pamelump, are you listening?

*   *   *

"I can't feed myself," she said crossly, "you know that."

"I'll put them where you can reach. If you really want to do it, you'll find some way."

"Prove myself?" she said.

She might only be playing right now, but if she got depressed again, she might do it in a fury without really meaning to. I went to her mother's room and took pills from different bottles so it wouldn't notice.

"If you take too many, it doesn't work," she said. "There was a man in the papers."

We tried to work it out, but we didn't really have a clue. I left the pills on her reading lectern.

Next day, Mrs Geldenhuys rang my mother's work.

"Wendy darling, Pamela's had an accident. Smashed up her poor face. Mrs Geldenhuys says she'd love to see you."

Pamelump was all puffy with bruises and cuts. She had a black eye, but, much worse, she had knocked out two front teeth and split her tongue open. That was drastic. She needed her teeth for so many things and false ones would just fall out if she tried to pull a string with them. Her tongue was too sore to press buttons, though it would've healed in time. Her hair hung over her eyes, a bad sign. She was always arguing with her mum to cut it. It was thick and long, gave visitors something nice to exclaim over. "What lovely hair." Don't notice the slab in the bed. Pamelump complained that, as she couldn't push it away behind her ears, she'd rather it wasn't there to torment her. They compromised and she always had it in a plait. Now it just flopped.

I was shocked. She looked beaten, just lying back on her cushions, crying.

"I'm sorry, Pamelump, I'm so sorry."

"Now do you see?" Her voice was thick. "I can't do anything. I've smashed two teeth and I can hardly talk."

She looked at me, one eye half-closed, one piercing.

"Wendy, I'm begging you. You kissed me because you love me."

I nodded.

"Please give me those pills. I fell out of my chair trying to get them."

I was angry and deserted and hurt, but I still did not want her to die. Most of the pills spilled into a video case when the chair tipped; in the fear for Pamelump, no one had noticed. I picked them out and held them in the palm of my hand. I would give them, one by one, to Pamelump whose mouth hurt so much she could hardly swallow. Twenty of them. I must dip my fingers into my cupped hand twenty times and feed her as I'd fed her hundreds of times before. If she wanted to change her mind, she could stop before any one of the pills.

"For pity's sake, Wendy," she said, after the third mouthful, "it's not a game."

So I gave her the rest four at a time to make it quicker.

"Wait with me," she said.

I stroked her hair and kissed her. I was eleven years old, nearly twelve. I knew that she would die and that I had killed her. That no one would ever understand. Anything. Why I loved her. Especially not that. I would never see her again. Never talk to her again. Never play another moving game or swim in the pool. And I would never be able to speak to anyone else about her. They would talk of murder and affliction and what is now called euthanasia; they would not talk about the terrible loneliness, about my lack of power: I could not, for all my efforts, make a world she wanted to live in. She would see the bougainvillea waving on the stoep; she could not touch it.

I have written this just as I remember. When Pamelump closed her eyes, I waited a long time. Then I went out onto the stoep and began to pick bougainvillea. I left them on Pamelump's window sill.

Funny Women

Shay Youngblood

Miss tom was not a pretty woman, she was handsome like a man. Tall, broad-shouldered, big-boned, lean and lanky like a man. Her soft silver hair was cut short and curled tight around her nut-brown, smooth and narrow face. She had silver side-burns, thick eyebrows that almost met across the top of her face, dark black eyes that could see through almost anything, and a silver mustache, like a man. Kids, and some grown folks, who didn't know Miss Tom were always asking her if she was a man or a woman. Miss Tom was patient with small children and strangers, so she would say in a deep, husky voice:

"Don't judge a book by looking at the cover."

Her chest was flat as a man's, her hands were big, thick and callused. But she had a woman's eyes, dark, black eyes that held woman secrets, eyes that had seen miracles and reflected love like only a woman can. Her walk was slow and deliberate like she had somewhere to go, but wasn't in any hurry to get there.

Me and Miss Tom were friends, good friends. She taught me how to fish, throw a knife, carve a piece of wood, tame birds, and believe in a world of impossibilities. She lived in a big, white house next door to Miss Rosa. It was a nice old house with long porches that wrapped around its sides and green shutters; behind them, lace curtains whipped in the breeze. She had lived there with Miss Lily for as long as I could remember. Miss Lily was real sick, in the hospital with a fever. Big Mama said the doctors didn't know anything, so it was no surprise when they said Miss Tom couldn't visit Miss Lily because what she had might be catching.

When Miss Tom came by our house with a fishing rod over her shoulder headed for the river, I asked her if I could go. She nodded her head and waited under the chinaberry tree in the yard while I went in to ask Big Mama, who I knew would say yes.

I got my fishing pole and ran out. Big Mama stuck her head out the door and hollered at Miss Tom.

"Hey Tom, how you making out? I hear Miss Lily sick. You need anything?"

"I'm doing pretty good so far. Me and your youngun going to catch my supper and yours too I reckon." Miss Tom winked down at me.

"You tell Lily we all praying for her when you get chance to see her."

"Thank you. I appreciate your prayers and I'll tell her you praying for her. We all is. See you 'fore sundown."

"Tom, don't you drop my baby over in the river. She got some things to do round this house when she gets back. Y'all take care." Big Mama waved us on.

I put my hand in Miss Tom's, and she held it kind of light as if she might break it.

"I'm sorry about Miss Lily," I said and gave her hand a squeeze.

"Me too, baby. You and me both," she said, squeezing back.

It was early in May and spring was in every strawberry bush, chinaberry tree and lime-colored leaf. The sky was crispy, deep blue and full of white fluffy clouds. The sun was so bright it hurt my eyes to look at anything white or shiny. Down by the river it was quiet, nobody around but us.

"What we got to catch with today?" I asked Miss Tom.

"We got a sardine, some Vienna sausages, and fresh bacon," she said, laughing that deep, rough laugh of hers. "These old crafty swimmers do like that fresh bacon." Then, after a while, like she remembered something terrible, the smile and the light in her face was pinched out like a flame.

I guessed Miss Tom was worried about Miss Lily. Her mind seemed to be miles off. I had thought she and Miss Lily were kin or sisters for the longest time, it was the only reasoning I could make out, them living together like that. When I asked Aunt Mae if they were sisters, she said:

"They sisters all right, but it ain't by blood."

I didn't know what she meant, so I left it alone then. I knew Miss Tom was different from other women, and not just because of her mustache and the mannish way she walked or the deep rough way she talked. She was just different. I heard folks say she and Miss Lily were funny, but I never noticed anything funny about either one of them. They were serious women.

In silence, Miss Tom fed our hooks, and we threw the lines in. We leaned back into the shade of a pine tree on a soft bed of pine needles. After a while the sun caught us strong in the face. Miss Tom squinted directly into the sun, and when I looked up a few minutes later, tears were running down her face like twin rivers.

"Miss Tom, you all right?" I asked, taking her big, rough hand in mine, trying to give her some comfort.

She heaved a few times, like she would soon let out a shout, then she got up and walked to the edge of the river bank and stood there looking in. With her back to me, she breathed in deep a few times with her whole body, then calmed down easy and came back to sit next to me. She wiped her face with a clean white handkerchief, then blew her nose in it.

"I got a lot on my mind, baby, but Miss Tom ain't gonna jump in yet. I needs to clear my head. Miss Juliette heavy on my mind."

"Who is Miss Juliette?" I asked. "You mean Miss Lily?"

"Miss Juliette is the most beautiful creature on God's green earth. She better get over this fever, we got things to do, we got plans. We going back to New Orleans . . ." Miss Tom said, like I wasn't even there.

She was real quiet for a few minutes, but I kept my eyes on her. I was real confused. I'd never heard tell of anybody around named Miss Juliette. Now, Miss Tom didn't talk much, said she didn't like to waste words saying nothing, but without warning, out of nowhere, without me even asking, she dived deep into a story simply because there was one that needed telling. She began in that deep, husky voice of hers that would've put me to sleep except the story kept me on the edge of those pine needles, and my eyes steady on Miss Tom.

"I growed up in a house wid six brothers on the banks of the Mississippi River. Six mens and me till Mama had Juliette. I member it like it was yesterday . . . the midwife coming in the middle of the night sending the boys out and making me boil water and tear up sheets. Way after a while I heard Mama in the bedroom hollering, grunting like her bowels wanna move, then I hear a baby crying. I peep behind the curtain in time to see the midwife hold up a ugly lil wrinkled up red baby.

"It was clear to be a white man's child, most probably Mr Boone, who Mama kept house for. Mama called her Juliette after Mr Boone's dead wife. It was a pretty name for such a ugly lil worm as that. My name rough, fit me like a glove, Tom. My grandmama's mama name me after her mama, Tomasina Louise Perry. That's what was wrote in the family Bible. But since I was little, the boys and Mama call me Tom, and treat me like I was a boy, no different from the other six. I believe sometimes even my Mama forgot.

"I was five years old when Juliette was born, but I was the one learn to bathe her, feed her and sit up all night wid her by the fire rocking wid her till she could sleep. She growed into such a pretty child. Long, black hair Mama kept in two plaits, so soft I would rub my face in it, taking hollow breaths of it, trying to take her in. She was a white man's child, all right, her skin was white as Jesus Christ's. She was built slim, but strong and long-legged, and them eyes of hers was green and gold like cats' eyes. You look in em too deep and you was liable to be sucked in. She was strong-willed and we spoiled her rotten by giving her everything she thought she wanted. Yes m'am, she growed to be pretty as a picture. I was proud to walk the two miles into town wid her on my back to show her off. Folks who didn't know us ask me whose child she was. When I say she my sister, they fall out laughing like it wasn't possible. When she say I'm her sister, they laugh more, cause I looked like a boy even then. Even then I would've cut my arm to the sleeve to please her. When she was four, she demanded we call her Miss Juliette. The poor child thought she really was white, and to keep our precious Juliette happy, we called her Miss Juliette, Queen of the Mississippi, till she wasn't round to call no more.

"After Juliette was born, Mama had to go work in Mr Boone's fields picking cotton. That left mostly me to take care of Miss Juliette. We slept in the same bed every night for sixteen years. For sixteen years we never spent a night apart. I never loved nobody like Miss Juliette, nobody . . ."

Miss Tom stopped suddenly. She looked up at the sun again and stared out at the water like she was blind. Finally she pulled a corncob pipe from the front pocket of her overalls and a pouch of sweet-smelling tobacco out of her back pocket. Without even looking down to see what her hand was doing, she pinched a bit of tobacco and stuffed it into the bowl of the pipe that was cradled in her other hand. She struck a match on the bottom of her boot, and for a few minutes was swallowed up in a cloud of sweet smoke. Miss Tom said some things to make me know she was way off somewhere. The next thing she said opened up a world of impossibles and never-even-dreamed-of ideas.

"It just seemed like we was always in love and loving one another. Sometimes I'd think about her being my blood sister and worry about going to hell for loving her that way. We started loving one another different the summer it was too hot to sleep. The summer the boys was all out possum hunting wid Uncle Trey and Mama was sleeping by Mr Boone's house. I must've been thirteen, and Juliette was bout eight. It was dog awful hot and nobody was home 'cept us, so we figured it was safe to sleep naked. My lil sister turned to me in her sweet lil whispering voice and say, 'Tom, hold me to you like you do when it's cold. I'm scared.' 'It's too hot to be all hugged up, Miss Juliette. Go on to sleep,' I say to her, kinda rough. Then I was sorry cause her feelings was hurt and she start to whining like a broke record, and I couldn't refuse her nothing. It was all in a natural move that I cradled up next to her lil body spoon fashion. Somehow in the middle of the night, we was laying face to face, me still holding her in my arms. By the moonlight she was almost too pretty to look at, like a angel. I member I closed my eyes and counted stars. Afterwhile I felt a soft something all over me, tingly kinda. I could feel the berries stand up on my bosom and then a nice easy rubbing on my nature. It felt so mighty wonderful I knowed it was a dream, so I kept my eyes shut tight trying to hang on to a good feeling. Can you blame me, Lord? I'd had so many bad dreams.

"Pretty soon I was moving against the softness, till I found relief. Behind my eyes was still a bunch of stars so I counted em till all the lights went out. I heard a whispering in my ear, then felt my hand being moved to a soft spot.

" 'Tom, do me. Do me now, it's my turn.'

"I heard her whispering like cool air through the trees. She put my hand between her legs. She was laying on her back looking over at me, holding my hand on a spot as soft as goose feathers and melted down like butter. Then I loved her all over wid my eyes closed and I make out like it was a dream, so we wouldn't go to hell. I'd been having bad dreams. Since I was eight, my oldest brother had used me like a woman. The first time he did it to me, it hurt and I tried not to move so I wouldn't wake up lil Juliette, so I'd make out like I was having a bad dream, cause if it's a dream, you wake up, daylight come, and it's passed. Me and Juliette had good dreams together. The night me and Juliette start loving one another different, I make out like we was dreaming. She kept her eyes closed too. I give her a bath with my kisses all round her face and neck and the lil bumps on her bosom and all over the soft spot between her legs."

Miss Tom stopped again, and was quiet as the fish sleeping in the river. The sun poured down on us heavy, scorching between the branches. So quiet, I could hear birds singing and branches falling in the woods behind us. My line got a bite, but Miss Tom didn't even look up as I pulled the little wiggling baby fish out of the depths of the river. I unhooked it and without Miss Tom even telling me, I threw it back to its mama.

"Growing up in a four-room shack on the Mississippi River in a house wid six men, I dreamed a lot. But after loving Juliette in that way, things was different. My brother didn't come to me no more. Juliette stopped that. She didn't make out like she was sleeping no more. When my brother come, she would kick him, bite him, scratch him, so he just quit and pretty soon left Mississippi to find a job out West. Juliette was jealous in a vicious kinda way, but she had a good heart. She wouldn't let no boys come round to court me. Not that they was tearing down the door, but some old men who was widowers wid children, and needed another hand on they farm, would come round looking me and Juliette over. She would put the dog on em.

"For sixteen years we slept in the same bed, loving one another like it was natural. Then Mama died of TB, and Uncle Reb and Aunt Taylee come to fetch Juliette. They said they only had room for her. Mr Boone say me and the boys could stay on the land and work it.

" 'You and the boys grown,' Aunt Taylee say to me. 'You can make it on your own. You near bout a old maid. Humph! At twenty-one years old you need to be married. If you fixed up some and shaved off that mustache you might look more like a woman.'

"Juliette's heart broke in two when I told her she had to go, but I promised I'd send for her. She cried all the way down the road. I cried late that night into a pillow filled wid the smell of her. After the funeral, and after Juliette left, me and Booker T., my youngest brother, set out for New Orleans on a shrimp boat wid everything we own wrapped in a piece of newspaper tied wid string. I kept a lock of Juliette's hair in a lil bag wid some roots in it round my neck, and I touched it when I wanted to dream. After a week the only job I could find was washing dishes in a whorehouse. Booker T. got a job working on the shrimp boats the second day we was there. We rented a lil room in back of a stable yard and took turns sleeping on the lil cot they call a bed. Other times we'd sleep in a old raggedy chair wid the springs popping out. New Orleans was full of big, pretty houses and pretty mulatta women, though none could compare to Miss Juliette. Out the blue one day, Booker T. say:

" 'Tom, I bet you down at the shrimp boats they don't know you from a man. Your lip hair and sideburns thicker than mine.'

"Don't you know they went for it? I got a job shrimping the very next day. Soon after that I got into a trade school for colored men, and me and Booker T. was living in a boarding house wid separate rooms. He was feeling his nature and took to drinking and bringing women to his room. All I worked for was Juliette, all I thought about was her sweet pink smile, black cloud hair and loving her soft lil body till daybreak. I almost had the money to send for her when me and Booker T. got a letter that froze my blood. Uncle Reb and Aunt Taylee was sending Juliette to school up North. She got a scholarship to a school in Canada, a teaching school. You could've knocked me over wid a feather.

"I was lonesome for a lot of years, but fate led me to meet a woman like me. She was a real woman though. She liked to wear fancy dresses, put on bright jewelry, dash herself wid loud perfume, and paint herself up. I was still doing men's work, and even after hours we went out wid me dressed like a man. She was named Ruth, but sometimes when we lay loving one another, I call her Juliette. Most times Ruth be so drunk she never member what I call her or what we did. The only way I could love her was if I membered Juliette, my eyes shut tight counting stars and dreaming, wid Juliette.

"It was twenty-two years before I heard from Juliette again. I got a letter in a handwriting that wasn't hers, begging me to come to her in Georgia, this very town, in the very house I live in today. The letter said she was sick and wanted to see me one last time 'fore she died, she said not to tell nobody else, I was the only one she wanted to see. The letter was signed, 'I will always love you, your gentle sister, Juliette.'

"I packed everything I owned in a suitcase like I did when I left Mississippi and never looked back. I left Ruth a lil piece of money and told her I was leaving and didn't know if I'd be back. She cried some and I hugged her one last time at the train station but I never looked back. All the way on the train I never once stopped thinking bout Juliette. Sometimes I'd wake up, and my face be wet from crying in my sleep.

"When I got to the address she wrote she lived at, I got a surprise. It was a big fine house for a colored woman, I figured she might work there. Indeed, a white woman met me at the door. I had on a new gray suit and stiff brim hat. I stood there wid my hat in my hand in a sweat.

" 'Excuse me m'am,' I say. 'I'm looking for Miss Juliette Perry. This address she sent me say she live here.'

"The woman look me up and down in a friendly sort of way, kinda curious.

" 'You Tom?' she ask me.

" 'Yes'm.' I answer polite as you please.

" 'I'm Lily. I been taking care of Juliette. She ain't well at all. I'm the one wrote to you. Why you dressed like that? You hiding from something?'

" 'No m'am. This the way I have to live to find work. Only work a colored woman can get where I been is cooking, cleaning, washing, or whoring, and I ain't partial to none of them.'

" 'You don't have to call me m'am, I ain't white,' she say, smiling at me.

"You could've bowled me over wid a dime. She had them light colored eyes, dark straight hair and white, white skin. She was young too. Couldn't have been more than twenty. She ask me to come in the house, took my hat and bag and led me to the kitchen.

"Juliette had been sick for more than a month. While we was sitting at the kitchen table, the woman tell me what happen in them twenty-two years that was missing. She say Juliette moved to New York when she finished school and started passing for white. She was teaching school up there, and Lily was one of her students. Lily was passing too. They kinda helped one another out and was soon living together. Juliette wanted to teach in the South, teach colored children to read and figure, and she got Lily to come wid her to study under a colored doctor to help heal coloreds. They was living here three years when Juliette was struck with this sickness.

"Then Lily showed her to me. My Juliette lay in a big, iron bed pale as a ghost and delicate like a dried-up flower withering amongst all them quilts and plump pillows. I walk up to the bed and whisper her name real low. Her eyes open and shut like bird wings. When she see me, her eyes light up the dark circles all round em. First thing she say is that she sorry for all these years gone.

" 'Tom, I knowed you'd look just like you do.' Then she just look at me, us not talking for a long time. Finally she say:

" 'You know, I ain't got much time, so I want you to come closer to me and listen.' I did like she wanted. I sat on the bed close to her and took her cool, dry hand in mine, and I heard Lily go out the room and close the door. Juliette sit up and speak stronger. She was still a beautiful creature. I tried to drink her up, swallow her whole wid remembering.

" 'Tom, I wanna love you one last time before I go. I wanna love you wid my eyes open. I learned how to do that wid Lily, and I wanna give you something and take something of you before I go. And Tom, I want you to take care of Lily. She ain't got nothing and nobody in this world to claim her but me. This is my house, now it belong to the two of you. Promise me you'll do it Tom, promise me.'

"What could I do, 'cept like always?

" 'Miss Juliette, I would die for you if I could.' She squeezed my hand wid a strength she didn't look to have.

"She didn't make love like a dying woman, but slow and natural, like a woman in love, and I loved her back wid everything in me till we was both wet wid loving and empty of all but love. After she fell asleep I got up and washed myself, then I bathed Juliette's body as if she was my sleeping child.

"When I went out to the kitchen to get a pitcher of drinking water, Lily was slumped over the table crying her eyes out.

" 'Why? Why you have to love her like that? Ain't she sinned enough wid me? You her sister, and it just ain't right,' she wailed, like death was on her.

"She looked more like Juliette wid every tear that drop. I hadn't noticed so much before how much they look alike. Where Juliette was tall and lean, Lily was on the short side and kinda plump, but they could've passed for sisters and probably did when they was living up North like white women.

" 'I love her as much as you do,' was all I could tell her.

"I put my arm round her and let her cry. That night I slept in the bed wid Juliette, and Lily slept on the floor next to Juliette's side. We went on like that till Juliette died, two weeks later, leaving us in mourning, loving her even into the grave. After the funeral, me and Lily stayed up all night talking about Miss Juliette. When it was time to turn the lights out, I took Miss Lily's hand and we went into Juliette's bedroom and lay down together, and we been sleeping in the same bed every night, ever since."

Miss Tom let out a cry so sharp, I dropped my fishing pole and it slid in the river. I took her big, rough hand in mine and felt my throat tighten up and tears fall.

"Miss Juliette, I can't lose you twice. Lord, don't let her go . . ." Miss Tom said with grief deep in her heart.

We sat there crying on the banks of the Backbend River as the sun, a big red ball of fire, fell gently between the trees. Miss Tom seemed to come around after a while. She looked over at me through her tears.

"Lord forgive me for what this child have heard this evening but you and me both know it's the truth. If you in heaven God please spare me losing Miss Juliette a second time."

With not another word, Miss Tom got up, dusted off the seat of her overalls and started gathering up our stuff. She took my hand and whistled an old blues song as we walked home in the dark. Her telling me that story clicked the lock on our friendship and was never spoken of again, but that was the last time Miss Tom took me fishing. Like she predicted to Big Mama, my interests turned to boys and other young folks, but I never forgot Miss Tom or her story.

Miss Lily eventually got over her fever and continued to heal folks in the community. She and Miss Tom probably still live in that big, old white house on Sixth Avenue, loving each other with their eyes open.

Magic Eight Ball

Marion Douglas

When I turned ten, my mother made the decision I could help out with the greenhouse work and at that time she made the transition from mom to boss. Like many children that age – even Lois Wilde, who was never given to fads – I was convinced by my parents' inscrutable behaviour that I had been adopted, purchased actually, from a factory outlet of newborns, plucked from a row of infants displayed – because greenhouses represented the retail context most familiar to me – in seedling trays. By way of response to this change in status from child to employee, I constructed a family tree that excluded both my boss, Franny, and my father. A continuous work in progress, my revised family tree included Alice the Goon and Popeye, Dale Evans and Roy Rogers, Elizabeth Taylor, several Mouseketeers, Walt Disney himself and, at the very top, like a Christmas tree ornament, Hayley Mills.

Those days, greenhouse work was not what I had in mind. I could not generate a fondness for seedlings and, despite reassurances to the contrary from the boss, was unable to convince myself that potting soil had no relationship to toilets. But more importantly, most importantly, work was an obstruction to my relationship with Lois Wilde. In the weeks following my tenth birthday, I assured and reassured Lois that the play room remained open as always, my parents did not disapprove of her or her mother, and that she should, no, *must*, continue to get off the bus at my stop. From there, the two of us sneaked from poplar tree trunk to poplar tree trunk, past the greenhouses which propagated themselves I was sure through some underground root system (every other month, another seemed to appear), to the house and upstairs into the play room. If we managed this without being seen, I was free until dinner-time. It was as if, on a day-to-day basis, Franny could not recall my existence until I had entered her field of vision. When I first read Piaget, it occurred to me that my mother suffered serious lapses of object permanence.

The play room was the best part of the house. Upstairs, it was the one bedroom nobody used for sleeping. My parents occupied the large and gabled room facing the road, I had the little one with the chandelier – a light fixture originally intended for a haunted house and purchased by my father at an auction – and Lois and I had the play room. I think the fact that Franny never once came looking for us there convinced me Lois and I had entered some territory most adults, at least my parents, had forgotten or never learned about, their third-grade readers for example or a multiplication table beyond twelve. For whatever reason, the play room had all the potential of a book illustration, admired again and again until you yourself slipped into the clothing worn by Heidi or felt an odd elongation of the neck similar to Alice's in Wonderland.

The play room is where Lois and I invented the McCrackens. The McCrackens were the small and life-like family which arrived with my dollhouse, the Christmas I was six. Initially unremarkable, the McCrackens took on an identity when Lois began visiting. She and I spent hours decorating the play room in a manner we thought would reflect the McCrackens' character and lifestyle. This was not always easy. The McCrackens had money but Mr McCracken was a tightwad, so we were constantly having to make do. Using some bricks and planks, we made a sideboard. On it, we placed a tea set and an old electric kettle Lois brought from her house. We had a little end table we covered with a table cloth and on it we placed seasonal decorations, yellow leaves in a bowl, spring flowers, crab-apples. Life magazines supplied photos to be cut and framed with twigs and bits of cedar shingle. Using a couple of real frames found in a shed on my parents' property, we hung reproductions Lois clipped from an art history book belonging to her mother. With these, we took particular care, because they were a McCracken inheritance from rich relatives in Europe.

Then, in the spring of 1964, to my utter and complete stupefaction, I arrived home from school to find the McCrackens' house on the kitchen table, the McCracken family and all of their furniture stuffed into a paper bag. Upstairs in the play room, all the decorations and artwork had been removed and the walls papered with images of the seven dwarfs, unwelcome and menacing figures heigh ho-ing their way to work. My old crib lay in pieces on the floor, awaiting assembly.

"I'm pregnant," Franny said. "You're going to have a little sister or brother."

The possibility that Franny might become pregnant had never, ever occurred to me: she was so unlike other mothers who routinely became pregnant, mothers whose bodies were rounded and cushiony, as if developing babies might, or at least could, be curled up inside a breast or beneath generous rolls of fat. Franny was straight and without hiding places. I understood that she had given birth to me in the same way I understood Bible stories – as an unlikely tale the adults believed I should believe.

That very day in health class at school, I had read about a woman in the United States who, upon arriving home from the state fair to find her house burned to the ground, lost all of her hair. If only my body could communicate such eloquent ruin. Standing in the doorway to the play room, I pulled at my brown braids, willed each of my follicles to clench itself shut and free my hair in a stark act of protest. This was too much. But not one hair was lost. I dragged the McCracken house out to the dark and musty shed that had contained the picture frames. I gathered up the artwork and moved it out as well. Then I called Lois Wilde with the news.

A couple of years passed with the McCrackens, their house and all its furnishings languishing in a shed in what must have been near-absolute darkness. That particular building was used as a repository for items to be kept out of the way and eventually auctioned off. When this might happen was never made clear.

"Someday that'll be worth something to somebody," my dad would say of a broken pulley or a green garden hose that had sprung leaks.

The door to the storage shed would then open and the item in question sequestered for the process that would miraculously invest it with value. Sometimes, I liked to sit in that shed and enjoy the pleasing melancholy of objects growing older. The McCrackens seemed well-suited to this environment; they, or at least Mrs McCracken, had always had a rare, unappreciated quality to her and now here she rested, becoming more exceptional with each passing day.

It stood to reason that the McCrackens, finding themselves in dire economic straits, would need to sell their house. When I knew I was alone and nobody could possibly hear, when Franny and dad and my new brother Stephen were away to Calgary or the neighbouring village of Flax, I would entertain myself by auctioning off the McCrackens' home, making the sounds I thought auctioneers made. "Who'll give me ten, ten, ten . . . this is a beautiful piece of workmanship! Who'll give me ten thousand dollars for this exquisite dollhouse? It came over from the old country. Ten thousand. Who's going to make a bid? Come on, somebody start us up here. Come on, you stupid people," I would eventually say. "You stupid, stupid people."

The bidders' lack of interest in my dollhouse would invariably force a move into oration. What I wanted in the shed, really, was to position myself in front of a crowd, exhorting, upbraiding and offering explanations. Since no one would buy my priceless dollhouse, I would carry on, I would teach them. I would explain why old people should worry more. I would shout about the dangers of nuclear destruction. I would describe in great detail pictures I had seen of the nuclear winter awaiting us. I urged them not to be so complacent. Have you not eyes to see? Ears to hear? I demanded, making the easy shift from auctioneer to television evangelist. Nuclear weapons will kill us all. Show me that you are willing to shake off the evil prejudices of the cold war, the yoke of nuclear power. Stand up and renounce their evil hold upon you. Stand up, you cowards, I was saying (my tendency was to become abusive), when the shed door opened and there stood Lois Wilde. I do not think my body has since experienced such a radical transition from triumph to humiliation. It was as if my entire circulatory system braked and changed direction: as if the white blood cells became red and vice versa in a blindingly rapid exchange of uniforms.

"What are you doing?" asked Lois.

My embarrassment was caused only in part by the ridiculousness of my behaviour. It was made unbearable, held over a hot, hot flame by a glass blower or the devil or a vengeful someone whose pants had perhaps fallen down in school, by the fact of Lois Wilde's discovery. Had it been Barbara White or Lesley Munro, the other two girls in our grade seven class, I would not have cared so much. Barbara and Lesley were chemically bound, a boring atomic team, one of those blue or red knob-headed representations we had in our science text. Always together. On the way home from school, they planned to wear the same colours the following day. Who cared about Barbara and Lesley? To myself, I called them the molecule.

But Lois. The unfortunate truth in grade seven was that neither Lois nor I had a best friend. And this was a rather bright and radiant and difficult truth that could not be ignored. We had been friends; it seemed logical we should continue to be; but now we weren't. What could possibly be the problem? So important was this issue, I imagined groups of puzzled adults discussing and analyzing the situation. Why don't the Wilde and the Raine girl spend more time together? they asked one another, over cards.

My ears turned red because I knew the answer: I was in love with Lois Wilde. I was in love with Alexander Mast, too, an Amish boy (and a safe choice, I must have thought, in his suspenders and black vest, his cultural harness), so I knew what the word meant; I had thought about it at length and even composed a few definitions, definitions being an area in which I excelled; given the job of Minister of Education, at age twelve I would have made definitions a subject area. What Is Love? I asked the back page of my math scribbler.

Love is an expanded and slightly shameful feeling, like stretched-out elastic bands from old underpants.

Love is food, prepared by another mom: poached eggs, that which is unfamiliar and has to be eaten. It brings on a fear of gagging.

Love is *Lady Chatterley's Lover* and all of the reasons it is not to be taken from the shelf at home.

Love is your very own eyes turning bright as the headlights of a car when Alexander Mast comes into sight.

I could have gone on and on. Love was a diverse group of events and thoughts and waste products and, in Alexander's case, I carried this group deep inside me, in a place where I could easily control its waxing and waning. If I wanted to magnify and grow this warm pablum of love, I had only to walk close to Alexander at recess or goad him into teasing me or chasing me. All very easy, because Alexander liked me, too. If he grabbed my arm, the feeling rose from my stomach to a place between my ears from which more than a dozen imperatives could be issued at once, all clearly heard, all different, a sort of NATO response: run, touch him, kiss him, don't even think such a thing, are you crazy? Wrestle with him, go and see what Lesley and Barbara are doing, make him chase you, just go inside, go inside the school, go inside where it's dark, sit at your desk for a while. And that took care of the waning.

With Lois, the feeling, although the same, existed outside my body. It was like a poltergeist but not frightening exactly; a natural phenomenon, a comet, the northern lights, swamp gas, UFOs. If I went looking for it, I might see it; if I didn't, I wouldn't. It was at Lois's house, it was in Lois's clothing and also her mother's car, it hovered over her desk at school, it was buzzing slightly within the McCrackens' house. Groups of scientists from the National Research Council would have been hard-pressed to identify it, much less explain it.

Our school had only two classrooms: one for the first four grades, the other for grades five to eight. The grade seven class was small and occupied a single row of desks. At the beginning of the year, because of my inability to see the board, I had been seated in the very front desk. By spring, I had glasses kept in a beige case with a gold clasp, the opening and shutting of which made me feel important, glamorous even, as if I might have connections to Hollywood or at the very least, a clerical position in the entertainment industry. I removed my glasses, snapped them into their case and massaged the bridge of my nose at least twenty times a day, so exhausting was my work. Lois, two desks behind, easily became Hayley Mills, passing by from the set for Pollyanna. The voice of our teacher, Miss Brilz, was in actuality that of Agnes Moorehead suggesting, insisting, that Lois and I were twins, separated by feuding parents.

Thanks to my optometrist, the final weeks of seventh grade passed in an extravaganza of daydreams, all of which cast Lois Wilde in leading roles. And even though we were not officially friends, did not even speak for days at a time, as if we were both victims of a hurtful misunderstanding, my anticipation of the long summer days ahead included some index of Lois; plans formed in my head around a vastly pleasing but missing detail.

So it is not surprising that she appeared that day, if you believe at all in the unstoppable commotion of the vital organs that can't seem to get what they want, all the talk that is heard on the skin, in the abdomen, at the back of the throat and inside the knees. Lois must have picked up on the general murmur. She had just decided to drop by. No reason, really. And, not surprisingly, she had thought I was being hurt – logical enough, considering the loud haranguing of my audience. I was fine, I told her and offered no further comment – Lois was frankly too cute to be expected to suffer long-winded explanations. Besides, the combination of her beauty and my adoration often left me speechless, especially since she had begun to wear her dark hair in a style similar to that of the twins in *The Parent Trap*. Like them, she wore jeans and T-shirts. Lois did not follow what we experienced then as trends; stretchies, for example, the tight, nylon predecessors of the modern stirrup pant, were not her style. She would have looked as ridiculous in stretchies as Alexander Mast.

"The McCrackens!" Lois said, soon after she realized I was not hurt and was merely behaving like Billy Graham. "They've been in this shed all that time. We have to bring them out. They'll be turned into albinos by now. We should make them some little sunglasses. Do you have any black construction paper? If you don't, I can go home and get some from my mom."

"Actually, I think I do." And for the remainder of June, in the long spring evenings, the McCrackens made several trips from the shed to the slanted daylight beneath the one big and half-dead poplar tree. They carried on, a little disoriented, in their paper glasses, adapting as best they could. Their house had been sold to a collector, I told Lois, we'd have to leave it in the shed.

That summer, we moved the McCrackens and their furniture into a corner of one of the greenhouses. Because Lois was not required to be home until midnight, we stayed up late, playing until five minutes before her curfew so that, when she left, she left in a hurry on her CCM, out the laneway in the standing position, bobbing with that piston quality, like a boy. As I watched I imagined the walls and rooms of air I knew she would pass through, one minute warm, then down into the coulee. The hair on my arms stood up.

We had made a net hammock for Mr McCracken out of an onion bag and four knitting needles, sharp ends sunk in pots of sand. The effect was pyre-like. We both knew he could not get out of there and was likely starving but, oh well. Mrs McCracken had stopped making meals anyway. The kids fended for themselves, but there seemed no need to worry. Everyone was still in sunglasses because of the brilliance of the lighting. Lois said we can't see them but there is an audience outside watching us, people sometimes halfway up the hillside, depending on the size of the house. She talked that way because of her mother, who had connections to theatre.

I asked Lois if the Stanton twins were in the audience.

"Most nights," she answered. "They see better in the dark, so some nights they like to waddle out here."

The Stanton twins were two old fellows from the village whose sole occupation was people-watching. Seated on the bench outside the Flax Home Hardware store, they watched. That was the work they did, in exchange for their disability pensions. A strange choice, this watching, since they were blinded with cataracts. Their eyes, cloudy like bits of ice in a glass of Pepsi, seemed always to drip and melt with a tender enthusiasm when Lois and I came into view. Whether alone or together, we elicited comment: All by yourself today? Where's your little friend? Aren't you two the happy pair? Around the Stanton twins, I could always feel my love for Lois take form, bunch up in my hair like a gnarly tat or make itself into a brownish smear on the back of my pants.

"I really wish the Stanton twins weren't in the audience," I said to Lois one night.

"You can't make people stay home," she said. "But, with their night vision they probably can only see the people around them in the audience out there. The greenhouse is likely just a kind of blur to them. I seem to have heard that they hate it when the streetlights come on at night, because then everything goes blurry for them. Everything's opposite for them." Lois had a way of seeming to have heard important bits of information.

I moved my transistor radio into the greenhouse and we listened to a station received only at night. W-O-W-O. Suddenly, we were living in an apartment in Chicago. It was apparent that Lois had a job and I kept house.

"A man jumped in front of the train today," Lois would say. "I think I've seen him before. I tried to save him, tried to talk him out of it. 'Don't you want to live any longer?' I asked. He jumped anyway. There was nothing anybody could do."

Despite my auctioneering and Hollywood fantasies, despite my adoration of Lois, I was not at ease with this type of pretending. I could imagine the Chicago apartment and I could picture us in it, but I could not comfortably play along. I contributed by making observations of an inventory sort.

"We have an oil cloth on our table," I said. And, "We need to get a trilight lamp."

I drew floor plans of our apartment and arranged and rearranged the furniture.

Lois began to bring a jack knife and whittle pieces of wood. We had lawn chairs. We had a balcony. The street was always busy. The McCrackens were our neighbours.

Mrs McCracken dropped in like a character in a situation comedy, making preposterous announcements. She wanted to hop the train to New York; there were some important auditions she didn't want to miss. She was in a hurry; she had a coffee date with a Senator. She wanted to get out of this damn blue skirt; she hated it. Lois agreed to whittle off the plastic, pleated skirt Mrs McCracken had never been without. She whittled until all of Mrs McCracken's bottom half was bandaid-coloured, her top half remaining blue and short-sleeved. Lois made legs, with a V-shaped notch at the top.

"Do you have a pen?"

Through the yard, lit by its single bulb on a pole. I had to cross the circle of light quickly because the rule was, inside it, I could not breathe; my oxygen was outside of that area, in the grey space where the poplar tree's branches moved unexpectedly and creepily like a bad puppet show. In the kitchen, my parents had left a light on like always, a dim one over the counter, and I easily found a pen, a great find, and the giving of it to Lois passed through me like the breeze out in the puppet branches.

With great concentration, Lois drew a little triangle of hair on Mrs McCracken and then leaned her against a small pot. There she was, transformed, her transformation an odd feeling like too much pudding but not in the stomach, lower.

After that, Mrs McCracken always visited half naked, something we overlooked and also anticipated. When Lois was not around, Mrs McCracken had to be hidden in a pot of vermiculite. If she were found, the Stantons would have something to talk about that would make their collapsing, sinking eyes light up. I began to make sure I was in the greenhouse before Lois arrived. I wanted her to ride in the laneway and see me, having already got Mrs McCracken out of her hiding place. I wanted her to know that things went on between Mrs McCracken and me when she wasn't there.

In the fall of 1966, Mr McCracken slipped into a coma for all eternity. The story was that, in the move from the greenhouse to the barn, Mr McCracken had caught a chill which rendered him vulnerable to a form of dust virus, several of which infected the barn. The possibility of disease and fire made the barn a more dangerous home but the greenhouse had become too public: Mrs McCracken objected to being on display.

"We live in a glass house and we do throw stones," she said. Also, "I need some damn privacy." A move was absolutely necessary.

The upstairs of the disused barn offered quantities of hay and straw, housed there it seemed to me since the dawn of time, in two dizzyingly attractive lofts. The straw was stored in hard-edged and urine-coloured rectangular bales which we set to arranging, as soon as we had finished a sort of palliative shrine for Mr McCracken – nothing more than a bridge constructed of three bales off in a darkened corner. There, wrapped in toilet paper, suspended in his hammock safely above the threat of rats and mice, he rested in peace.

In the barn, no effort was made to replicate the greenhouse floor plan; instead, we created a version of the upstairs of my parents' house. We made the walls as high as we possibly could, four bales up; then, with the help of an overturned box, settled bales above the entrances to make door frames. The McCracken children were immediately quarantined in separate bedrooms because of the dust virus scare. Both being shorter than three inches in height, they were easily kept from harm in Mason jars with two layers of cheesecloth secured with elastic bands serving as lids. And there they stayed, little specimens without a medium. Very little was known about the dust virus; the experts were not in agreement on the period of quarantine.

This left Mrs McCracken, Lois Wilde and me to make a life for ourselves. There was a small coma pension from Mr McCracken's former employer but this barely covered the rent. With her nudity, at first an embarrassment, now a cause – Yes, I'm naked. So? You are, too, under those cheap clothes – there were some barriers to employment until I hit upon the solution of a television broadcast from the apartment. Mrs McCracken was so worldly wise, she could provide advice or simply answer questions you might have on your mind. "Ask Mrs McCracken" would be the name of the show. I imagined myself with an executive position, someone in charge of research.

Lois used her jack knife to convert the dollhouse bedroom vanity into a desk by chopping off the plastic mirror. With this, and a piece of ink-blue bathroom tile from a Wilde family home renovation project, we created a studio for Mrs McCracken. Behind her, we propped a map of the world, glued to cardboard. The barn was wired. We found an outlet near the stairwell and, using an extension cord and goose-necked desk lamp, created studio lights. I was in heaven. Mrs McCracken, the studio, the blue tile in the lamp light, Lois Wilde, the straw house and the smell of what I considered museum-quality dust were a miniature, contained, planned, site of pleasure to me, like the intricate model of the township's future the Flax village reeve had brought to school one day, with its groups of plastic trees and Monopoly houses. It was as if the architecture of my love for Alexander Mast and Lois Wilde had been studied, on a molecular level, understood and constructed in the upstairs of my parents' barn.

The first few broadcasts were slow; we even made a test pattern. Then Mrs McCracken found her stride.

Eugenia Wilde, Lois's mother, was third-generation Mercury Township, and thus from a successful farming family. When she and Allister married, her parents, Margaret and Harold Favell, retired into town, allowing Allister and Eugenia to move into the farm house. Eugenia needed space. The land was rented to a neighbouring farmer. Not long after Lois was born, Mrs Wilde began a Bachelor of Arts degree. She completed her Master's degree in philosophy, just prior to Lois, leaving behind her yellow banlon cardigan and moving away for good. Fourteen years of commuting to the University of Alberta. To review lecture notes, she kept a reel-to-reel plugged into the lighter in the front seat of the car. When Eugenia drove us anywhere, Lois and I had to sit in the back seat.

Lois's mother sought ever-expanding circles of acquaintanceship; she liked entertaining. People from the university visited, frequently staying overnight – it was such a lovely spot. Mr Wilde seemed never to be there; his work took him away on business trips, he was an avid hunter, maybe he too fell ill with a dust virus and was consigned for periods of time to a pyre in the garage – hard to say where Mr Wilde was, much of the time. In a small community, the Wilde situation, as it was called, generated talk with a nuclear proficiency. This gossip mill fuelled Lois's own personal cold war. Still, she had an exaggerated notion of the locals' censure of Eugenia Wilde.

"They think she's a floozy. They think she's a drug addict. They think she has crackpot ideas," she told me, up in the barn.

"They like her plays," I said (Eugenia also more or less ran the Flax Little Theatre). "My parents liked the last one. Everybody applauded, didn't they? What more do you want? Nobody ever jumps out of their car and applauds for my parents' perennials."

"Do you think your parents would let me live here, if I worked for free in the greenhouses?" she asked.

"I honestly don't know," I said, thinking, Franny, most likely yes; Dad maybe not.

Ask Mrs McCracken. There were a host of unanswered questions. It began with the magic eight ball. Remember those? The pyramidal floating body inside a black ball of viscous liquid yielded up its oracular messages – *outlook not so good*, or, *it is decidedly so*, or, *cannot predict now*. This quickly reached its limits and, by her own account, bored Mrs McCracken to tears.

The medium idea was Lois's, from a movie she had seen at the drive-in. This was the format. We were to write out one question for Mrs McCracken before the show, to be read by the opposite (Lois's word) person. She who did not read, shook the eight ball and served as the medium or the voice of Mrs McCracken. In other words, you were guaranteed the job of answering your own question. Until, that is, I proved my inadequacy as a medium with the first question I handed Lois.

"Will Alexander Mast ever run away from the Amish?"

A vigorous shake of the eight ball. "*Ask again later*," I read, relieved, thinking that settled that.

An expectant look from Lois was intended as my cue to continue, but my childhood years were burdened by a form of cue-resistance, a tendency to balk. Like one completely unprepared, one who had never done a moment's practice being encouraged to perform a musical piece or a figure-skating routine, my face reddened, my thoughts milled in directionless groups.

"Look at Mrs McCracken. Let everything else blur." Lois had inherited some of her mother's directorial talent. "Empty your mind and answer the question."

"The answer is," I intoned in the low monotone I felt befitted the brainwashed and the living dead, "the answer is *ask again later*."

"No, that's not the answer. You're Mrs McCracken. She's not a zombie. She's way more than just the magic eight ball. OK. Listen. Watch. Read the question."

I obeyed. "Will Alexander Mast ever run away from the Amish?"

I watched Mrs McCracken absorb Lois's gaze as if it were light and she were colour. Her small, plastic frame changed, took on some animation, I swear to it. And then, in the voice of authority, someone who had never harboured a moment's doubt, Lois began to speak.

"*As I see it, no.* Of course Alexander Mast will never run away from the Amish. Think about it. What's he going to run away with or to? He has to quit school, the minute he turns sixteen. He doesn't have one non-Amish friend, except Julia Raine. Cuteness does not equal running away. Look at Lorne Hogan. He's not Amish and he's certainly not cute and he ran away."

"How does Mrs McCracken know Lorne Hogan?" I asked, suspicious.

"Why wouldn't I know him? I've lived here all my life, ever since I came from Eaton's."

Now the voice of Lois. "All right. Read my question to Mrs McCracken."

I read, "Is Allister Wilde really the biological father of Lois Wilde?" I had no idea this was the sort of question we would be asking Mrs McCracken.

The eight ball was unambiguous. "*Yes,*" Lois read the watery message, "don't be ridiculous. People talk nonsense, especially here in Mercury Township. You've got to understand people have nothing better to occupy their minds. Lois Wilde and Allister Wilde have the same hair and eyes; it's genetic proof. Whoever started that talk about Lois Wilde being the possible daughter of somebody else has shit for brains. People talk nonsense here in Mercury Township."

Who started that talk? I would have asked, had I not already asked one question beyond my allotment. And anyway, when our eyes met, blink, the spell was broken and Lois had become a former medium. But only because the authority exiting Lois had entered me, wiring my insides with a jumble of cables and current and volume control, someplace noisy with pleasure, a drive-in movie, perhaps, with a speaker attached to the car door. Hayley Mills dropping by, at last, to ask if I might want to visit the set.

"Maybe we should check on the kids," I said, by way of diversion. "I don't think they're all that sure the dust virus can't get through cheesecloth."

Lois saw no reason not to.

Later, I would return to the barn alone, hold the eight ball in the lamp light and await the change, the arrival of the medium, someone frankly devilish at the wheel of a rusted, smoking half-ton truck. But nothing of the kind happened. Then I picked up Mrs McCracken and, lying on my back, placed her on the space between my nonexistent breasts. And it was as if I had found the reverse gear on my crushes; I could feel their warm knowledge backing into me, parking, brake lights on, then off. If at all possible, I would have grown a layer of skin over Mrs McCracken and kept her there. So what if she made a weird lump?

I think I was waiting for the days to shorten. "Ask Mrs McCracken" was broadcast Saturday nights. Throughout September and October, I kept an eye on the little barn window with its partitioned moments of late evening sky, a blue that seemed, like the shirts of Alexander Mast, to undergo washing after washing, slowly fading to gray. By the time the sky had darkened to the indigo of Mrs McCracken's studio floor, it was eleven o'clock and Lois was expected home. Once daylight savings time had been got rid of, though, there was a change: the minute we entered the barn, we were moved along, east against the sun's progress and into much later time. When everyone else was turning the dial to hockey, our prairie clock was setting itself over the Atlantic Ocean, the sky outside already the darkness of waves most people never see. And this, for reasons I could not articulate, was good.

The use of the barn's overhead lighting became necessary – two old bulbs from the time electricity was first invented, I guessed; the light cast an inspirational mood, a moment of reverence seemed fitting. "And with just the flick of a switch," Lois liked to say when we arrived.

November temperatures were a problem, so Lois supplied blankets. Eugenia Wilde did not pay much attention to domestic details; entire pieces of furniture probably could have gone missing without comment and at this I marvelled. In my home, any effort to "traipse" off to the barn carrying blankets would have been observed from a greenhouse and stopped. Julia, what are you doing with those blankets? Nothing. Then nothing them back inside right now.

And Mrs McCracken was a little moodier, so time had to be taken before the show to assess her state of mind or just give her the stage.

"Be careful," Lois might say in the voice of the medium, "I've got a damn hangover. It's not easy being mom and dad to a couple of ungrateful kids in jars." Or, "Stop staring at me like you've never seen a half-naked person before." Or, "Get me my magic eight ball; I want to ask it a question."

"Is Mr McCracken ever going to come out of his coma?" Lois would ask impatiently. And immediately came the resolute answer, "*Don't count on it.*"

"Are the kids OK?"

"*Most likely.*"

"Will somebody, someday, write a play about my life and will it be a big Broadway hit?"

"*Signs point to yes.*"

Mrs McCracken had a right to her mood swings, she said, we asked so many questions. And we did. We – meaning Lois – now asked whole strings of questions requiring strings of answers.

"Is Eugenia Wilde now, or has she ever, had an affair with that Professor Byrne she keeps talking about?"

"*It is decidedly so,*" Lois reported from the eight ball, then expanded.

"What do you think they were doing, that time he came to stay for the weekend and Mr Wilde was in Saskatoon? They weren't playing checkers, I assure you. You saw them kissing when you came back from the greenhouse one night – thank God we got out of that fishbowl – and they were embarrassed, as well they should be. But it's not such a huge deal. I've stepped out on Mr McCracken a couple of times. Well, can you blame me?"

"Does Mr Wilde know?"

"*Yes, definitely.* Next question."

"Well, does he care?"

'*As I see it, yes.* Mr Wilde does and does not care. Eugenia Wilde talked him into that open marriage agreement and he tries to make the best of it. Once, he had an affair with a woman in a motel in Edmonton. They were at the same motel, so it just kind of happened. He felt bad but also a little good, because it cancelled out Professor Byrne."

"But didn't Eugenia like Professor Byrne?"

"*Signs point to yes* but why, I don't know. Professor Byrne looked like Ed Sullivan, all hunched over in a suit. I guess there's no accounting for taste. It's marriage that's the problem, anyway. No offence to Mr McCracken, but marriage is silly. Don't ever get married. God, you two are making me tired."

"What about Julia's mom? Has she ever had an affair?"

"*My sources say no.* Julia's mom is not interested in an affair. She is interested in greenhouses and money."

"Julia's dad?"

"*No.* Julia's dad is not interested in affairs either. He is also preoccupied with greenhouses and getting the meals on the table. Julia's parents are not the type to have extra-marital affairs. They don't wear caftans or make frequent trips to Edmonton."

"If Eugenia and Allister Wilde were killed in a car accident, would the Raines adopt Lois Wilde?"

"*Most likely.* They need somebody to help out in the greenhouses and Lanny Shepherd is no good to them."

"Hmmm," Lois said, sceptical. "Do you know the Stanton twins?"

"*Don't count on it.*"

"Do you know the Stanton twins?"

"*Without a doubt.*"

"What exactly is wrong with them?"

"They have cataracts; that's why their eyes look the way they do. And they don't ever get away so they have nothing better to think about than everybody's business."

"Do the Stanton twins talk about Lois Wilde?"

"*Cannot predict now.*"

"Yes, you can. Come on. How come when Julia and I, I mean Lois Wilde, weren't friends they said to me once in this sissy voice – why aren't you friends with the little Raine girl? You both stick to yourselves too much."

"I think I just answered that with my previous comment about not getting out of Flax ever. Plus, the Stanton twins like to see everybody in pairs, like them."

"Except for now that we are friends, I mean Julia and Lois are friends, when they see us together they make a sound like this: hussy, hussy. Why?"

"*Cannot predict now.*"

"Why?"

"Oh, I don't know. I'm tired. I don't have an answer to everything. It's hard having a husband in a coma."

"Do you know the Stanton twins?" Lois asked with renewed intent, shaking the eight ball again, in need of a more fruitful response.

"*It is certain.*"

"Well, then, give me an answer. When the Stanton twins see us together, why do they make a noise that sounds like hussy, hussy?"

A deep sigh from Mrs McCracken, then, "The Stanton twins live in a dream world. They make everything up. When they were children, they spoke their own language and had to go to a special school for the first two years. After that, they had a tutor. Mr and Mrs Stanton were too old to cope. They just let their twins go until they were driven to an early grave. Nobody even knows which one is Russell and which one is Berty. So who knows what hussy hussy means? It could mean the square of the hypotenuse is equal to the sum of the squares of the other two sides or it could mean, I think you're a little hussy, hussy – twice, because there are two of you."

A pause, followed with, "Are the Stanton twins homos?"

"*As I see it, yes.*"

"How do you know?"

"I just know. I've lived in Chicago long enough to be familiar with such things. There are signs."

"Like what?"

"They walk and talk like sissies."

"I could have told you that," I interrupted. I was the technical director; I had a right to interrupt. It had been my idea to turn off the overhead lights for the broadcast. That meant Lois climbing down the ladder, out of the mow and switching off the lights, then returning to the cosy, dusty gloom of our straw house, our triangular party hat of lamplight. The best part was our position behind the lamp, on the blankets, in the space where the light was kept in grey abeyance, never invited. It was there, the night of the hussy hussy line of questioning, I first observed to Lois that, for a boy, Alexander Mast looked a little bit like Hayley Mills, don't you think?

In the eighth grade, we were introduced to what was called the new maths. The new maths was about a future certain people, such as the mathematicians and space explorers, knew was on its way, a representation of what might be expected. First of all, binary notation, binary code, base two. Everything could be made to be understood in a series of zeros and ones. 111010=58. So futuristic I worked on converting the alphabet to binary code, tried to translate a poem by Archibald Lampman, covered an entire page of foolscap with ones and zeros, all to the enthusiastic approval of Miss Brilz.

Then we turned a page in the mathematics text and there was algebra. It almost made the binary system seem like a cheap gimmick. I loved algebra. Let X = the unknown. Let X = Hayley Mills, I wrote in my notebook. Alexander Mast = X. Lois Wilde = X. Therefore, Alexander Mast = Lois Wilde.

Late November, and I was waiting for Lois out in the barn. I had had to schedule an emergency session with Mrs McCracken, because of developments at school. I, for a change, had questions.

Lois's mother had volunteered to stage the Christmas concert, a situation Miss Brilz found pleasing as she could continue to devote herself full-time to academic instruction. Eugenia Wilde had decided upon a production she called *Joy to the World*, a musical revue offering jazzed up versions of Christmas carols accompanied by interpretive sorts of dance. Eight grades, eight carols, eight dance routines. The student body, as Mrs Wilde called us – an image of a 47-headed ton of flesh springing to mind – made up the choir, with the separate grades breaking rank for the dance portions.

As eighth-graders, we were privileged to have the opportunity to perform the finale and title piece – *Joy to the World*. Alexander Mast was not allowed to dance, so the four girls were to be done up in flapper-style dresses for a 1920s number. Lois fomented resistance but Barbara and Lesley loved the idea. I was firmly in Lois's camp but stopped short of ever making a critical comment about the director.

The more complicated costumes were to be sewn by the retired high school home economics teacher, Miss Maudsley, who visited the school to take measurements. Even in retirement, Miss Maudsley continued to wear the white nurse's uniform she had worn during her teaching years, a uniform that implied domestic science, hygiene and professionalism. One by one, she took us behind the piano, with her tape measure.

Miss Maudsley had an overbite and breathed loudly like a bull dog. There was some problem with her nasal passages and the acoustics behind the piano amplified its effects, so that the general impression was one of telephone breathing from a suspense movie.

"Raise your arms," she said.

Miss Maudsley found what she considered to be my bust line, then my waist. Then came the instruction, "Raise your skirt."

I took a moment to admire the blonde wood of the piano back; I looked over it to the grade eight class. Not one girl wearing a skirt, all in trousers. Had she asked them to lower their trousers?

In her white uniform, Miss Maudsley was creaking to her knees.

"Raise your skirt."

In order to wrap the tape around me, she practically had to rest her cheek on my right hip. Thank God, thank God I had put on leotards. The morning was cool but it had warmed up and I had considered taking them off at recess. Thank God, thank God.

Pulling the tape tight, Miss Maudsley drew up close to where the tape came together above my pubic bone. Leaned forward to read the number. Worse than when a dog tried to sniff you there and everyone was watching. OK. I dropped the skirt. The effort of standing caused the bulldog breathing to intensify. Through the magic of body chemistry, I managed to walk to my desk as if nothing had happened. Lois was watching.

"She practically squeezed my tits, back behind the piano," Lois said at lunch-time, out on the playground. "She had the tape measure like this –" Lois began an imitation of the breathing "– and she's fiddling around trying to get it right at the spot where my tits are biggest and she kind of rubs her hand here. Did she do that to you? Oh, right, you don't have tits, yet. I keep forgetting."

"No," I say. "She didn't do much. Just measured. It was kind of creepy, being back there with her."

Since the Christmas concert rehearsals began, Mrs McCracken had been drinking, for no particular reason other than she felt like it. Her drink of choice was the vodka martini. There had been several questions in the past couple weeks about other kids' views of Eugenia Wilde. Their thoughts on *Joy to the World – a musical revue*. Even requests for predictions: will people laugh at me in that flapper girl dress? Is there any possible way I might be able to get the dust virus before December 21?

Mrs McCracken was friendly when intoxicated and kinder in her judgments.

"Who cares what the other kids think? Chances are, they aren't thinking anything. And as for Barbara and Lesley, they love the idea of showing off in some trashy dresses. They adore your mother for giving them this opportunity. They're both certain a talent scout will show up for the concert and, by January 2, they'll have been signed up with the June Taylor dancers. Stop worrying. If anyone should be worrying, it's me. Look at the family I have: comatose and quarantined. I think it's time we moved out of this damn barn; it's been nothing but trouble."

And a few changes had been made to the set, all by Lois. Now a little martini glass stood on the end of a swizzle stick, entering the straw like a sceptre. Tiny rectangles of paper, like those of a TV broadcaster, lay on the desk. Lois had even made a small but still disproportionately large typewriter from cardboard, and this sat on a brick at right-angles to Mrs McCracken's desk. The brick also supported an empty two-ounce vodka bottle from Mr Wilde's most recent flight to a convention in Ottawa.

When the overhead light went off, I knew Lois had arrived. I clicked on the studio light and there she was. We wrapped ourselves in the blanket and got ready to roll. I had my questions ready.

"Do you know Miss Maudsley?"

"Definitely."

"How much difference to a pattern would skirt material make?"

"What?" Mrs McCracken had never before sought clarification.

"How much difference to a pattern would skirt material make?" I repeated. "Why did she have to ask me to raise my skirt when she was measuring me? Couldn't she have measured me without that having to happen?"

No visible reaction from Lois. No disgust from Mrs McCracken. Just the usual smooth transition from question to answer. "She's an old home ec. teacher who probably wanted to be famous. She probably wanted to be a famous designer and maybe she still thinks she might be someday. Or maybe she thinks she is so she has to do things the right way, like a famous designer would. You'd be amazed how many people go around thinking they're movie stars or Liberace."

"What do you think she was thinking about when she said 'Raise your skirt?' "

"Thinking? I would suggest she was thinking next to nothing. It's a big effort for her just to breathe. She's got some kind of problem like adenoids that never got removed, or a blockage like that flap at the back of your throat – I seem to have heard it was enlarged. Thinking about breathing takes up a lot of Miss

Maudsley's mental energy. You could imagine what that must be like, if you need to think to breathe."

After a very short while, Lois said, "Let's lie down. We can get arranged with the blanket." And we did, with me in front on my side and Lois behind on hers, we curved ourselves around the studio lamp, a crescent shape of girls, the dark side of the moon. Lois put her arm around me and it was as if Hayley Mills had just dropped by and together we were gigantic movie directors, watching the action in back of the lights. Lois had a couple of half-hearted questions about her dad's trip to Ottawa. Then there was quiet and the loft filled with a familiar happiness, as if my crushes were out driving around together, turning on their headlights, sweeping down one side of the coulee and up the other. If I lifted up my shirt – raise your shirt, I thought spookily – I was sure to see a glow behind my skin. If I stood, the lights shining from behind my ribs could have illuminated Mrs McCracken's set.

Which was when Lois kissed the back of my neck. And, with an enormous grin, I turned to her and she kissed me on the lips, a long kiss, and I wrapped my arms around her. Whoa, my mind said to itself – this was more happiness than my body could contain. It leaped out of me onto the straw in yellow and green grasshopper-sized fragments of light.

Then on came the overhead bulbs, ruining everything, and my dad's voice. "Julia? Is Lois up there?"

"Yes," I said, reaching out to extinguish the studio light, as if the whole set was wrong, which it was. We weren't supposed to have an extension cord in the barn. The wiring was no good.

"Her mother called. She wants her home. They have company." No mention of the cord.

"I forgot the damn Hubbards were coming over."

In my room, I stayed up late doing algebra homework. How pleasingly the numbers and symbols moved back and forth across the equations. After that, I made the remarkable discovery that Lois's name was practically a binary structure: IOIS, I wrote. Lois Wilde was a girl of the future.

About two weeks prior to the staging of *Joy to the World*, Mr Wilde learned he was being promoted to a junior executive position in Winnipeg. The Wildes would be moving. I repeated this statement to myself as if it were a paradoxical formula, the new maths at its most innovative. An actual moving van would arrive at their front door on December 31. Atlas. This was the sort of event common to Hayley Mills and girls who had been to Hollywood. So Lois did equal Hayley Mills, after all. Algebra did not lie.

Lois began to speak of junior high school – an institution foreign to Mercury Township. She made reference to our visits with Mrs McCracken as mental. I returned to the studio a couple of times alone, climbed the ladder in the dark smell of tinder-dry alfalfa and switched on the lamp. Not one question for Mrs McCracken. I had nothing to ask. I wanted Mrs McCracken to ask me a question: How do you know Lois will never come back to the studio?

I just know, I said. I know it the way an ant knows its way around the ant-hill. Obviously, it's not saying to itself, left, right at the next corridor, down the steep grade and then another right to the sugar pantry. I'm not saying Lois won't come back to the barn but I know it's true. I can read it somewhere inside me. Not that an ant can read words but maybe it can recognize certain signs and bumps like Braille.

And there was the revue to think of. Lois became increasingly irritated by the demands of the dance routine and the costume. She was looking for an out and made some headway by locating the definition of flapper in the dictionary. "Free from social and moral restraints," Lois read to her mother at one of the final rehearsals. "Do you really think it's a good idea to go ahead with this? Do you really think Barbara and Lesley's mothers are going to be happy with their daughters dancing around up here, free from social and moral restraints?"

"They don't care," Barbara and Lesley said in perfect unison.

"Well, I care," Lois said at recess. "Only my mother would want to stage some crappy musical with flappers. She wants me to be just like her; she wants to raise me as a slut. Well, you know what? I might be very sick the night of the concert. I might just be puking my guts out."

"Don't make me do the musical revue alone with the mole-cule. Don't do that to me, Lois," I said.

With her head full of spring-loaded plans, Lois looked me in the eyes. I was sick with worry for the next forty-eight hours but, the night of the concert, there was Lois – a flapper in a murderous mood.

Then a surprising affair. In the social hour after the show, my father invited the Wildes for dinner, the day after Boxing Day. They, that is Eugenia, accepted the invitation gushingly.

In the days that followed, I contemplated the preparatory work needed before Lois Hayley Mills Wilde could be permitted entrance to my bedroom. This immature family tree, I thought, should go. It had been developed to the point it now covered three sheets of Bristol board and included a woman from a Maidenform bra ad, Perry Mason and Della Street, Princess Anne and Eric Burden and the Animals, to name a few. There were no rules governing lineage, so any group or individual could qualify for family status. Ridiculous, really. Very childish. But I didn't want to get rid of it – or anything, upon further thought, other than the sissy jewellery box with the twirling ballerina, which I hid in my closet.

Being Christmas, my parents were busy with the poinsettia trade and I was supposed to help, or at the very least be watching Stephen but instead, and very inconveniently, I fell suddenly ill. Some sort of greenhouse virus, I suggested, contracted from mistletoe, from the family of potentially deadly berry viruses, I said to my father with all the drama I could muster.

Five days passed – were viewed, rather – on the movie screen suspended between my eyelids and the spackled ceiling of my room. Through some assemblage of cameras and projection equipment, my parents' made their debut, the thermometer again and again with boring regularity, a series of enormous tumblers of ginger ale, even the doctor with his Pepto-Bismol breath. Smellovision, I thought, just in time for the holidays.

Christmas morning, the gifts came to my bed, hydrofoiling above and around my feverish brain. Everyone stood and watched. Escaped from the screen, now they resembled people I had seen in a book of optical illusions, made to look large by being placed in a tiny room. My brother came and went, came and went until finally he had worn himself down to his regular size and demeanour. On the afternoon of the twenty-seventh, out of sheer boredom, he ordered me out of bed and, to my surprise, I found I was better. I had survived. My recovery had timed itself to accommodate Lois Wilde and her parents. What luck I had, I really was very lucky. Ageing but vital groups of antibodies moved through my bloodstream, carrying streamers, throwing ticker tape: this was certainly the life.

Moments later, in the shower, I observed for the first time two small breasts in the making.

"They're here," I heard Stephen shouting from downstairs.

And, lucky me again, I had just finished dressing; my hair looked great and I was downstairs in a minute, the smell of turkey and stuffing and cooked turnip causing a hard shove to the lining of my stomach but never mind. Before Lois had even begun to unbutton her coat, there I was in my harlequin-checked Christmas jumpsuit.

"Do you want to go and see Mrs McCracken?"

"No, I told you, that's mental what we were doing out there." First the peacoat, then the new and yellow banlon sweater were hung in the hall closet. Lois was beautiful. Her response ricocheted off me easily enough, the way my occasional cruel comments no doubt bounced off the rubbery skin of the molecule. Briefly, and with humour, I saw myself as possessing a blue knob for a head, much smaller pink knobs for breasts.

"What do you think junior high will be like?"

"How should I know?"

"I guess there will be lots of rooms full of grade nines."

"I guess." (Elongated with sarcasm.)

"I wonder if you'll have more of the new maths."

"That's really been on my mind, Julia."

There was nothing particularly wrong with this conversation, I decided. Lois was nervous about moving. I would be, too. She had always liked my little brother, so it made perfect sense that she would want to play with his new Tinkertoys. And I was still a little weak from the virus. Better for me just to relax.

It wasn't until we sat down to eat that I began to make sense of the situation, began to appreciate the difference between Lois' family and mine. Their clothing, for example.

Lois's black dress had me planning to fling my red and green Christmas jumpsuit into the furnace, the first chance available. Mrs Wilde was in a purple velvet dress, while my mother had on her stock pair of green plaid and slightly pilled slacks with a navy turtle-neck. Both men wore white shirts and pants, but my dad's were the kind that would never get him sent to Winnipeg. When I tried to gauge what the Wildes might think of my parents, I arrived at a wordless void into which tumbled nothing other than the certain knowledge that the Wildes were infinitely superior. Maybe they didn't know that. But I did. So why had I never noticed it before?

"Are you going to take Lois up to your room?" my mother asked, after dinner.

Upstairs, we sat on the bed, stale from my five delirious days of breast-growing. Lois, ever unpredictable, did not ridicule my family tree: paid no attention, in fact. She was restless, she said, bouncing to her feet, had to keep moving. And I was still probably quite sick, she thought. "Usually, with these things there's some kind of relapse," she said.

"How about a game of Cootie?"

"Nah."

"Monopoly?"

"I might go look at Stephen's room."

Lois and my brother busied themselves with his jigsaw puzzles and I, like a chameleon, took on the seven dwarfs pattern of the wallpaper. Became invisible. And then she was gone. The Wildes had so much packing to do.

The next morning, there was Lois's sweater in the hall; when nobody was looking, I moved it to my bedroom closet.

In the final afternoons of eighth grade, Miss Brilz was allowing me to help the younger children finish their topographical map of Canada. While the grade fives and sixes, in constant consultation with the Gage Canadian School Atlas, sculpted and painted their way through eastern Canada, I had single handedly and grumblingly constructed the west coast. As far as

I was concerned, elevation was an irrelevant feature and, far from being the exemplary substitute teacher I was supposed to be, spent large periods of time creating rows of pointed Dixie cup breasts, flattening them and starting all over again. If I didn't get out of this damn kindergarten soon, I'd go nuts. And, to add to my annoyance, Lois Wilde was coming to visit. She and her dad would be dropping by someday soon. *Her* junior high school ended in the middle of June; *they* were on a six-day cycle. Lois was someone whose life now conformed to another calendar, living in an altogether different galaxy with six-day weeks and perhaps an extra month thrown in. I began to worry for the first time that the world awaiting me after grade eight might be more plastic than I could imagine or endure. Topographical maps seemed inadequate preparation for a future that might structure its years in binary notation.

The day the map was finally complete, Lois and her dad were already there when I arrived home from school. This threw me, as I had envisioned hours of waiting that would settle into ennui, utter boredom and eventually, I hoped, a coma much like Mr McCracken's.

I began by ignoring Lois, with an indifference I thought would chill her to the bone. But, like some flawed gelatin product, Lois was not one to be chilled. She gave off a certain heat, in fact, a teacherly kind of incandescence, like Miss Brilz on the topic of the great depression.

"I have something for you," she said.

"Oh, yeah; me, too. I've got your sweater. It's up in my room," I said. She could follow me, if she wanted.

"Thanks," Lois said, placing the yellow sweater on my desk chair where I watched it slide to the floor and pool in a square of sunlight. It was the colour of lemon pie-filling, I saw for the first time, the instant variety, and therefore much too bright. Hayley Mills would never have chosen such a garment.

"I've had some testing done at my school," Lois announced. "They're putting me in the enrichment class next year. They say I have a mental age of eighteen. Even though I've just turned fourteen."

"I know you're fourteen now."

"Well, not really," Lois said. And pulling some folded, ragged-edged papers from a pocket, she added, "I brought this to show you. It's from the Reader's Digest. I found it in the school library and ripped it out, it was so interesting." She looked at me the way I looked at Miss Brilz when busy with my rows of breasts, hoping she would and would not see. "Anyway, it's about . . . you know . . . that time in the barn when I touched you. Well, it has these graphs and percentages and it says that –" and here she began to read, with the confidence of the smartest girl at the science fair, "– under age fourteen, a large proportion of girls might experiment with another girl but, by age eighteen, seventy per cent will know for sure whether or not they're [very brief pause] lesbians." The enunciation of this word had obviously required some practice, as it made its appearance with a bulky self-consciousness, the spoken equivalent of a Kotex pad worn for the very first time.

"But you're not eighteen, in real time," I said.

"I'm eighteen in mental age time. Which is just as real, if you ask the school psychologist. And I know for sure I'm not and, by the time I'm twenty-eight, I'll be eighty-five per cent sure."

"But that's not what it means," I said, studying the array of bar graphs. "It means by age twenty-eight, eighty-five per cent of the women in the survey who were that way said they knew."

"Well, whatever. I'll be in the eighty-five per cent who knows they're not and I'll be one hundred per cent sure. Why don't you just read it yourself, little miss mathematics? It's you I brought it for. And anyway, I better see what dad's up to. We're not staying for long."

Left on the bed with my glossy sheets of statistical probability, I felt as if I had just made a visit to the doctor, and not the local doctor: oh, no, I had seen the specialist, someone from farther away, paid to impart certainty. The yellow sweater lay on the floor and I made no move to pick it up until after Lois had left, after she had sat in the kitchen for more than an hour talking to my parents in her eighteen-mental-years-old voice, after she had waved goodbye and said *adios*, as if Spanish were the first language of those living in Winnipeg. Then I placed the sweater inside the suitcase beneath my bed, the same suitcase

where I had, one day in April or May, stored the McCracken
family.

The sight of Mrs McCracken caused a sudden and odd
desire: I wanted her back. I had to admit, I missed her. Even
thought about taking her to school with me the next day, inside
my trouser pocket. Maybe I would stand her, if for only a
moment, in my flour and water Rocky Mountains, facing west-
ward to the ocean, like an explorer or at least someone who
might want to make an intelligent comment. I knew I wouldn't
though. Too easily I could imagine the voice of Miss Brilz saying,
silliness and hijinx are one thing but a miniature woman with
ink-drawn pubic hair was quite another. Even though she would
never have made such a comment. And I laughed a bit to myself.
Instead, I went looking for the masking tape and, with several
pieces bandaged over and across her small body, I fastened Mrs
McCracken to the family tree, at the top, a little above Hayley
Mills.

The Lobster Queen

Susan Hampton

I don't know what I thought of her then. I know that the details don't matter. It could have been any two women, a thirty-year-old, a fourteen-year-old, falling in love, on a wharf anywhere in the world. Chinese women, for instance. They were very cold. They held each other through their coats, on the wharf.

The older one always woke early and had her first cup of tea by five-thirty. She had ironed a hanky and put it in the pocket of the coat she loaned the girl. On the wharf later, the girl put her hand in the pocket. It was still warm.

It may have been a year after when the girl's father found a letter she had hidden in a sock. She had forgotten writing it. Later she realizes there are forgotten areas all through her history, spread like fishing-nets over the landscape, nets which turn to clouds so areas of nothingness occur. The empty territory of the psyche. In this country, the body blurs sideways from the shock of what the nothing must contain.

We are not the same women we were. Everything has changed. When I looked back, I could remember some things about the girl. I know there are major blur areas. At this point, the details do matter.

In summer they began to fish from a rusted wreck at the end of the breakwater. It was dangerous to walk on, especially in the half-light before sunrise. They were usually the only ones there. At low tide, they walked to the bottom of the ship and fished for yellowtail swimming in the hold. The girl said she was tempted to dive in, the water was so green. Her friend said, "Don't be crazy, there's sharks."

The woman stood up and rigged her rod with a live yellowtail and cast into the sea. When she caught her first tailor, she filleted it and used that to bait both lines. "Tailor eat tailor," she said to the girl, casting again in one smooth action.

Every movement the woman made, the girl copied her. At first, she cast so wildly the hook swung behind her and caught her trousers. They were laughing into each other's faces, in a light nor'-easter wind.

"Here," the woman said, and she took the hook out. Then slowly she turned the girl around and kissed her on the mouth.

"Do it properly," the girl said. "You know what I mean. Kiss me properly."

The deck of the *Adolf*, wrecked in 1907 on top of six other ships, swayed beneath her. She held the woman for balance, and breathed in her breath. She tasted of sea wind and being outside and early light.

The woman looked at her for a long time, at first with a hot longing, then sadly, and then, with a kind of line across her face, she bent to pick up her rod and demonstrated the cast. The girl watched each movement, the tanned fingers releasing the reel clip, the slow backward arch of the back, the forward movement as she cast out so far the sinker was a tiny plop, invisible. The arms straight, strong, exactly in the direction where she wanted the bait to land. She did all this without speaking, then squatted and lit a cigarette.

Waiting for the schools of tailor to come in was like all waiting, a suspension, a positive quietness of the body, the tingling edge of any part of her body knowing it would leap at a movement of the line.

"How will I know," the girl asked, "whether it's waves moving the line, or a fish?"

"Your fingers will become sensitive," the woman said, showing her how to rest the line on the tip of her index finger, teaching her when to wind in a bit, when to let it out.

When the first tailor hit the line they stood and braced themselves, the sensation of a fish was so definite after all, and for twenty minutes they were reeling them in, shining and white, taking them by the gills and unhooking them, casting again.

Sometimes they forgot to rebait the hook, everything went so fast, and they caught fish anyway, by the fin, by the gills, because the school was so thick.

After the catch, fifteen or twenty fish at that time of year, they squatted to clean them. The girl watched the woman's fingers fly, scales lifting to the air like sequins, the knife expertly opening the belly, guts being flicked into the sea, the carving of fillets, never a mistake, the roe sacs of pregnant ones, blood on the fingers, sometimes the birds collecting, surrounding them.

The woman let down a bucket on a rope and hauled up water from the hold. They washed the fish. Squatting either side of the bucket they stared at each other, the girl's green eyes soaking blue from the woman's, till the woman leaned back and put her hands to her face. She breathed in, looking through her fingers at the girl, and smiled, shaking her head slightly, wry. At this time the girl knew what the gesture meant, without knowing why.

There would be more waiting at the house. Waiting was a part of everything that happened. The girl waited on the step, or on the chiller near the door, while the woman made tea in an aluminium pot.

Sometimes she disappeared to do other things and the girl didn't know where she was. Sounds would tell her – the dog barking at a man who came in asking for a haircut, water running, a bath being run.

"Get in," the woman said to the girl, "I'll come later and wash your back."

In the car, on the lounge watching TV, she held her hand out to the girl. At sundown she opened a bottle of beer and began to cook for the men. She walked the girl home at night. Before they came to the gate, she took the girl's head in her hands; holding her face, she kissed her once, not "properly", but breathing in, holding the breath.

In winter, the girl stayed in the kids' room once or twice, when the kids were away. In the bed they opened mouths, necks, arms, bellies, but there were places the girl could not touch her; these were her frozen zones, this was what she told the girl. Something is wrong, but nothing is ever explained. Later the girl will write the letter and hide it, unable to post it in case the opening of questions closes everything that has happened. She will hide it in a sock, and forget it. It will not exist.

At certain times of the year they went up the river in a long rowboat the woman hired from Mr Lindstrom, the dwarf. He lived in a small house he'd built himself opposite the mangrove flats, and kept bait in two long freezers. A wooden ladder leaned against each freezer, and sometimes the dwarf sat on one of these ladders while his customers worked out where they would fish, and what bait would be needed. He would recommend one thing or another depending on the wind and the tide. There was a windsock in his front yard and a hand-painted notice saying PIPPIES. CHICKEN GUTT. WORMS. PRAWNS. YELLOWTAIL.

It was early winter and there was frost on his lawn. The girl stopped at the small door and looked back at the marks their sandshoes had left in the frost. They bought the packets of bait and he followed them across the road to the river. The woman thanked him and headed out along the jetty. He stood there watching her movements, the darting of a cormorant behind her, smoke from the industries across the river, then ripples in the mudflats beneath them.

"This is not a rewarding liaison," the dwarf said flatly. The wispy curls on his large head shook themselves in the river breeze. He was standing on the bank, and the girl had stepped down onto the jetty, so they were looking directly at each other. The girl noticed his eyes had kind lines around them.

"I've asked her to go away with me," the girl said.

The dwarf looked out at the rowing boat, where the woman was storing the tackle bag, the buckets, the picnic.

"She won't go away. She had no family when she came here."

"I don't think she's happy."

"Who is happy? Tell me this. She will never take the children away."

The girl turned to look. The early light had turned the river pink. In the boat the woman sat quietly waiting

"You must find someone else to love," the dwarf said.

"It's too late."

"You will never get to know her."

"Maybe not. It doesn't stop the love."

"No."

"Does everyone know about us?"

"They have guessed. In the town, they call you 'the boys'. They won't say anything."

"There's nothing to say."

"No." The dwarf took her thin hand in his pudgy one and held it softly. His white hairs lifted and settled again on his head. "Tell her to take you up into Fullerton Cove," he said, "to the whiting hole. She knows where it is."

They have lit a fire on the beach, and cooked a snapper for lunch. The woman turns to sit facing the sea and lights a cigarette. She smokes it without saying anything. The girl considers how these two years have happened. She is sixteen and nothing has changed; there are no explanations.

Her fingers are not as sensitive as the woman's. She has learnt to tell the difference between the way a tailor and a bream take the hook; how a flathead is exciting, sudden, and swims hard, how a crab will suck and so on. She has learnt the woman's language, which she will forget later, but now seeing a man further down the beach dragging a fish on a rope and bending, rising, putting worms in the tin on his waist, she says, "Must be whiting about." The woman nods.

The woman has not much use for words. Most of her talk is saved for the dog, and the girl has learnt that a mood can be judged by this. If the woman is happy with the girl, she will speak to the dog with such affection and endearments the girl is sure it's for her.

"You darling thing. Look at those beautiful eyes. Come here now and let me cuddle you, gorgeous thing you are. What a girl!"

At other times the dog sits under the table, waiting, till the woman says "I don't want to SPEAK to you." None of her moods seem to be related to anything, as far as the girl can see.

On the beach the woman put her cigarette out and said, "My mother was a good swimmer." There was a long silence.

"She was in the state team, before she had me. They said," (she looked down towards the wreck, towards the city) "they didn't know who my father was. I think he was rich, but he never came near her again after I was born, except once when I was in the Home."

The girl considered this information carefully. It was the longest speech the woman had made in the time she had known her.

"Why were you in the Home?" the girl asked.

"My mother died when I was one," the woman said.

Suddenly she had lost her straight back, she seemed smaller than before. The girl wanted to take her in her arms.

Could she be reached out for? She was staring straight out to sea. The girl moved and sat in front of her. Now they had locked vision. The woman's eyes had turned into wells reflecting the sea, the fine lines radiating to the edge of the iris seemed painted there like markings on a lizard. She kept her eyes focused on the girl and made slight movements of her head from side to side. Eventually she looked away and lit two cigarettes. She passed one to the girl.

The girl smoked the cigarette because it tasted like the kiss. How many thousands of cigarettes she smoked later because of the memory of the kiss.

The girl realised she was on some sort of path. The way was not clear, but there was a fellow traveller. Later the path would be crowded with women but the girl was not to know this. When she looked ahead now she saw two solitary figures, parting and coming together again, but always parting.

She thought about the woman's mother. The woman could not let herself be held, by a friend, by a *child*, whom she now turned to abruptly – "I want you to swim," she said. "Go and get in the water."

The girl put down the snapper bone she was sucking on and walked towards the water. There was a boat in the distance, too far away to see her clearly. She took off her jeans and jumper and stood naked for a while, breathing, telling her body not to feel the cold. She bent to a low dive and stroked out to the first wave, which went over her like a tunnel. Underwater she opened her eyes and saw how green it was, a yellow green light like columns of buildings in other civilisations, then the discrete grains of sand, each one with its edges and vertices. She breast-stroked along the bottom, holding her breath as long as she could – almost a minute – and then came up to face the horizon, gasping slowly so it wouldn't show, and continued out beyond the waves. There was *The Lobster Queen*, the boat her friend was never allowed to go on because it belonged to her husband, and women were thought to be bad luck on fishing boats.

The girl could see the husband and his deckhand moving about, shaking fish from the net. The men didn't look up.

She turned and arrowed back to the waves. Ahead of the breakers, she trod water and began to take deep breaths. When the wave was three lengths behind her, she began to swim fast. The wave collected her like a giant hand and she ducked her head and held her arms straight out in front, fingers stretched. Then slowly she brought her arms back to her sides and came in fast on the beach, head first. The wave eddied and she stood up, an aviator, elated, the saltbush in the distance dancing, each leaf an oiled sparkling green.

"Don't you ever do that again," the woman said. "You had me frightened half to death, staying under so long."

The girl bent and nuzzled her face into the dog's neck, nuzzling and pretending to bite, then she dug her fingers in near the dog's tail and brought them backwards through the fur to the neck, growling, and the dog growled with her.

Late in the afternoon they went back to the beach for another throw. Squinting, the girl could make out cars on the breakwater and people fishing off the wreck. Then the woman had something on her line and reeled in fast.

"Huh, I thought it was a bloody fish, the way you pulled it in," the girl said. She stood looking down at a heap of tangled line on the hook.

"No, no. We can use this," the woman said. She had a hook in her mouth and the sun was shining on her eyebrows and teeth, on her straight nose. Her disappointed face.

The girl helped her undo the line, feeding the end through tangles, then holding it as the woman got progressively further away while unknotting it. Talking to herself about breaking-strain and bream. Then she came back and showed the girl how to tie it on to another line so it would be long enough.

"This is a blood knot; will you remember how to do it?"

"Yes."

"Will you remember how to do it when I'm dead?"

"Yes."

At seven o'clock the sheet of wet sand was streaked in pink and orange from the setting sun. The woman stood, a hand in her cardigan pocket, nudging at the sand with a toe. "Remember when we used to dig out pippies with our feet? Bucketfuls." The girl caught up with her and said, "Come on, let's walk." They went through wave edges and past an old man worming. He had a smelly piece of mullet tied on a string, and was dragging it across the sand after each wave receded. Every so often, he bent down and pulled a long worm out of the sand, and dropped it in a tin tied to his belt. His rod was standing upright in the sand further along. "Must be whiting about," the girl said. The woman grunted.

That night, they went to the hotel and sat in the lounge bar with the other women. They played the jukebox and drank beer till late.

When the girl went to the toilet, the woman followed her in and stood with her back to the door, watching the girl pee. When the girl finished, the woman pushed her gently to the side wall and put her arms on the wall and brought her face close and kissed her on the mouth. Through the wall, the girl could hear "Put your sweet lips a little closer to the phone, Let's pretend that we're together, all alone" and in her mouth she could hear the woman humming the same song against her tongue and her teeth. Then the woman sat and peed, while the girl watched.

"You go out first," the woman said.

It was the first time the girl had been drunk, and she realised how many times she had seen the woman drunk and not recognised it. She also thought, as they were driving home, she could top the woman's drink up at night – that helping her get drunk would make things happen. Half the night, she lay awake thinking about this; it was a moral decision she could make. Her body told her to do it. Her mind said no; her mind won.

In the morning when the girl came into the yard amongst the halfmade lobster pots, fish traps, string nets, bits of planking, oil drums, she saw the woman on the step cleaning out her tackle bag. With a minimum of words, and slowing the action of her hands so the girl could follow, she showed her rigs for different fish, when to use a trace, a swivel, and what size sinkers were needed. Then she took the reels off and squatted and showed the girl how they worked, and how to clean and oil them.

"This is an egg-beater," she said, "and this is what the ratchet's for. This is an Alvey reel, or a sidecast. It's better for the beach."

The girl looked at this one – it was the classic type you saw in books with people fishing, a plain reel, made of bakelite like the old radios.

"I'll get one of these, one day," the girl said.

The woman looked at her and said, "You'd be better with an egg-beater."

The girl ignored this. She would get what she wanted. It would never be just a matter of fishing.

Later the woman took her to the shed and showed her the sinker moulds, and pieces of lead they'd collected at the tip, or from people's roofs. They weighed the lead in their hands like butter. For some time they stood in the green light at the bench where her husband's cousin made their sinkers. "My cousin", she called him, but the girl knew he was her husband's cousin. It was the tall man who came to have his hair cut in the kitchen.

The woman was in a good mood that morning. She talked quietly about the tides and times of year and what fish liked to eat. She talked about the different shapes of the insides of fish, she said that mullet could only be netted or jagged because they wouldn't take a hook, and how they had a black lining to their gut.

"Groper do this," she said, squatting on the lawn near her tomato beds, opening and closing her mouth as she brought her head closer to the girl, who leaned in, her hair brushed by a sheet on the washing line. The woman sat back, grinning, and said, "Now, that's enough."

"How is your boyfriend?" she said, after a long time. "Do you have a boyfriend at work? What about the man who came into the restaurant?"

"I want you," the girl said. "Now."

"Now, now," the woman said, and went to fill the copper at the end of the shed. In the middle of the day her husband would come home. The shed had low windows at the back which let in the greenish light. Standing there watching, the girl realized that although the woman said she didn't have any love left for her husband, although they rarely spoke and then only to abuse each other, the abuse was the form their passion now took, it was their way of staying together, and the truth was the woman liked to do things for him – but only when he wasn't home. These things were done at certain times of the day – washing his overalls, filling the copper, ironing the shirts he wore to the club in the afternoons. The ironing lay on the floor in neat piles near her tools – the saw, hammer, chisels, brushes – things she needed to fix the house.

He kept his tools separate in the shed, where he spent most of his time when he wasn't on the boat. He had a kettle and tea things in the shed, where his friends visited him. He had a fridge there, and bales of wire and a cocky in a cage. When he came home he would stand in his overalls, wreathed in steam over the copper boiling his lobsters. Then he would take the catch to the co-op, come home and have a bath, put on his ironed shirt and go to the club and get drunk. He did this every day. At night he came home at ten, took his tea out of the oven and ate it alone, grumbling, while she watched the late news. They didn't do anything together except sleep in the same bed. Once the girl had sneaked into their bedroom. There were little piles of clothes everywhere, and the racing pages from the paper. The girl thought that maybe they had a flutter together, now and then, but she would never know this. It was the permanent mystery of adults who seemed to choose not to be happy. They could not give up the things they had because the things were known and clear and warm. If they were warm with abuse it was just another kind of heat.

The girl could see that the man was jealous of her, and that he didn't know what to do about it. Sometimes as she passed the shed he growled at her, which was his way of saying hello, and she would smile and ask how he was, but usually he pretended she wasn't there. He listened to the races on his little radio.

Sometimes the kids tried to talk to him, but he would tell them to get out of his way, he said he was worried they'd get a hook in their foot, or put their hands in his copper of lobsters.

The girl thought he might be uncomfortable because the boy looked like a girl, and the girl looked like a boy, but she never knew. Her own father was not good at speaking to children. So the man seemed normal, but more so. She tried not to think about him. Once he asked if she would like a naughty and she said no and thanked him, and went away with her throat burning.

She had forgotten writing the letter to the woman, and not sending it. Who are we, what are we doing? she had asked. Why is this so strong? Where are the others? She had obviously hidden it in the sock. Her father was waving it in the air and speaking crudely, in his insulted state, and then he hit her once, hard, on the face. When she became conscious she was lying on the bed. He was continuing with his sentences.

Later, her father went to visit her friend, trying three hotels and then the house. He told the woman he'd ring up the market where she worked and explain to them just what kind of person she was. He advised her never to touch his daughter again.

Ten years later, the girl found out this had happened. She had rung her sister and the sister said, "Just like when Dad –" and the story came out.

"When did this happen?" she said, "this visit of Dad's – when I was sixteen? What – seventeen? When I was at the restaurant?"

"Look," her sister said. "I thought you knew. Didn't anyone tell you?"

"No, nothing," she said.

"Well, look. I think you were sixteen. I used to lie for you, say you'd gone to another friend's place. You were seeing her for two years, three years – were you doing it? You never said."

"I don't know. Not exactly. Not completely."

The phone call left her in shock for days. In the kitchen, looking at her quince tree through a small pane of blue glass, she understood why she'd hated her father. Or why the hate was as strong as the love. Before, her rage had been blind. Her father's face appeared and she bared her teeth.

So many years later, it became clear why the woman had suddenly turned cold towards her. When she visited, the woman would hardly acknowledge she was there. There was no news about which cousin had sunk someone's boat because that bloke had stolen lobsters from his traps. No affectionate talk to the dog who now sat on the girl's lap, or beside her on the step, as if to console her. There were the visits and there was silence. The woman never sent her away, and never said why she had changed. When the girl asked if something was wrong, the woman shrugged, and got up to make more tea.

Sometimes there were strange fish in the sink.

"What's this you've caught?" the girl said. She leaned over, smelling it.

"Trevally," the woman said.

"What did you catch it with?"

"Beach worms," the woman said, talking for a while about the habits of trevally.

When the girl tried to talk about things other than fishing, personal things, the woman was silent or changed the subject. She moved her lips around without opening her mouth. She shrugged a lot, and looked out the back door. She always had her hand on the brown dog beside her.

They sat looking at the husband's nets drying on stumps on the back lawn. The husband was watching his lobsters cook, and turning his head to the side now and then to say something to his cocky. He had found the cocky caught in wire on the riverbank, injured, and brought it home and nursed it for months. Sometimes he put the cocky on his shoulder, and fed it with cheese.

The woman made the girl tomatoes on toast and tea with milk and sugar. Then she opened the fridge and took out a lobster she'd taken from her husband's catch the day before.

"Come here," she said, beckoning with the lobster's feelers. At the bench, she showed the girl how to open the lobster, laying it on its back and making a neat cut down the centre of the tail up to the head, and opening the shell away. Now she took a round segment from near the tail and held it to the girl's mouth.

The flesh was moist silk against her tongue. It was as though every sweet flathead fillet she'd ever eaten was a preparation for this craving in the mouth. They set to and devoured the lot, grasping legs and cracking them open and sucking out the flesh. They ate the lobster's brain. They up-ended the shell and drank the juice. Then they wrapped what was left and put it in the bin out of sight.

When they sat down again, the woman's face seemed to set in its lines till she looked like a statue. Sometimes this had happened at night, when she was tired. She sat very still, without speaking.

The dog came in and put its paws on the girl's lap, and looked into her face. Its eyes were a deep gold flecked with brown like a river stone seen through water. Eventually the woman said, "Maybe you ought to get a boyfriend. Don't you think?"

"If you want me to," the girl said.

Free Love

Ali Smith

The first time I ever made love with anyone it was with a prostitute in Amsterdam. I was eighteen and her name was Suzi; I don't think she was much older than I was. I had been cycling round the town in a bad mood and had come upon the red light district quite by chance; it was the most pleasant red light district I've ever got lost in. The women there sit on chairs in windows that are lined with furs and fabrics, they sit breast-naked or near-naked, draped with gowns and furs. It took me a while to work out that they were probably scowling at me so contemptuously not just because I was staring but because I wasn't business.

It was evening and I'd been out cycling by myself. I had wandered down a back street and had stopped to put my jumper on, and my bike had fallen over and the chain had come off. It was when I stood the bike up against the wall of a building to get a proper go at the chain that I noticed the cards stuck by the door. Several of them were in English, one said *Need To Relax? Take It Easy No Rush Ring Becky*. Another said *Dieter Gives Unbeatable Service Floor 2*. Another said something about uniforms and domination and had a drawing of a schoolgirl on it. I was just laughing at them to myself when I saw one at the bottom in tiny writing and several languages, Dutch, French, German, English and something eastern, and the English line said *Love for men also women, Suzi 3rd floor*. The also was underlined.

That's when I left my bike standing and found myself going up the old staircase; on the third floor there was a door with the

same card stuck on it and my hand was knocking on the door. I
had a story ready in my head in case I wanted to get away, I was
going to say I was lost and could she direct me back to the youth
hostel. But she came to the door and she was so nice, I took to
her at once and wasn't the least bit scared.

The flat had one room and a bathroom off it, some chairs
and the bed and a hanging bead thing curtaining off the kitchen
area like in photographs of the sixties. On the wall there was a
poster of the lead singer from A-Ha, A-Ha were big at the time
in Europe and she said she liked him because he was a man but
he looked like a woman. I remember I thought that was a very
exciting thing to say, I hadn't heard anyone say anything direct
like that before. I come from a small town; one night my friend
Jackie and I had been sitting in a pub and two girls had been
sitting at a table on the other side of the room; they looked
conventional, more so than we did really, they had long hair,
were wearing a lot of make-up, and it was when I glanced to see
what kind of footwear they had on that I noticed one of them
had one foot out of her high-heeled shoe and was running it up
and down the other one's shin under the table. This was a very
brave thing to be doing now that I come to think about it;
chances are if anyone had seen them they'd have been beaten
up. At the time I pointed it out to Jackie and she said something
about how disgusting it was, I think I even agreed, I never
wanted to disagree with her on anything.

The prostitute spoke English with an American accent. She
said she had an hour and would that be enough for me, and
though I hadn't a clue I said yes I thought so. I showed her my
hands all oily from the bike and said I should maybe wash them,
and she sat me down in one of the old armchairs and, bringing
a cloth and a washing-up bowl over, washed and dried them for
me. Then she did this thing, she put my hand to her mouth and
put her tongue between my fingers at the place where my fingers
meet my hand, and she pushed it in, going along between each.
I think my head almost blew off just at her doing that.

She gave me a cup of very strong coffee and a glass of red
wine, she told me to help myself from the bottle of wine she left
on the little table next to the chair, then she put her arms around

my neck and kissed me, and loosened my clothes, and undid my jeans, and I sat there, amazed. She took my hand and took me on to the bed, she didn't even pull the covers back, we stayed on top, it was August, warm, and afterwards she showed me what to do back though I did have a pretty good idea. When eventually she looked at her watch and at me and smiled and shrugged her shoulders, we got dressed again and I took out my wallet and thumbed through the guilder, but she put her hand over mine and closed the wallet up. It's free, she said, the first time should always be free, and when she saw me to the door, she said would I be in Amsterdam long and would I like to come back. I said I would very much like to, and went down the stairs in such a daze that when I came to my bike I got on it and tried to cycle it away, completely forgot about the chain and nearly hit my chin off the handlebars. So I pushed it back to the youth hostel and I felt as I walked past the reflections of the tall buildings curving in the leafy surfaces of the canals that life was wondrous, filled with possibility. I stopped there and leaned on the railings and watched the late sun hitting the water, shimmering apart and coming together again in the same movement, the same moment.

When I arrived back at the hostel, Jackie put the chain back on for me. Jackie and I had been friends since school; she'd been in the year above me, and we'd stayed friends now we were both students. We'd saved our summer money to go on this trip. I'd been serving in the souvenir shop on the caravan site since the end of June and she'd been behind the bed and breakfast counter of the tourist information board; we made a pittance but it was enough to get us return tickets for a cheap overnight bus to Amsterdam.

Jackie was blonde and boyish and golden in those days. One day I had simply seen her, she was sitting on the school wall by the main door and I had thought she looked like she was surrounded with yellow light, like she had been gently burnt all over with a fine fire. At a party we'd sat in a dark corner and Jackie had nudged my arm, her eyes directing me to a handsome thuggy boy lounging on the couch opposite watching us, her mouth at my ear whispering the words, see him? Tonight I only have to smile, you know, that's all I have to do.

I had thought this very impressive, and had held her head for her later in the upstairs bathroom when she was being sick after drinking a mixture of beer and wine; we sat on the stairs laughing after that at the girl whose party it was going round the living-room hoovering up other people's sick into one of those small car hoovers; after that we had been friends. I don't know why she liked me, I think because I was quiet and dark and everybody thought I must be clever. I'd thought Jackie was beautiful, I thought she looked like Jodie Foster on whom I had had a crush, she looked like Jodie Foster only better. I'd thought that when we were at school and I thought it then, even though Jodie Foster's film career had hit rather a low spot at the time.

I'd had these thoughts for years and they were getting harder and harder to keep silent about. I didn't really have a choice. Once we got to Amsterdam and she saw there were people selling big lumps of hash in the street, she was filled with moral outrage, that's what she was like. But the overnight bus had been a great excuse to lean my head on her shoulder, to have my nose in her yellow hair and pretend I was asleep, which meant I was very tired the first day we were in Amsterdam, going round in a stupor telling myself it was worth it.

Already Jackie had made contact with a boy from Edinburgh whom we met in the youth hostel kitchen, his name was Alan; already they were big friends and he'd suggested she should go and watch him sword-fight at a tournament that night, which is why I cycled off in a terrible mood. I was in really rather a good mood by the time I came back to the hostel, and Jackie, who hadn't gone to the sword-fight after all, went into a sulk because I was happy for some reason and because when she asked me where I'd been I wouldn't tell her.

Nothing could spoil my holiday after that, I didn't care any more. And that's when Jackie started being unusually nice to me; this was confusing because, although we were best friends we were pretty horrible to each other most of the time. The next day she hired a bike too and we cycled up and down by the canals and the crammed parked cars, we drank beer and ate ice cream under restaurant parasols, we visited the Van Gogh Museum and Rembrandt's House and the Rijksmuseum full of old Dutch paintings, we went to a shop where they made shoes while you watched. The day after, we cycled to a modern art gallery; downstairs they had a room sculpture where people were sitting round a bar and their faces were made of clocks. We wandered this gallery for a while and upstairs I lost Jackie and fell asleep on one of the wooden seats. When I woke up, she was sitting very close to me, her arm on my shoulder. I sat up and she didn't move away; we sat there looking at the picture I'd fallen asleep in front of, it was a huge rectangle of red paint with one thin strip of blue paint down the left hand side. Her leg was pressing firmly into my leg. Do you like this? she asked, looking at the picture, and I said I did, and she suggested we should go and visit the Heineken factory now.

At the Heineken factory they give you a tour of where and how the beer is made, all the steps in its brewing process, how it's bottled, how the labels are stuck on and where it goes after that. At each stage they give you a generous glass of beer and everyone on the tour shouts cheers or *pröst* and drinks it. Then they take you into their office for after-tour drinks. By the time we'd done the Heineken tour, we were so drunk we shouldn't have been cycling at all and had to leave the bikes against a tree and lie on our backs in a park, laughing at nothing and looking at the sky. It wasn't as if we'd never been drunk together before, but somehow this time it was different, and we sat in the grass in the late afternoon and I told her all the things I'd felt for years now, and she looked at me woundedly, as if I'd slapped her, and told me she felt exactly the same. Then she put her arms round me and kissed my mouth and my neck and shoulders, we were kissing in the middle of Amsterdam and nobody even noticing. Even after the Heineken wore off, the afternoon didn't, it lasted for the rest of the holiday, me with my arm through hers on the street, at nights in the youth hostel dormitory Jackie reaching up from her bunk below mine to press her hand into my back, us holding hands between bunks in the dark in a room full of sleeping people. Very romantic. Amsterdam was very romantic. We took photos of each other at the fish market, I still have that photo somewhere. We went boating on a lake and took pictures of each other rowing.

The day before we were supposed to be leaving, on the pretext of going out to do some mysterious present buying I cycled back to the red light district and left my bike at the bottom of the stairs again. I had to wait this time for half an hour. Suzi remembered me, I know for sure, because afterwards she sat up, looked at her watch, smiled and ruffled my hair, saying, it's sad darling but the second time you have to pay. It was good, but not as good as the first, and it cost me a fortune. On top of which I had to buy Jackie a present; I remember it was expensive but I can't remember what it was I actually bought her. I think it was a ring.

Of course, when we got home, we stopped being able to do things like hold each other's arm in the street, though we did manage to snatch a little time after hours in the back gardens of unsuspecting people, in lanes and alleyways between houses or garages, in the back of her father's van parked in the dark by the river. Otherwise it was downstairs at either of our houses after everybody else had gone to bed, on the floor or on the couch, one of us with one hand over the other's mouth, both of us holding and catching our breath.

The first place we really made love was arriving back home after Amsterdam in the women's toilets at the bus station, hands inside clothes, pushed up against the wall and the locked door in the minutes before her father was due to come and take us and our rucksacks home. It was one of the most exciting things I have ever done in my life, though Jackie always called it our sordid first experience. About a month after, I walked past the tourist information board and saw through the window in the back office Jackie heavily kissing the boy who worked on the Caledonian Canal tourist boats. I thought that remarkably more sordid, I remember. But then, what people think is sordid is relative after all; the person who saw us holding hands between our seats at the theatre one night thought it sordid enough to tell our mothers about us in anonymous letters. We both had a lot of denying to do and that's something that certainly brought us closer together at the time. We had that to thank them for. Recently Jackie and I lived in the same city again for a while, and we were always nice to each other when we'd meet occasionally in the street. We both know we owe each other that, at least.

But I date the beginning of my first love from that August in Amsterdam, and we lasted over five years on and off before we let go. I think about it from time to time, and when I do the picture that comes first to mind is one of the sun as it breaks apart and coheres on the waters of an unknown city, and I'm there, free in the middle of it, high on its air and laughing to myself, a smile all over my face, my wallet in my pocket still full of clean new notes.

PRESENT TENSE

Present Tense

The first five stories in this section all conform to the easiest definition of lesbian fiction: they are about getting (or failing to get) the girl. There the mutual resemblance ends. These stories deal with the tensions of contemporary adult erotic life, from a Puerto Rican disco to the Irish countryside. Some could be described as peculiar romances; others refuse all such consolations.

The first two stories feature contrasting loner heroes, but both authors treat them with a deft touch. Jane DeLynn's "Puerto Rico" is anti-romantic in structure as well as treatment; its cynical protagonist is always in some sense alone. Though she wants to escape herself and "fraternize with the natives", this Don Juan's search for holiday sex ends up leading her through a cultural minefield. She is aware enough of her ignorance and prejudices to satirize them, but not enough to escape them. Her difficulties with Spanish grammar stand for more profound gaps in comprehension. DeLynn's people are foreign countries to each other, and no "guidebook for special persons of special tastes" will help a traveller find her way.

Dale Gunthorp's protagonist in "Kermit's Room" is as isolated as DeLynn's, but for different reasons. Instead of sex she seeks out "bareness" and tries to reduce her all-white living space to a blank. She fights against the seductiveness of things and the nagging voices of consumerism. But from behind this obsessive, existentialist narration emerges an old-fashioned comic romance based on the irresistible attraction of opposites.

I wanted to find her, but all I did was dust her satsuma peelings with the careful touch of a forensic investigator, and hoover around her bootprints.

In Marnie Woodrow's "In the Spice House", the world of spices the narrator discovers through her enigmatic lover evokes the non-rational nature of their desire. Many lines in this story work on two levels, creating a lushly erotic atmosphere: "It has to cook really slowly and for a long time. Do you mind?" But what gives it real substance is its tragic ending, the briefness of this particular encounter. We can taste each other, Woodrow seems to suggest, but never be truly satisfied.

The last two stories in this section are both, in different ways, about ethics. In each case, letting yourself fall in love cuts against the grain of a community, and causes irreparable pain to other people. Mary Dorcey's "A Country Dance" could be summarized, at the plot level, as a tale of two women evading the threats of rural homophobia, but the real drama is their private one. The narrator is old enough to recognize the repetitiousness of romance, but not yet immune to it. This is a story of friendship and age, self-deception and desire, all played out with exquisite pacing over one long evening at "a Friday night country dance, surrounded by drunken males who have never before seen two women dance in each other's arms."

Michelene Wandor's "Some of My Best Friends" is set in a very specific milieu – British gay leftist activism of the mid-1980s – but explores a more timeless conflict between individuals and their settings. It's about the personal and the political, the enemies within and without, and the disruptive qualities of love in a time of battle: "we sat down on opposite sides of the kitchen table and i said well, this is a how dye do." This story of bereavement still manages to make fun out of squabbles over words. With delicacy and balance, Wandor writes about wanting, with the best motives, "to have your cake and eat it".

Puerto Rico

Jane DeLynn

One of the things I like to do when I travel is fraternize with the natives, and of the many ways to do this, sex is perhaps the best. You can walk down the streets, of course, and follow a person dressed in a certain style in the hope they will lead you to a certain kind of place, but it is easier and far more certain to buy a guidebook – a guidebook for special persons of special tastes. It will supply you with the names and locations of bars around the world, and something of the kind of person and experience you are likely to encounter in these bars. There are guides for men and women – and no doubt for some of the other sexes, too.

I was staying by myself in a guest house in the Condado area of San Juan. Although it was a guest house for persons of special tastes, which I had been told would be good for someone who was traveling on her own, I found it extremely difficult to engage anybody in conversation. This was a while ago, after people like us had gotten over the initial excitement of beginning to talk about ourselves and our condition both to ourselves and to the world outside, but when we were still supposed to be kindly disposed towards each other – not just women and women, or men and men, but women and men as well – and the lack of friendliness there surprised me. Disillusionment had already begun to set in, a disillusionment similar to that in love when you realize that the two who thought they were one are really two after all, but a kind of consensus was around whose intent was maybe not so much to hide this realization as to pretend it was not important. The more we hid it, of course, the more important it became, but I had made efforts to overcome my natural cynicism concerning the possibility of change in the behavior and attitudes of human beings towards one another, and I was not yet willing to admit that these efforts had been in vain.

I suspect that this is too sophisticated an analysis of the situation, that in fact I was at a place and with people who had never been particularly interested in the initial excitement I'm referring to, who therefore would not have suffered any disillusionment, whose friendliness or lack of it was less a matter of consensus than of simple preference. Quite possibly these were people who refused to admit they were different from the world around them; very likely they were people who refused to discuss the subject at all. I couldn't tell, I could only guess, because nobody was talking to me. Most of the people not talking to me were Americans, but people from other parts of the island or the Caribbean were managing to ignore me too.

One problem was I was the only woman traveling alone. Even if the others were not in couples, they were part of a group. Although this happened constantly, somehow I never managed to anticipate it; I kept expecting to encounter other solo adventurers similar to me in everything but hair color. I wondered why it had been suggested I come here, to that part of the Caribbean which most resembles Miami Beach. I would stroll down the Condado looking at the big hotels and their kidney- or heart-shaped pools with intense disgust, wishing I were on a tiny island with straw huts whose thatched roofs leaked in the rain. I felt contempt for the women and men sitting around the pools with triangles of aluminum-covered cardboard under their chins reflecting the sun onto their faces as they drank pineapple daiquiris and listened to Gloria Gaynor singing "I Will Survive" on their ghetto-blasters. These were the years before Walkman, and disco was big then; for the first time in my life I swam to a beat. Perhaps it was appropriate; I was swimming in a city. The swimming didn't calm me; it only set me up for the things of night.

The guidebook suggested several bars where tourists might feel welcome, but since I travel so as not to be me, I decided on a local bar, a place where the natives went. If I were going to reject or be rejected, I wanted it to be with a different kind of person than those whom I rejected or who rejected me in Manhattan. That afternoon I practised my Spanish. *Cómo se llama?* – What is your name? – though it is said in the third person, as if you were talking to someone about somebody else. *Quiere usted bailar?* – Do you want to dance? – a bit formal, but the book was clear about not using *tu* when you didn't know someone – even someone you might end up exchanging saliva with a couple hours later. The *usted* worried me; it had an ugly Germanic ring.

There was an outside bar at our guest house, where people would gather in the evening before going out to dinner. I sat there with a cuba libre, partly to kill time, partly to see what the women were wearing, partly because of my ineradicable hopes. A Puerto Rican man in his early forties sat down next to me; he was slightly overweight, but good-looking in the Latin way. After a few minutes of silence he asked me if I was having a good time.

"Not really," I said.

"No? I am always so happy here."

"Maybe if I knew somebody. I think I should have gone to someplace tiny, with hardly any people."

"I have just the spot for you," he said. "Vieques. I go there all the time – it's a little island off the coast. Twenty minutes on the airplane and you're there." I wrote the name of the island down, and the airline that flew there.

"The women here aren't very friendly," I said, glancing at the couples locked in their claustrophobic worlds. I expected him to be sympathetic, but he shrugged.

"What can you expect? They're on vacation. They come to this place because they know it's safe."

"I'm on vacation too," I protested. He bought me a drink. He told me he was married, but sometimes he came here to get away from his wife, who lived on the other side of the island. "Do you want to have dinner?" I asked him.

"I'm sorry, I'm meeting some friends." I hoped he would ask me to join them, but he didn't. No doubt they were men, going to some male place where they didn't want to be bothered with someone like me. I talked with him till he left to dress for dinner.

The women drank their pre-dinner cocktails in their silk shirts and gold chains, white pants with pleats in them, makeup. What they wore was of no use to me; I had nothing like that in my hotel room, nor in my closet back home, nor would I have wanted to.

I decided to wear a pair of gold jeans a friend had stolen from a chic Italian boutique in New York; they were too tight for her and she had given them to me. If the label of this boutique had not been on the pants I could not have brought myself to wear them; they looked like they came from one of those cheap places that lined Union Square before it got cleaned up. "Puerto Rican stores," my mother used to call them, and though I had protested I had secretly felt that she was right. And yet, I had not seen anything remotely resembling gold jeans on anybody in San Juan. On the contrary, people here seemed to dress more formally and conservatively than in New York City. I told myself that was because I hadn't yet gone to the bars where women like me hung out. I told myself that in any case I didn't care what people thought, at least I would be noticed: I was tired of being invisible.

In my gold pants, before dusk, I walked towards town on the main road of the Condado. You would have thought I was leading a parade: almost every car that passed had to slow down and shout something out the window to me. *Hija de puta, puerca, vendámelos, prostituta!* – even women stopped to shout mean and half-intelligible things at me out the windows of their white convertibles. I was glad I didn't know Spanish better. My face burned but I refused to go back; I didn't like them any more than they liked me.

When I couldn't take it any more, I retreated into a dark and empty restaurant, where I ate some mediocre *carne asada*. Now that the effect of the cuba libres had worn off I felt a bit depressed, and I ordered a double espresso to wake myself up. My bravado was gone and I wished I was back at the motel reading a book or lying on the sand. But if I began to pay attention to that coward's voice within I would never be able to do anything or go anywhere, so I forced myself to head for the disco. According to the map, it was near the restaurant where I had eaten, but I was unable to find the street. I asked people directions but this was no help, either because my Spanish was bad or because people were deliberately misleading me on account of my gold pants.

After half an hour of fruitless wandering I hopped in a taxi. The man shook his head and refused to move. In the luxury of his being unable to understand me, I told him in English that he was a closety faggot, that his wife was a whore, that I had fucked his daughter's brains out all last night. When I stopped scream-ing he got out of the cab and, motioning me to follow him, led me across the street and down a little alley. He stopped in front of a building. It was the place I was looking for. He refused my tip.

I walked up the stairs to the entrance to the disco. The man who took the money seemed worried I didn't know what kind of place it was and kept pointing to several men standing together by the door. "*Sí, sí, yo comprendo*," I assured him, but he wouldn't take my money. Through the closed door I could hear the music. It was Latin rather than disco, but New York is in many ways a Latin city and I felt at home. Finally two women came up the stairs together; they were holding hands and, when I didn't pass out from astonishment or shock, the man finally accepted my money and let me follow them in.

The front room was an old-fashioned bar with large "antiqued" mirrors and flocked red wallpaper and banquettes; it didn't exactly resemble any bar I had ever been in, and yet it felt familiar, like a dream of a bar. Beyond it was the dancing area, a huge room with a mirrored revolving ball that hung from the ceiling and reflected colored lights onto the floor, the walls, your eyes. It was not yet eleven, but the rooms were already crowded.

The biggest difference from what I was used to in New York was the clothing. Whereas on Christopher Street in the Village, men walked around in jeans, plaid shirts, cowboy boots, and carefully trimmed three-day-old beards, here the iconography was more direct: close-fitting pants made at least partially of some synthetic material, pullover knit shirts in bright colors or dress shirts in stripes and patterns, clean-shaven faces with coconut-smelling pomade slicking down their hair, highly polished pointy shoes as contoured as their pants hugging their crotch.

But it was the women who were the real surprise. Either they wore high heels and fancy low-cut dresses that sharply outlined their bodies, huge amounts of dark mascara and bright red lipstick swabbed on their faces, or they had on dark blue or black suits, white shirts, and wingtip cordovan shoes, their faces plain and unmade-up, with short, slicked-back hair. Some looked like flowers and some looked like men, but either way they didn't look anything like me – or the blue-jeaned hippies, tweed-blazered businesswomen, or polyestered secretaries you saw in New York bars. I had seen women dressed like this before, back when we were just beginning to talk about ourselves with excitement, in bars where women who knew nothing of this talk still dressed in ways that were a sign of the past we were trying to destroy. In an odd and embarrassing fashion they had excited me, these women that bound their breasts to hide the fact that they were women, these women that would not let you touch them "down there" because they could not admit they were not men, and I had often wondered what it would be like to go home with one of them. But they were too butch for me to come on to them, and I was not femme enough for them to come on to me.

Everyone in the bar stared at me – perhaps it is more accurate to say they stared at my gold pants. Those who did not have the guts to stare at them directly were staring at them in the mirror, where, amidst the black and gray and brown pants, the brown legs with black stockings, shone two pillars of gold. Suddenly I remembered my bad luck with Latin women. In all the nights I had spent at bars I had never succeeded in persuading a *latina* to come home with me. The closest I had come was dancing for about an hour with a *puertorriqueña* at the Sahara. We kissed a little, then she asked me what I liked to do in bed. When I told her she said she was sorry, but I was not what she needed me to be.

I realized my eyes had focused on a woman in a dark blue dress with high black heels. She seemed to be looking at me too, with deep brown cow eyes like those of someone I used to love, though at the moment I could not remember who this was. It made me feel as if I knew her, so I got up the nerve to walk over to her.

"*Quiere usted bailar?*" I asked. She looked at me strangely. "*Quiere usted bailar?*"

"*No comprendo.*"

"*Quiere usted bailar.* You know, *dance,*" I said in desperation, pointing to the dance floor. She walked away. I started to follow her, thinking she was leading me to the disco area, but she went over to some people she knew. She said something to them and they began giggling at me. I turned to my right. A woman stood near me; I didn't even know what she looked like. Who cared what she looked like if only she would help me get away from this spot? "*Quiere usted bailar?*" I asked.

"*Quieres bailar?*" she said back.

"*Si,*" I said, and began heading for the dance floor.

"*No,*" she shook her head, then repeated: "*Quieres bailar?*"

"*Si. Quiero bailar.*" I took her hand, but she shook it off. I pointed to the couples dancing. Again she shook her head.

I was dying to leave, but I forced myself to go back to the bar and order a drink. A cuba libre – coke to keep me up, rum to calm me down, *libre* for all the faggots stuck in Castro's prisons, though I didn't know about this then. Perhaps, I should say, I didn't want to know about this then. I drank it quickly, with my eyes straight ahead, then I ordered another. So what if I got drunk? It would change the state of my mind, if not to something better, then to something different.

I tried to smile to show I was at ease, but of course it is difficult and unconvincing to do this when you know that the people who are looking at you know you have no reason to be so. In spite of my attempts to think ego-enhancing thoughts, all I could envision was the hideous walk down the Condado, the parade of epithets pouring out of cars. I remembered the vacation I had pictured: empty curved beaches surrounded by palms, women of various sexes all in love with me. What had been going through my head that of all the places in the world I ended up here? What was the matter with me that I unfailingly chose the wrong bar, the wrong clothing, the wrong person? Surely it couldn't be accident; either God had something in for me, or a perverse worm inside me was intent on compensating for an undeserved good fortune that years ago I had thought I had had.

"She was trying to tell you how you say," said a man's voice at my shoulder.

"What?"

"*Quieres bailar*. Do you want to dance."

"*Quieres bailar*," I repeated. "That's much prettier."

"*Usted* is formal."

"*Sí*, I know. But the *libro*—"

"*Quieres bailar*?" he said.

"*Yo comprendo*," I said. "*Quieres bailar*."

"No," he said. "Do you want to dance?"

I assumed it was pity. He was tall for a Puerto Rican, dark and somewhat younger than me. He wore a knit shirt and tan pants with a slim black belt and, like everybody on the dance floor except me, was a wonderful dancer. The music was disco now and we did the hustle, then it switched to a salsa beat. After each dance I stopped to give him a chance to move away, but despite my inadequacies he kept on dancing with me. No woman would be so kind.

I tried to imitate the movements of the people around me as they undulated to the music. After a while I began to sweat, and the heat and wetness aided my exertions. Or perhaps it wasn't that I was actually dancing so much better, but that my self-consciousness about how I was dancing began to disappear. The sexiness I secretly believed was always hidden within me began to rise to the surface, and I felt I could seduce my partner, or anyone – that it didn't depend on how I danced or looked but merely on how I felt about how I danced or looked. I told myself the stares I had been and was still receiving expressed not hostility, but admiration for my sexiness and guts. Women liked odd things, that was why heterosexual women fell into bed so easily with women like me; all you had to do was ask. Women who liked women were far more discriminating, but the women in this bar who were dressed like women resembled heterosexual women much more than they resembled gay women; in fact, they looked far more like heterosexual women than the heterosexual women I knew in New York.

The man I was dancing with told me his name was Juan, that he sold televisions in an appliance store, that he lived with an older man named Carlos who was in Mexico City for a week on business. Juan was not supposed to make love with anybody else, but perhaps he would tonight. If Carlos found out he would end the relationship. Spanish men – and women also – were incredibly jealous. Juan had broken off with his previous lover, whom he had lived with for four years, because he had found out that he was cheating on him with a woman. Juan had discovered this just before they were going on a vacation together, and, as it was too late to cancel the reservations, he had said nothing until they arrived back at the San Juan airport. As they were standing at the baggage pickup, he told his lover he would never see him again.

"Was he gay or straight?" I asked.

"My lover." He almost spat. "He is a pig."

I wondered if I was supposed to sleep with Juan in return for his asking me to dance, in some kind of revenge for his ex-lover's betraying him with a woman.

At a lull in the music – that period every half-hour when you're supposed to buy a beer – Juan excused himself to go to the bathroom.

I felt sweaty, hot, sexy. Again I saw the woman with the dark blue dress, the high heels, the cow eyes, staring at me.

Almost with a swagger I walked over to her.

"*Quieres bailar?*" I asked, with a slight Castilian lisp, holding out my hand.

She looked at me in disgust, then walked away, in a language anyone could understand.

Juan didn't return from the bathroom. The next day, I went to the airport to fly to Vieques, but the pilot of my tiny plane told me the Navy was in the midst of its annual maneuvers there and I should go to Culebra instead. Culebra was like Vieques, only smaller. There was a guest house but it was expensive; if I wanted, I could stay with the pilot in the house the airline rented for him on Culebra, so that he could fly emergency flights to San Juan if anybody on the island got sick during the night. There was no hospital on Culebra.

Many interesting things happened to me on Culebra. I learned to scuba dive, I rode a pony bareback on the beach, I woke at dawn when the cocks began crowing, I watched white puffs from naval artillery rounds floating over the beaches of Vieques, I listened to "Rumours" by Fleetwood Mac – the pilot's favorite album – a minimum of three hours every day.

One night around eleven, I sat in the co-pilot's seat next to him for twenty minutes as he took a girl who had a stomachache and her family to San Juan (emergency flights were free so there was a tendency for people to get sick in the middle of the night). On the return flight, he shut off all lights but those on the instrument panel and told me to take over the controls. There were lights in the sky above and lights from the sky reflected on the water below and there were lights on the island ahead, and though I thought I was keeping level, he told me I was descending at two hundred feet a minute. Back home, I let him put his hand in my vagina. There was already a tampax in there and when his hand pushed on it I got an orgasm. It was the first time I had gotten one that way. In the morning, when he tried to do this again I told him no, it had been a one-time thing due partly to his astonishingly strong marijuana.

The next afternoon he brought two young women – girls, really – back with him on the evening flight. They were blond and from Argentina and their fathers had big jobs in the government. When the pilot lit a joint, they told him what a degenerate he was, he was lucky he was an American; in Argentina it was considered worse than murder. The pilot listened to this calmly, then passed me the joint. I didn't really feel like smoking, but to show them that I was lucky to be an American, too, I took a few hits. I passed it to them and they took it – even though one of their fathers was big in the Security Police and had devised a way of taking care of people like us, they'd pour gasoline on the prisoners' mattresses and set them on fire and watch everybody burn to death. They giggled as they said this, perhaps because they thought they were funny, perhaps because they were smoking marijuana for the first time – at least, they said it was the first time.

That night we went to the local island dance. There was no disco or Fleetwood Mac; the band used no electric or electronic instruments; the people scarcely moved their feet; yet it was the sexiest dancing I had ever seen in my life. The pilot, the scuba dive instructor, the two Argentinian girls, and I were the only non-natives there, and though I felt conspicuous, it was in a different and better way than in the bar in San Juan. The pilot danced with one Argentinian girl and the scuba dive instructor danced with the other. I danced with several teenage boys who got a kick out of me, *la gringa*.

At a break in the music, we went off into the bushes and smoked more of that astonishing marijuana. Roberta, the girl whose father was big in Security, began telling us more tales of torture and murder. The pilot and scuba dive instructor did not seem at all fazed by this, and as I got higher I began to wonder if maybe such things weren't weird at all, if maybe they were absolutely common, a state of affairs everyone knew about but me, that for all I knew existed in the United States, only I didn't know people important enough to tell me about it – or maybe even people had told me about it but I had pushed it out of my mind and was only now bothered about it because I was high and in some strange place where I felt more outside of things than usual. Did not horrible things happen every day on the streets of New York and did I not manage to ignore them?

I also realized men would do anything to get laid.

I walked over to where the teenage boys I had danced with were. But it was a teenage girl I faced as I asked, "*Quieres bailar?*"

She looked astonished, so I repeated the question.

"*No comprendo*," she said.

"*Muy simple. Quiero bailar contigo. Quieres bailar conmigo?*" The kids disappeared. Some older man came over and started shouting at me. I laughed, it was like an undubbed movie on the Spanish cable station in New York.

"Are you crazy?" the pilot ran over. He and Roberta dragged me away.

"*Quieres bailar?* Isn't that right? What didn't she understand?"

"You want to get me thrown off the island?" asked the pilot.

"You know what we do to people like you back home?" asked Roberta. She had the same evil smile as when she had talked about the burning marijuana prisoners. I smiled back, then grabbed her head and stuck my tongue in her mouth.

"*Quieres bailar?*" I asked. The pilot laughed as I led her out onto the dance floor. She kept saying it was disgusting and I kept telling her she loved it, that everybody in the world was really gay and the point of marijuana was to enable people to admit this big secret. I also told her I knew she was just making up this stuff about her father, that deep down she was really the same as the pilot and me. I don't remember if I believed this as I was saying it.

The other girl had gone off with the scuba instructor, so by the end of the dance it was just the pilot, Roberta, and me. She pretended she was going to sleep alone, but the pilot and I joined her on her bed with a bottle of rum. Sometimes I passed out from the marijuana and the rum, and sometimes the pilot passed out, but Roberta was always there, ready in her strange way for whoever was awake. One time I woke up and saw her and the pilot in the moonlight. It was beautiful but very far away and I had a reluctance to interrupt them, the way I hate being interrupted during a movie. I fell asleep again, and when I woke up I found I was biting her breast. She screamed for the pilot to help, but he just sat smoking a joint.

"*Mira,*" I said, sitting up on top of her. I took the joint out of the pilot's mouth and held it near her right breast. I began talking to her softly, mostly in English but using the few Spanish words I knew, telling her I was going to do to her what her *padre* did to the *maricones* and *marihuanistas*. As I talked I squeezed the nipple of her other breast, which got hard, then I leaned down and kissed her. Then I sat up and brought the hand with the joint next to her nipple.

She didn't move. "You don't have the guts," she said.

I lowered my hand. I *didn't* have the guts, but it was not so much the act I was scared of as the memories.

But my excitement was gone, and I let the pilot take over.

When the girl and her friend left the island the next day, they warned the pilot and the scuba dive instructor and me not to come to Argentina, because Roberta would tell her father all about us and he'd have us arrested and thrown into prison and we'd never get out. They were giggling when they said this. Then they took our photographs and gave us their addresses. The scuba instructor kissed his girl goodbye, while I got on the plane with the pilot to fly them to the mainland. We didn't give them our last names or addresses.

There were passengers with us on the way back too, so I didn't get a chance to take over the controls.

"Did you believe those stories?" I asked the pilot when we got back to the house.

"Did I believe what?" he asked. He popped open a beer and lit a joint, then we headed off to a dinner of some famous local fish we had expressly ordered the restaurant to catch for us that day.

Although I stayed on Culebra till I got my scuba certification, I never did manage to get one of the local *puertorriqueñas* to dance with me. I'm an outsider in their world, as they are in mine, as the Argentinian girls surely are in a country no longer run – if it ever was – by their fathers' friends. In New York I continued my quest, going to Latin bars in a man's suit and a pair of Oxford shoes borrowed from a friend who likes to dress up. One night I finally succeeded, but it didn't mean what it should have, because I am who I am and not who I am not, and the girl I brought home quickly realized it.

Kermit's Room

Dale Gunthorp

I am a tidy person. To me, tidiness is space – bare clean open-ness around me.

This isn't any kind of lifestyle statement – I'm not trying to imitate a Zen garden or those neo-minimalist interiors of converted warehouses along the Thames. I want the opposite of statement: I want to wipe the thumbprints of my life off my environment; I want to make silence.

So I live in one room with nothing in it that is beautiful, and as little as possible to fall over, dust or put away. This room has a tightly stretched cord carpet, an over-sized bean-bag on which I read, think and sleep, a microwave oven, a large fridge-freezer (in which I store my knives, plates and the like) and, on a coffee table, the portable computer in which I file away my thoughts. All these items are white. I have a bathroom, also white – white tiles, soap, towels, loo-paper.

Because every inside must have an outside, my white room is part of a flat; and the flat is on the thirteenth floor of a 1960s block, where the lifts don't work, the cacophony of messy lives surrounds me, and the neighbours tip their rubbish down the stairs. This, however, doesn't matter to me. It took time, but I worked to desensitize myself to the block until it became only the dark approach tunnel to my hidden safe space, and I heard nothing from beyond my walls but an amorphous hum, dissolved in the rotation of the globe.

Apart from doing a job (and, in working hours, I enter another compartment of consciousness), I limit my dependence on the outside world to the local library. I can't see the point of fiction or poetry, and too much clever wordplay has made me suspicious of philosophy, but otherwise I read anything. I especially love dictionaries, but I will read about the construction of Victorian sewers or particle accelerators, the migration of birds, the logic of postal codes, anything. I take out one book at a time, otherwise I'd read several together. But reading does fill up my head with distractions, so I'm working towards rationing myself to four books a week.

It took me years to get to this point, but I'm still far from the bareness I need. The weakness is not my job or the block, but that my private space isn't the bareness it seems. It has a secret compartment: I have another room. This is heaped, floor to ceiling, with Things, and they all derive from me. I desperately want to get rid of them but, when I confront them, they put up a strenuous fight – this one claiming rights because it belonged to Grandma, the next because it cost more than I could afford, the third that I might want to read it one day, and the television grouching that if I got an aerial, I could watch programmes which would improve my mind.

So my home has never quite become the place of peace I want it to be. I come in from work, lock the door and, like falling snow, the quiet descends about me. A wonderful moment. But then, like as not, I start to fiddle. I open the fridge, and take out the carton of milk. I want to throw the carton away but, before I can do that, I must drink the milk. So my first unease will be an ice-cold lump in my stomach.

My second is the sound, first a whisper, like mice, of Things from behind the closed door of the other room. In honesty, I must admit that this confrontation is usually started by me. Having emptied the milk carton, I need to throw it away. But, since the waste disposal chute also doesn't work, I must climb 260 steps to the bin. It isn't sensible to climb these twice for such a small load. So I edge towards the closed door, and then the muttering begins – "spare me, I belonged to Grandma" and so on.

This is the point at which I could easily give up, but I know I must struggle on for the ultimate tidiness. I've been kept on course by a passion which began in me when my schoolmates were discovering boys, horses or Julian of Norwich. I discovered instead that I must, at some time before my death, experience one clear, pure, unmuddled thought. I always knew I could do it, if I could make myself able to receive; if I could empty my brain of clutter. Often and often, the thought came so close – I could almost see it hesitating just out of my field of vision. It would watch, nod and quiver, like a bird trying to decide whether it's safe to take the bread you put down for it. On the best days, I sensed it draw breath, preparing itself to come to me. But every time this happened, Things would intervene – my shoe-lace mutter "tie me", the kettle boil, or the red lettering on the notice from the Water Board light up like neon.

But I'd try, and try again, make myself go quiet, wait for the thought to return, try not to first-guess it. I knew I couldn't know and didn't need to know what it would be. It needn't be big or important, anything about the riddle of the universe. It just had to be utterly itself, and not a projection of me or any other transient thing. I never lost faith that, when it came, I would understand, without words, how all spirit is connected; I'd be able to believe at last that my consciousness is woven into the fabric of life, not a blind scuttling thing sealed up in the cravings of my psyche.

Of course, I never spoke about this project. People – meter-readers and the like – think me queer enough when they come to my flat, though all they ever say is how tidy it is.

Then at 8.30 p.m. on Tuesday 15 November last, I met some-one who changed all that. We met at the library, in fact we collided there – both of us reaching for the manual on electric wiring. She gestured to me to take it; I gestured to her, and so, like two polite footmen in a doorway, we got jammed in, each trying to give precedence to the other.

She broke through the impasse, said: "This is getting silly." She had a gritty voice, like a smoker, though she didn't smell of anything unpleasant, only of car undersides. I yielded, and pushed the book her way.

She half accepted. "Okay," she said, "I'll get it stamped, so long as we go round the pub and sort out who takes it home."

Panic hit like a tidal wave. I couldn't breathe, couldn't think, couldn't tell the floor from the ceiling. I could do nothing, but my hands were flapping, making white flags in front of me, and torrents of words were frothing out of my mouth. I heard the last of them: they were telling her to come up to my place for a glass of milk. And then there was terrible silence.

She shook the hair out of her eyes and looked at me, slowly and slightly sideways, like a dog when you say hello to it in the park. "Okay –" she was speaking carefully " – if that's better for you." I nodded furiously. "Well, okay. But on condition we call at the offie for something to liven it up with."

We paused at every landing on the way to my flat. She was out of breath because she doesn't do thirteen flights four or six times a day, and I because I was so embarrassed. Words were still gushing out of me, and every one got it so wrong that I had to add another half-dozen to cover up. First I tried to explain that I hadn't turned down the pub suggestion because I'm a fuddy-duddy or a Born Again or under orders from the AA, but because I don't carry money on me.

She gave me that quick all-seeing laser glance you get from store detectives. "If it's a few bob you're short, I can help you out for a day or two."

This was even more embarrassing. I have plenty of money, but I keep it in the bank. As this made me sound like a skinflint, I then had to explain that I have to put my money out of the way. If I don't, every object in every shop window yells "buy me": it's because I'm so bad at saying no that the room with the shut door is as dreadful as it is. This was a lot to have to admit to a stranger, but there was no other way out.

She took this quite seriously. "So what do you do," she said, "when they yell 'steal me'?"

I knew then that she, like me, has a different way of looking at the world, and my heart bounced on the springs of my chest as if it could hear the footsteps of an approaching thought.

She marched into my room, leaving bootprints on my white carpet and flinging her cap, muffler, gloves, overcoat, backpack, bag of lumpy shopping, the manual on wiring and a half-bottle of whisky on the beanbag, and the first thing she said was: "What a tidy flat."

It had been, until she walked into it. It became even less so. She added lashings of whisky to the milk I'd poured in two glass tumblers, pulled a satsuma out of her shopping, squeezed its juice into the drinks, and left the peel on top of my computer. (I eat fruit peelings, so that I don't have to climb the stairs to throw them away.)

Then, handing me a glass, she flopped down on the beanbag. "Okay, to business," she said. "Why do you want a book on electric wiring?"

My room has four wall sockets. I explained that I wanted to get rid of them.

"You could pass them on to me."

The sudden stab under my shoulder-blade made me aware that I didn't want to give them to anyone; I wanted to put them away in the room with the Things. So, muttering with shame, I told her to take them.

"Thanks," she said. "Then I'd better have the book, too, so that I can get them out of your place, and put them into mine."

Another stab told me that I wanted the book, too. I countered this attack by gulping down half of her peculiar cocktail. The satsuma acid went straight up my nose and the alcohol crumpled my knees. I sank onto the far end of the beanbag. "Please, take the book." We were sitting back to back, which must have seemed an odd way to have a coversation. Nonetheless, I had stopped myself from doing something odder – throwing open the room with the Things and telling her to take them all.

She leaned back, and said, over her shoulder, "Thanks. But shouldn't you ask me where I'm taking your sockets, to make sure they go to a good home?" Then she laughed, a sort of stuttering starter-motor ironic laugh, implying that they were going to a dreadful home. It wasn't necessary. I knew that already from her greasy finger nails and the dandruff on her collar.

"It's a wreck of an old Victorian terrace in Stratford," she said, "four storeys tall, held together with tie irons, and it rattles like an old man's teeth when the tube trains pass underneath. I bought it, at auction, just days before it was to be condemned, and now I've got the Council on my back, demanding that I make it habitable. I've got the lights going after a fashion, but they flicker when I turn the water taps. On the plus side, there's a car-breaker's yard next door, so I pick up any amount of metal and rubber to seal up gaps and keep the weather out."

I wasn't shocked; I just couldn't understand how anyone could live like that. "Don't you worry terribly?" I said.

"What about? If it falls down, my loan-shark loses money, not me. If the roof leaks, I have upside-down car bonnets to catch the drips. I'm burning up the worm-eaten timbers, so I keep warm. It's a great place. I'm thinking of taking tenants, but I'm fussy about company."

I was relieved to know that somebody so loose had standards. "I'm fussy, too," I said, "that's why I live alone." But, when she gave another of her stutter-laughs, it crossed my mind that she might take this for a hint that I wanted to be her tenant, so I had to explain that I prefered to live alone because I needed to make my life very simple, so that I could think simply.

"Simply about what?"

It isn't easy to explain to someone that "what" isn't the point. It's the process, the reception of something true in itself, no matter what it is about. "I want to have a thought that just comes to me," I mumbled.

She laughed again. "Watch it, or you'll be hearing voices."

I hear voices all the time. The voice I wanted to hear was one which passed from no throat to no ear. "In a way, that's what I want, but not any person's voice, or anything at all from my environment."

"In that case," she said, "the thought will begin and end with yourself."

What did she mean? What I most want is to exclude self from the thought.

"Because, thoughts have roots and leaves and branches," she said, now leaning so far back that I could feel the touch of her hair. "If they're all inside your head, the thought will grow entirely out of you. And nothing will control it. Before long, you'll think you're Napoleon."

I was almost relieved to hear her say that. I've never had delusions about being anybody other than me, but I've wondered what he thought when he was in exile on St Helena. Did he live in hope that the French fleet would rescue him, or did he accept that it was all over and try to work out what, if anything, all those wars and deaths and chaos amounted to? "I'm interested in Napoleon, but I wouldn't want to be him," I replied.

"Well," she said, "you're on the way to it. You've got his smile. And you're five-foot two, and have a Napoleonish face, a little bird's face. I'd think you were French if your library card didn't call you 'Ms B. Preston'." She leaned round to face me and tossed the hair out of her eyes. "What does the 'B' stand for?"

I'm funny about my name. It's a common enough name, but somehow it makes me squirm. And I'm funny about being identified. My hands began to make their fluttering white flag, so I sat on them and said nothing.

"Okay." She slithered back to her place at the other end of the bean-bag. "No need to tell me. I'll call you Bonaparte."

I could hear a giggle in her voice, but what she said was so kind that I melted, and said I was an exile of sorts, but hoped my isolation was chosen rather than imposed. "You could," I said, "call me Hermit." This idea, a new one, so pleased me that I added, "So long as you can promise that someone with a name that sounds like 'Kermit' won't be taken for a frog."

"Why not? I love frogs," she said.

She left soon after, with the book and my socket-fittings. "See you at the library, some day," she said. "Goodnight and thanks for the milk, Kermit."

I didn't sleep that night. It wasn't the mouse voices from behind the closed door. It wasn't anything near a hovering thought. It was her. Her satsuma peelings were still on my computer, her bootprints on my carpet. She'd turned my place into a tip, but I knew she had something crucial to do with my thought.

At work next day, I raised clouds of dust, searching folders that hadn't been touched in decades. In the work compartment of my consciousness, I am a financial archivist and am currently trying to balance the accounts of the National Health Service for 1967. But what I was looking for that day was her. I wanted to find her name. I don't have and never use a telephone, but I wanted her number.

She is small, smaller than me, and skinny as a weasel. Her eyes are bright but concealed by that great bush of hair, so I couldn't judge the colour: the impression I had was of blackness. Her skin is pallid now; in summer it would be berry brown and her dark, thick hair would flash red. You'd never pick her out in the street; there is something underworld and concealed about her. But there is also something exotic. As I totted up the cost of bandages, hospital linen, dangerous drugs and even ambulances which had disappeared into cracks in the wall in 1967, I guessed that her forebears came from somewhere in the Balkans, and that her name was Gabrielle, the messenger, or something of that order. I called in at the library at lunch time and again after work, but the messenger was not there.

I was in a peculiar mental state when I left the library that evening – disappointed, yet at the same time excited. I picked up supper at Safeways (ricotta cheese ravioli with cauliflower) but didn't feel hungry. At the third level of the staircase, I sensed the thought. But it was only the old woman from Number 1306, who walks her cat in the wasteland downstairs. As she approached, that starter-motor laugh came to me, and with it a gritty voice saying "That's a powerful-looking tiger at your heels, ma'am." Of course, I knew I'd only imagined the voice, but my hands rushed into their white flag, and they dropped my supper into the old woman's basket. "For the cat," I said, and charged off. Then I was furious with myself. Everybody knows cats don't eat cauliflower.

I got in, closed my door, and tried to go quiet. The thought was still close. But my eye kept latching on the satsuma peelings, bootprints and mark of her tumbler on the coffee table. The only thought that came to me was that the messenger had brought me these three signs, and I had to work out what they meant.

All this time, there was silence from the Things behind the closed door, but not from the block. I remembered how, years ago, the noise used to cut through my nerves. I would walk round, frantic, my hands to my ears, moaning aloud: "These people's lives are so messy; they spend all their time relating to each other; they have no outside." And I could feel, dense as storm clouds, their furious energy swirling round and round and swallowing itself up, like a vortex, like a body with cancer consuming its own cells.

That night, all those sounds came back, with a weary echo, as if they'd been stored up in the walls. Over my head, Number 1408 was hammering. At my feet, Number 1208 was watching *The Bill.* On my left, 1307's children were screaming, and 1309 was beating up his wife.

But that night, the noises didn't wound me. ("Shit, caught my thumb." "The guy's a wally, not a bloody murderer." "Mummy, Jason's hogging the ball." "George, please put down the scissors: that's my best dress.") I found them curious. I had no desire to save the battered wife or her best dress, or to know whether the wally was the killer or not, but I did sit there wondering what Gabrielle would have done. She would get involved. She would hold the plank square for the man who was hammering, and then take a few spare nails away with her; get Jason to surrender the ball; turn down the television; punch George in the solar plexus. I was still wondering as I lay wide-eyed in bed. And then I began to wonder what she would do if my thought went instead to her. I didn't think she could have one of her own; she gets too involved with things on the side. But even so, she was someone who could hear; someone in some way grounded.

Nobody understands my anguish at being imprisoned in a human brain and walled off from the forces of life, so I want nobody for my friend. But by the time the early morning lorries were churning up the street, I wanted to bump into her again, and to have money in my pocket for whisky at the pub. This was a cheap fantasy: I would almost certainly never see Gabrielle again.

That seemed to be the case. Days and then weeks passed, but she was never at the library. I made various small preparations. I took Grandma's little change-purse out of its box in the other room. It felt strange to the touch, its fine silver mesh so sinuous and cold, like the skin of a snake, its black velvet lining hard and shiny where the old copper pennies had rubbed it. I was aware that it didn't look like a proper purse; that it would be a long and embarrassing struggle with its clasp when I tried to pay for whisky. Yet I knew Gabrielle, who laughed at many things, wouldn't laugh at that.

Then, I looked up Stratford on the map: it's a sprawling tangle of roads, rivers, railways, canals, and dotted red lines: a place where any house could be big and ramshackle and next door to a car-breaker's yard. I wanted to find her, but all I did was dust the satsuma peelings with the careful touch of a forensic investigator, and hoover around her bootprints.

During this period, my Thought was hovering. I had several half-thoughts that seemed to be preludes to it. They weren't of the right kind, but they did seem to penetrate below the surface. One evening, I had an image of the dress George had cut up – I didn't see its colour, but knew the cut and texture of the fabric, and how it slithered in the blades of the scissors. Another night, it came to me that even the best human institutions – I had in mind the accounting procedures of the National Health Service – become corrupted in use. Several times, I saw the sun glinting crookedly off the windows of her house. The best was a sudden flash of perception that thought is an electric current; you can't hold it, keep it; it has to pass through you. And I had been blocking the thought that wanted to come to me because I had no way to pass it on. With a flush of real joy, I believed I could receive it, if I could give it to Gabrielle.

But the only message she sent was negative. Four weeks after our encounter, the manual on electric wiring was back on the library shelves.

I became somewhat depressed after that. I disciplined myself out of hearing her voice in every choking carburettor, but the din and squalor of the block intruded more and more, and Things from the other room began to creep into my space. Some nights, the milk in my refrigerator was sour. The days grew darker and the nights gloomier, and the only thought of any consequence that came near me was that nothing we can comprehend is of any value.

*   *   *

Then, one night when I was without hope or any thoughts at all, she was there – in the library, in the DIY section. She had her back to me, hair springing up around her woollen scarf, boots square, backpack over one shoulder and a plastic bag of shopping disgorging at her feet. The sheer power of her presence made me feel faint. Then I doubted that she was she. I'd thought so much about her, but I'd never imagined her like this – so scruffy yet somehow so in control.

She turned. I flinched, as if she'd made the gesture of a mugger. "Beg pardon." She shook the hair out of her eyes. "Oh, hi," she said, and the grit in her voice shivered my nerves. "Well, if it isn't, um, Bonaparte."

"Kermit Bonaparte, the same," I said.

"The very one." She hesitated. "Thanks for the socket-fittings."

"They don't flicker, I hope."

"Flicker?"

"I mean, when you turn the taps on."

Her laugh was shot through with irony. "That was a manner of speaking."

The house? I hoped the house wasn't also a manner of speaking. "How's the house in Stratford?"

"Oh, the car-breaker's yard is expanding. Didn't I tell you? No? Well, they made the offer you can't refuse. I'm making enough on the deal to go for a fantastic place, a warehouse in Barking Creek."

I was now utterly calm, almost relieved. My Gabrielle was not a property speculator; my Gabrielle lived like a water-rat beside a canal in Stratford. I pushed the silver-mesh change purse to the very bottom of my coat pocket. "Sounds like you made a killing."

"Well," she scratched at her woolly hat. "I did something to earn it. I made improvements. Your sockets came in handy."

"I'm so glad," I said. This was a lie. I was now utterly indifferent to the sockets. In fact, I felt so detached from it all that, just to fill the gap in the conversation, I let the long-rehearsed, but now irrelevant, words trickle out of my mouth: "Fancy a quick one round the pub?"

I didn't know it until they were hanging in the air between us that nobody with my voice and manner can use those words. Coming from me, this was too familiar, and so impertinent. I had squandered my moral advantage. She would reply that she was "rather busy", had someone waiting for her. This would not upset me; it would probably be true. Most people rush from one appointment to another. Anyway, I no longer cared whether she saw Grandma's little purse or not. And even if it did matter, her refusal wouldn't be a rejection of me: it would just be the way things are.

My mind was furiously sorting these conflicting thoughts when I heard the predictable words: "Great idea, but I'm rather busy this evening." But, as I struggled to phrase a reply which could save something of my dignity, I realized that she had said something different: "Great idea, but I'd rather make it your amazingly tidy flat."

Sometimes, you can have so much of an extraordinary thing that you can't take it in. I was anxious about what she would make of the carefully preserved satsuma peelings, about what George would be doing to the remains of his wife's wardrobe, about all the Things that had invaded my room, about everything that now made my white space vulnerable. But there was also a half-bottle of shockingly expensive single malt whisky on top of the microwave, and so I said, "Okay, if it's no bother to you." And she laughed her big stuttering starter-motor laugh which nobody ought to do in a library.

"I'd forgotten your dreadful stairs," she said, clutching her ribs as we paused at the third landing. "And they smell like a backstreet urinal."

They do, rather. I hadn't noticed the smell for years; now I realized that I found it oddly comforting. Perhaps that's why dogs sniff trees. "I'm fond of this place," I said.

"You *do* have weird tastes."

We clambered on to the next landing, where we again paused: "I get to like it more and more," I said, surprising myself. "Sometimes this block feels like the real world."

"You like it that much? What it is to be a thinker!" Her laugh bounced up and down the stairs. "So what's the news on the great Thought?"

And then, while her laugh still echoed through that piss-soaked concrete tunnel, the thought came; it just dropped on me, casual as a spider. It is still with me and it is, as I'd hoped it would be, very simple. It is, my darling Gabrielle, that you exist.

And for the brief while I do truly know that, everything exists and is beautiful and necessary.

In the Spice House

Marnie Woodrow

When I first met you I didn't know a bay leaf from a Maple Leaf. The idea of tossing leaves into a perfectly good sauce frightened me. But you were so confident, holding your head high as you marched me to the Spice House in Kensington and took me down the aisle where the bay leaves lived. We visited six countries with our nostrils: you put your smooth-warm hand on my arm by the tins of hearts of palm. There had been no kiss between us, not then, but you pointed to the packets of saffron and I was all over you with my mouth.

That afternoon you took me to your little apartment. We usually met for very public coffees and lunches, platonic interludes in crowded spaces. Movie theatres, libraries and darkened bars were unconsciously avoided. But as you set the grocery bags down to struggle with the uncooperative lock on your door I was oblivious to our sudden *aloneness*. Instead I studied your perfectly rolled shirtsleeves and the back of your very fine head. I lost myself in a reverie of trying to guess your hat size, trying to imagine the way your skull tilted when you were listening intently. Oh you: beautiful.

I stepped into your apartment with hungry eyes and a greedy stomach. The sunsplashed hallway, the numerous healthy plants, the window at the end of the hall: I took them all in, eye-gulping the details. You took my hand and led me past a small room with no door: your *reading room*. A shrine of books, but not nearly as important as your kitchen. I knew that you would take me to the kitchen first.

"It's a really small place," you warned me on the street-car, as though I would mind.

We stood in the doorway and looked in at the kitchen. I saw a fairly large room, well-equipped, with shelf after shelf of mason jars, full of powders and spices that were clearly labelled by your neat hand. White refrigerator, red stove, a ceiling fan spinning above our heads as we moved into the room. A light perfume of foods previously cooked tangoed with the mingling perfumes of herbs hanging to dry.

"Sit down," you said, and pointed to a small bed in one corner of the room. There was no kitchen table, there were no chairs.

"Your bed is in the kitchen?" I asked. I worried that you were odd, that you had other strange habits I hadn't detected. Perhaps your passionate niceness was a smoke-screen for strangeness.

"It's a small apartment. I told you," you said, turning to the shelves and touching various jars.

I went to the corner and sat on the edge of the bed. My deep desire for you didn't guarantee an absence of fear. My hands were damp as I watched you bustling with the groceries. I didn't want my nervousness to threaten the development of our romance.

"A friend of mine in New York has a bathtub in her living room," I offered.

You nodded in acknowledgement and continued tossing cut vegetables into a large pot. There was a moment's pause as you made stern-faced selections from your spice-collection. Royal choices: you held each jar of spice like each was a precious trophy or an urn of sacred ashes.

Soon a gorgeous smell began to leak out of the pot and into the room. You sautéed shrimp and talked to me, grinning happily and winking. The smells combined and grew more intense as we talked. My hunger was becoming a drunkeness, teased by the wild aromas of your lunch-making.

"The stew has to simmer for quite a while," you said, sitting next to me.

"What kind of stew is it?" I asked.

"It's an Indian vegetable stew, but I like to add shrimp. I hope you like it. But it has to cook really slowly and for a long time. Do you mind?"

I *did* mind, because the smell was intoxicating and unbearable. The room was full of the warmth and the tingling tickle of the meal; and there was my ache for you. The two longings inseparable, my hunger was confused in its priorities. My head swam with the perfumes of your culinary seductiveness.

That first afternoon in your apartment: the wild exquisite smell of your skin and of spices. We rocked together on the bed while the stew grew thicker and hotter; we simmered like the pot on the stove: ground and stirred weeks of built-up wanting.

You sat up and announced, "Lunchtime." It was nine o'clock at night. The sky had blackened outside the window. You stood naked at the stove and stirred your potion, an unforgettable sight in shadows.

Naked, we ate the stew in bed, a divine meal with your thigh resting against mine. We said nothing: there was the scraping of our spoons and the traffic outside, the fridge purring. I discovered that the kitchen was the perfect place for a bed. Stomachs full and heads full of fading spices, we slept on the bed in the corner of your kitchen, soundly and all night.

Before you, I never cared what went into my mouth in the way of nourishment. My appetite was scarce, dispassionate. Love, too, was sporadic and thoughtless, and I had certainly never tasted authentic passion.

You always insisted that I meet you at the Spice House. Often I arrived there early, to drive myself crazy with anticipation. I'd lurk behind stacks of Ethiopian bread, behind veils of sweetgrass: to watch your entrance. Once, in a playful mood, you brought me to the edge of a ribald moan in a shadowy corner of the shop, next to a giant drum of curry powder that burnt my throat and nostrils as I gasped in pleasure. Your hand could always stir me just so.

We met like that on Saturdays: in the Spice House and then on to your house. You'd put something torturously good-smelling on to simmer or in to bake, like some people put soft music

on, and we would end up eating lunch at midnight, propped up
by pillows.

You gave me your Saturday, your Sunday morning. Questions
were distasteful to you and you swatted them away like flies. Of
me you wanted to know everything, but you insisted you could
not offer the same revelations. In my blind contentment, I
agreed to your conditions.

One Saturday you didn't show up at the Spice House. I waited
until the shopkeeper asked me to leave. You weren't a *telephone
person*; wouldn't have one, wouldn't use one. I went home and
wondered if I had the right to drop by your house. I wandered
around my own kitchen, its cupboards filled with the little bags
of spice you sent me home with every Sunday morning. Neatly
labelled, carefully tied.

"Someday we'll get you some nice jars for your spices," you
said. You never came to *my* apartment.

Unable to eat but absolutely starved, I took the bus to your
little apartment.

Your lock was cheap. You didn't answer my knocking, my soft
calls. I remember thinking it was far too easy to get in. The doorknob was in my hands in pieces after a few frantic wrenchings.
The smell of burning food was strong and I ran down the hallway to your kitchen, blinded by the black smoke that filled the
apartment and stung my eyes.

I stood in the doorway. Hanging there, you said nothing,
offered no explanation.

I turned off the burner, sat on the bed in the corner of your
kitchen and looked up at you. There was a wooden chair on its
side on the floor. A chair I had never been offered and had never
seen in any other room.

Your father gave me the urn with your ashes inside.

"I guess you're the girlfriend," he shrugged. He drove off,
back to a distant city I hadn't known you were from.

I went back to your little apartment with the urn and put a
key in the new lock. Your mother asked me to deal with your
belongings, your things. Your nice jars, the white refrigerator

and red stove. Strange to suddenly have a key, to have access to your secrets. But I decided I would not read anything, wouldn't look in drawers, wouldn't scan the spines of your books with curious eyes.

The big pot you liked best I filled with water.

One by one, I pulled jars from shelves and dumped their contents into the water as it boiled. Incompatible spices were mixed together. I threw them all in. I cried as I dumped and scooped your ashes into the pot. The smell was heady, rancid and peppery. I lay down on the bed and took a deep breath, missing you and feeling hungry; the confused appetite I had always enjoyed in your little apartment.

When the soup had cooked down to a thick, grainy sludge I turned off the heat. All those weeks, I had been so cold, unable to warm myself in any way. I undressed in your kitchen, shivering near the red stove. I carried the pot of acrid soup to the side of the bed and sat down. Ladling the warm mixture onto my belly, I smeared myself with the pasty soup of spices and you. I massaged it into my breasts and thighs, remembering our Saturday afternoons, every one.

Completely covered, mummified in the warm paste, I stretched out flat on the sheets and studied the chair you never offered me. It sat upright by the white fridge. I realized as I made myself warmer with eager muck-covered fingers that I had known you almost longer in your death than I had in life.

The next morning I dressed without washing, pulled my clothes over the crust on my skin. I took the urn to my apartment. I filled it with one of the bags of spice you had given me. I have a nice jar now and six chairs to offer no one.

A Country Dance

Mary Dorcey

On the arm of your chair, your hand for a moment is still; the skin smooth and brown against the faded, red velvet. I touch it lightly with mine. "Maybe what she needs is more time," I say.

The air is dense with cigarette smoke, my eyes are tired. You stare past me and begin again to fidget with a silver bracelet on your wrist. I make my tone persuasive: "Time to regain her identity, a sense of independence, and ..."

The words are swept from me in a sudden upswell of sound as last orders are called. The climax of the night, and so much left unsaid, undone. Every man in the room is on his feet, shoving for place at the bar, the voices bluff, seductive, as they work for one last round.

"Here, John, two large ones ..."

"Pat, good man, four more pints ..."

You ignore them, your gaze holding mine, your attention caught once more by the hope of her name.

"What did you say about independence?"

"I said you need it, need to cultivate it." Something perverse in me all at once, wanting to disappoint you. Your eyes drop, slide to the fireplace where the coal burns with a dim red glow.

"Ah, I thought it was Maeve you meant."

And what matters after all which way I put it? In these stories, aren't all the characters interchangeable? The lights are turned up full now, the evening over. And you as much in the dark as when we started. If I had used less tact; if I had said straight out what everyone thinks, would it have made a difference? I twist the stub of my last cigarette into the glass ashtray. No, whatever

I say, you will hear what you choose. Your misery safely walled beyond the reach of logic, however much you may plead with me to advise, console. If you were not fully certain of this, would you have asked me here tonight?

"Time, ladies and gents, please – have you no homes to go to?" The barman turns, the great wash of his belly, supported just clear of the crotch, tilts towards us. He swipes a greasy cloth across the tabletop, forcing us to lift our drinks: "Come on now, girls."

I take another sip of my whisky and replace the glass emphatically on the cardboard coaster. You clasp your pint to your chest, swilling the dregs in languid circles.

"I don't think I can bear it much longer."

I look at you; your dark eyes have grown sullen with pain, under the clear skin of your cheek a nerve twitches. Years ago, I would have believed you. Believed your hurt unlooked for – believed even in your will to escape it. Now, too many nights like this one have altered me. Too many nights spent in comforting others, watching while each word of sympathy is hoarded as a grain of salt to nourish the wound. On the blackness of the window, I watch beads of rain glance brilliant as diamonds, each one falling distinct, separate, then merging – drawn together in swift streams to the ground. Why try to impose reason? Let you have your grand passion, the first taste of self-torment – never so sweet or keen again.

"Look, will you have another drink?" I say in a last attempt to cheer you, "They might give us one yet."

Instantly your face brightens. "Thanks, but you've bought enough," you say, and add lightly as if you'd just thought of it, "Did you see someone has left a pint over there – will I get it?"

Without waiting for a reply, you slide your narrow hips in their scarlet jeans between our table and the bar. You reach for the pint of Harp and a half-finished cocktail. The barman swings round. "Have you got twenty Marlboros?" you ask, to distract him. While he roots on a shelf above the till, you slip the drinks over to me and turn back with a smile. Seeing it, placated, he tosses the cigarettes in the air, beating you to the catch. "What has such a nice-looking girl alone at this hour?" he asks, his voice oiled, insistent. You stand and say nothing. Your smile ransom enough. "Go home to your bed," he says, and throws the pack along the wet counter.

"Jesus, the things you have to do around here for a drink." You fling yourself down on the seat beside me, close so that our knees and shoulders touch.

"You don't have to," I say.

"Is that right?" you answer and raise one sceptical eyebrow. You pick up the cocktail glass and hold it to your nose. "Is it gin or what?"

"I don't know and I certainly don't want it."

Fishing a slice of stale lemon from the clouded liquid, you knock it back and reach for the Harp.

"Easy on," I say, "you'll be pissed, at this rate."

You take no notice, your head thrown back, drinking with total concentration. I watch Pat, the young barboy, guide customers to the door. A big woman, her pink dress stretched tight across her thighs, is hanging on his arm. She tells him what a fine-looking lad he is, and laughs something caressively in his ear.

"Ah, wouldn't I love to, Molly, but what would Peter have to say?" Slapping her flanks with the flat of his hand, he winks across at me, and slams the door behind her. Outside, in the carpark, someone is singing in a drunken baritone: "Strangers in the night, exchanging glances, wondering in the night . . ."

"At this stage of the evening," I say, "everyone is wondering."

"About what?" you ask. You run your fingers idly through your long hair, puzzled but incurious.

"Nothing," I reply. "A silly joke – just the crowd outside singing."

You have noticed no singing, much less the words that accompany it. Your gaze is fixed resolutely on the uncleared tables – you have spotted one more in the corner. It's obvious now that you have no intention of going home sober, but we cannot sit here all night and I do not want Paddy to catch you lifting leftovers.

"Well, if you want to stay on," I say smiling at you, as though it were the very thing I wanted myself, "why don't we finish what we have in comfort, next door?" I look towards the hallway and an unmarked wooden door on the far side. You are on your feet at once, gathering our glasses, not caring where we go so long as there is a drink at the end of it.

A thin Persian carpet covers the floor of the residents' lounge. On the dim papered walls hang red, satin-shaded lamps with frayed gold fringing, and three framed prints – hunting scenes – men and animals confused in the dark oils. A few of the regulars have drawn armchairs up to the fire. Pipe tobacco and the scent of cloves from their hot whiskeys hang together in the air. A man is kneeling over the coal bucket, struggling to open the tongs. He has the red face and shrunken thighs of the habitual toper. "What the bloody fuck is wrong with this yoke anyway?" he says.

"Here, let me," leaving him the tongs, you lift the bucket and empty half its contents into the grate. You rattle the poker through the bars, shifting the live coals from front to back. Dust crackles. After a moment, shoots of yellow flame break from the new untouched black.

"Nothing like a good fire," the man announces, rubbing together his blue-veined hands, "I always like to build up a good fucking fire."

His eyes follow the line of your flank, taut and curved as you bend to the hearth. His tongue slides over his bottom lip. "Always like to build up a good fire," he repeats, as though it were something witty.

He looks towards me; suddenly conscious of my presence and gives a deferential nod. "Excuse the language," he calls over. He has placed me then as protector, older sister. And why not, after all? Is it not the role I have adopted since that first day I met you in Grafton Street, walking blinded by tears, after one of your quarrels? Did I not even then, that first moment laying eyes on you, want to protect you, from Maeve – from yourself – from that reckless vulnerability of yours, that touched some hidden nerve in me? But it was not protection you wanted, it was empathy. You wanted me to look on, with everyone else, impassive, while you tormented yourself struggling to retain a love that had already slipped into obligation. Though you would not see it – you would see nothing but your own desire. Night after night, following her, watching; your wide, innocent eyes stiff with pain, while she ignored you or flirted with someone else. Waiting because at the end of the evening she might turn, and on an impulse of guilt ask you to go home with her.

"The last one, I think, do you want it?" You hand me an almost full pint of Guinness – brown, sluggish, the froth gone from it. I accept with a wry smile, why not – nothing worse than being empty-handed among drunks, and you clearly will not be hurried.

"Are they residents?" you ask with vague curiosity, looking towards the threesome on the opposite side of the fire.

"No, just regulars," I say, and none more regular than Peg Maguire. Peg who is here every night with one man or another, drinking herself into amiability. A woman with three children who might be widowed or separated – no one asks. With her blonde hair piled above her head, lipstick a little smudged at the corners, her white coat drawn tight about her as though she were just on the point of departure, Peg – shrewd, jaunty – always careful to maintain the outward show. "But you know country hotels: once the front door is shut you could stay forever." I should not have said that, of course, it encourages you. You will have to stay over with me now, I suppose, you are long past driving.

I take a deep draught of the bitter stout, letting it slip quickly down my throat, and to keep this first lightness of mood, I ask you about the college. You are bored, dismissive. Second year is worse than first, you tell me – the life drawing is hopeless, you have only one male model and he wears a g-string; afraid of getting it on in front of women. "Anyway, I haven't been there for a week – too stoned," you add as if that exonerated you. Tossing your head back to sweep the hair from your face. For which of us, I wonder, do you present this elaborate disdain.

"You'll come to a sorry end," I warn you. "All this dope and sex at nineteen destroys the appetite." I have made you smile, a slow, lilting smile, that draws your lips from white, perfect teeth.

"Is that what happened to you?" you ask.

"Perhaps it is. I would say I have decayed into wisdom. A forty-hour week and a regular lover – no unfulfilled lust masquerading as romance."

"Don't tell me you are not romantic about Jan," you look at me intently, your eyes at once teasing and solemn, "when anyone can see you're mad about her."

"That's one way of putting it, I suppose. At least the feeling is mutual so there is no aggravation."

"And what about Liz?" you ask. "Was it not very hard on her?"

"Oh, Liz had other interests," I say. "There was no heartache there."

I have shocked you. You want fervour and longing, not this glib detachment. Should I tell you I am posing, or am I? Is there anything I cherish more than my independence? You lean forward, the cigarette at your mouth, gripped between thumb and forefinger, urging some story of need or rejection.

"You know, it is possible for people to care for each other without tearing their souls out," I hear my voice, deliberately unemotional. "All this strife and yearning is a myth invented to take our minds off the mess around us. Happiness distracts no one." And what is it that impels me to disillusion you? Is it only that this intensity of yours so clearly hurts no one but yourself? With impatience you fan the trail of blue smoke from your face and cut me short.

"Ah, you are always so cynical. You would think thirty is middle age the way you go on. Anyway it's different for you. You have your work – something you really care about. It's all different."

And so, maybe it is. What answer could I give you that would not be twisting the knife?

You stare into the fire, blazing now. The flames bouncing up the chimney throw great splashes of light about the room. Dance on the red brown of your hair. You have finished your cigarette. Your hands in your lap are curiously still – palms upturned. My own lean, fidgeting. I look about the room, at the rubber plant in the corner, the gilt-framed mirror above the mantel-piece – from it my eyes stare back at me, to my surprise still bright and sharp; a gleaming blue. I notice the faint tracing of lines at the corners. First signs. Give up the fags for good next week – get a few early nights. I look towards you. Your lips are at the rim of your glass, sipping at it, stretching it out. Do you dread going home so much?

"You can stay over with me, you know. Anna is in town – you can have her bed. Maybe you would come jogging in the morning – do you good."

Roused for a moment, you regard me slowly, from shoulders to thigh, appraising me. "Aw, I'm not in your shape," you say. "I wouldn't last more than a mile."

"Well, you can walk while I run," I answer, but your gaze has slipped back to the fire, watching the leap of the flames as if they held some private message. We sit in silence, lulled by the heat and alcohol until I break it to ask – "What are you thinking?" Foolish question, as though you would tell me. But you do, holding my eyes to yours, you answer slowly: "I was wondering if I might ring Maeve – she could be . . ."

"At this hour? You are incorrigible." I do not try to hide my irritation. "I thought you said you were going to keep away for a week . . ."

You begin to smile again. For a moment, I wonder if you are playing with me. Then your face shuts, suddenly, as though a light had been switched off. "You are right, of course. I'd forgotten."

And why should I strain to follow these moods? If it were not that you look so forlorn, huddled in your chair, like an animal shut out in the rain.

"You are inconsolable, aren't you?" I say, hoping to tease you out of it. "Tell me, have you not, even for five minutes, been attracted to another woman?"

You turn away abruptly, as though I had struck you, and ask over-loudly; "Do you think we can get something to take away?"

"Is it a drink you want?" one of Peg's friends calls over. He has been listening to us for some time, his gaze flickering between us like a snake's tongue. "I'll get you a drink," he offers.

"It's all right, thanks," I say quickly.

"No, no, I insist. Name your poison, girls." His speech is slurred. Conscious of it, he repeats each sentence. "Pat will give us a bottle – no trouble." He hauls himself up from his chair, clutching the mantelpiece. Peg grabs at his arm.

"Pat has gone off hours ago – don't bother yourself."

"No bother. Got to get these lassies a drink. Can't send them home thirsty," he rolls a watering eye at us.

"And what would you know about thirst – you've never been dry long enough to have one." Peg is an old friend and wants no trouble with me. "Sit down, Frank, and don't be annoying the girls."

"Who's annoying anyone, Peg Maguire – certainly not you – not if you were the last bloody woman on earth."

We have set them bickering between themselves now. Time to go. But you are edgy, persistent. "Is there really no chance of another drink?" you ask Peg. She lowers her voice and gives you a conspiratorial look.

"What is it you want – would a six-pack do? If you come with us to the Mountain View, I'll get you something there. They've a disco with late closing."

"The very thing," Frank roars. "A disco tit. Let's all go. Two such lovely young women need . . ." he staggers to his feet once more and begins to sing. "I could have danced all night – I could have danced all night and still have begged for more. I could have spread my wings," he wheels his arms in a jagged circle almost knocking Peg's glass, "and done a thousand things, I'd never done . . ."

"Will you for God's sake hold on to yourself," Peg snaps furiously, and pushes him forward.

"Are you right then, girls," she nods towards us. "I'll give you the lift down and you can walk back. It's only ten minutes."

Well, that has done it. There will be no stopping you now. We will not get home, till you are soused. And why should I try to deter you? Have I anything better to offer? All the tired virtues. Useless. I should be exasperated by you, dragging me all over the country as if a pint of stout were the holy grail. But something about you halts me. As you move to the door, something exaggerated in you – the turn of your shoulders, your head thrown back as though pulling from harness. Defiance and vulnerability in every line. Something more than youth. Something more than me as I was before I learnt – and who was it who finally taught me? – the hard-won pleasures of realism and self-sufficiency. Yet if I had the power to bestow them on you, this very instant, would I want to?

In the unlit carpark we find Peg's Fiat and pile in – Frank pulling me towards his knee: "If you were the only girl in the world and I was the only boy." Rain slashes at the windscreen, one wiper stuck halfway across it. Peg seems to drive by ear. Wet fir trees arching over us make a black tunnel of the road. The road to God knows where. I recognize none of it, letting myself be carried forward – lapsing into the heedless collective will. All needs converging in the simple drive for one more drink. "Nothing else would matter in the world today ..." Frank's whisky breath encircles us. We reach tall, silver gates, pass them, and sluice through rain-filled craters in the drive, the wind snapping at our wheels. A furious night – clouds blown as fast as leaves across the sky. Lights ahead – the tall Georgian house bright in welcome. Braking almost on the front steps, Peg jumps out, leaving the door wide: "I'll put in a word for you." We follow, our faces lowered from the rain. In the hallway with the bouncer, her blonde head bent to his ear, she is confidential, explaining that we want only a takeaway – no admission. Solemn as a mother entrusting her daughters. Then she turns back to the car and her boys waiting outside. She throws a wicked grin at me over her shoulder – why? – "Enjoy yourselves, girls," and she is off.

Out of the night – into a frenzy of light and sound. We push through the black swing doors. Red and purple light, great shafts of it, beat against the walls and floor. The music hammers through my chest, shivering my arms. A man and woman locked together, move in a tight circle at the centre of the room. In the corner, beside a giant speaker, two girls on stiletto heels dance an old-fashioned jive. We push through the wall of shoulders at the bar, country boys shy of dancing. "Two large bottles of stout," I order. The barman reaches for pint glasses and shoves them under the draught tap. "Bottles – to take away." I call across to him. But it is useless, he has already moved to the far end of the counter to measure out whiskey.

"We will just have to drink them here," you say, putting your mouth close to my ear so that I feel the warmth of your breath. So be it – at least we are in from the rain for a while.

We choose a corner table, as far from the speakers as possible, but still I have to shout to make you hear me.

"It's easier if you whisper," you say, bringing your lips to my ear once more, in demonstration.

"You are used to these places, I suppose." It is years since I have sat like this. Though so little has altered. The lights and music more violent maybe, the rest unchanging. Nobody really wants to be here, it seems. Young women dressed for romance display themselves – bringing their own glamour. The men stand banded in council, shoulders raised as a barrier, until they have drunk enough. The faces are bored or angry. Each one resenting his need, grudging submission to this ritual fever.

You finish half your pint at one go and offer the glass to me. I down the remainder and together we start on the next, laughing. A rotating light on the ceiling spins a rainbow of colours; blue, red, gold, each thrust devouring the last. Smoke hangs in heavy green clouds about us. As though it were the fumes of marijuana, I breathe it deep into my lungs and feel suddenly a burst of dizzy gaiety . . . the absurdity of it all – that we should be here. And back to me come memories of years ago – adolescence, when it might have been the scene of passion, or was it even then absurd? The pace slows and three couples move to the centre of the floor. "I don't want to talk about it – how you broke my heart." The voice of Rod Stewart rasps through the speakers in an old song. But a favourite of yours. We have danced to it once before – in the early hours at Clare's party two weeks ago, when Maeve had left without you. You stand beside me now and in pantomime stretch your hand. "Will you dance with me?" You walk ahead on to the floor. Under the spotlight your white shirt is luminous – your eyes seem black. You rest your hands on your hips, at the centre of the room, waiting.

"If you stay here just a little bit longer – if you stay here – won't you listen to my heart . . ." We step into each other's arms.

Our cheeks touch. I smell the scent of your shirt – the darkness
of your hair. Your limbs are easy, assured against mine. Your
hands familiar, hold me just below the waist. We turn the floor,
elaborately slow, in one movement, as though continuing something interrupted. The music lapping thigh and shoulder. "The
stars in the sky don't mean nothing to you – they're a mirror."
Round we swing, round; closer in each widening circle. Lost to
our private rhythm. The foolish words beating time in my blood.

I open my eyes. The music has stopped. Behind you, I see a
man standing; his eyes riveted to our bodies, his jaw dropped
wide as though it had been punched. In his maddened stare I
see reflected what I have refused to recognize through all these
weeks. Comfort, sympathy, a protective sister – who have I been
deceiving? I see it now in his eyes. Familiar at once in its stark
simplicity. Making one movement of past and future. I yield
myself to it; humbled, self-mocking. Quick as a struck match.

As if I had spoken aloud, with a light pressure of my hand,
you return to consciousness and walk from the floor.

I follow, my skin suddenly cold. I want as quickly as possible
to be gone from the spotlight. I have remembered where we are:
a Friday night country dance, surrounded by drunken males
who have never before seen two women dance in each other's
arms. All about the room they are standing still, watching. As we
cross the empty space to our table, no one moves. I notice for
the first time Brid Keane from the post office: she is leaning
against the wall, arms folded, her face contorted in a look of
such disgust, it seems for a moment that she must be putting it
on.

"Let's get out of here – as soon as you've finished your drink,"
I whisper.

"What – do you want another drink?" Your voice rises high
above the music that has begun again. I stare at you in amazement – is it possible that you haven't noticed, that you don't yet
know what we've done? Can you be so naïve or so drunk that
you haven't realised whose territory we are on?

And then someone moves from the table behind and pushes
into the seat opposite us. Squat, red-faced, his hair oiled across
his forehead. He props an elbow on the table, and juts his head

forward, struggling to focus his eyes. His pink nylon shirt is open, a white tie knotted about the neck.

"Fucking lesbians," he says at last, "Are you bent or what?" The breath gusting into my face is sour with whisky. We look towards the dancers writhing under a strobe light and ignore him.

"Did you not hear me?" he asks, shoving his face so close to me, I see the sweat glisten on his upper lip. "I said are you bent – queers?" He drives his elbow against mine so that the stout spills over my glass.

A familiar anger rips through me, making my legs tremble. I press my nails into the palm of my hand and say nothing. I will not satisfy him so easily.

"What were you saying about the music?" I throw you a smile.

"I asked you a question," he says. "Will you give me a bloody answer?" He runs the words together as though speed were his only hope of completing them.

"I said it's lousy," you reply, "about ten years out of date."

He looks from me to you and back again with baffled irritation and his voice grows querulous. He asks: "Look, would one of you lesbians give me a dance?"

A friend has joined him now, leaning over the back of your chair, a grin on his lips sly and lascivious.

"Will you not answer me?" the first one shouts, "or are you fucking deaf?"

Drawing my shoulders up, I turn and for the first time look directly into his eyes. "No," I say with warning deliberation, "we are not deaf, yes, we are lesbians and no, we will not give you a dance."

He stares at us stupefied, then falls back into his seat, breath hissing from his chest as though a lung had burst. "Jesus, fucking, Christ."

You give a whoop of laughter, your eyes wide with delight. It seems you find him hugely amusing. Then you're on your feet and across the room in search of the toilet or God knows another drink.

I have my back turned to him when I feel the pink-sleeved arm nudging mine again. "Hey, blondie – you've gorgeous hair," he says, giving an ugly snigger. "Did anyone ever tell you that?" It is a moment before I recognise the smell of singed hair. I reach my hand to the back of my head and a cigarette burns my fingertips. With a cry of pain, I grab hold of the oily lock across his forehead and wrench hard enough to pull it from the roots. He stretches his arm to catch hold of mine but I tear with all my force. "You fucking cunt!" he screams.

Suddenly someone catches hold of us from behind and pulls us roughly apart. It's the bouncer – a big red-haired man in a grey suit. When he sees my face he steps back aghast. He had plainly not expected a woman.

"I don't know what you two want," his voice is cold, contemptuous, "but whatever it is, you can settle it between you – outside." He drops the hand on my shoulder, wheels round and walks back to his post at the door. At the sight of him, my opponent is instantly subdued. He shrinks back into his seat as though he had been whipped, then slowly collapses on to the table, head in his arms.

You return carrying another drink. I wait until you are sitting down to whisper: "We have to get out of here, Cathy – they're half savage. That one just tried to set fire to my hair."

"The little creep!" you exclaim, your eyes sparking with indignation. "Oh, he's easily handled – but the rest of them, look."

At the bar a group of six or seven are standing in a circle drinking. Big farm boys in tweed jackets – older than the others and more sober. Their gaze has not left us, I know, since we walked off the dance floor, yet they have made no move. This very calm is what frightens me. In their tense vigilance, I feel an aggression infinitely more threatening than the bluster of the two next us. Hunters letting the hounds play before closing in?

"I think they might be planning something." I say, and, as if in response to some prearranged signal, one of them breaks from the group and slowly makes his way to our table.

His pale, thin face stares into mine, he makes a deep bow and stretches out his hand. "Would one of you ladies care to dance?"

I shake my head wearily. "No, thanks."

He gives a scornful shrug of the shoulders and walks back to his companions. A moment later, another one sets out. When he reaches us, he drops to one knee before you and, for the benefit of those watching, loudly repeats the request. When you refuse him, he retreats with the same show of disdain.

"They can keep this going all night," I say, "building the pressure. With their mad egotism, anything is better than being ignored." And I know also what I do not say, that we have to put up with it. They have us cornered: under all the theatrics lies the clear threat that if we dare to leave, they can follow, and once outside, alone in the dark, they will have no need for these elaborate games.

"What can we do?" you ask, twisting a strand of hair about your finger, your eyes attentive at last.

"I'll go off for a few minutes. Maybe if we separate, if they lose sight of us, they might get distracted.'

Five minutes later, pushing my way through the crowd to our table, I find you chatting with the one in the pink shirt and his mate, smoking and sharing their beer like old drinking pals. How can you be so unconcerned? I feel a sudden furious irritation. But you look up at me and smile warningly. "Humour them," I read in the movement of your lips. And you may be right. They have turned penitent now, ingratiating: "We never meant to insult you, honest, love. We only wanted to be friendly." His head lolling back and forth, he stabs a finger to his chest: "I'm Mick, and this is me mate Gerry."

All right, then, let us try patience. At least while we are seen talking to these two, the others will hold off.

"You know, blondie, I think you're something really special," with the deadly earnest of the drunk, Mick addresses me. "I noticed you the second you walked in. I said to Gerry – didn't I Gerry? Blondie, would you not give it a try with me? I know you're into women – your mate explained – and that's all right with me – honest – that's cool, you know what I mean? But you never know till you try, do you? Might change your life. Give us a chance, love." He careens on through his monologue, long past noticing whether I answer or not. On the opposite side, I hear Gerry, working on you with heavy flattery, admiring your eyes (glistening now – with drink or anger – dark as berries), praising the deep red of your lips – parted at the rim of your glass. And you are laughing into his face and drinking his beer. Your throat thrown back as you swallow, strong and naked.

Mick has collapsed, his head on the table drooping against my arm. "Just one night," he mutters into my sleeve, "that's all I'm asking – just one night. Do yourself a favour." His words seep through my brain, echoing weirdly, like water dripping in a cave. Drumming in monotonous background to the movements of your hands and face. Half turned from me, I do not hear what you answer Gerry, but I catch your tone; languorous, abstracted, I watch you draw in the spilt froth on the table. Your eyes lowered, the lashes black along your cheek, one finger traces the line of a half moon. Behind you I see the same group watching from the bar; patient, predatory. My blood pounds – fear and longing compete in my veins.

And then all at once, the music stops. Everyone stands to attention, silent. The disc-jockey is making an announcement: the offer of a bottle of whiskey, a raffle, the buying of tickets – gripping them as the music and dance never could. This is our moment, with Gerry moving to the bar to buy cigarettes and Mick almost asleep, slumped backwards, his mouth dropped open. I grasp your hand beneath the table, squeezing it so that you may feel the urgency and no one else, and look towards the green exit sign. We are across the floor, stealthy and cautious as prisoners stepping between the lights of an armed camp. At the door at last, "Fucking whoores – you needn't trouble yourselves to come back," the bouncer restraining fury in the slam of the swing doors behind us.

And we are out.

Out in the wet darkness. The wind beating escape at our backs. I catch your hand. "Run and don't stop." Our feet scatter the black puddles, soaking our shins. The fir trees flapping at our sides beckon, opening our path to the gates. So much further now. The moon will not help – hidden from us by sheets of cloud withholding its light. We run blind, my heart knocking at my ribs; following the track only by the sting of gravel through my thin soles. "Come on – faster." The gates spring towards us out of nowhere – caught in a yellow shaft of brightness. A car rounds the bend behind us, the water flung hissing from its tyres. We dodge under the trees, the drenched boughs smacking my cheek. The headlights are on us, devouring the path up to and beyond the open gates. The window rolled down, I hear the drunken chanting – like the baying of hounds: "We're here because we're queer because we're here because we're ..." "Great fucking crack, lads ..." Gone. Past us. Pitched forward in the delirium of the chase – seeing nothing to left or right. A trail of cigarette smoke in the air.

"All right – we can go on now," you say, laughing, drawing me out from cover. "Do you think it was them?"

"Yes, or worse. We had better be gone before the next lot."

We run on again, through the wide gates to the main road. The alcohol is washing through me now, spinning my head. My heart is beating faster than ever, though the fear has left me. You are beginning to tire. "We are almost there," I urge you, marvelling that you can still stand, let alone run. The rain darts in the gutter, the leaves slithering under our feet. Jumping a pool I slip towards you. Your arm outflung steadies me. You're laughing again – the long looping kind you do not want to stop. "You're worse than I am," you say.

The moon all at once throws open the night before us, scattering in sequins on the tarred road, silver on the hanging trees. I see the house massed and still in its light.

"We are home," I say.

You slow your pace and let go of my hand. Your eyes under the white gleam of the moon are darker than ever – secretive.

"Are you laughing at me?" I ask, to capture your attention.

"I'm not – really," you answer, surprised.

I lift the latch of the gate, softly so as to wake no one. How am I to keep this? To keep us from slipping back into the everyday: the lighted, walled indoors – all the managed, separating things. And what is it I fear to lose? Any more than my desire – dreaming yours. Any more than a drunken joy in escape?

The cat comes through a gap in the hedge, whipping my shins with her tail. I lift her to me and she gives a low, rough cry.

"She's been waiting for you," you tell me.

I turn the key in the kitchen door. You step inside and stand
by the window, the moonlight falling like a pool of water about
your feet. I gaze at your shoes for no reason; at the pale, wet
leather, muddied now.

"Well, that looked bad for a moment," I say, putting my arm
round you, not knowing whether it is you or myself I am consol-
ing. "Were you not frightened at all?"

"Oh, yes, I was," you answer, leaning into me, pulling me
close. "Yes."

And so, I have been right. So much more than comfort. I
slide my lips down your cheek, still hesitant, measuring your
answer. And you lift your open mouth to meet mine. I have
imagined nothing, then. Everything. All this long night has been
a preparation – an appeal. You untie the belt of my raincoat. I
feel your hands, still cold from the night rain, along my sides:
"I'm freezing. Are you?"

"Yes."

"Are there beds anywhere in this house?"

"We might find one."

You laugh. I take your hand and silently, as though fearful of
waking someone, we cross the hall together and climb the
wooden staircase.

The room is dark but for a shaft of moonlight which falls
across the double bed, with its silver and wine red quilt, that
waits at the centre of the floor. I light a candle by the window.
You sit on the cane chair and unlace your sneakers, slowly, knot
by knot. Then stand and drop your clothes – red jeans and white
shirt – in a ring about them. I turn back the sheets and step
towards you. Downstairs the phone sounds, cracking the darkness like a floodlight. It rings and rings and will not stop. "I had
better answer it," I say and move to the door.

"Who was it?" When I return, you are sitting propped against
the pillow, easy as though you spent every night here. I cannot
tell you that it was Jan, feeling amorous, wanting to chat, imagining me alone.

"Jan . . ." I begin, but you do not wait to hear. Reaching your
hand behind my head, you pull my mouth towards you. I feel,
but do not hear the words you speak against my lips.

The rain drives at the window, shivering the curtains. The wind blown up from the sea sings in the stretched cables. Your body strains to mine, each movement at once a repetition and discovery. Your mouth, greedy and sweet, sucks the breath from my lungs. I draw back from your face, your long dark hair and look in your eyes: you are laughing again – a flame at the still black centre. Your tongue seals my eyelids shut. Your hands, travelling over me, startle the skin as if they would draw it like a cover from muscle and bone. We move – bound in one breath – muscle, skin and bone. I kiss you from forehead to thigh. Kiss the fine secret skin beneath your breast, the hard curve of your belly.

The wind moans through the slates of the roof. The house shifts. Beneath us the sea crashes on the stones of the shore. Your voice comes clear above them beating against mine, high above the wind and rain. Spilling from the still centre – wave after wave. And then, a sudden break; a moment's straining back as though the sea were to check for one instant – resisting – before its final drop to land. But the sea does not.

You lie quiet above me. I taste the salt of tears on my tongue. "Are you crying? What is it?"

"No, I'm not," you answer gently, your head turned from me. Maybe so. I close my arms about you, stroking the silk of your back, finding no words. But it does not matter. Already you have moved beyond me into sleep. I lie still. Clouds have covered the moon, blackening the window of sky. I cannot see your face. Your body is heavy on mine, your breath on my cheek. I soothe myself with its rhythm. The rain has ceased. I hear once more the small night sounds of the house: the creak of wood in floor-boards and rafters, the purr of the refrigerator. Then suddenly there comes a loud crash – the noise of cup or plate breaking on the kitchen's tiled floor. My breath stops – you do not stir. I hear the squeal of a window swung on its hinge. A dull thud. Footsteps?

Before my eyes a face rises: mottled cheeks, beads of sweat along the lip. A wild fear possesses me that he or his friends have followed us, come here to this house in search of us. I slide gently from under you. I creep to the door and stand listening for a moment, breath held, before opening it. Silence . . . Nothing but the hum of the fridge. And then . . . a soft, triumphal cry. Of course – the cat. How well I know that call. Elsie has caught a rat or bird and brought it home through the window. In the morning, there will be a trail of blood and feathers on the carpet. Time enough to deal with it tomorrow.

I go back to bed. Lifting the sheet, I press near to your warmth, my belly fitting exactly in the well of your back. I breathe the strange, new scent of you. A shudder goes through my limbs. I reach my hand and gently gather the weight of your breast. I feel the pulsing through the fine veins beneath the surface. You stir, sighing, and press your thighs against mine. You murmur something from sleep – a word, or name. Someone's name.

My arms slacken. I taste your tears, again, on my lips. In the morning what will we say to each other? Drunk as you were it will be easy to forget, to pretend the whole thing an accident. No need then to prepare an attitude – for Maeve (when she calls, as she will, as before, thanking me for taking care of you), for Jan – for ourselves. The night is fading at the window. The bare branch of the sycamore knocks on the wall behind us. Words echo in my mind, the words of the song we danced to, foolish, mocking: "The stars in the sky mean nothing to you – they are a mirror." And to me? What was it I said this evening about romantic illusion? I reach out my hand for the candlestick on the table. As I lift it, the flame flares golden. My movement has woken you. You regard me, for an instant, startled. How childish you look, your forehead smooth, your eyes washed clear. Was it only your hurt that set a cord between us – that lent you the outline of maturity? "I thought I heard a noise downstairs," you say.

"Yes, but it was nothing," I kiss your eyes shut. "Only the cat with a bird," I answer as you move into sleep, your cheek at my shoulder. "Nothing."

Far out to sea, a gull cries against the coming of light. For a little longer, night holds us beyond the grasp of speech. I lean and blow the candle out.

Some of My Best Friends

Michelene Wandor

Don't get me wrong. I have nothing against politicos. Some of my best friends are politicos. Always have been, ever since I discovered politics. it's something about their energy, their pigheadedness, their impossible visions about making the world a better place as long as you agree to see it their way. the ones i like the best are the ones who rabbit on and on about collectivity, about getting rid of leadership, about giving the power back to the people, or whatever slogan they happen to have made up that amounts to the same thing. These are the people who go on about working collectively in the most persistent and egomaniacal way, and always somehow manage to end up in the centre of things, never doing any actual work, but always talking the loudest and being the most dynamic. sorry. i didn't mean to go on about politicos, it's just that once I get going i just go on and on about it. the other thing is that i'm probably driving you mad by sometimes having capital letters and sometimes not. i'm sorry about that, but it's because my left arm is still in a sling, and sometimes I feel like pressing the shift button and sometimes i don't. I always do for apostrophes, because there's nothing i hate more than words without their apostrophes. so this will look a bit like those long long tracts which all those american 1960s poets used to write, because they were all so in love with their typewriters, and instead of "and" they used to have "&", partly because it was quicker to write, partly because it was technological, and i've just noticed that you have to press the shift button for that as well, so i'll see how i go.

i'm a terrible digresser, a picker up of anything that happens to be floating down the street, bits of paper, people – I'm not fussy, i just like talking, but i better concentrate a bit more – i read somewhere recently that the b vitamins or do i mean the B vitamins have something to do with your concentration, so maybe i need a few more of them.

well. where shall i start? i expect you want to know how i got my arm in a sling. i expect you want to know a bit more about me. the two go together, i think. i just am not quite sure where the best place is to start.

i'll start with Howell. no, I won't. i'll just say a bit more about me – not much, i promise, my name is Tara Black. that's the name i'm known by, though it isnt – im not going to use any upper case any more from now on – my real name. my real name doesnt matter. i decided to call myself tara black after the Avengers – sorry, i boobed – and it took me ages to decide. i thought about honor, after honor blackman, but im not blonde and anyway the name honor is too moral by half. then i thought about diana, after rigg, but if theres one thing i cant stand its all those matriarchal sort of politicos, i mean mothers are perfectly all right in their own way, but ive never been into worshipping anything or anyone and im not too keen on archetypal myths or any of that rubbish either. just things, real things that happen that you know about. and then there was tara king, in the final series of the avengers. now, i think she was the least successful of the three, and i wasnt about to call myself king, that would be like the other side of the matriarchal coin, but i have always liked the sound of tara. its got a sort of fanfare ring to it, and also its something you can just throw off on your way out the door – ta ra, everyone, so its a name that comes and goes just as you want it to, and i like things that are useful. the black was because i always fancied honor blackman, and i just hope no one thinks im being racist about it all. there was a great load of hullabaloo when the festival started about whether i should change my name in case the black women got upset and i didnt dare let on then that black wasnt my real name anyway.

i wont tell you much about my background; ill just say that my life really started about ten years ago, in the middle of the

1970s, when i discovered all these wonderful politicos and they discovered me. until then i had got up in the morning, gone to my office job in the petroleum company, gone home to my little flat, cooked my dinner, gone out to the films with friends, found the occasional lover, never really fell in love, and went home to visit my parents in brighton some weekends. then one evening i went to a film and there were all these women in trousers, and i wore trousers anyway, so it wasnt that, but i realised that the film id come to see was about women who loved one another, and i promise you i didnt know about the word lesbian then, id just got on with it and not known what it was called. now none of my politico friends believed me when i said this to them, oh, they said, but werent people hostile to you, didnt you get flak, werent you for gods sake, oppressed. but i honestly wasnt. ive always been a bit of a loner, and i like men, some of my best friends are men, but i just didnt fancy going to bed with them. until howell, that is. but ill come to that in a minute. but what about our invisible history, they all said, well, i said, after i failed history o level, i didnt think it had much to do with me anyway, so why should who i go to bed with matter. you can imagine that all this didnt go down at all well, but there you go. thats me. anyway, after this film event, i got to know more and more of them, and eventually gave up my job and went to work at the arts centre where the festival was going to take place. just at reception, answering the phone, booking tickets, that sort of thing, nothing creative, just being around sort of thing.

anyway, the festival was already being organized when i started working there, and i was roped in to do dogsbody things, like phoning people up, writing letters, helping to book groups, acts. oh, yes. the festival was a gay arts festival, the sort of thing thats been happening quite regularly over the past few years in london, and the people at the arts centre already had a routine that i fitted into. and that was how i first met howell. hes one of the live wires in the gay arts group, knows lots about lots, is very dynamic, has long wavy blond hair, bright blue eyes, an amazing smile and a wonderfully crooked nose. ive just reread that sentence, and boy, it is like the description of a film star, written by someone besotted. i tell you, it was the strangest thing. when howell first came to the arts centre after i started work there, we were all having a meeting. id sat myself at the end of the room where there werent any people smoking, and the other end of the room was a haze of smoke.

howell came dashing in late – he was always late for everything – apologizing, and although nobody noticed it, i could see that the air just cleared around him as he walked in. it was as if he brought with him some sort of aura, that made the air round him clearer and brighter than the air round everyone else. reader, i fancied him. now i didnt know this at the time. it was not a feeling i recognised. i had never had it before, and all i felt was perked up, terrific energy, my heart beating faster. it was quite a different feeling from the one i got when i fancied women. that feeling was warm, magnetic, a little anxious, but secure and comfortable. what i felt when howell walked into the room was insecure, vibrant, sparkling and shivery.

the meeting carried on, and whenever i could i darted looks across the room at howell. i knew he had noticed me, because he is a restless sort of person who looks round at everyone all the time, but i was very careful never to catch his eye. at the end of the meeting someone asked for two central co-ordinators, one for the men and one for the women, and i volunteered and howell volunteered and there we were.

now it took about another month to get the festival under way, but from the minute the meeting ended, howell and i were inseparable. we all went off to the pub to have a drink, and he and i got into a corner and started sorting out paperwork and we got on like a house on fire, as they say. we met for breakfast, before the arts centre opened the following morning, because there was so much to do. at first we just talked work and organization, right, because that was what we had to do, and we were both obsessive and workaholics, for the first week we worked busily and crazily and wonderfully, organizing, liaising, finding the same people pains in the arse to deal with, and the same people co-operative and reliable. howell had a sort of easy charm about him, and at another meeting, he was asked to take on press and publicity, because everyone thought that with his blond hair and blue eyes and direct gaze he would wow any of the media contacts, whatever their sex and whatever their sexual orientation. funny, that phrase. id never heard it until i got involved with all these politicos and i thought it was a bit stupid to say that when you really meant who they fancied, but then i suppose they were trying to legitimize – there it is again, another of those long words – something they felt had been suppressed. you can tell i got quite good at picking up all the terms, but then i was always good at languages at school, mum said.

anyway, howell, with what i now realized was his usual dynamism, did a real blitz on the press and whatever he did, worked. lots of interest got shown – much of it salacious, probably, but what the hell. we had a really successful press conference in which howell was the front liner, and to all the snidey, gay-baiting questions, he made brilliant little throwaway quips, so that he managed to make people laugh while at the same time absolutely showing that he would not be put down. some of the women were really pissed off with him afterwards, because they said he was just using his macho talents to play the camp clown, but i thought he was just great, and if his little act meant that we would get press coverage, what the hell, then some of the other women said i didnt have a political view of it and i said, no, i didnt, i left that to them. because by this time something had already happened.

that was that howell and i had made love and slept together. not at one and the same time, you understand; the one followed the other as the night follows the day, and this particular night followed the day on which we got the first obscene phone call, and the first letter with abuse printed all over it. the abuse was amazingly comprehensive, and it isnt worth reproducing really, its just enough to say that it lumped together every minority you can imagine, as well as being anti-gay, as if it imagined that this festival was somehow going to take over the world. i must say in a funny sort of way it sounded as terrified as some of my politico friends sounded euphoric about the festivals, all passion and form. well, perhaps thats not very clear.

we reported all the obscenities to the police. i was a bit shocked after the first one, i must say, and it took howell ages to reassure me that whoever it was wouldnt be lying in wait for me.

we went off and had a kebab after work and then he could see i was still in a bit of a state so he offered to come home with me. i was grateful, putting off the moment of being alone, and when we got to the house i automatically went to give him a kiss, as we all did to each other, and somehow, and this is absolutely true, the kiss turned into something really quite other. it went on for ages and ages, as if we were both hungry for something we never knew we had wanted. then, breathless, our mouths and faces wet, we stood back from each other, let go and just burst out laughing. i opened the door, he came in, i put the kettle on and when id put the coffee in the cups we sat down on opposite sides of the kitchen table and i said well, this is a how dye do. the best how dye do ive said for a long time, he said. i liked that, i said. me too, says he. were not supposed to, i said. no, he agreed, have you ever done that before, i asked. not with a girl – sorry, woman, he said. no, nor me, i said – i mean, nor me with a man. and that was just a kiss, he said. i looked at him. we both burst out laughing again. thats my overwhelming memory of that evening, us laughing. it didnt seem shocking or surprising, it was strange and unfamiliar for both of us, and because neither of us ever had to think about contraception or anything like that, we didn't, as they say, go all the way, but I will tell you for sure that we both came with great amusement about how different it all was.

in the morning we were both a bit more sober about the whole thing and tried to work out exactly what the hell had happened. were we going straight, for heavens sake, given that we were such good friends even that didnt seem too bad an idea. we were actually more worried about what other people would think than what we thought. we asked one another whether we were in love and since neither of us had ever been in love with a member of the opposite sex, we had no idea how to answer the question, but i must say it had the hallmarks of love and romance – you, know, you walk past someone in a room just on your way to do something perfectly functional like put on the kettle and you cant resist a quick touch of a piece of skin, or you have a sudden impulse to kiss a bit of exposed neck, or bend down and bite a rather nicely rounded bum and then you simply carry on with being functional. we decided, in deference to the feelings of our friends, not to tell anyone about it. anyway, we didnt know what there was to tell.

on the way to work i had a thought. what, i said, if we were simply bi-sexual. you know, sometimes you fancy one sort of person and sometimes you fancy another. oh no, said howell, thats worse than going straight. i mean, that is wanting to have your cake and eat it. a most capitalist and venal thing to do. id have thought you could argue it as most liberating and progressive, i said, and then i saw the look on howells face and added, but then that sounds rather wishy-washy and very sixties, and he leaned over and gave me a quick peck behind the ear.

now we didnt know it at the time, but someone must have seen us. we were just round the corner from the office anyway. for that first day we thought we were behaving quite as usual. looking back, i think we were both oblivious to everyone and everything, and im sure people must have noticed. it wasn't till the following morning that i felt we were being avoided. you know how they say everyone loves a lover, well, this was sort of the opposite. we must have been exuding goodwill and happiness, and i swear we said nothing, were careful not to make any obvious little gestures towards one another. but there you are, people must have noticed, after a few days of avoidance from people, during which, incidentally, the phone and postal abuse got worse, one of the directors of the arts centre took us both off to lunch, ostensibly to talk about work. but as soon as we got settled in this little italian restaurant, she spoke up. we were throwing a spanner in the works, we were behaving appallingly, we were flirting and generally carrying on like school-children and it either had to stop or we would have to leave. what were we, straights or something.

we were quite shocked, i suppose, wed been naive, i think, in assuming either that we could keep things hidden or that somehow there would be no problem. i wont go into the lengthy tos and fros with all the various people over the next few days, arguing that we could no longer be part of the whole thing, that gay meant gay, that bi-sexuality was liberal and just refusing to accept the radicalism of alternative sexuality. we tried very hard;

there were meetings at which we explained that we didnt entirely understand it ourselves, that we were experiencing a new kind of sexual attraction – new to us, that is – and that we were not abandoning any radical sexual causes. we found ourselves developing an argument for bi-sexuality, which didnt go down at all well with the hardliners, some of whom said we should be sacked forthwith, and not allowed in the building again. well, it was all very shocking, and we clung together even more. once i said to howell that if it hadnt been for all the fuss, we might never have done it more than once and he sort of agreed. it wasnt just that we were being defiant, it was that we felt like outcasts, like people who had to prove that we were serious about what we were doing, and that meant we began to be more blatant about it while everyone else wrangled on about whether or not we should be sacked. we held hands in public, we kissed now and again, and if we did not go out of our way to be obtrusive in showing our affections, we stopped making any effort to hide them while we were at work.

the festival was nearly upon us, and because we were both so important to its co-ordination, the rows about whether to sack us or not went on and on, while we went on working. the very hardline group that thought we should be thrown out – men and women who normally wouldnt have agreed about anything were absolutely united about this – began to get very fed up when they realized we couldnt be got rid of as easily as all that, and some rather awful things started happening. i found dogshit – well, i suppose it was dogshit – on my chair when i arrived in my office. rotten food was left on top of files, both howell and i got a new sort of hate mail, which we just added to the general anti-gay abuse which was still pouring through the post. we still laughed a lot, but there was a tension there underneath, because we could never just get on with our friendship or relationship or affair or love or whatever it was. any sense of romance in the conventional sense went quite soon, and we had to work hard to make a space where we felt relaxed with one another. one sunday we went off for a very long walk in epping forest, which was lovely. we came back to find my bedroom window smashed, a brick in the middle of the room with an obscene message written on it. we couldnt work out who the hell sent it and then thought it didnt matter anyway.

the day before the festival was due to start, there was a final checking-up meeting. all the plans for the opening, the press nights, all the organization was gone over, and then when all the business was finished, there was a silence, a few rustling of papers, and one of the people most hostile to us spoke up. he had two things he wanted to say, the first was to do with the torchlight procession that night, which was to wind round central london, singing and dancing and celebrating. he announced the time of departure. then he paused, and said that he and his group had decided that if howell and i were anywhere near the building during the festival, they would boy-(and girl)-cott all the events. there was a silence. a lot of the events were being run by them, and everyone knew that the festival would collapse without them. i could tell that everyone was waiting for us to say something. i didnt feel angry or hurt, just very very tired. howell and i had been very silent during all the other meetings, i said, since we had been prepared to abide by the majority decision, but since that decision had not yet been arrived at, perhaps they would let us decide ourselves. howell interrupted me. we have to talk about it, he said. yes, i agreed. well talk about it tonight and let everyone know tomorrow morning. the official opening isnt till lunchtime. well all be here, so if we can all get together at twelve, well have decided something by then. you havent got much option about what you decide, said the opposition. howell said wed still like the evening to think about it all, because we would probably want to make a statement. there was a silence and even the opposition didnt seem to want to push the point. the meeting finished, everyone avoiding our eyes again.

once out of the meeting room, everyone broke into a frenzy of last-minute preparation. the street theatre group changed into their costumes for the procession and great fun was had by everyone as the rock band tuned up. the floats arrived and somehow there seemed like an excited, united feeling about it all. howell and i joined in, and feeling towards us relaxed a bit from some people as we all got carried away by the knowledge that after all the hard work, it was all going to really happen.

the procession began moving off at about seven in the evening. lots of people had turned up, there was an accompanying posse of police who were all very good-humoured, and by about eight the last stragglers had left the centre. they were all due to get back somewhere about midnight. howell and i waved the procession off, and then turned round to go back and finalize some last-minute details. we avoided one anothers eyes, knowing that our evening was going to be a lot more soul-searching than any of those people on the procession could imagine.

when we got back into the building it was terribly quiet after the days excitement. howell and i began going over the press arrangements to check that everything would run smoothly. and then i had a thought. howell, i said, i dont think theres anyone else in this building. rubbish, said howell, there are all sorts of people finishing lastminute things off – theres the lighting – no, i said, i bet everyone else has gone.

we went round that building with a toothcomb. no one else was there. you could tell that people still had bits and pieces to do – well, i said, theyll come back and finish later. that procession was obviously too exciting to miss.

we locked the front door, to prevent the idly curious from wandering in, and went back to work. it was a quiet evening and we worked with hardly a word. by about ten o clock we had finished and the moment could not be put off any longer. well, said howell. well, i said, i dont want to make any statement. i just want to go home and never come back. good, said howell, so do i. ive never really been a politico, i said, well, not like some of the others think they are. howell said, oh, i dont know. theres different ways of being political. anyway, i said, thats what i want to do. and theres another thing. i know, said howell. yes, i said, i know you know. howell said it for me: that we shouldnt see each other for a little while, until after the festival perhaps, and then we could see what we both felt. well, i said, if were both thinking the same sort of thing, it must be a good sign. we looked at each other. then, without saying anything, we went into the theatre and made love on the stage, in the middle of a jumble of a set, using the cushions that were there, adjusting soft lighting and putting on a billie holliday record. we lay there for a little while, still very quiet, then i got up and got dressed and went off to have a pee. i put a kettle on and made some coffee, put it on a tray with some biscuits and went back into the theatre.

just as i pushed the swing doors open, the explosion happened. i was thrown backwards, out of the theatre and my left arm got caught in the doors.

the hospital did a marvellous job with my arm. they actually sewed it back on – after, that is, they had found it, thrown on the other side of the theatre. there was nothing they could do for howell.

i was in hospital for a while. the inquest and funeral all happened while i was still in hospital, and i cried. i had lots of visitors, with much sympathy and support. the police investigated, but could not find any sure source for the people who had planted the bomb. some of the politicos were annoyed because they felt the police hadnt tried hard enough, and had just dismissed it as one loony gesture towards a lot of other loony people. i dont know about that. that may be the right way to look at it. quite frankly, i didnt care whether they found out or not. it wouldnt bring howell back; it wouldnt change anything important.

when i came out of hospital there was a memorial meeting arranged for howell, at the arts centre. i went. some people avoided me completely, a few others – the ones whod come to see me in hospital – were friendly, as usual, and full of excited chat about the festival the following year. the arts centre would be rebuilt and the insurance was going to pay for the new lighting board they always wanted. i had a momentary impulse to ask if there was a job going, but because i knew it was an ironic impulse, i didn't say anything, just said ta-ra as i left the building.

after the meeting i left london and came back to brighton. my left arm is still in a sling, although it isnt like that all the time. its just that i have to rest it as well as move it, if you follow me. i think of howell very often. i wonder whether he was a martyr, willing or unwilling; hes been taken up by lots of his friends as a martyr, and thats fair enough for them. perhaps if howell had been in their shoes he would have felt the same. anyway. last night i met a woman i liked a lot. i fancied her, even. shes married, has a daughter and seems perfectly happy as she is. but there was something in her eyes when she looked at me. ill always recognise that sort of look. its exactly the same look howell had in his eyes at that first meeting.

some of my best friends are still politicos.

FAMILY VALUES

Family Values

It's a loaded phrase. "Family values" has been used to evoke the very particular ideals and prejudices of conservative nuclear families, on the understanding that queers have no families and no values. In this section it is used in a very different and broader sense to evoke a sense of shared life – whether in families of ancestry, birth, upbringing, or the unpredictable "chosen families" lesbians are putting together for themselves.

In Dorothy Allison's shattering story of child neglect and abuse, "River of Names", the narrator's lesbian identity is much easier for her to own up to than her family one. What makes this story so subtle is the critical eye it casts on the articulation of childhood trauma: the self-hatred of the survivors, the awful tricks of memory, and the falsity inherent in storytelling, especially literary storytelling. What comes between the narrator and her easy-going girlfriend is the knife of the past.

"What did your grandmother smell like?"
I lie to her the way I always do, a lie stolen from a book.
"Like lavender," stomach churning over the memory of sour sweat and snuff.

The next two stories, from New Zealand and Canada, respectively, are about characters negotiating with so-called ethnic family values in a new world. The title of Annamarie Jagose's "Milk and Money", about a family of "hybrid exotics", alludes to a wonderfully suggestive Indian legend about immigration.

The narrator's beloved twin sister Flytalker is aphasic because of brain damage, but the story reinterprets this as the hopeful speechlessness characteristic of new arrivals in a strange land. Is assimilation the only option, the narrator asks, or can the old names be treasured?

> We left home in search of other women like us, with short hair and long memories; the words Flytalker had tattooed on her inner thigh were, *You have thrown away the rule book.*

In Shani Mootoo's slice-of-street-life "Out on Main Street", the narrator and her girlfriend – "cultural bastards", in their own flippant formulation – have to work out how "out" to be, as a butch and a femme, but also how to order the right pastries in an Indian sweet-shop. As in Marnie Woodrow's story, food and sex speak for each other: "Check out dese hips here nah, dey is pure sugar and condensed milk". What makes this story is its language, a dazzling mixture of dialect slang and erudite diction.

> And de women dem embarrass fuh so to watch me in mih eye, like dey fraid I will jump up and try to kiss dem, or make pass at dem. Yuh know, sometimes I wonder if I ain't mad enough to do it just for a little bacchanal, nah!

The families lesbians make for themselves in adult life bear the mark of those in which they were raised. Jane Rule's subtle story "Middle Children" stands out among lesbian fiction of the early 1970s for being about something other than two women falling in love. Its clever governing idea is that middle children will adapt the skills of diplomacy and adaptation they learned in their families of origin to the very new kinds of community they find themselves forming later. Though the narrator and her lover are discreet and old-world in their values, they can also mock themselves, and the story shows the utter confidence they have in their love, despite the fact that they never stand up and declare it to outsiders. (This story is a valuable corrective to the idea that semi-closeted relationships are necessarily neurotic and doomed.) Something else that is remarkable about "Middle Children" is the way it associates a long-term relationship with a fabulous sex life. "It's simply not true," as the narrator coyly observes, "to say such things don't improve with practice."

Set in the age of AIDS, but conjuring up all the passionate rituals and familial structures of the butch-femme bar scene often associated with an earlier era, Jenifer Levin's chronicle of the life and death of "La Bruja" combines urban grit and old-style Hollywood romance. "Over the years I'd see her sometimes," begins the narrator with misleading casualness, as she gathers up all she can say about a woman she never exchanged more than a few words with until the very last time they met. This story is a love affair that happens in imagination, in the gaps between elusive glimpses. It's about how the lives we end up leading are haunted by those we don't; about dividing your loyalties between your realities and your dreams.

Levin also shows the way parenting can creep into a life; many lesbians find themselves in a maternal role by accident, as it were, when they get involved with women who already have children. "Lesbian mother" is still often thought of as a contradiction in terms. In Madelyn Arnold's story "See You in the Movies", a recently divorced woman embarks on one long and terrible drive with her kids and her girlfriend that ends up being nothing like the movies. This story is a funny and fractious dialogue piece about the unnerving changes of life, about how to be a lover and a parent at the same time without losing your mind. With bitter wit, Arnold makes the point that two women, like any other couple, have needs "like different roads on the same map".

Elise D'Haene's story "Self-Deliverance" is an unsentimental study of a chosen family made up of three powerfully characterized individuals. She alternates the narative point of view between the two lesbians ("we don't call each other girlfriends") and a gay man whose families of origin have failed to give them the love they need. This story is about waiting tables and waiting to escape: "I can't tolerate the ordinariness of my days. I'm thirty now, not eighteen, and I'm still as stuck as a snowball on a wet mitten." Like Anna Livia, Elise D'Haene explores an appalling act of love: helping someone die. This three-way love story is a heartbreaking study of family values, in the best sense.

River of Names

Dorothy Allison

At a picnic at my aunt's farm, the only time the whole family ever gathered, my sister Billie and I chased chickens into the barn. Billie ran right through the open doors and out again, but I stopped, caught by a shadow moving over me. My cousin, Tommy, eight years old as I was, swung in the sunlight with his face as black as his shoes – the rope around his neck pulled up into the sunlit heights of the barn, fascinating, horrible. Wasn't he running ahead of us? Someone came up behind me. Someone began to scream. My mama took my head in her hands and turned my eyes away.

Jesse and I have been lovers for a year now. She tells me stories about her childhood, about her father going off each day to the university, her mother who made all her dresses, her grandmother who always smelled of dill bread and vanilla. I listen with my mouth open, not believing but wanting, aching for the fairy-tale she thinks is everyone's life.

"What did your grandmother smell like?"

I lie to her the way I always do, a lie stolen from a book. "Like lavender," stomach churning over the memory of sour sweat and snuff.

I realize I do not really know what lavender smells like, and I am for a moment afraid she will ask something else, some question that will betray me. But Jesse slides over to hug me, to press her face against my ear, to whisper, "How wonderful to be part of such a large family."

I hug her back and close my eyes. I cannot say a word.

*　　*　　*

I was born between the older cousins and the younger, born in a pause of babies and therefore outside, always watching. Once, way before Tommy died, I was pushed out on the steps while everyone stood listening to my Cousin Barbara. Her screams went up and down in the back of the house. Cousin Cora brought buckets of bloody rags out to be burned. The other cousins all ran off to catch the sparks or poke the fire with dogwood sticks. I waited on the porch, making up words to the shouts around me. I did not understand what was happening. Some of the older cousins obviously did, their strange expressions broken by stranger laughs. I had seen them helping her up the stairs while the thick blood ran down her legs. After a while, the blood on the rags was thin, watery, almost pink. Cora threw them on the fire and stood motionless in the stinking smoke.

Randall went by and said there'd be a baby, a hatched egg to throw out with the rags, but there wasn't. I watched to see and there wasn't; nothing but the blood, thinning out desperately while the house slowed down and grew quiet, hours of cries growing soft and low, moaning under the smoke. My Aunt Raylene came out on the porch and almost fell on me, not seeing me, not seeing anything at all. She beat on the post until there were knuckle-sized dents in the peeling paint, beat on that post like it could feel, cursing it and herself and every child in the yard, singing up and down, "Goddamn, goddamn, that girl . . . no sense . . . goddamn!"

I've these pictures my mama gave me – stained sepia prints of bare dirt yards, plank porches, and step after step of children – cousins, uncles, aunts; mysteries. The mystery is how many no one remembers. I show them to Jesse, not saying who they are, and when she laughs at the broken teeth, torn overalls, the dirt, I set my teeth at what I do not want to remember and cannot forget.

We were so many we were without number and, like tadpoles, if there was one less from time to time, who counted? My maternal great-grandmother had eleven daughters, seven sons; my grandmother, six sons, five daughters. Each one made at least six. Some made nine. Six times six, eleven times nine. They went on like multiplication tables. They died and were not missed. I come of an enormous family and I cannot tell half their stories. Somehow it was always made to seem they killed themselves: car wrecks, shotguns, dusty ropes, screaming, falling out of windows, things inside them. I am the point of a pyramid, sliding back under the weight of the ones who came after, and it does not matter that I am the lesbian, the one who will not have children.

I tell the stories and it comes out funny. I drink bourbon and make myself drawl, tell all those old funny stories. Someone always seems to ask me, which one was that? I show the pictures and she says. "Wasn't she the one in the story about the bridge?" I put the pictures away, drink more, and someone always finds them, then says. "Goddamn! How many of you were there anyway?"

I don't answer.

Jesse used to say, "You've got such a fascination with violence. You've got so many terrible stories."

She said it with her smooth mouth, that chin nobody ever slapped, and I love that chin, but when Jesse spoke then, my hands shook and I wanted nothing so much as to tell her terrible stories.

So I made a list. I told her: that one went insane – got her little brother with a tire iron; the three of them slit their arms, not the wrists but the bigger veins up near the elbow; she, now *she* strangled the boy she was sleeping with and got sent away; that one drank lye and died laughing soundlessly. In one year I lost eight cousins. It was the year everybody ran away. Four disappeared and were never found. One fell in the river and was drowned. One was run down hitchhiking north. One was shot running through the woods, while Grace, the last one, tried to walk from Greenville to Greer for some reason nobody knew. She fell off the overpass a mile down from the Sears, Roebuck warehouse and lay there for hunger and heat and dying.

Later, sleeping, but not sleeping, I found that my hands were up under Jesse's chin. I rolled away, but I didn't cry. I almost never let myself cry.

★　　★　　★

Almost always, we were raped, my cousins and I. That was some kind of joke, too.

> *What's a South Carolina virgin?*
> *'At's a ten-year-old can run fast.*

It wasn't funny for me in my mama's bed with my stepfather, nor for my cousin, Billie, in the attic with my uncle, nor for Lucille in the woods with another cousin, for Danny with four strangers in a parking lot, or for Pammie who made the papers. Cora read it out loud: "Repeatedly by persons unknown". They stayed unknown, since Pammie never spoke again. Perforations, lacerations, contusions, and bruises. I heard all the words, big words, little words, words too terrible to understand. *DEAD BY AN ACT OF MAN.* With the prick still in them, the broom handle, the tree branch, the grease gun . . . objects, things not to be believed . . . whisky bottles, can openers, grass shears, glass, metal, vegetables . . . not to be believed, not to be believed.

Jesse says, "You've got a gift for words."

"Don't talk," I beg her, "don't talk." And this once, she just holds me, blessedly silent.

I dig out the pictures, stare into the faces. Which one was I? Survivors do hate themselves, I know, over the core of fierce self-love, never understanding, always asking, "Why me and not her, not him?" There is such mystery in it, and I have hated myself as much as I have loved others, hated the simple fact of my own survival. Having survived, am I supposed to say something, do something, be something?

I loved my Cousin Butch. He had this big old head, pale thin hair, and enormous, watery eyes. All the cousins did, though Butch's head was the largest, his hair the palest. I was the dark-headed one. All the rest of the family seemed pale carbons of each other in shades of blond, though later on everybody's hair went brown or red and I didn't stand out so. Butch and I stood out then – I because I was so dark and fast, and he because of that big head and the crazy things he did. Butch used to climb on the back of my Uncle Lucius's truck, open the gas tank and hang his head over, breathe deeply, strangle, gag, vomit, and breathe again. It went so deep, it tingled in your toes. I climbed up after him and tried it myself, but I was too young to hang on long, and I fell heavily to the ground, dizzy and giggling. Butch could hang on, put his head down into the tank and pull up a cupped palm of gas, breathe deep and laugh. He would climb down roughly, swinging down from the door handle, laughing, staggering, and stinking of gasoline. Someone caught him at it. Someone threw a match. "I'll teach you."

Just like that, gone before you understand.

I wake up in the night screaming, "No, no, I won't!" Dirty water rises in the back of my throat, the liquid language of my own terror and rage. "Hold me. Hold me." Jesse rolls over on me; her hands grip my hipbones tightly.

"I love you. I love you. I'm here," she repeats.

I stare up into her dark eyes, puzzled, afraid. I draw a breath in deeply, smile my bland smile. "Did I fool you?" I laugh, rolling away from her. Jesse punches me playfully, and I catch her hand in the air.

"My love," she whispers, and cups her body against my hip, closes her eyes. I bring my hand up in front of my face and watch the knuckles, the nails as they tremble, tremble. I watch for a long time while she sleeps, warm and still against me.

James went blind. One of the uncles got him in the face with home-brewed alcohol.

Lucille climbed out the front window of Aunt Raylene's house and jumped. They said she jumped. No one said why.

My Uncle Matthew used to beat my Aunt Raylene. The twins, Mark and Luke, swore to stop him, pulled him out in the yard one time, throwing him between them like a loose bag of grain. Uncle Matthew screamed like a pig coming up for slaughter. I got both my sisters in the tool shed for safety, but I hung back to watch. Little Bo came running out of the house, off the porch, feet first into his daddy's arms. Uncle Matthew started swinging him like a scythe, going after the bigger boys,

Bo's head thudding their shoulders, their hips. Afterward, Bo crawled around in the dirt, the blood running out of his ears and his tongue hanging out of his mouth, while Mark and Luke finally got their daddy down. It was a long time before I realized that they never told anybody else what had happened to Bo.

Randall tried to teach Lucille and me to wrestle. "Put your hands up." His legs were wide apart, his torso bobbing up and down, his head moving constantly. Then his hand flashed at my face. I threw myself back into the dirt, lay still. He turned to Lucille, not noticing that I didn't get up. He punched at her, laughing. She wrapped her hands around her head, curled over so her knees were up against her throat.

"No, no," he yelled. "Move like her." He turned to me. "Move." He kicked at me. I rocked into a ball, froze.

"No, no!" He kicked me. I grunted, didn't move. He turned to Lucille. "You." Her teeth were chattering but she held herself still, wrapped up tighter than bacon slices.

"You move!" he shouted. Lucille just hugged her head tighter and started to sob.

"Son of a bitch," Randall grumbled, "you two will never be any good."

He walked away. Very slowly we stood up, embarrassed, looked at each other. We knew.

If you fight back, they kill you.

My sister was seven. She was screaming. My stepfather picked her up by her left arm, swung her forward and back. It gave. The arm went around loosely. She just kept screaming. I didn't know you could break it like that.

I was running up the hall. He was right behind me. "Mama! Mama!" His left hand – he was left-handed – closed around my throat, pushed me against the wall, and then he lifted me that way. I kicked, but I couldn't reach him. He was yelling, but there was so much noise in my ears I couldn't hear him.

"Please, Daddy. Please, Daddy. I'll do anything, I promise. Daddy, anything you want. Please, Daddy."

I couldn't have said that. I couldn't talk around that fist at my throat, couldn't breathe. I woke up when I hit the floor. I looked up at him.

"If I live long enough, I'll fucking kill you."

He picked me up by my throat again.

What's wrong with her?
 Why's she always following you around?
Nobody really wanted answers.

A full bottle of vodka will kill you when you're nine and the bottle is a quart. It was a third cousin proved that. We learned what that and other things could do. Every year there was something new.

You're growing up.
 My big girl.
There was codeine in the cabinet, paregoric for the baby's teeth, whiskey, beer, and wine in the house. Jeanne brought home MDA, PCP, acid; Randall, grass, speed, and mescaline. It all worked to dull things down, to pass the time.

Stealing was a way to pass the time. Things we needed, things we didn't, for the nerve of it, the anger, the need. *You're growing up*, we told each other. But sooner or later, we all got caught. Then it was, *When are you going to learn?*

Caught, nightmares happened. *Razorback desperate*, was the conclusion of the man down at the county farm where Mark and Luke were sent at fifteen. They both got their heads shaved, their earlobes sliced.

What's the matter, kid? Can't you take it?
Caught at sixteen, June was sent to Jessup County Girls' Home where the baby was adopted out and she slashed her wrists on the bedsprings.

Lou got caught at seventeen and held in the station downtown, raped on the floor of the holding tank.

Are you a boy or are you a girl?
 On your knees, kid, can you take it?
Caught at eighteen and sent to prison, Jack came back seven years later blank-faced, understanding nothing. He married a

quiet girl from out of town, had three babies in four years. Then Jack came home one night from the textile mill, carrying one of those big handles off the high speed spindle machine. He used it to beat them all to death and went back to work in the morning.

Cousin Melvina married at fourteen, had three kids in two and a half years, and welfare took them all away. She ran off with a carnival mechanic, had three more babies before he left her for a motorcycle acrobat. Welfare took those, too. But the next baby was hydrocephalic, a little waterhead they left with her, and the three that followed, even the one she used to hate so – the one she had after she fell off the porch and couldn't remember whose child it was.

"How many children do you have?" I asked her.

"You mean the ones I have, or the ones I had? Four," she told me, "or ten."

My aunt, the one I was named for, tried to take off for Oklahoma. That was after she'd lost the youngest girl and they told her Bo would never be "right". She packed up biscuits, cold chicken, and Coca-Cola, a lot of loose clothes, Cora and her new baby, Cy, and the four youngest girls. They set off from Greenville in the afternoon, hoping to make Oklahoma by the weekend, but they only got as far as Augusta. The bridge there went out under them.

"An Act of God," my uncle said.

My aunt and Cora crawled out down river, and two of the girls turned up in the weeds, screaming loud enough to be found in the dark. But one of the girls never came up out of that dark water, and Nancy, who had been holding Cy, was found still wrapped around the baby, in the water, under the car.

"An Act of God," my aunt said. "God's got one damn sick sense of humour."

My sister had her baby in a bad year. Before he was born, we had talked about it. "Are you afraid?" I asked.

"He'll be fine," she'd replied, not understanding, speaking instead to the other fear. "Don't we have a tradition of bastards?"

He was fine, a classically ugly healthy little boy with that shock of white hair that marked so many of us. But afterward, it was that bad year with my sister down with pleurisy, then cystitis, and no work, no money, having to move back home with my cold-eyed stepfather. I would come home to see her, from the woman I could not admit I'd been with, and take my infinitely fragile nephew and hold him, rocking him, rocking myself.

One night I came home to screaming – the baby, my sister, no one else there. She was standing by the crib, bent over, scream- ing red-faced. "Shut up! Shut up!" With each word her fist slammed the mattress, fanning the baby's ear.

"Don't!" I grabbed her, pulling her back, doing it as gently as I could so I wouldn't break the stitches from her operation. She had her other arm clamped across her abdomen and couldn't fight me at all. She just kept shrieking.

"That little bastard just screams and screams. That little bastard. I'll kill him."

Then the words seeped in and she looked at me while her son kept crying and kicking his feet. By his head the mattress still showed the impact of her fist.

"Oh no," she moaned, "I wasn't going to be like that. I always promised myself." She started to cry, holding her belly and sobbing. "We an't no different. We an't no different."

Jesse wraps her arm around my stomach, presses her belly into my back. I relax against her. "You sure you can't have children?" she asks. "I sure would like to see what your kids would turn out to be like."

I stiffen, say, "I can't have children. I've never wanted children."

"Still," she says, "you're so good with children, so gentle."

I think of all the times my hands have curled into fists, when I have just barely held on. I open my mouth, close it, can't speak. What could I say now? All the times I have not spoken before, all the things I just could not tell her, the shame, the self-hatred, the fear; all of that hangs between us now – a wall I cannot tear down.

I would like to turn around and talk to her, tell her . . . "I've got a dust river in my head, a river of names endlessly repeating. That dirty water rises in me, all those children screaming out their lives in my memory, and I become someone else, someone I have tried so hard not to be."

But I don't say anything, and I know, as surely as I know I will never have a child, that by not speaking I am condemning us, that I cannot go on loving you and hating you for your fairy-tale life, for not asking about what you have no reason to imagine, for that soft-chinned innocence I love.

Jesse puts her hands behind my neck, smiles and says, "You tell the funniest stories."

I put my hands behind her back, feeling the ridges of my knuckles pulsing.

"Yeah," I tell her. "But I lie."

Milk and Money

Annamarie Jagose

Everything is travelling, our father translates for us. Outside the window the light catches on the semi-cactus blooms of the dahlia; an unpicked head of broccoli is shot through with small yellow flowers; unseen, a codling moth larva is beginning its slow burrow to the heart of a Cox's Orange. *Everything has a journey in it.* We see no reason to disagree. After all, we are the direct result of twentieth-century mobility, hybrid exotics tamped down in someone else's soil and taught to call it our own. Our childhood catechism – Mynish, Bombay, London, Edinburgh, Igls, Dunedin – tracked our parents' convergent journeys and helped us make sense of ourselves. Now our trajectory takes us here, one thousand kilometres north to another hilly harbour city, to this white and grey, upstairs/downstairs house we share with Evie and Di.

Six months, a year later our mother is still writing *Are you settled in yet? I hope you are both settled in.* We try to reassure her with accounts of new friends made, progress reports on our vegetable garden – *we've already eaten our first crop of zucchini; tomatoes and peas are on the way* – and anecdotes from my job. She is not reassured by our careful letters. Another truth is visible between the lines: we are not settling in; we are always approaching, never arriving, looking for new ways to continue our asymptotic journey.

In November 1960, before we met her (but as we were about to make her acquaintance), our mother kept a day planner. She called it her diary but a glimpse between its faded red covers reveals no sign of the sort of social engagements that caused *The*

Times of India to dub her "the Galway Princess". Instead the year is bundled into cycles of twenty-eight – sometimes twenty-nine, less often twenty-seven – days. A block of five days marked in scarlet is counterpoised with a block in black, the latter also distinguished by a slight one degree rise and fall in the otherwise soberly consistent temperature recordings.

Our parents pondered these inscriptions in much the same way as later, and on foreign shores, they were to linger over the pages of the *Yates Garden Guide*, marking their place with a finger while leafing ahead with cautious anticipation, noting temperatures and growth cycles with the thoughts of seeds – the thin black/white spurs of the marigold, calendula's warty horseshoe, the generous bulge of the scarlet runner bean – bursting and swelling in the fecund backpastures of their minds. Our parents were, as our father was to tell us proudly, "practitioners of the rhythmic method".

Forgive him: English is not his first (or second or third) language.

Despite this, or perhaps because of it, vocabularies are life-lines for our parents. It was Flytalker who taught me this. Words are their parachutes, safety nets, inflatable liferafts. The desperate determination with which they accumulated them only accentuated, for us, the perilousness of their situation. Probably you are wondering how Flytalker, whose moist buzzing lips remain, to this day, untrafficked by coherent sound, came to be so aware of the word's seductive power. Or perhaps, prepared to accept this situation, you are hooked on the barb of a more pragmatic problem: namely, given Flytalker's aphasic condition, how did she teach me anything?

Or I have misjudged you completely and you are shuffling from foot to foot, anxious in your politeness for this impropriety to end, for correct etiquette to be observed, for introductions all round so you can resume your seat with an easy heart and enjoy yourself as proceedings unfold. Do not think you are only being mocked. In this respect you resemble our "intended reader": that is, our mother who had such utmost respect for rules that she did not distinguish between the Ten Commandments and the requirements for membership to the Willingdon Club, between the Tarikats and the instructions that accompanied a backgammon set; who in the moment of her starkest grief and bewilderment was only able to say to the two of us, "You have thrown away the rule book."

Last night when Flytalker and I came home from the pictures, Evie's light was still on and as we passed her doorway she called us in. At first we couldn't see her. Evie's bedroom is always a breathtaking orchestration of disarray; the walls are a kinetic display as the breeze from the permanently open window tugs at the hundreds of pieces of paper tacked up there (telephone messages, quotations copied from books, newspaper articles); clothes are tangled up in sheets which lie half on, half off the bed, weighted down here and there by books and, tonight, a two-bar heater; drawers from her desk and dresser are pulled out and lie strewn or stacked about the room, filled with paints, crayons and, the one in front of the window, a collection of cacti.

"Evie?" I say tentatively, but then we see her. She is standing absolutely still, spreadeagled, against an enormous bull's-eye freshly painted on the back wall, the contrast between her naked flesh and the uniformly concentric lines further emphasised by the steely gleam of the knives which surround her.

People never tired of passing comments about Flytalker and me. About our brown skin and unpronounceable names; about Flytalker's off-balance walk and swollen hot-water bottle head; about the fist-sized hole the butcher's wife claimed to have seen one day in my chest, the light from the plate glass window behind me illuminating a roughly circular patch on the inside front of my shirt. *Something spooky about those kids. Half castes. Honest, the size of my fist, like a big torch. Well, you just stay away from them or we'll see what your father has to say.* We skirted these the way we skirted small acts of cruelty in the playground but the words we cherished even after we left home in search of other women like us, with short hair and long memories; the words Flytalker had tattooed on her inner thigh were, *You have thrown away the rule book.*

"Good movie?" asks Evie; then, while we are still staring openmouthed, she gestures at the knife between her legs. "What d'you reckon? Is this too phallic?"

It is difficult to give a considered opinion. Flytalker and I exchange glances; we have just recognized the blade in question as our only breadknife.

Later, before going to bed, the three of us have a cup of tea at the kitchen table. Evie shows us the flyer that inspired her performance art. It is from the Women's Art Gallery in town and invites submissions for a nine-day exhibition tentatively entitled "Lesbian Re/presentations". As soon as Flytalker sees the flyer, she acts as if it were a personal letter addressed to her. She reads it through and then folds it up and puts it in her pocket, takes it out again to reread highlights and, when she finally goes upstairs to bed, it is still, casually but firmly, in her hand.

I have never been to England but I imagine it is like the laundromat at the end of our street; no matter what you take down there, you always leave with a more homogeneous load. Our parents were both processed by England's wash-rinse-spin cycle. When our mother arrived in the country, she was seventeen years old and had never been away from home overnight. In her passport under *Ainm an tSealbhóra* was written Mairéad Keenan; twenty-four hours later she was Margaret, renamed by her staff nurse who, on learning her name, said, "We'll have no such foolishness here." Our father was more jocularly teased out of his inheritance, his king's name. His first landlady said Jamshed sounded like somewhere to store preserves and that he looked like a Jim to her. Our parents are Margaret and Jim now. They recognized the protection offered by their new names and learned other words to go with them. Our mother learned to say *supper* when she really meant tea and our father learned *kipper*. He even learned to like them. Now that we too have left home, Flytalker and I always keep an ear open for our new names and their associated vocabularies.

In the morning on my way to work I stick my head around Evie's door to ask if we need anything special from the vegetable market. Evie and Di are curled up in bed, asleep. On the wall at the foot of the bed, Evie's figure is still picked out in stainless steel.

When Flytalker and I left home we travelled up the coast by train and caught the *Aramoana* across the strait. It was 31 October and, standing on the foremost part of the deck, we commemorated the twenty-second anniversary of another doubled voyage. On the last day in October our parents sailed from Bombay on the P & O liner, the *Stratheden,* to Sydney via Colombo and Perth. Somewhere between Colombo and Perth, our own voyage began although our parents were, as yet, unaware of it. They boarded the ten-thousand-ton Huddart Parker liner TSMV *Wanganella* in Sydney with no idea of the contraband they had stowed away. We were conceived in the single bunk of a double cabin with the waves crashing against the porthole; in that impossible gap between scarlet and black, menstruation and ovulation; at some unspecified point between two known land masses.

Our parents were amazed and a little taken aback that their little family had doubled so easily. In February, when our mother was three months pregnant, our father, unable to open his mouth without talking about gestation, infants and educational prospects, managed to write home to his sister: *My dear Jeroo, we had a nice time here the other day collecting apples from our garden and Margaret made 3½lbs of jelly and bottled it.* Once Flytalker and I were old enough to understand, as our father was now calling it, the miracle of our birth, we plagued our parents for further clues, gloating over that blue breach between Ceylon (as it was then) and Australia like twin discoverers of a new world. The only irregularity we ever learned about was that during the trip our father put his watch forward, in anticipation of South Pacific time, while our mother honoured Indian clocks until she stepped ashore in Wellington. This cleavage of time allowed us to be conceived both at two in the morning and seven-thirty the night before. An interesting irrelevance, that's all, for when has synchronicity been regarded as prophylactic?

Ever since Evie's stint as the knife thrower's assistant, Flytalker has shut herself up in her room, emerging infrequently for meals and maintaining her secrecy about what's going on behind her closed door. Tonight Di is out and I am cooking *brinjal pakora,* partly because I am hungry and bored but really because I know that their seductive spiciness will waft upstairs and flush Flytalker from her room when nothing else can. The peaflour batter is sitting to thicken and my knife, recently removed from Evie's wall, hesitates, pressing into but not piercing the eggplant's purple/black skin. There is a movement in the corner. Evie emerges from beneath a dusty tarpaulin which is, I now notice, handpainted with the yellow/brown/green splotches of army camouflage. Her face is red, with excitement or confinement I can't tell, and she has a cobweb clinging to her hair.

"I've been under there since you got home and you never noticed. Do you think that's more subtle than the knife throwing, politically speaking?" she asks. "What's for tea?"

Flytalker's favourite photograph of herself appeared in the *Otago Daily Times* in February 1962, accompanying an article about the new superintendent of the public hospital and his family. We are not so much a family as a molecular structure. Our father is standing in the background, shoulders diagonal to the square edges of the photograph, feet planted solidly into the earth as though afraid of falling off. Our mother looms large in the foreground, the white border of the photograph cutting her off below the breasts. Both parents are slightly out of focus. The effort of learning new vocabularies – *Otepoti, bring a plate, pohutukawa* – has fuzzed their edges. Slightly off-centred, I am six months old, raising myself on my hands like an abandoned seal cub on an ice floe. My image is so crisp you can see the blades of grass sprouting between my fingers. I am leaning over, our father is straining towards, our mother is glancing backwards over her shoulder at a smudged patch of grass (bobble-headed, baby-sized) on my immediate left. The editor thought it best to airbrush Flytalker from the picture. He felt the community would be suspicious of a doctor who could not safeguard his own family from hydrocephalus.

Chilli and *garam masala* perfume the air and Evie and I are just starting on the first batch of *pakora* when Flytalker comes in. She takes after our father's people who long ago fled their land on ill-constructed rafts, taking with them their sacred flame, forced to ask for sanction in a foreign kingdom. Our father's people sat opposite the king and his court: in this strange place, their language was like so much dirt on their tongues. The king called for an empty bowl and indicated, by filling it to the brim with milk, that there was no more room in his kingdom. Our father's people produced a gold coin and carefully,

carefully slid it into the milk. Not one drop spilled: they could stay. See Flytalker's wise smile; see her wet lips, always open, always silent: she too promises to introduce richness into that gap you never knew you had.

Dudh; rupee. Bainne; arigead. Milk; money.

Two months after our sixth birthday our father discovered, while shaving one morning, a pinprick of white on his cheek between the corner of his mouth and the fleshy lobe of his right ear. He recognized it immediately from the streetside advertisements of ayurvedic practitioners in Bombay: "White Patches? Immediate Cure Guaranteed." When the bleached dot was the size of our little fingernail, Flytalker and I noticed it for the first time and, fascinated, we began to assess its daily colonization of our father's face. First it concentrated on increasing its surface area but, once established, it ran a line down to our father's chin and, bulging sideways, claimed the better part of his nose. Here its territorial expansion ended and Flytalker and I began to interpret our father's piebald markings: maps having failed us before, we decided in favour of an epidermal cartography.

Less lofty representations of our father's affliction abounded. Flytalker was kept in at school after an altercation with a group of our classmates who had to be persuaded that our father was not trying to be a white man. When our father got home from work that night, the first thing he did was remove one of their milk teeth from her knuckle and stitch closed the small gash that remained. The second thing that he did was to sit us both down and retell the by now familiar story of our ancestors, the bowl of milk and the gold coin. When he got to the line, "Not one drop spilled: they could stay?", which Flytalker and I had always imbued with a certain triumph of spirit, he looked at us most seriously.

"Now you understand what our promise to the world has been," he said. "And I expect you to honour it as I have honoured it – assimilation without disruption."

Our father had taken our glittering history of resourcefulness and strength and turned it into something cringing and compliant. We could not bring our eyes to meet his, to challenge his interpretation. Someone was missing the whole point of the story: we hoped it wasn't us.

The lilac invitation to the exhibition opening said, *The Women's Art Collective is proud to present "Lesbian Re/presentations." Opening Friday 7.30, women only.* Coming straight from work, I am pleased to see a crowd already gathered at the gallery. A fifteen-foot diving platform has been installed just inside the door. At the very edge of the board, frozen in a diving position, is Evie wearing an old-fashioned, black-and-white, bathing costume. Below her on the floor, a small goldfish bowl filled with water is waiting. Its label reads "Patriarchal Woman". Evie winks at me as I pass.

I am looking around for Flytalker and then I see her. Or rather I see her exhibit. It is across the room, surrounded by several women, yet even seen like this, in part and from a distance, it is unmistakably hers. At closer range, it takes my breath away, makes me both vulnerable and inviolate, flensing my skin and replacing it with a new hide. Its gallery label reads *Sculpture, 1 m 34 cm by 76 cm* but the newness of its form defies such easy classification. Like a Mobius strip, its inside is its outside and it seems to swell and contract fluidly, according to the idiosyncratic pulsing of its aqueous heart. We are all in here somewhere: our settlements and our migrations, our compromises and our negotiations. Here are our grandparents whom we never met; here, between the blurrings and the sharp focusing, Jamshed and Mairéad are reconstituted; here are our contradictory watch faces, our tattoos, our milk and gold coin. There is a foreign familiarity to the whole piece that draws me in and, with a thoracic ache, I recognize at last the precise proportions (although not the size) of the cavity in my chest.

Flytalker is standing opposite, watching me. Our eyes connect and a high tide swells up inside my skull, something inside my head casts off its moorings and drifts. Our secret and complex selves, so often held apart by barriers and borders, come together to stand solidly at a knot of intersecting lines. We have not been given the new names we were waiting for: we have made them up for ourselves.

Out on Main Street

Shani Mootoo

1.

Janet and me? We does go Main Street to see pretty pretty sari and bangle, and to eat we belly full a burfi and gulub jamoon, but we doh go too often because, yuh see, is dem sweets self what does give people like we a presupposition for untameable hip and thigh.

Another reason we shy to frequent dere is dat we is watered-down Indians – we ain't good grade A Indians. We skin brown, is true, but we doh even think 'bout India unless something happen over dere and it come on de news. Mih family remain Hindu ever since mih ancestors leave India behind, but nowa-days dey doh believe in praying unless things real bad, because, as mih father always singing, like if is a mantra: "Do good and good will be bestowed unto you." So he is a veritable saint, cause he always doing good by his women friends and dey chilren. I sure some a dem must be mih half sister and brother, oui!

Mostly, back home, we is kitchen Indians: some kind a Indian food every day, at least once a day, but we doh get cardamom and other fancy spice down dere so de food not spicy like Indian food I eat in restaurants up here. But it have one thing we doh make joke 'bout down dere: we like we meethai and sweetrice too much, and it remain overly authentic, like de day Naana and Naani step off de boat in Port of Spain harbour over a hundred and sixty years ago. Check out dese hips here nah, dey is pure sugar and condensed milk, pure sweetness!

But Janet family different. In de ole days when Canadian missionaries land in Trinidad dey used to make a bee-line straight for Indians from down South. And Janet great-grandparents is one a de first South families dat exchange over from Indian to Presbyterian. Dat was a long time ago.

When Janet born, she father, one Mr John Mahase, insist on asking de Reverend MacDougal from Trace Settlement Church, a leftover from de Canadian Mission, to name de baby girl. De good Reverend choose de name Constance cause dat was his mother name. But de mother a de child, Mrs Savitri Mahase, wanted to name de child sheself. Ever since Savitri was a lil girl she like de yellow hair, fair skin and pretty pretty clothes Janet and John used to wear in de primary school reader – since she lil she want to change she name from Savitri to Janet but she own father get vex and say how Savitri was his mother name and how she will insult his mother if she gone and change it. So Savitri get she own way once by marrying this fella name John, and she do a encore, by calling she daughter Janet, even doh husband John upset for days at she for insulting de good Reverend by throwing out de name a de Reverend mother.

So dat is how my girlfriend, a darkskin Indian girl with thick black hair (pretty fuh so!) get a name like Janet.

She come from a long line a Presbyterian school teacher, headmaster and headmistress. Savitri still teaching from de same Janet and John reader in a primary school in San Fernando, and John, getting more and more obtuse in his ole age, is headmaster more dan twenty years now in Princes Town Boys' Presbyterian High School. Everybody back home know dat family good good. Dat is why Janet leave in two twos. Soon as A Level finish she pack up and take off like a jet plane so she could live without people only shoo-shooing behind she back . . . "But A A! Yuh ain't hear de goods 'bout John Mahase daughter, gyul? How yuh mean yuh ain't hear? Is a big thing! Everybody talking 'bout she. Hear dis, nah! Yuh ever see she wear a dress? Yes! Doh look at mih so. Yuh reading mih right!"

Is only recentish I realize Mahase is a Hindu last name. In de ole days every Mahase in de country turn Presbyterian and now de name doh have no association with Hindu or Indian whatsoever. I used to think of it as a Presbyterian Church name until some days ago when we meet a Hindu fella fresh from India name Yogdesh Mahase who never even hear of Presbyterian.

De other day I ask Janet what she know 'bout Divali. She say, "It's the Hindu festival of lights, isn't it?" like a line straight out a dictionary. Yuh think she know anything 'bout how lord Rama get himself exile in a forest for fourteen years, and how when it come time for him to go back home his followers light up a pathway to help him make his way out, and dat is what Divali lights is all about? All Janet know is 'bout going for drive in de country to see light, and she could remember looking forward, around Divali time, to the lil brown paper-bag packages full a burfi and parasad that she father Hindu students used to bring for him.

One time in a Indian restaurant she ask for parasad for dessert. Well! Since den I never go back in dat restaurant, I embarrass fuh so!

I used to think I was a Hindu *par excellence* until I come up here and see real flesh and blood Indian from India. Up here, I learning 'bout all kind a custom and food and music and clothes dat we never see or hear 'bout in good ole Trinidad. Is de next best thing to going to India, in truth, oui! But Indian store clerk on Main Street doh have no patience with us, specially when we talking English to dem. Yuh ask dem a question in English and dey insist on giving de answer in Hindi or Punjabi or Urdu or Gujarati. How I suppose to know de difference even! And den dey look at yuh disdainful disdainful – like yuh disloyal, like yuh is a traitor.

But yuh know, it have one other reason I real reluctant to go Main Street. Yuh see, Janet pretty fuh so! And I doh like de way men does look at she, as if because she wearing jeans and T-shirt and high-heel shoe and make-up and have long hair loose and flying about like she is a walking-talking shampoo ad, dat she easy. And de women always looking at she beady eye, like she loose and going to thief dey man. Dat kind a thing always make me want to put mih arm round she waist like, she is my woman, take yuh eyes off she! and shock de false teeth right out dey mouth. And den is a whole other story when dey see me with mih crew cut and mih blue jeans tuck inside mih jim-boots. Walking next to Janet, who so femme dat she redundant, tend to make me look like a gender dey forget to classify. Before going Main Street I does parade in front de mirror practising a jiggly-wiggly kind a walk. But if I ain't walking like a strong-man monkey I doh exactly feel right and I always revert back to mih true colours. De men dem does look at me like if dey is exactly what I need a taste of to cure me good and proper. I could see dey eyes watching Janet and me, dey face growing dark as dey imagining all kind a situation and position. And de women dem embarrass fuh so to watch me in mih eye, like dey fraid I will jump up and try to kiss dem, or make pass at dem. Yuh know, sometimes I wonder if I ain't mad enough to do it just for a little bacchanal, nah!

Going for a outing with mih Janet on Main Street ain't easy! If only it wasn't for burfi and gulub jamoon! If only I had a learned how to cook dem kind a thing before I leave home and come up here to live!

2.

In large deep-orange Sanskrit-style letters, de sign on de saffron-colour awning above de door read "Kush Valley Sweets". Underneath in smaller red letters it had "Desserts Fit For The Gods". It was a corner building. The front and side was one big glass wall. Inside was big. Big like a gymnasium. Yuh could see in through de brown tint windows: dark brown plastic chair, and brown table, each one de length of a door, line up stiff and straight in row after row like if is a school room.

Before entering de restaurant I ask Janet to wait one minute outside with me while I rumfle up mih memory, pulling out all de sweet names I know from home, besides burfi and gulub jamoon: meethai, jilebi, sweetrice (but dey call dat kheer up here), and ladhoo. By now, of course, mih mouth watering fuh so! When I feel confident enough dat I wouldn't make a fool a mih Brown self by asking what dis one name? and what dat one name? we went in de restaurant. In two twos all de spice in de place take a flying leap in our direction and give us one big welcome hug up, tight fuh so! Since den dey take up permanent residence in de jacket I wear dat day!

Mostly it had women customers sitting at de tables, chatting and laughing, eating sweets and sipping masala tea. De only men in de place was de waiters, and all six waiters was men. I figure dat dey was brothers, not too hard to conclude, because all a dem had de same full round chin, round as if de chin stretch tight over a ping-pong ball, and dey had de same big roving eyes. I know better dan to think dey was mere waiters in de employ of a owner who chook up in a office in de back. I sure dat dat was dey own family business, dey stomach proudly preceeding dem and dey shoulders throw back in de confidence of dey ownership.

It ain't dat I paranoid, yuh understand, but from de moment we enter de fellas dem get over-animated, even armorously agitated. Janet again! All six pair a eyes land up on she, following she every move and body part. Dat in itself is something dat does madden me, oui! but also a kind a irrational envy have a tendency to manifest in me. It was like I didn't exist. Sometimes it could be a real problem going out with a good-looker, yes! While I ain't remotely interested in having a squeak of a flirtation with a man, it doh hurt a ego to have a man notice yuh once in a very long while. But with Janet at mih side, I doh have de chance of a penny shave-ice in de hot sun. I tuck mih elbows in as close to mih sides as I could so I wouldn't look like a strong man next to she, and over to de l-o-n-g glass case jam up with sweets I jiggle and wiggle in mih best imitation a some a dem gay fellas dat I see downtown Vancouver, de ones who more femme dan even Janet. I tell she not to pay de brothers no attention, because if any a dem flirt with she I could start a fight right dere and den. And I didn't feel to mess up mih crew cut in a fight.

De case had sweets in every nuance of colour in a rainbow. Sweets I never before see and doh know de names of. But dat was alright because I wasn't going to order dose ones anyway.

Since before we leave home Janet have she mind set on a nice thick syrupy curl a jilebi and a piece a plain burfi so I order dose for she and den I ask de waiter-fella, resplendent with thick thick bright-yellow gold chain and ID bracelet, for a stick a meethai for mihself. I stand up waiting by de glass case for it but de waiter/owner lean up on de back wall behind de counter watching me like he ain't hear me. So I say loud enough for him, and every body else in de room to hear, "I would like to have one piece a meethai please," and den he smile and lift up his hands, palms open-out motioning across de vast expanse a glass case, and he say, "Your choice! Whichever you want, Miss." But he still lean up against de back wall grinning. So I stick mih head out and up like a turtle and say louder, and slowly, "One piece a meethai – dis one!" and I point sharp to de stick a flour mix with ghee, deep fry and den roll up in sugar. He say, "That is koorma, Miss. One piece only?"

Mih voice drop low all by itself. "Oh ho! Yes, one piece. Where I come from we does call dat meethai." And den I add, but only loud enough for Janet to hear, "And mih name ain't 'Miss'."

He open his palms out and indicate de entire panorama a sweets and he say, "These are all meethai, Miss. Meethai is Sweets. Where are you from?"

I ignore his question and to show him I undaunted, I point to a round pink ball and say, "I'll have one a dese sugarcakes too please." He start grinning broad broad like if he half-pitying, half-laughing at dis Indian-in-skin-colour-only, and den he tell me, "That is called chum-chum, Miss." I snap back at him, "Yeh, well back home we does call dat sugarcake, Mr Chum-chum."

At de table Janet say, "You know, Pud (Pud, short for Pudding; is dat she does call me when she feeling close to me, or sorry for me), it's true that we call that 'meethai' back home. Just like how we call 'siu mai' 'tim sam'. As if 'dim sum' is just one little piece a food. What did he call that sweet again?"

"Cultural bastards, Janet, cultural bastards. Dat is what we is. Yuh know, one time a fella from India who living up here call me a bastardized Indian because I didn't know Hindi. And now look at dis, nah! De thing is: all a we in Trinidad is cultural bastards, Janet, all a we. *Toutes bagailles!* Chinese people, Black people, White people. Syrian. Lebanese. I looking forward to de day I find out dat place inside me where I am nothing else but Trinidadian, whatever dat could turn out to be."

I take a bite a de chum-chum, de texture was like grind-up coconut but it had no coconut, not even a hint a coconut taste in it. De thing was juicy with sweet rose water oozing out a it. De rose water perfume enter mih nose and get trap in mih cranium. Ah drink two cup a masala tea and a lassi and still de rose water perfume was on mih tongue like if I had a overdosed on Butchart Gardens.

Suddenly de door a de restaurant spring open wide with a strong force and two big burly fellas stumble in, almost rolling over on to de ground. Dey get up, eyes red and slow and dey skin burning pink with booze. Dey straighten up so much to over-compensate for falling forward, dat dey find deyself leaning backward. Everybody stop talking and was watching dem. De guy in front put his hand up to his forehead and take a deep Walter Raleigh bow, bringing de hand down to his waist in a rolling circular movement. Out loud he greet everybody with "Alarm o salay koom." A part a me wanted to bust out laughing. Another part make mih jaw drop open in disbelief. De calm in de place get rumfle up. De two fellas dem, feeling chupid now because nobody reply to dey greeting, gone up to de counter to Chum-chum trying to make a little conversation with him. De same booze-pink alarm-o-salay-koom-fella say to Chum-chum, "Hey, howaryah?"

Chum-Chum give a lil nod and de fella carry right on, "Are you Sikh?"

Chum-chum brothers converge near de counter, busying deyselves in de vicinity. Chum-chum look at his brothers kind a quizzical, and he touch his cheek and feel his forehead with de back a his palm. He say, "No, I think I am fine, thank you. But I am sorry if I look sick, Sir."

De burly fella confuse now, so he try again.

"Where are you from?"

Chum-chum say, "Fiji, Sir."

"Oh! Fiji, eh! Lotsa palm trees and beautiful women, eh! Is it true that you guys can have more than one wife?"

De exchange make mih blood rise up in a boiling froth. De restaurant suddenly get a gruff quietness 'bout it except for a woman I hear whispering angrily to another woman at de table behind us, "I hate this! I just hate it! I can't stand to see our men humiliated by them, right in front of us. He should refuse to serve them, he should throw them out. Who on earth do they think they are? The awful fools!" And de friend whisper back, "If he throws them out, all of us will suffer in the long run."

I could discern de hair on de back a de neck a Chum-chum brothers standing up, annoyed, and at de same time de brothers look like dey was shrinking in stature. Chum-chum get serious, and he politely say, "What can I get for you?"

Pinko get de message and he point to a few items in de case and say, "One of each, to go please."

Holding de white take-out box in one hand he extend de other to Chum-chum and say, "How do you say 'Excuse me, I'm sorry' in Fiji?"

Chum-chum shake his head and say, "It's okay. Have a good day."

Pinko insist, "No, tell me please. I think I just behaved badly, and I want to apologize. How do you say 'I'm sorry' in Fiji?"

Chum-chum say, "Your apology is accepted. Everything is okay." And he discreetly turn away to serve a person who had just entered de restaurant. De fellas take de hint dat was broad like daylight, and back out de restaurant like two little mouse.

Everybody was feeling sorry for Chum-chum and Brothers. One a dem come up to de table across from us to take a order from a woman with a giraffe-long neck who say, "Brother, we mustn't accept how these people think they can treat us. You men really put up with too many insults and abuse over here. I really felt for you."

Another woman gone up to de counter to converse with Chum-chum in she language. She reach out and touch his hand, sympathy-like. Chum-chum hold the one hand in his two and make a verbose speech to her as she nod she head in agreement generously. To italicize her support, she buy a take-out box a two burfi, or rather, dat's what I think dey was.

De door a de restaurant open again, and a bevy of Indian-looking women saunter in, dress up to weaken a person's decorum. De Miss Universe pageant traipse across de room to a table. Chum-chum and Brothers start smoothing dey hair back, and pushing de front a dey shirts neatly into dey pants. One brother take out a pack a Dentyne from his shirt pocket and pop one in his mouth. One take out a comb from his back pocket and smooth down his hair. All a dem den converge on dat single table to take orders. Dey begin to behave like young pups in mating season. Only, de women dem wasn't impress by all this tra-la-la at all and ignore dem except to make dey order, straight to de point. Well, it look like Brothers' egos were having a rough day and dey start roving 'bout de room, dey egos and de crotch a dey pants leading far in front dem. One brother gone over to Giraffebai to see if she want anything more. He call she "dear" and put his hand on she back. Giraffebai straighten she back in surprise and reply in a not-too-friendly way. When he gone to write up de bill she see me looking at she and she say to me, "Whoever does he think he is! Calling me dear and touching me like that! Why do these men always think that they have permission to touch whatever and wherever they want! And you can't make a fuss about it in public, because it is exactly what those people out there want to hear about so that they can say how sexist and uncivilized our culture is."

I shake mih head in understanding and say, "Yeah. I know. Yuh right!"

De atmosphere in de room take a hairpin turn, and it was man aggressing on woman, woman warding off a herd a man who just had dey pride publicly cut up a couple a times in just a few minutes.

One brother walk over to Janet and me and he stand up facing me with his hands clasp in front a his crotch, like if he protecting it. Stiff stiff, looking at me, he say, "Will that be all?"

Mih crew cut start to tingle, so I put on mih femmest smile and say, "Yes, that's it, thank you. Just the bill please." De smartass turn to face Janet and he remove his hands from in front a his crotch and slip his thumbs inside his pants like a cowboy 'bout to do a square dance. He smile, looking down at her attentive fuh so, and he say, "Can I do anything for you?"

I didn't give Janet time fuh his intent to even register before I bulldoze in mih most un-femmest manner, "She have everything she need, man, thank you. The bill please." Yuh think he hear me? It was like I was talking to thin air. He remain smiling at Janet, but she, looking at me, not at him, say, "You heard her. The bill please."

Before he could even leave de table proper, I start mih tirade. "But A A! Yuh see dat? Yuh could believe dat! De effing so-and-so! One minute yuh feel sorry fuh dem and next minute dey harassing de heck out a you. Janet, he crazy to mess with my woman, yes!" Janet get vex with me and say I overreacting, and is not fuh me to be vex, but fuh she to be vex. Is she he insult, and she could take good enough care a sheself.

I tell she I don't know why she don't cut off all dat long hair, and stop wearing lipstick and eyeliner. Well, who tell me to say dat! She get real vex and say dat nobody will tell she how to dress and how not to dress, not me and not any man. Well I could see de potential dat dis fight had coming, and when Janet get fighting vex, watch out! It hard to get a word in edgewise, yes! And she does bring up incidents from years back dat have no bearing on de current situation. So I draw back quick quick but she don't waste time; she was already off to a good start. It was best to leave right dere and den.

Just when I stand up to leave, de doors dem open up and in walk Sandy and Lise, coming for dey weekly hit a Indian sweets. Well, with Sandy and Lise is a dead giveaway dat dey not dressing fuh any man, it have no place in dey life fuh man-vibes, and dat in fact dey have a blatant penchant fuh women. Soon as dey enter de room yuh could see de brothers and de couple men customers dat had come in minutes before stare dem down from head to Birkenstocks, dey eyes bulging with disgust. And de women in de room start shoo-shooing, and putting dey hand in front dey mouth to stop dey surprise, and false teeth, too, from falling out. Sandy and Lise spot us instantly and dey call out to us, shameless, loud and affectionate. Dey leap over to us, eager to hug up and kiss like if dey hadn't seen us for years, but it was really only since two nights aback when we went out to dey favourite Indian restaurant for dinner. I figure dat de display was a genuine happiness to be seen wit us in dat place. While we stand up dere chatting, Sandy insist on rubbing she hand up and down Janet back – wit friendly intent, mind you, and same time Lise have she arm round Sandy waist. Well, all cover get blown. If it was even remotely possible dat I wasn't noticeable before, now Janet and I were over-exposed. We could a easily suffer from hypothermia, specially since it suddenly get cold cold in dere. We say goodbye, not soon enough, and as we were leaving I turn to acknowledge Giraffebai, but instead a any recognition of our buddiness against de fresh brothers, I get a face dat look like it was in de presence of a very foul smell.

De good thing, doh, is dat Janet had become so incensed 'bout how we get scorned, dat she forgot I tell she to cut she hair and to ease up on de make-up, and so I get save from hearing 'bout how I too jealous, and how much I inhibit she, and how she would prefer if I would grow *my* hair, and wear lipstick and put on a dress sometimes. I so glad, oui! dat I didn't have to go through hearing how I too demanding a she, like de time, she say, I prevent she from seeing a ole boyfriend when he was in town for a couple hours *en route* to live in Australia with his new bride (because, she say, I was jealous dat ten years ago dey sleep together). Well, look at mih crosses, nah! Like if I really so possessive and jealous!

So tell me, what yuh think 'bout dis nah, girl?

Middle Children

Jane Rule

Clare and I both come from big families, a bossy, loving line of voices stretching away above us to the final authority of our parents, a chorus of squawling, needy voices beneath us coming from crib or play pen or notch in tree. We share, therefore, the middle child syndrome: we are both over-earnest, independent, inclined to claustrophobia in crowds. The dreams of our adolescent friends for babies and homes of their own we privately considered nightmares. Boys were irredeemably brothers who took up more physical and psychic space than was ever fair. Clare and I, in cities across the continent from each other, had the same dream: scholarships for college where we would have single rooms, jobs after that with our own apartments. But scholarship students aren't given single rooms; and the matchmakers, following that old cliche that opposites attract, put us, east and west, into the same room.

Without needing to discuss the matter, we immediately arranged the furniture as we had arranged furniture with sisters all our lives, mine along one wall, hers along the other, an invisible line drawn down the center of the room, over which no sock or book or tennis racket should ever stray. Each expected the other to be hopelessly untidy; our sisters were. By the end of the first week, ours was the only room on the corridor that looked like a military barracks. Neither of us really liked it, used to the posters and rotting corsages and dirty clothes of our siblings, but neither of us could bring herself to contribute any clutter of her own. "Maybe a painting?" Clare suggested. I did not know where we could get one. Clare turned out to be a painter. I, a botanist, who could never grow things in my own room before where they might be watered with Coke or broken by a thrown magazine or sweater, brought in a plant stand, the first object to straddle the line because it needed to be under the window. The friends each of us made began to straddle that line, too, since we seemed to be interchangeably good listeners, attracting the same sort of flamboyant, needy first or last or only children.

"Sandra thinks she may be pregnant," I would say about Clare's friend, who had told me simply because Clare wasn't around.

"Aren't they all hopeless?" Clare would reply, and we middle children would shake our wise, cautious heads.

We attracted the same brotherly boys as well who took us to football games and fraternity drunks and sexual wrestling matches on the beach. We used the same cool defences, gleaned not from the advice of our brothers but from observing their behaviour.

"Bobby always told me not to take the 'respect' bit too seriously if I wanted to have any fun," Clare said, "but I sometimes wonder why I'd want 'respect' or 'fun'. Doesn't it all seem to you too much trouble? This Saturday there's a marvellous exhibit. Then we could just go out to dinner and come home."

We had moved our desks by then. Shoved together, they could share one set of reference books conveniently and frugally for us both. We asked to have one chest of drawers taken out of the room. Neither of us had many clothes, and, since we wore the same size, we had begun to share our underwear and blouses to keep laundry day to once a week. I can't remember what excuse we had for moving the beds. Perhaps by the time we did, we didn't need an excuse, for ourselves anyway.

I have often felt sorry for people who can't have the experience of falling in love like that, gradually, without knowing it, touching first because pearls have to be fastened or a collar straightened, then more casually because you are standing close together looking at the same assignment sheet or photograph, then more purposefully because you know that there is comfort and reassurance for an exam coming up or trouble in the family. So many people reach out to each other before there is any sympathy or affection. When Clare turned into my arms, or I into hers – neither of us knows just how it was – the surprise was like coming upon the right answer to a question we did not even know we had asked.

Through the years of college, while our friends suffered all the uncertainties of sexual encounter, of falling into and out of love, of being too young and then perhaps too old in a matter of months, of worrying about how to finance graduate-school marriages, our only problem was the clutter of theirs. We would have liked to clear all of them out earlier in order to enjoy the brief domestic sweetness of our own sexual life. But we were from large families. We knew how to maintain privacy, a space of our own, so tactfully that no one ever noticed it. Our longing for our own apartment, like the trips we would take to Europe, was an easy game. Nothing important to us had to be put off until then.

Putting off what was unimportant sometimes did take ingenuity. The boys had no objection to being given up, but our corridor friends were continually trying to arrange dates for us. We decided to come back from one Christmas holiday engaged to boys back home. That they didn't exist was never discovered. We gave each other rings and photographs of brothers. Actually I was very fond of Bobby, and Clare got on just as well with my large and boisterous family. Our first trip to Europe, between college and graduate school, taught us harder lessons. It seemed harmless enough to drink and dance with the football team travelling with us on the ship, but, when they turned up, drunken and disorderly at our London hotel, none of our own outrage would convince the night porter that we were not at fault. Only when we got to graduate school did we find the social answer: two young men as in need of protection as we were, who cared about paintings and concerts and growing things and going home to their own bed as much as we did.

When Clare was appointed assistant professor in art history and I got a job with the parks board, we had been living together in dormitories and student digs for eight years. We could finally leave the clutter of other lives behind us for an apartment of our own. Just at a time when we saw other relationships begin to grow stale or burdened with the continual demands of children, we were discovering the new privacy of making love on our own living-room carpet at five o'clock in the afternoon, too hungry then to bother with cocktails or dressing for dinner. Soon we got quite out of the habit of wearing clothes except when we went out or invited people in. We woke making love, ate breakfast and made love again before we went to work, spent three or four long evenings a week in the same new delight until I saw in Clare's face that bruised, ripe look of a new, young wife, and she said at the same moment, "You don't look safe to go out."

In guilt we didn't really discuss, we arranged more evenings with friends, but, used to the casual interruptions of college life, we found such entertainment often too formal and contrived. Then, for a week or two, we would return to our honeymoon, for alone together we could find no reason not to make love. It is simply not true to say such things don't improve with practice.

"It's a good thing we never knew how bad we were at it," Clare said, one particularly marvellous morning.

When we didn't know, however, we had had more sympathy for those around us, accommodating themselves to back seats of cars or gritty blankets on the beach. Now our friends, either newly wed in student digs where quarrelling was the only acceptable – that is, unavoidable – noise, or exhausted by babies, made wry jokes about missing the privacy of drive-in movies or about the merits of longer bathtubs. They were even more avid readers of pornography than they had been in college. We were not the good listeners we had been. I heard Clare being positively high-minded about what a waste of time all those dirty books were.

"You never used to be a prude," Sandra said in surprise.

That remark, which should have made Clare laugh, kept her weeping half the night instead. I had never heard her so distressed, but then perhaps she hadn't had the freedom to be. "We're too different," she said, and "We're not kind any more."

"Maybe we should offer to baby sit for Sandra and lend them the apartment," I suggested, not meaning it.

We are both very good with babies. It would be odd if we weren't. Any middle child knows as much about colic and croup

as there is to know by the time she's eight or nine. The initial
squeamishness about changing diapers is conquered at about
the same age. Sandra, like all our other friends, had it all to learn
at twenty-three. Sometimes we did just as I had suggested,
sitting primly across from each other like maiden aunts, Clare
marking papers, I thumbing through books that could help me
to imagine what was going on in our apartment. Or sometimes
Sandra would call late at night, saying, "You're fond of this kid,
aren't you? Well, come and get him before we kill him." Then
we'd take the baby for a midnight ride over the rough back roads
that are better for gas pains than any pacing. I didn't mind that
assignment, but I was increasingly restless with the evenings we
spent in somebody else's house.

"You know, if we had a house of our own," I said, "we could
take the baby for the night, and they could just stay home."

I realize that there is nothing really immoral about lending
your apartment to a legally married couple for the evening so
that you can spend a kind and moral night out with their baby,
but it seemed to me faintly and unpleasantly obscene: our bed
. . . perhaps even our living-room rug. I was back to the middle
child syndrome. I wanted to draw invisible lines.

"They're awfully tidy and considerate," Clare said, "and they
always leave us a bottle of scotch."

"Well, we leave them a bottle of scotch as well."

"We drink more of it than they do."

I didn't want to sound mean.

"If we had a house, we could have a garden."

"You'd like that," Clare decided.

Sandra's husband said we could never get a mortgage, but
our combined income was simply too impressive to ignore. We
didn't really need a large house, just the two of us, though I
wanted a studio for Clare, and she wanted a greenhouse and
workshop for me. The difficulty was that neither of us could
think of a house that was our size. We weren't used to them. The
large, old houses that felt like home were really no more expensive than the new, compact and efficient boxes the agent thought
suitable to our career-centered lives. Once we had wandered
through the snarled, old garden and up into the ample rooms of

the sort of house we had grown up in, we could not think about anything else.

"Well, why not?" I asked.

"It has five bedrooms."

"We don't have to use them all."

"We might take a student," Clare said.

We weren't surprised at the amount of work involved in owning an old house. Middle children aren't. Our friends, most of whom were still cooped up in apartments, liked to come out in those early days for painting and repair parties, which ended with barbecue suppers on the back lawn, fenced in and safe for toddlers. Our current couple of boys were very good at the heavy work of making drapes and curtains. They even enjoyed helping me dig out old raspberry canes. It was two years before Clare had time to paint in the studio, and my greenhouse turned out to be a very modest affair since I had so many other things to do, cooking mostly.

We have only one room left now for stray children. The rest are filled with students, boys we decided, which is probably a bit prudish, and it's quite true that they take up more physical and psychic space than is ever fair. Still, they're only kids, and, though it takes our saintly cleaning woman half a day a week just to dig out their rooms, they're not bad about the rest of the house.

Harry is a real help to me with the wine-making, inclined to be more careful about the chemical details than I am. Pete doesn't leave his room except to eat, unless we've got some of the children around; then he's even willing to stay with them in the evening if we have to go out. Carl, who's never slept a night alone in his life since he discovered it wasn't necessary, doesn't change girls so often that we don't get to know them, and he has a knack for finding people who fit in: take a turn at the dishes, walk the dogs, check to see that we have enough cream for breakfast.

Clare and I have drawn one very careful line across the door of our bedroom, and, though it's not as people proof as our brief apartment, it's a good deal better than a dormitory. We even occasionally have what we explain as our cocktail there before dinner when one of Carl's girls is minding the vegetables; and, if we don't get involved in too interesting a political or philosophical discussion, we sometimes go upstairs for what we call the late news. Both of us are still early to wake, and, since Pete will get up with any visiting child, the first of the day is always our own.

"Pete's a middle child," Clare said the other morning, hearing him sing a soft song to Sandra's youngest as he carried her down the stairs to give her an early bottle. "I hope he finds a middle child for himself one day."

"I'd worry about him if he were mine," I said.

"Oh, well, I'd worry about any of them if they were mine. I simply couldn't cope."

"I just wouldn't want to."

"There's a boy in my graduate seminar . . ." Clare began.

I was tempted to say that, if we had a family of our own, we'd always be worrying and talking about them even when we had time to ourselves, but there was still an hour before we had to get up, and I've always felt generous in the early morning, even when I was a kid in a house cluttered with kids from which I dreamed that old dream of escape.

La Bruja

Jenifer Levin

Over the years I'd see her sometimes, red lips, whiff of perfume, sweat on fur, smelling Marlboros and Rémy and Coke and with sometimes-flashing, sometimes-softening eyes she'd slice a path through all those dykes to the bar. Brought the night air in. Everybody looked. But Labruja, just like royalty – she looked at no one. Then she'd sit. Her first drink always on the house.

Watching her, the steely-shelled dark wanting deep down in me tingled every time. Along with that pull – in the hands, in the hips. Go, it said, go to her. Not that I'd dare. The fact is I was too young, too broke, too stupid. Too soft. Soft butch. Yes. Truth is the thing you never admit.

But someone older, tougher, wiser, handsome and hard like stone, dressed fine with a good tie and polished shoes and a fierce face, would appear to light her cigarette. There were still some of them around – I mean, they never really left – dykes you didn't fuck with. She'd barely touch the lighter-holding hand.

Then I would feel it drop around them both: a shining glass bubble, magnet of hearts and cunts, sealing them off from the world.

I grew. Life was not kind. Sometimes it stabbed me bad and I'd wish for the courage to die, or to kill. In the middle of despair came these dreams of Labruja. Just this picture I kept in my head of her: a walking thing of high-femme glory that no pain of the world could touch or beat out of me. All this, and I'd never even spoken to her. Yet imagined her every day. And that, just that, was a reason to go on.

Meanwhile real life happened. I got older, smarter. Had some women and affairs. Learned how to be: how to treat women right, how to worship their hair and full painted lips. And then later on, how to mess both up real good. Grease in your comb on the sheets. A couple times I even fell in love – got my heart smashed, and smashed up some others. But one night after work, I was having a beer and whooosh, the bar door opened to wind-burning ashes, and someone slinking by – Labruja. This time I caught her eye. That glance made me shake. And I noticed I was standing, foamy beer all over the table.

Petie yanked my jacket. "Where you think *you're* going? Child, better watch out for that witchy witch. She's high femme, high *drama,* burn you up and break you. Okay, you been warned."

By now, though, Labruja had looked away. Schlitz dripped down on my trousers, and all my friends were laughing. I shoved through elbows and thighs to find some place more quiet. No one was fighting or kissing in the stairwell, but it smelled like piss. I let the sour dark cool off my sweat. Sometimes, there just aren't enough corners.

Got out of the bar habit and stopped going much. But one Pride Day in June, after marching and parading and pretending to die with all the fags near that church, I went to some block party downtown. I was covered with sun and dust. Sleeveless T, black jeans. I'd been working out a lot and felt good, and some pretty girls were looking. There were speakers like rocket launchers set up, everyone busy bumping with everyone else to the drum-beat blare. It was twilight. And across the street, moving slowly in an invisible circle all her own, was Labruja. Dancing. She wore a flowery light-print dress. Not as much makeup. She'd put on weight, too, so her hips were round, breasts pressed out against cloth flowers with soft fullness, and as I pushed my way over closer I could see her skin was tight and clear, the lips full red like a heart. She'd almost lost that ragged raw edge I remem-bered, looked like she was out of the life. The music stopped. Speakers crackled over the musical boom. Between buildings the sky got darker. She twirled around once more, opened her eyes. Then saw me. And smiled. I reached without thinking, took her hand like a treasure so our palms sparked against each other's, and bent down to kiss it. "Labruja," I said, "you look beautiful."

Her eyes seemed dangerous for a second, then tender.

"Oh, honey, *call* me."

Some big dyke like a *thing* stepped in: leather boots, harsh handsome face, pale bloody eyes stabbing rage. "Who're you?" she said, and spun me around to face her.

Scared me at first. Then I got it together, said to myself, Addy, you are not some fucking punk. And to her, "What's the matter?"

"The lady's with me, is what." She was big, and raw – harder, wiser, tougher than me – but in that second what I saw was that she was vulnerable, hurt by the world a lot worse than I, in a way nobody could ever fix. Usually in those situations I'd back off, be a buddy, say hey, no harm intended. This time, though, her hurt fed my meanness. This time, too, was Labruja. Labruja of my dreams, getting hustled away from me now in someone else's big T shirted arms.

So I shouted stuff after them I never otherwise would have: "Hey, you got a problem? Well fix it at home, bro. The lady looked at *me*." And I was still shouting while they disappeared past fire hydrants and cement into shadows, when a couple of other dykes grabbed both my arms, saying Shut up kid, calm down, don't take it like this. Nice-looking kid like you, you'll get your own woman some day – Labruja's with Mick now, understand? She is Mick's. That's all.

More years passed. I got to feeling good in an older, grown-up way, and I was just about cock of the walk late one spring-time afternoon, stepping out of work early and down to the gym to lift hard, do sit-ups, biceps, get pumped, that nice rush and the so-fine scent and flesh swell after shower, after towel-down. Bag of wet sweats in one hand, I was on the street whistling, breeze in the air, my shoes very shined. Remembering this rumor someone had passed on to me the other night: *Now's your chance, sweets. Mick left the bitch!* Well, I was ready. Old enough. Tough enough. Handsome enough. Had a job. Paid my own way. No major fuck-ups, no, no more. Just one more fine stud bouncing down a breezy springtime city street, quarters in my palm, heading for the nearest pay phone. This time I'd do it. Call that Labruja. This time, she was mine.

First phone had the receiver ripped out. But I maintained what you'd call serenity. Another corner. Quarter went in and I was whistling, heart thumping, waiting and waiting but no dial tone. I banged it a couple times with my fist but nothing slid back. Now there was one quarter left. So I headed for another bunch of phones a block away, my mouth dry and sweat starting at the roots of my hair. This one had a dial tone. I put in the quarter, punched all the right buttons.

Then a woman – I'd seen her here and there at some places, maybe, only now she was walking with a little boy of about three – brushed past. The kid got in her way and she tripped, dropped two brown bags of groceries at my feet. A ketchup bottle smashed, mayonnaise splattered – all over my shoes. The kid fell on his knees, and he was crying.

"Shit!" I yelled.

"Oh, God, sorry!" she yelled, and started to cry, too. I let the receiver dangle, stooped to help with their fucking groceries. The kid was really screaming. She was sobbing something about how it's food or rent and what the fuck was she gonna do now. I helped her pick up bruised apples, a box of smashed eggs. Out on the Drive it was rush hour, major traffic tie-up. Cars waiting at exits spewed and honked. My breezy springtime city turned into a whirling circle of chaos and sound, and in the center of it I was helping some bitch and her brat pick up their ruined groceries while the receiver of my dreams dangled close by, and I was ignoring a phone call I'd waited my whole life to make.

Later I stood covered with foodstuffs. Pressed the phone to my ear. Hello I said, vacantly. Maybe Labruja had answered it before, but now it was dead. I set it quietly back on the hook.

Sometimes gentlemanhood takes over. I let it do that with this grocery bitch and kid. Wiped off cans and bottles. Crammed as much stuff as I could into my gym bag.

Here, I said dully, I'll help you home.

Gee, she sniffled, that'd be great.

I pulled out some gum and gave it to the kid to shut him up. He paused with it halfway to his mouth, stared tear-stained and imploring up at her.

"Go on, sweetheart, you could have it."

Her voice was tender.

He was soft brown like her, with somebody else's eyes.

We walked slowly as he toddled along chewing happily, away from park and Drive, shortcutting through the projects. Past a couple of dumpsters, brick, concrete. She lived up some flights, and in the dim light when we paused on landings I saw that she was not beautiful really but sweet, with a shining on her cheeks and way down deep in the eyes that told me yes, she was kind.

Her place was a little cozy crazy bright hole, plant-littered, toy-littered, that sucked you right in and made you want to stay. I helped her unload crushed containers of food, watched as she put them away. Just as I was about to leave, the kid had to go potty. I waited while she mopped up his rear end. He seemed happy now so I gave him another piece of gum.

"Take off your shoes," she said. "I'm real sorry, I will clean them."

She set my shoes on newspaper, pulled out a cloth and brush and buffer, black polish, rags. I sat on her sofa barefoot, watching. How she bent gently over those shoes, with humility and care. How her fingers were gentle and strong. The kid sat on my lap, just like that.

"He likes you." She offered up the shoes. Taking them, I touched her wrist. Skin rubbed. Eyes met. "Hey," she said softly, "you wanna stay for dinner?"

"Okay," I told her.

But it was like I wasn't in charge of my own voice. Some ache inside of me spoke instead, a deep sore aching mixed with quiet calm mixed with a desire that I didn't even know I'd had, but I could feel without knowing somehow that here, in here – if I stayed – she might ease it.

So I stayed.

I never really left.

That was Rosa.

★   ★   ★

More years passed. Things with me, Rosa, and the kid were great. If we had problems, we'd work them through. I didn't have much to complain about. At night sometimes she'd just touch and pull me in, her femmeness and hunger washing over me with every move of her soft woman body. What I had with them gave me a warm strong solid core inside. But the warmth lived right next to a darkness. It was the other part of me, the part of dream and unquenchable desire: a hard persistent shadowy butch thing that left me always restless, always somehow far away from what I loved and had. I kept that part pretty quiet. Most times, didn't even touch on it myself. Things were too damn good.

One cold late winter in the middle of all this wonderfulness, the kid had vacation and she decided they gotta go to Miami and see his grandma. She and he will fly super-saver; four days later come back to me. I helped them pack. Kissed and hugged them good-bye. Put them on the bus to LaGuardia. Missed them.

"Yo," said Petie later that night, on the phone, "you heard?"

"Heard what?"

"Shit. La bruja. She's at St Vincent's. She's dying."

"Whaddaya mean dying?"

"I mean like, *dying*. I mean I guess the life caught up with her."

I worked out hard at the gym. Picked up a video on my way home. In the kid's room I turned down his blanket, just so, the way I did every night, so that the bed was waiting for him – even though they wouldn't be back for days. I got to sleep around midnight. There were voices in my dream. *Child*, they said, *your heart is your own.*

Next morning was Saturday. I bathed and dressed, combed and polished to kill. Money in the pocket. And rubbers. I was packing, for the first time in years. The cock buckled on with leather sat there with its base above my cunt, the rest of it strapped back between thighs, a faint bulge swelling out against my baggy jeans crotch. It was unfamiliar for a minute or two, my walking clumsy, self-conscious, then I got the rhythm, then I had the power, power of a dream, power of a lover, and I walked outside so sure of dreams and of the realness and power of desire, for the first time in forever.

It was cold, streets and trees bare, the wind blowing garbage around an early weekend morning stuck in the winter chill between snows. I stopped at the Korean guy's fruit stand and stared at the roses. One stood alone, silvery soft naked, strange, like shaped metal on fire.

"I'll take that one there."

"That platinum rose. Rare, only one left, ten bucks."

I didn't argue. Made sure he wrapped the stem and tied it with white ribbon. Then, holding it close, I hailed a cab heading west.

St Vincent's, I said, off of Seventh.

They gave me a pass at the desk. I was up elevators and down halls, dodging wheelchairs and carts. Peeking around the corner of a dark room. Thumping heart. Shy.

"Labruja. You remember me?"

She was propped on pillows, her makeup fresh. "Addy, honey," she said smiling, "of course!" and offered a hand, very gracious. I took it gently, turned it to kiss. Ran a figner over it and could feel veins. I sat on the side of the bed and sensed for a second the sharp knob of a knee against my back. She moved it discreetly away with a faint swish of white sheet.

I noticed bouquets and vases of flowers, cards and presents on the little table next to her bed. They were all pretty, all expensive, crowding each other out. Too many for the nightstand to contain. Then I looked down at the single, dumb little rose in my hand and felt small for a second, shabby, still too young for her somehow. The lady had plenty of friends and admirers. She hadn't exactly been waiting for me all these years. But I offered it anyway.

"Here, every pretty girl deserves flowers."

This made it almost okay. Labruja held it to her cheek a second. Then guided my chilled hand to her nose, mouth, and cheek and breathed deep.

"God, you smell like outside! Like the air, I mean, like the world. Oh, it smells so good!"

"You can't die, Labruja," I blurted. "Because of women like you, I never killed myself." I sat back and apart then, my fingers suddenly clumsy without hers. Surprised because I had no idea that's what I felt or would say, but there, there it was, and it was true.

She gave a little gasp. And cried. The tears made mascaraedged rivers through rouge, powder, foundation. I dabbed at them with a hanky.

We talked some, quietly. Shyly at first. About her life. Mine. We'd never really spoken much before. Then she lay back on the pillows, very tired, and took my hand in hers again.

"I want to run away," she said, sadly, "but I can't."

Already an idea was ringing in my head. I reached through bouquets for the phone.

Yes you can, I said. Let me take you.

After the call I turned away while she dressed. I found her coat in a closet near the bed. It was long, long-sleeved, covered the hospital ID around her wrist. Then we were walking slowly, casually, around hallway carts and wheelchairs and trays of unclaimed lunch, through the antiseptic smell, avoiding nurses' eyes. And down. In a dream haze. And out – on the street, among cabs, in the cold. Tears came to her but didn't flow. A taxi stopped and I opened the door. Trembling, I helped her inside.

"Uptown," I said. "To the Waldorf Astoria."

Rich people's hotel lobbies are all carpets and glass, lights, terracotta, gold, and everyone bustling silently. No they are not silent but muffled, muted, their voices refined and footsteps hushed. So that's how it was: the whole big rich unfamiliar place surrounded me and her but we moved forward through it in the same warm protective bubble that had carried us this far. I sat her down on a chair.

Petie met me, eyes darting everywhere, all done up in his uniform of wine-scarlet with bright gold tassles. The little hat brim over his face, sort of ridiculous, and at the same time all business. He spoke without looking at me, nervous, and handed over the keys.

"Twelfth floor, number 1285. You got until noon tomorrow. Then the next shift comes on and it's scheduled to clean." His voice had gone husky, there was stubble on both cheeks. I figured he was on the juice again. Personally, I wouldn't touch that stuff, but it was none of my business anyway.

Thanks, I muttered, sweating.

And keys in hand, I floated across the carpet like I belonged there with all the muffled, smart-dressed servants and guests, to the soft, plush lobby chair where Labruja sat next to a mound of someone else's high-polished leather luggage, pale and waiting, half a smile on her lips. I offered my arm. Very gentlemanly. And together we travelled to the row of silently blinking elevator buttons. Out of the sides of their eyes people glanced at us sometimes, glanced again, seemed puzzled, turned heads ever so slightly to stare in that discreet don't-ask way of the wealthy and polite. Something in the eyes turned hard and self-satisfied once they'd seen that yes, we both were women, and no, we could not fool them. Poor straights. They'd be disappointed if they'd known that I didn't even want to – fool them, that is. I was too far away from their life to try, and the woman on my arm took me farther. So we waited, Labruja and I, and we floated up together noiselessly in the glass-shining, brass-shining elevator. Down hallways with carpets that absorbed our feet. Where the lighting was delicate, kind on her exhausted face and eyes. Where the shake of her hand and the flush of her fever was hidden, known only to me now, and I held the shake of her and the flush of her in my own hands and heart.

Labruja, I said. Just that – her name.

And opened the door.

Silent flick of a light switch. The carpets, smooth walls, sparkling polish of things. Plush sofa and chairs. Gilt-edged mirror. Heavy thick drapes to pull across windows sparkling out on city skyline. A little pint-sized refrigerator stocked with snacks wrapped in pretty French and English packages. A bar with every kind of fancy booze under the sun. All these things were there for us. Maybe Petie'd kill me later, but I had to try stuff out. Poured spring water for the lady – she couldn't stomach anything else, she said – and popped a soda can for me. Sure I thought about champagne. But Labruja wasn't drinking hard stuff, not any more. I decided maybe I wouldn't either.

She was like a kid for a while, asking me to bring her things to look at: the room service menus, the special thick glossy entertainment magazines. Me? I was a willing servant. In between doing what she bid, bringing hotel knick-knacks to her, taking them back to their places, I sat next to her on the sofa fingering velveteen and cushions, and we talked. We talked the afternoon away. Flicked on the TV – cable – with a multi-purpose smooth-buttoned remote. There'd been a scent to her when we came in, I realized. Hospital disinfectant, alcohol swabs, very medicinal. Now, though, it was gone. She turned the TV off. Talked some more, this time about Mick. The first thing that brought them together, she said: Mick was strong.

I didn't know whether to believe her or not.

"I want to feel someone strong again," she said. "I think I'd like to feel you that way, strong and alive."

I'd only been waiting my entire life.

I leaned over closer to her heat and fever. Then I just pulled her up and onto me. Her legs and arms wrapped around, riding.

I rested against a wall, holding her. She was frail, childlight, so easily supported. I moved my hands on her ass and thighs slow, pressing her down, moved my hips up into pure woman smell and nylon. That's when she felt it for the first time, and breathed out once, loud, surprised, "*God*, hon."

The bed was king-size, pillow-littered, a vast thing to get lost on. I rolled over it into her mouth and hair. She pressed fingernails against my neck. Then something fierce got me moving on top of her so hard and blurred and fast I forgot who I was, and pulled back for a moment, blinking, when she called out in pain. She made one great effort then, pushed me down by the shoulders. Crawled on top of me, very graceful, older, wiser, knowing and smiling, rubbing against my thighs and belt.

"Stay still, hon." She pushed off my jacket. Unbuttoned my shirt, pulled the tails of it out to each side, unbuckled my belt and teased down a zipper, then briefs, then reached between my legs and the cock sprang rubbery free.

"Mmmm-mmmm. That for me?"

"Yes, baby."

"Well," she said, "I got a present for you, too." She went into one of my pockets and pulled out a rubber, and the plastic wrapping crackled. I reached. "Uh-uh," she said, "let me." With one expert motion it was on, little waiting bubble at the tip for a sperm that does not exist except in the hard strong make-believe love-fucking of the mind. She rolled to one side and peeled her nylons off. Then crouched over me again in nothing but the dress, and came down on top of me, slowly, while I guided the cock inside.

"Aaah," she sobbed, hurting, and took it all in. Then just sat on it and on me breathing fast, tears streaming. I reached up under soft flaps of dress to hold her hips. Ran my thumbs across her belly, across all the bumps of scars.

"They cut everything out of me, hon."

I licked one finger, touched it to her clit, and she moaned. "Not everything."

"Be soft, hon," she said. "Go slow."

I rocked up into her with a sure, smooth motion that made her lips part and eyes flick shut, then open, made her smile sweet. It was something that in my daydreams I always meant for her to feel. Meant for her to know just who and what I could be for her here, in this room, in this place, in the shadows, just for her: a lover who knew how to wait, and knew how to move, to hold back, give, fuck, caress, take, a woman who was old enough and ready enough, tough enough, soft enough, wise enough now, and in love. Who had come to find her still alive – finally, yes, and not a moment too late.

Sometime during that afternoon we had all our clothes off, strewn over floor and bedcovers like unnecessary things, and in the heavy, peaceful curtain-drawn quiet lay side by side on damp sheets, half asleep. I was totally naked, not even packing. She ran a hand in circles on my belly.

"So smooth. Mine's ruined."

"No, baby."

"Mick never let me touch her."

"Hmmm. But you wanted to?"

"Oh," she mumbled, suddenly shy, "yeah. Sometimes. What about you with your lady? You let her touch you?"

"Well, sure, sometimes."

"You *soft*," she teased. Then, very serious, "See, stay that way. Stay nice and strong and soft for your lady. Stay good to her."

Then she slid a finger inside me without even asking, and something escaped from my mouth, a piece of my guts, like a breath or a sound. What all the surgery had left criss-crossed her belly, a dark red death messenger. Platinum petals. But the rest of her was still alive, her hands and eyes seeking life.

"You just *let* me," she whispered fiercely. "Stay right there, like so. Give it to me. Give it to me. Give it to me, honey."

I showered in a bathroom like a palace. Later I cleared marble shelves of all the special little containers of shampoos and conditioners and stuffed them into a bag.

When I drifted out with the steam she was dressed. Feverish, weaker than ever, but sitting there in the quiet-draped dark smiling. She hadn't bathed. "I want to smell like today," she said, "for as long as possible."

I left the key and a ten on the dresser. Big spender. But in the elevator all that floating peace inside started to be pulled down, pushed apart, like shattered glass, ruined light. Grace and mercy left me. I had no idea what time it was. Stepping out into the cold of a bitter winter weekend night told me it was late, and my insides went desolate. A cab stopped and the hotel hop opened a door for Labruja. I gave him a couple bucks. Watching her fold herself slowly, achingly inside, I knew for sure then how weak she was, how little time she had, so when I climbed in after her I sent all the bad fear feelings inside me away and pressed her hands between mine. St Vincent's, I told the guy, downtown, take Seventh. And please take it easy, the lady doesn't feel good.

I'm sorry, he said, no problem.

Shampoos rattled in her purse.

"Should I call you?" I whispered.

"No, I don't think so, hon."

We were silent. But partway downtown in that cab on that night-lit city avenue we turned to each other, suddenly laughing. Roaring. It came from deep in the gut, warm, delicious, spiced like life. I understood then that this was the last time I'd ever see her, my desire and dream, my Labruja. Because somehow she was mine. Oh, sure, maybe other people's, too. But also *mine* in a way that she'd never been before. And as long as I lived – which, for sure, would be longer than she did – I could have her this way.

At the hospital's main entrance we were both still smiling. I got out to open her door. She staggered by, utterly exhausted, but with a fiery look to her, brushed my cheek with her lips. I watched her walk unsteadily away. She waved once without turning. Last I saw she'd taken out the platinum rose, which was wilted with cold and crushed, but she was holding it to her nose, breathing deep. She was entering the lobby, her patient wristband showing from beneath a coat sleeve. She turned once to blow me a kiss. Then entered the revolving door of shadows and of glass, dancing, reeling on feverish feet, spinning round and around.

A couple of days later, Rosa and the kid came back. I met them at LaGuardia. We went home together in the bus.

The kid was happy because he got some toys and shit from his cousins. Rosa looked great. Said it was good to see everyone but she'd missed me. Yeah, I said, I missed you too. Then she was quiet.

That night we fixed spaghetti with meatballs. I made tomato sauce from scratch. The kid helped, stirring in onions. And our whole place got that warm home family air, covering us all in a kind of blanket of closeness, familiarity, and affection. We ate, caught a couple shows on TV. Bathed the kid, tucked him into bed, and it was my turn to read a story. Later I headed for the kitchen to help clean up and found myself drying dishes.

"Coffee?" Rosa took out the can. I said sure.

"Tried calling you the other night," she said. "You weren't home."

"Huh," I mumbled, "which night?"

"Oh," she said, "the one before last."

I was glad she couldn't see me. But gentlemanhood kicked in fast and helped me save my sorry butt. I stayed right on my toes. "Oh," I said, very casual, "that. Well, I was pretty beat, baby. I just turned in early, must've turned off the phone."

"Ah."

Soon the coffee was bubbling away, filling the warm kitchen with a homey, fine perfume.

"You know," she said, "Angie called the day before I left. She told me something about that ho, you know, the one used to go with Mick? Well, she said the bitch is dying."

"Uh-huh," I said. "No kidding?"

Then, before I knew it, an almost-full can of El Pico came sailing through the air, bounced off the kitchen cabinet, leaving a big scarry dent in wood, just about an inch above my head. It crashed into the sink, and I wheeled around to face her.

"What the fuck?"

Her face was burning, eyes and mouth anguished slits. "That," she hissed, "that's for turning off the phone."

I spent a few nights on the couch.

Winter slowed us down.

Springtime the kid was doing great at school, Rosa got back to her old sweet ways, I kept up pretty steady at the gym. Since that one night, no more coffee cans got tossed my way.

I heard through the grapevine that so-and-so was with so-and-so, and this one had left that one to go there – fucking dykes and their affairs, you know, all of us hopping around on this board of a city like a bunch of Chinese checkers. In my heart center settled that big sure steadiness again: Rosa, and me, and the kid.

Desire is one thing with a mind and a heart of its own. It picks us up, spins us around in the brilliant cloud world of extreme unction, crisis times, life and death, a soul-world of always-passion, gold hotels, and of dreams. Then it spits you out real good. Me? Like most folks, I move most times in the touchable, nondream, material world of real things: a job, a home, a woman and child. Just me. In all my soft butchness, hard womanness, all my heart's truth and lies. Nobody's savior. Nobody's angel.

Labruja died that spring. They had a service at the Community Center. I heard that Mick cried.

One afternoon, weeks later, I was lying near the window in our bedroom after work, waiting for Rosa and the kid to come home. A leaf blew past the fire escape, riding on what looked like a puff of something thicker than air, like silver smoke. I saw it through the turned-up blinds. And I thought: Desire. Petals. Labruja.

My woman and kid, they are so *real*. Kindness. Anger. Love. What I need, for my life. And I am what they need, too. This I know, deep down inside.

But I've got this other desire inside for things that don't have a whole hell of a lot to do with the life that happens to me, to most of us I guess, day after day. Call it crazy butch dreaming – Petie does. The hard buried part. The not-woman, not-man, just-butch darkness in me. That could love and want Labruja.

See, she was real, too. Not what I needed – but what I *wanted*. What I almost never grew up enough for.

The leaf blew by. Puff of smoke. Lipstick trace. A dream. Lucky me. To get, in life, what I wanted. And to also give back something. And, no matter how many cans of El Pico go sailing past my head, to be smart enough to shut up about it.

Femmes. They're a mystery to me. Mine, or hers, or yours – oh, we think we're so tough, but none of us ever own them. Yet among them *sometimes* are the ones just looking at keeps your dreams alive, so you can go on surviving yourself. It's this passion they have for what you are in your own butch heart. It never dies in them – it's something you can count on. Keeps you going when you'd rather not. It caresses you free of shame. So no matter who you love in everyday life, you will never stop dreaming of them. Every living day. Gods or goddesses or demons give me this: my dream femmes, these special tender women whom you want without end but also somehow without selfishness. I mean, without coveting. See, women to me are love. Also, desire. But that's not all they are.

Alone, I'm mostly my own butch shadow. Watching the drift. Wanting the dream. Inside the shadow, desire rises. Then the magic. And love. All but unspoken. Says one word, one yearning, a name. Always and forever to me – Labruja.

Some women, you're glad they've lived. And not just for yourself.

See You in the Movies

Madelyn Arnold

Early traffic was whooshing past and everything was going just swell, except they were just the bittiest bit off schedule. They might arrive late. Ginny looked to the rear-view mirror at her children. Katie Lee was about lost in the blankets, her fluffy hair the exact honey color of the stuffed giraffe and two of the teddies. Johnny Allen's red head nearly matched his father's sleeping bag – from that musty, buggy hunting gear of Phil's. And no need to think of Phil any more on *this* trip.

Things were *under control* – except of course John Allen's sucking on his thumb, which strictly speaking, at that exact instant, Ginny was not obliged to notice.

"Hon?" She nudged Barb. "Barb, honey, I don't suppose you want to drive, would you, hon?" Barb's salt-and-pepper head rolled gently. Ginny generally preferred that Barb be butch.

"My God, we're moving." Barb yawned. "What time is it?" Barb was a freckle-faced broad-shouldered thing with kissable lips and a butch streak that was cute in a little round person. Ginny leaned down for a peck, weaving the van all over the road. Which woke Barb.

"You," said Barb, "are the Morning Type –" The way Mama would have said "round-heeled". "When did we leave Harrisburg?"

"Practically eight!" said Ginny, the morning type indeed. It wasn't eight. "I thought we'd start in looking for some nice little place to eat!"

"But we've been driving since –" Barb stopped herself. She was even-tempered, nothing at all like Phil. "How far did you say this cabin was?"

"Not very . . ." sang Ginny, and launched into humming "There's a Coconut Grove," which she was very fond of humming sometimes.

She was just the littlest bit cross, although they were making fair time and should be at the lake by noon. A weekend at the old summer place, perfect surroundings and arm-in-arm; a picnic before they unpacked. A psychic reminder to Phil of what he had lost . . . The kids on the beach and everything lovely – unless they slowed down. If they slowed down, the lighting would be all wrong.

"An o-o-open be-e-each," she soothed for the thousandth time. "There's the loveliest little shore birds . . . and these little hawks. I think it's just about the only piece of Pennsylvania still undeveloped. And so-o-o sought after. Phil could just see it as time-share condos, but *nobody's* going to get that place while Mama's alive."

Phil was present only as a sleeping bag – he still stored it in the garage, so it wasn't like she didn't have any right – she hadn't asked him for a thing. The van didn't count.

Suddenly, Barb swan-dove over the seat –

A baby-sized denim behind was shining plainly in the mirror; a Volkswagen was passing on their left, with a ski rack full of baskets. Barb had hold of Johnny Allen – he'd tried to snag himself a basket right over Ginny's shoulder, right through Ginny's window.

She jerked round. Barb, in transit back, snatched the wheel, bringing them out of a swerve. Ginny hauled the rest of John Allen back in. She wanted to smack him.

"You get in here," said Ginny to John Allen, "and you keep your head, your hands and your body in here or we'll all turn right around and go straight back to Harrisburg, do you hear me?"

"It's too far," he whined. 'We *can't* go back this morning, it's too –"

"Want me to drive?" asked Barb.

"Whatever made you think you could have that gentleman's baskets for, when you hadn't even asked him! He probably sells them. He probably feeds his whole family selling those poor little baskets, and here you go and try to cheat him out of his – I have told you and I have told you that you leave your fingers off of other people's things –"

His eyes were suitably alarmed, so she didn't smack him. "Well, I know you didn't mean it. And *what* on earth is – Honey!" This to Barb. "Honey, why didn't you get a better hold of him? He could have fallen or got himself caught, or – Besides. That car was much too close; it could have clipped us –"

"More like bought at Bonwit's," Barb off-handed.

"Say *who?*"

But Barb was muttering at the window or the traffic. Up ahead, a bright sign read COUNTRY KITCHEN FARMS – BREAKFAST 24 HOURS. FAMILY ORIENTED DINING. Good. Ginny stood on the brake and slewed them across a crowded lane toward the almost-passed exit and into a parking lot. Barb went sideways; John Allen, the more experienced, hung on better. Little Katie Lee began to wail.

"They're hungry," chirped Ginny. "Now we're going to have a real nice breakfast, but we've got to hurry! We've got to be right at the lake by noon!"

"Are we there yet?" moaned John Allen.

Ginny power-rolled up her window and bounced cheerfully out of the van. "Every little body out!" She hauled a back door open and beamed at the kids, who didn't. "We'll be at the beach by picnic time! Do you have to go to the potty?" Johnny Allen shook his head. Then thought better of it, climbed out his door, and nodded.

Barb was looking a little frayed at the ends. "Barb, honey . . ." Ginny turned to face her, for a Private Talk. "I'll steer Johnny Allen, and you and Katie go freshen up and we'll all meet up inside, all right?"

"I want to see the trucks! I want to sit by the window!" said John Allen.

"I don't have to go with her!" wailed Katie Lee.

The parking lot was crowded, and every single window had its trucks.

"I want to see them jack up one of them eighteen-wheelers – brrrrrraaammmmm . . ."

"Now, honey," she said to Katie. "You just mind Barb and go over there to the ladies' room, and then we'll all meet up and have the nicest –"

"I don't have to do what *she* says," said Katie Lee. John Allen leaned back like his father and said, "She doesn't, you know."

"Then you come with Mama and John Allen can just be a big man and take himself. Barb can show you which door is the –"

"I know which one!" he said.

"Should I go get a table?" said Barb, inscrutable.

"Sweetie," Ginny said. "They're a little high-strung, they're a little hungry –"

"We may have to wait," said Barb. "There's quite a line –"

"Ma, can I have pancakes? Ma, can we have a table by the window –"

He was repeating himself, so Ginny turned round, expecting to see little Katie, but it happened she didn't. "Katie?" she said.

John Allen pointed. "I want to see all the big rigs. We gotta get a table by the *win*dow –"

"Honey, you run on and go to the potty, and come right straight back." There was an elderly gentleman standing at the screened restaurant door, talking to what appeared to be a waitress. "Ask that gentleman over there at the door where the men's potty is." John Allen skidded off, tripping and recovering himself again. More graceful than his father, at any rate.

Barb stood, hugging herself, close to frowning.

"You're just naturally good with kids," Ginny said encouragingly. "I guess that's because of the kind of work you do, but you just intuitively know when little ones are getting high-strung."

Barb was unreadable.

"I guess working with childlike adults, honey; well, in some ways I think it's just the same. You make yourself heard, and all of you have to back each other up on discipline. You just say what you think is right, and I back you up, and you do the same with me. You say no, and we both stick to it. It's like I told you, in three weeks you've done more with my kids than Phil ever will – unless John Allen gets himself a prize and Phil comes out to get his picture in the press. Don't worry about a little naughtiness. They're only testing you. Katie Lee's just trying to get your goat."

"Get my –?"

"It's an expression," snapped Ginny.

John Allen popped up under Ginny's arm. "I forgot my *truck*. Katie's locked the door, and I *can't* get my *truck*."

"Locked the –" Ginny leaned her tall frame down and peered in. There was her pretty little girl with two fingers in her mouth, behind the steering wheel. She tried the door. Yes, locked. Ginny felt in her pocket. There in the ignition were the keys. "Open the door, honey," she sang sweetly.

"Just unlock the door," said Barb.

"I can't!" snapped Ginny, pointing to the keys.

"Tell her what to do, then." Barb made a circular gesture in the direction of the door. "Get her to flip the lock up. She flipped it *down*."

"I want my truck," grieved John Allen.

The mechanism was one of those foreign things designed to frustrate burglars. The latch was below the base of the window, had to be tripped forward and then slightly upward into a slot.

"Push down on it," Ginny said evenly, pointing down. After a moment of sucking on her hand, Katie pushed and pulled on the unseeable latch with small, clumsy fingers.

"I can't," she cried, her face beginning to crinkle for a wail.

"We need a knife!" decided Ginny. "Honey," she said to John Allen. "You go ask that nice waitress for a flat butter knife."

"You can't open a latch like that from the side. Not with a knife. See? There isn't any way to reach the blade down to the lock. The lock is below the window, it's too far away, and besides, it curves up."

Damn, thought Ginny bloodily. "A hammer, then. There's probably a hammer we can borrow, or maybe just a big old rock –"

"This is in Phil's name, isn't it? You can't risk vandalizing his car! Think, don't you have another key somewhere? In your purse, say – right, of course, it's in the car – but maybe somewhere that –"

"Daddy puts one in a box!" said John Allen. "Daddy puts the box under –"

"John Allen," Ginny exclaimed. "Take this dollar bill and go in there and get yourself some of those chocolate mints –"

"Hey, can I get jujubes?"

"And you stay right there and wait by the candy case for Mama. *Do* you hear me?"

He had heard.

They had to do some fancy maneuvering but the magnetic keybox was fortunately *under* the engine block, in a line from the crest. "All right, babylove," crooned Ginny, lifting Katie. "Now let's all get us some nice breakfast –"

"I want jujubes too," said Katie as they quick-walked her off.

At John Allen's age they could only remember so much. The candy would probably help him forget to tell Phil ...

"We'll get you some nice raisins, Katiebabe," she said. "You hate jujubes."

No, they *weren't* there yet. She probably shouldn't have had Barb turn onto 36 so soon – they should have stayed on the interstate till they were closer to the lake, anyway. They seemed to be lost in a maze of little roads, largely unmarked, frequently blocked by horse-drawn buggies.

Breakfast hadn't quite been delightful. They hadn't been placed near a window; John Allen, cuddling his truck, had sat kicking the table and sinking down in his chair to where you could only see the misanthropic top eighth of his eyes. Katie Lee had chanted I *don't* have *to*, I *don't* have *to*, in a pathetic *sotto voce*, which after a while became I *want Daddy* as she took the tops off the little jellies on the table and smeared the goo on her chair.

Johnny Allen had filled up on candy, and Katie would only eat half a piece of pale toast to accompany little sugar packets poured into her milk, her water, and her juice. And Barb's egg. Ginny left a perfectly enormous tip, and when she couldn't help but look back at the damage, she saw that Barb had left a bigger bill on top.

* * *

"Is that a *Amish?*" yelled John Allen.

"Don't point –" began Ginny.

"Yes," said Barb, canting them all left to see past the little one-horse cart. They were going up a hill. There was no way of knowing what was coming, because they were stuck behind this primitive conveyance. A little boy on the back of the cart was making horrid faces at their van.

"That's not nice," said Katie primly. "That's not nice, is it, Mama?"

"No," said Ginny, brightly, looking up from the map. They shouldn't be going south, and this was south, wasn't it? "This road may be going the wrong way," she announced to Barb.

"*Imagine* that," said Barb.

"Are we the-e-e-re yet, Ma?" wailed Johnny.

"What is that river's name?" asked Katie, but nobody knew. A song, thought Ginny; we need a river song, now. And started right in singing about a river . . .

"Is this the Columbia?" whined Katie.

"This might be the Susquehanna, I think. I guess it has to be, because all the other rivers are so much smaller. Unless this is the Allegheny . . ."

"*You* think *everything* is the Susquehanna, Ma," said John Allen.

"The Susquehanna is all over the state," she said serenely, deciding she should include Barb in family talk. "The Monongahela is somewhere," she coaxed, "But the Columbia is in Oregon. Or – Barb, is the Columbia in Washington . . . ?"

"Want a Life Saver?" Barb said, reaching back over the seat. Both of them jumped.

"*They could choke,*" Ginny said. "And besides, it's between meals. Their uncle," she added, "*is a dentist.* I said, Honey, is the Columbia in Oregon or Washington?"

"Is what?"

"The *Columbia.* The Columbia *River.* Is it in –"

"I think it's in . . . Oregon. And Washington. And I think maybe Idaho, too? I think it starts –"

"Or in North Dakota. And you know, it's not that far across that little northern strip of Idaho, and it could go through Montana. What do you think?"

"You're thinking of the Mississippi," said Barb. "But that goes south and north."

"I think probably Montana, and –"

"Wyoming, Texas, Ohio, Pennsylvania and always remember the *Maine*. Only the Mississippi crosses that many states. Okay?"

"Do you think this is the Susquehanna?" Ginny coached.

"I do, I do, I do think it's the Susquehanna," snapped Barb.

"The kids are bothering you, aren't they?" whispered Ginny.

"The *kids?*" stage-whispered Barb.

"Mo-non-ga-he-la," John Allen said, testing the word. Then said it again. It was the kind of sound that kids are fond of making, and Katie joined him. Ginny turned her attention to timing again.

The vacation was being seriously slowed by the certainty of fifth-rate roads. Maybe Barb wouldn't mind speeding up just a little bitty bit, so they could make some time anyway. Ginny would have done it herself, but did not dare drive fast any more. Phil had claimed they might even put her in jail the next time, and he was a lawyer.

Barb was glaring at the cart ahead as if she had gone plumb out of her mind, as if she were going to snatch the little Amish boy baldheaded. Oh – the kids. Still chanting.

"All right." Ginny clapped her hands – once, twice. "That's enough –"

"Mo-non-ga-he-la," intoned the back seat.

Barb spoke up: "What would your father do," she said, "if he told you to shut up and you *didn't* do it?"

"He would, he would *knock me flat!*" yelled John Allen.

"He would – take *me* by the little toe, and start *peeling*," exclaimed Katie.

"It's just an expression," Ginny interjected. "Just one of those *things* you *say* –" Like "I just love kids." "I know, let's *all* sing a river song!" Anything not the Monongahela. Might as well go back to the song that had started it all. "Roll On, Columbia Roll On – Roll On Columbia Roll On!"

This got them upright and singing lustily, so sing-along songs seemed like a good idea. "Come on and sing," she said to Barb. "Come on, Tiger. Sing a little old bitty bit." Her left hand insinuated itself into Barb's tight back pocket. "We won't *criti*cize . . ."

On cue for once, Katie declared: "If *she* won't sing, *I* won't sing!"

"See, honey?" said Ginny. "See what you've done? We'll all sing songs together – just like in the movies!"

"I can't carry a tune in a bucket," said Barb, fixed on the road.

"A *basket*," sniffed John Allen. "You *can't* carry a *tune* in a *basket*."

Ginny opened her mouth –

"How do you know I can't carry a tune in a basket, Bub? I said *I* can't carry a tune in a *bucket* –"

"John Allen," said Ginny, "I don't like you correcting your –"

"– Harrisburgers carry tunes in *baskets,* but Yablonskis from New Rochelle carry tunes in buckets, and streetcars, and fedoras."

"– *elders*."

"Why is a tune in a *basket?*" Katie demanded.

John Allen chorused "What does 'fedora' mean?"

"Not so *loud*," said Ginny, and began to sing: "Whoopie ti yi oh –"

In fact, Barb had a marvellous voice, a trained voice, when she joined them for the chorus. Pretty ostentatious. "Git along little –"

"Doggie –" sang Katie.

"It's 'dogie', stupid!" said John Allen.

"Don't call her stupid!" snapped Ginny, and Katie began to wail.

They were about to lose the cart to a rightward road and enter what looked like an open mining shaft. "You've made your *baby sister* cry!" Ginny exclaimed.

"Naturally. You practically told her to," said Barb.

"How long is this tunnel?" yelled John Allen, plumping himself over the seat.

"Where," said Ginny to Barb, "did *that* remark come from?"

"Tropical Samoa," said Barb, "site of the ever-expanding Columbia River . . . Eighteen hundred miles," she added. "And don't yell in my ear."

At the next pit stop (this time they needed gas), although they had not yet recovered their time, the rest was welcome. So was the pop. Ginny had a guilty theory that soda pop kept children from being sick – or kept them at least from yelping about it.

There was a convenience store and one of those horrid road-side menageries, largely featuring marine forms. Amazing to have marine things this far from the coast. There were large and small cheap tanks loaded with murky greasy water and . . . *things*.

Even Johnny Allen seemed amazed. Barb held him up so that he could look at the crabs and lobsters from above while he criticized their glass surroundings. Katie, having been taken to the ladies' room and having drunk half a Sprite, crawled back into the blankets and fell asleep.

The tanks were not the only show at the tourist attraction. An incredible selection of expensive dolls stood in the office, above the chips. Ginny was glad her baby was staying asleep.

John Allen, ever the curious one, the star-bright inquisitive one, was staring at a ponderous tank, asking if the gross, slimy "manarays" were *monsters*. And how do they breathe?

At length a red-faced attendant with a feed bucket strolled around from the back of the tank and loomed over John Allen. "That's a mo-ray eel," he puffed. "Like a 'lectric eel. You seen one of them?"

"Yes," John Allen said. "And this isn't real e-lectric. It's only like a snake."

"Real smart little boy," said the man heavily, and grimaced. As Ginny stood, she was three inches higher in flats.

"My dad says places like these are just sucker bait."

"Does he," said the man, and Barb laughed fakely.

"Must bring a real lot of sunshine in your life," the man said heavily.

He finished throwing food in the tank ("He's doing that for the fish," said John Allen) and turned to leave. As the man was thumping up the few stairs to the service-station office, wiping his neck with what looked like a dipstick rag, Ginny finally found her ON switch: "Both my children are a great source of joy to me," she announced.

"Pleased to hear it –" The rest of his sentence was lost as he closed the door.

"Take it easy, honey," said Barb, and pulled her back.

Easing behind the tank, John Allen on its other side, Barb kissed her full and pleasantly and she wanted to kiss for several additional minutes.

Ginny took the wheel, and they were under way – Ginny insisting on a finger kiss or two because there were kids. On their way to the place she'd spent her honeymoon with *him*. She would reclaim it; it would be fine. And it is the nature of driving in cars to feel as if life is fairly all right.

During one of their trial separations before Katie was two, she had gone to all the Neighbours Talk programs at the local grade school, and there she met Barb. Talking about developmentally disabled adults and their abilities. One look, one good look at that pleasant face and frank stance and Ginny said to herself, *I have met a Lesbian*. She had always wondered about herself, and now she knew. And part of her had already known.

At the time, Phil was always dropping by in his newest car or with a selection of girls to pick up John Allen. And sometimes Katie. Ginny was jealous only of his arrogance.

Six months, she met Barb again at Meadowbrook Shopping Plaza and ended up charging $1,462 including sporting equipment, following Barb around the mall.

Barb had been buying for a group home. Phil didn't press charges. It came out of the alimony and Ginny had to give the Gold Card back.

Sometimes she wanted to call Phil and tell him about his successor. How would *he* feel that a woman had displaced *him*?

At the moment she was noticing the countryside again, beginning to slow the van. The trees came down to the road here. And there were pine trees. She hoped she could remember the exact point where you turned . . . She slowed the van a little. Whoops, seventy-five. A little more.

"Anyway," she continued, "it sure didn't bother Phil, and I didn't know any better. When we were married, my mother kept saying *no* lady really likes it, they're just animals and that's sort of a woman's work, you know – then they go punch a clock and you can go take yourself to the beauty shop –"

"Know why my dad says they have *live lobsters* in a tank in a restaurant where you eat, like, fish?"

"John Allen, adults are talking –"

"But you know why they keep them alive and cook them in a big pot *right there, where you see it* and you eat them and stuff?"

"Lobsters –" Ginny stopped. "Johnny Allen, did your daddy take you to the *Commodore Hilton?*"

"– So people can watch 'em *die*," he said cruelly.

"John Allen – Johnny Allen, they don't really die. It's not like they *feel* anything – they're just like *in*sects –"

"Insects die," he said.

"No, they don't. No, I mean they're not alive anyway, not like we are. They just jig around a little –"

"She talks nature into pseudo-animation," Barb said.

"Why do I get the feeling that somebody in this car is being critical of somebody else?"

"That's *you*," explained John Allen.

"And who was it who said we ought to get away and test the relationship?" said Ginny.

"It was the big one by Dad's office –"

"I said we needed to know each other better; I said we could leave the kids with their dad and –"

"Ma! We're supposed to be with Daddy this weekend. Aren't we? We didn't go *last* week –"

"*Tell me* he's wrong."

"It's Annie's place, too. Annie sleeps with Daddy."

"Don't tell me you're running out on a lawyer with visitation rights!"

"Now don't stir him up," hissed Ginny, touching the berm a little.

"Is Daddy going to be up at the lake?"

"I can't believe it. A man who abandoned his own children, taking up with those – And you side with him –"

"She means Dad," said John Allen. "Daddy says you'd try to tell God what to do, but nobody tells God what to do, do they?"

"I, always, enjoy, hearing, about your, father," syruped Ginny. "A gentleman, generous, in his, wisdom."

"Ma?"

"It's perfectly clear why I took the chance. It's your one week of vacation, your one chance to relax and enjoy us, get to be a part of us as a family – it was supposed to affirm my conviction that I was supposed to be with women. That I made the right choice, that the only thing actually wrong with my marriage was the –"

"Mama?"

"– wrong sex. It was right with women, we didn't have to mark out our needs like different roads on the same map and negotiate over –"

"A cartographer, that's what you are – dragging us down some path you alone can draw."

"I told myself a woman would *not* belittle the way I think, would *not* criticize the way I raise my children – she would know what I felt – I thought a woman would understand!"

"You certainly tell yourself a good deal. Don't you ever sit down and listen to yourself?"

"*Mom?*"

"Not *now!*"

"Yes, not now!" snapped Barb.

"Don't you raise your voice to him!"

"What am I *supposed* to do with him? I'm supposed to give him limits but I can't tell him I'm past *mine*?"

Both suddenly seemed to hear him. He was crying.

Guiltily, Ginny turned. "Johnny Allen, honey, what is it? What's the matter? Did Mama hurt your feelings?"

Sobbing, he outbreathed: "No-o-ot re-a-ll-y . . ."

"Well, what's the matter then?" Doing eighty again. She started to ease the pedal.

"How come," gulped John Allen, "Katie got to stay at that neat gas station and I had to stay in the car?"

      ★   ★   ★

Ginny made a left-hand U-turn over the grass of the dividing strip and jetted back. No one said boo.

Face smeared with dirt and tears, Katie was with her one hand gripping the thick pink fingers of the red-faced owner, and with the other a brand-new Baby Huggy; and looking frail and shocked. The fat man was fairly sweating nerves. They stood framed in front of the Pennzoil display, to the left of the station door.

The baby was safe. Tear-wracked and she didn't like that greasy man, but she was safe. How she had gotten back out of the car, Ginny couldn't imagine. But they had been otherwise occupied . . .

She could *see* the headlines now. Great for selling papers: SIMMONS COUNTY LESBIAN DIVORCEE STEALS, DUMPS CHILD AT WHAT-SIT MARATHON STATION. " *'I rest my case,' says Dad.*" Phil's brother didn't write for that rag for nothing.

Parking parentlike by the restrooms, Ginny climbed out and, absently aware that John Allen had dived for his door, said "Grab him," over her shoulder and slammed the door.

The man was standing stiffly, no longer worried now that he saw her. He was accusing her with his high chin, backthrown shoulders, formidable breadth of body, with his might-made-rightness. He was going to throw his weight around, and loud. Maybe he had already called the police. And *how* much would that blessed doll cost? If the baby had held it any closer it would have merged with her flesh. Her poor lonely baby girl –

Ginny eased back, looked into the car. John Allen had his fist wrapped around the door handle; she opened the door and leaned down. "John Allen, you stay in this car and keep your body entirely inside it and don't say a *word* that any soul can hear outside this car. You make a peep or make me any madder than I already am and we are going to find out that Daddy is not the only one who will blister your behind!"

His mouth popped open – his eyes went wide and he shut it.

It was probably empty, as such threats go. Probably.

She marched for the owner, with each stride steeling herself more furiously: *I should never have said such a thing; he'll repeat it at a custody hearing, I just know it.* By the time she reached the man – who had kept his eyes fixed on her – his shoulders had started to round.

She was in form.

"I see you have my daughter," she snapped. She focused on Katie, weepy, tired, dirty-faced. "Oh, sweetheart," she exclaimed. She refocused on the man: "I don't know what has been going through your degenerate mind, but don't lay another hand on this child. If she's in any way harmed . . ." She let it drop. "Darling, let Mama see you. Sweetheart-baby, has this man been being mean to you?"

"No-o-o . . ."

"How did he get you out of that car? I know you wouldn't just get out of that car when you were plainly told not to . . . She seems to be in one piece," said Ginny, and turned to glare at the owner, who had started to fade away.

The doll, it seemed, was free.

After a while, they were all safe back on the road.

"That," said Barb, "was incredible. You ought to get a job in the State Department."

"Do you really think so?" Ginny beamed.

"Yes," said Barb, looking cross. "Well, it's one thirty-four. Time to think *lunch* – right, Bub?"

"Yeah, and the dinosaurs!"

"What are you doing? Barb, you can't pull off here, this isn't what we planned. We can't eat our lunch till the cabin. Don't you remember?"

"John Allen and I have decided to see the dinosaur display, since we've been seeing the billboards since Peterberg. Besides, I'm hungry, if you're not. Dinosaurs make me hungry."

"Yeah!" said Johnny.

"Well we simply can't do it! We just lost time and we aren't scheduled to stop until we –"

"We'll just have high tea. We'll have high tea at the cabin. Real romantic."

"That's them! That's them! See that sign?"

They were passing a large sign that said: SEE THE ALLOSAURUS! BRING ALL THE KIDS!

"That's plastic! That's not a dinosaur!" snapped Ginny.

"I'm hungry," said Katie Lee.

"Now you've put it in her head! See here. Now you listen here. It was my planning this vacation and you said to me, you go ahead and plan this trip and –"

"Good planning doesn't keep folks from eating lunch. For that matter," said Barb with increasing firmness, "planning is not the same thing as running everybody's business."

"Yeah," said Johnny, and retreated all the way to the back.

She had tried so hard. After all they'd been through. After what Phil would say. And the papers could have said, too. And everything.

"You should see the look on your face," Barb said archly.

There came a tiny giggle from the back.

"I hope," said Ginny, a little flustered, "I hope you're satisfied, making me look foolish in front of my own children –"

"But, love, it will be all right. We'll get to the cabin, and we'll have a great – um – picnic supper and the kids will make sand castles –"

"I suppose."

"Lovely." Barb was nodding. "Honey, just like a – a fairy tale –"

"Just like in the movies." Ginny sniffed.

And she was *planning*.

Self-Deliverance

Elise D'Haene

1. It is important to have food in the stomach. Make it something you like: toast, apple-sauce, cereal are recommended.

So far, so bad. Every light I approached turned red. I needed to get strawberry ice cream so I went to the Quality Dairy on my way from work but couldn't get a parking spot so I thought, what the hell, I'll go to Kroger's, and only one checker's working so it took me about a half hour. I went to call Ginnie on a pay phone to remind her to pick up some flowers and lost two quarters. I was so worked up when I got home I went to the fridge to drink milk, which usually calms me, and discovered, not with my nostrils but with my taste buds, that it was sour. This about did me in, upset my already knotted-up stomach so much I had to run to the toilet. I had no toilet paper.

With my jeans at my ankles, I wobbled toward the kitchen like an ageing football player through a maze of old tires. The paper towel-holder wasn't holding paper either, just brown cardboard. My last resort was newspaper. I've got plenty of it, piles of it, sky-scrapers of ageing newsprint and magazines line the walls of my apartment. That's how I got my nickname, Alfie. It started at the restaurant. When I'm on break I bury my head in a book, a newspaper, a magazine, any kind of written material left behind by a customer. Victor, the owner, started teasing me. "What's it all about, Alfie?" It just stuck, that name, like gray gum on the bottom of your shoe. So anyway, I grabbed the thick classified section from some Sunday past, and wobbled back to the toilet. I tore a neat slice down the middle of the top page. After I wiped, I had this thought running through my head: '65 Mustang nu blk pnt/V8 $4,800. It's a good thing they don't print words on toilet paper, since I'd have to read every square inch before I used it. You know how bugs are at night, how various kinds just swarm together under the porch light? That's how it is with me and words.

I smell like fish and tartare sauce because today is Friday and we had fish and chips on special for lunch and the Lady's Madonna Circle from St Gerard's came in for their monthly luncheon. Of course Victor gives them to me, all twenty-seven of them, saying I was the only one he could trust to do it right. Which really isn't true. I'm the only one who'll put up with twenty-seven cackling Catholics who leave me a whopping twenty-five cents apiece. What's really annoying is this one woman, Dorothy O'Conner, actually counts the number of fillets on everybody's plate to make sure they all get the same amount. I tried to explain that the cook weighs the portions and that some pieces are bigger than others. That didn't go over well and she complained and Victor said give them what they want. So every time they come in, she walks to each table and reads me her list of who's short. Ginnie says I should spit on her food, but I can't, it doesn't make me feel better. I do, however, throw a few of her french fries in the trash. She doesn't count the french fries.

I made lots of mistakes today. Mixed up my orders, forgot to get this guy an ashtray after he asked three times and I thought he was going to punch me. Spilled-milk kind of mistakes, so no use crying, but I did. Every chance I got I ran to the bathroom and just bawled my eyes out. My busboy, Tony, covered for me even though he doesn't get much either when those ladies come in. I think he was worried and said something to Victor because Victor let me go early without having me clean my area or fill up the salt, pepper, and sugar containers. Victor pulled me aside, asked how Teddy was, and I mumbled, you know, the same, and then I walked out fast. Victor is Catholic, and I mean *very* Catholic, and I've heard all his opinions about Dr Kevorkian and I know he'd go ballistic if he knew what Ginnie and I are up to. The book I got said that we're supposed to act like nothing's unusual so that nobody gets suspicious. I almost blew it today, though, because when Dorothy O'Conner was saying, "Margaret Mary at table two, Kathleen next to her, and Doris, over there, all need one more fish fillet, dear," I came real close to pulling a Ginnie and telling Dorothy to go fuck herself and enjoy it for once.

My apartment is a mess, especially my bathroom, which I hate cleaning because when I was eight years old, cleaning the bathroom became my assigned lifetime chore. My brothers got good chores: raking leaves, taking out garbage, mowing the lawn, shovelling snow, and helping my father clean the gutters along the roof. These were good in my mind because they were all outdoors, out of the house, out of mom's reach, or grip (depending on her mood), out of her line of vision. Back then, I gagged at the smell of boy-piss, the sight of splashed brown stuff underneath the toilet seat, the mixture of hair, toenails, dust, and foot powder on the floor. My brothers would stuff washcloths, stiff as cardboard, behind the toilet with gooey and crusty white globs of some alien substance sticking to the crumpled mess. I had to pick them up and put them in the clothes hamper and when I did, I'd put on my mom's yellow plastic gloves and hold those washcloths out as far as I could from my nose.

Ginnie and Teddy can't believe how undomestic I am. Teddy wouldn't even use my bathroom, except the time he had an accident. Accident, meaning he was driving to the restaurant on his way to work and felt like he was going to have a bowel movement before his brain registered that he'd already had one. This was an early sign of his dementia. He was just down the street and called in a panic. I told him to come right up, I had some sweats he could wear, and boxer shorts. After I hung up the phone I ran for a sponge and scouring powder and scrubbed the tub. Teddy was crying by the time he got to my door and I just led him into the bathroom, rubbing the back of his neck, telling him it was okay, don't worry, get cleaned up, sweetie, you'll feel better. I called Victor and told him Teddy wasn't feeling well, then I called Ginnie and she went in and covered for Teddy. I feel tenderly toward Teddy, like a big sister, even though we're both twenty-seven.

I always wished I had been born years and years before my brothers so I could feel tenderly like that toward them, instead of being afraid of their unbelievably strong arms and legs that used to pin me down like a butterfly on paper. I was terrified that my limbs, like flimsy wings, would just crumple underneath them. There was a brutal hate coursing through their veins, a hate that laughed and drooled and poked and pounded, until they were bored or my mom snapped at them to go outside and play. I was left with handmarks, bruises, and sticky saliva on my face.

Long since my brothers got girlfriends and pinned them down instead of me, I've had this pressure on my chest, this weight in my body, and I'm always expecting to get slammed to the ground. Teddy's the first person I'd ever met that felt as pinned as I do, held down by some unseeable force that leaves us both gasping and struggling and trying to break loose. I wish I was more like Ginnie. She'll wrestle anyone to the ground who tries to get in her way. She's big, almost six feet tall, with strong arms and legs and a mane of dark hair. Sometimes, when wisps of her bangs hang down over her huge dark eyes, it's like she's got two bold exclamation points on her face. That's what Ginnie is to me, a big exclamation point.

At times, Ginnie and I sleep together. It started out that she would just show up at my door at any hour of the night, let herself in, and crawl into bed with me. She'll get real close, wrap her long legs and arms around me tight, and fall asleep. That's when I like to stay awake, feeling all six feet, all 163 pounds of Ginnie, like a sleeping stallion, exhaling and inhaling next to me. It's like nothing I've ever felt before. That weight in my chest dissolves and I can breathe, my wings are loose and I fly, fearless through the night. Since Teddy's been sick, Ginnie and I sleep together all the time. Sometimes, I guess you could say we make love. Ginnie will just bring her face close to mine and we'll start kissing and groping at each other like we're deep-sea diving, and one of us is out of oxygen. It's pretty frantic. We never talk about it, we don't call each other girlfriends, but I think it helps both of us, and I realize now that even Ginnie gets afraid.

She's coming over in an hour to help me pick out an outfit for tonight. I'd better clean out my closet, use those metal things called hangers instead of the floor for my clothes. She'll be disgusted if she gets a look at my wardrobe strewn everywhere like piles of donated clothes after a disaster. The only outfit I clean regularly is my waitressing uniform because Victor pulled me aside some time last year and talked to me about appearance and pointed to the stain on the back of my dress, that may have once been brown gravy, by then edged in a green growth of some kind. I agreed it was disgusting, but how often do you get a good look at yourself from behind? Then he pointed to my once-white shoes that were splattered with coffee, chocolate milk, soda pop, and bacon grease. Okay, I said, I'm not only a slob, I'm a clumsy slob, a bit dishevelled, but my tables are always filled, standing room only when I work the counter, and I tip out at night way ahead of the pack. Ask the busboys; I am exceedingly charitable with them, because without 'em, I'm nothing; they are the spine to my whole waitressing operation.

I get tipped better than Ginnie and even though she doesn't understand why, I do. The women who come in aren't threatened by me; my looks don't arouse envy, then hate, so they don't need to scrimp. I'm a plain Jane, like them. The men don't peck and paw and pinch me like they do to Ginnie, so they don't feel bruised, their egos don't wiggle limply between their legs like they do when Ginnie snaps her glare and has them begging for mercy. Teddy made good tips before he had to leave. Even the big, burly truckers tipped him well because they didn't have to spit faggot behind his back. Teddy just handed them faggot on a plate. He was the sideshow freak at the circus. "Fruit juice from the fruit." "Dairy from the fairy." "Straight up, or over easy, big guy?" He'd put himself down, let them laugh "with" him as he swished his hips into the back kitchen, where his smile would drop as quickly as the cigarette butts he dumped into the trash. This was Teddy's way of protecting himself from dissolving into a heap of quivering Jell-O. If some unknown guy came in and even seemed the teeniest bit aggressive, Teddy would ask Ginnie to take him. He's gotten beat up before, more than once. Bruises may fade on the outside, but you can't erase that particular look in the eyes, that look somebody gets when they see that fist coming at 'em. It's in Teddy's eyes all the time now. I guess death must look like a fist.

2. After eating, take two anti-nausea tablets.

Alf called to remind me about the flowers for tonight. I don't know what we'll do after Teddy dies. I was supposed to be in California by now. That alleged Hollywood agent I met at the airport in Detroit said long-legged dark beauties like me are in demand. I had two responses to his saying this to me: One, I wanted to kick him in the nuts. Did he think I was a fucking asshole born yesterday? Two, this is my only way out. I hate Michigan. I hate Grand Ledge. If I had to stay for the rest of my life, I would look for a ledge, way up high somewhere, and take a grand fucking leap.

Yesterday, I was driving by the high school and the cheerleaders were revving up the football team as they packed on a bus headed for Petoskey. I remembered that moment of horror in my senior year when Rich led me under the bleachers and was sticking his tongue down my throat and all I could hear were the cheerleaders screaming, "Eat a cowpie! E-A-T-A-C-O-W-P-I-E! Eat a cowpie!" The stomping students above Rich and me screamed in unison and I just vomited, lime vodka and a hot dog, partway into Rich's mouth which, I'm not sorry to say, was a peak experience. I swore at that moment that I would not live out my days in Grand Ledge, or anywhere near this godforsaken place. Even though I technically live in Lansing, the capital of the state, I can't tolerate the ordinariness of my days. I'm thirty now, not eighteen, and I'm still as stuck as a snowball on a wet mitten. I would have moved three years ago, I swear, with or without Alf and Teddy, but Teddy got sick and everything changed. We're his family. We take care of him. The four hundred dollars I had saved up for my plane ticket is gone. I sometimes feel like vomit is pooling up in my stomach and headed toward my mouth.

After I saw the cheerleaders I stopped at my mother's to pick up a flashlight and a casserole dish to make macaroni and cheese for tonight. She hardly looked at me, didn't ask how Teddy was, and told me to be sure I didn't break or crack her cookware. "Don't let Alf take it home with her." My mother hates Alfie because she's from a "low-rent" family. All that means is we own our piece of shit shoebox and they don't. I sometimes want to give my mother a heart attack and tell her I lick Alf's low-rent pussy every night. It's weird with Alf, but I love her, and I know she loves me. It's weird with my mother, but love doesn't enter the equation. She doesn't mention Teddy because it's widely known in the Grand Ledge area that Teddy Shepard is a homosexual and when my mother says "homosexual" she makes it sound like a kind of yellow pus oozing from a scab.

I ran into Teddy's mother at K-mart about three weeks ago. My shopping cart was filled with cotton swabs, adult diapers, plastic sheets, bottles of juice, and soft foods, all for Teddy. I spotted her in the women's clothing area going through a sale rack of sweaters designed by that famous TV star from "Charlie's Angels". She had a greedy, shit-eating grin on her face as she edged her fat elbow into the woman next to her. I couldn't help myself, I rolled my cart right over to her, nudged her with it, and announced loudly, "Mrs Shepard, remember me, I'm Ginnie, I'm a friend of your son, Teddy, remember you have a son, a homosexual son who is dying from AIDS! What the hell's wrong with you people?" I just couldn't hold my tongue. First she just glared at me, her jaw dropped along with the sweaters cradled in her arms; and then her eyes were like faucets and water gushed down her cheeks and landed on the sweaters pooled at her feet. I backed up slowly, wanting to apologize, but not wanting to at the same time. She started to say something, but it sounded garbled, like talking under water. My lower lip started to tremble and I noticed that a crowd of people stood stock still, staring at the space between Mrs Shepard and me, too frightened to make eye contact with either of us. Then I just screamed at them, "What the fuck are you looking at, fucking assholes?" I turned and got out of there fast, leaving my cart behind.

I went to the restaurant and pulled Alf off the floor. Victor gave me the evil eye, but didn't say anything, cuz he knows we're taking care of Teddy. We sat out back and I confessed what happened. Alf just shook her head, saying, "Oh, Ginn, oh, Ginn." She has a way of dipping her voice when she says my name like that, in response to whatever trouble I've gotten myself into. It usually makes me feel like crying, but I just bite the inside of my mouth and fix my eyes on the ground. Then she handed me a copy of the *Hollywood Reporter* to cheer me up. She started subscribing to it for me, underlining auditions and circling casting calls with a bright red marker. When I left and went over to Teddy's apartment, there were two grocery bags from K-mart on the stoop. On top were two of those sweaters, with a note from Mrs Shepard. "For you and Alf. Thank you for taking care of him." I shoved the sweaters behind a bush and walked inside with the bags. Teddy was asleep on the couch, and I looked at his face, a thin version of his mother, and I whispered, "I'm sorry." Which I am, but I'm still disgusted. She added a big tin of peanut brittle to the groceries, it used to be Teddy's favorite, and I wanted to scream again and slam my fist so hard into the folds of flesh around her stomach that she'd lose her fucking breath.

I've got to get out of here.

3. Combine the medications with the right dose of alcohol. This will multiply the toxicity of the drugs by about fifty percent.

I watched a documentary with Alf about that oil spill in Alaska, and thousands of dead birds and fish covered in black were scattered on the beach. And this oil slick was spreading everywhere. That's what it's like, inside my body, creeping real slow, like it's taking you over. Mostly, I stare at the ceiling or the TV cuz I won't look at myself anymore. Sometimes when Alf or Ginn get real close, hooking up a needle to the tube in my chest, or putting medicine in my mouth for thrush, I can see myself, my face, in their eyes. I ask them to stare at me, because it's like you're looking into a shiny, round marble and your cheeks puff out and your whole face is wide and round as if the flesh that has vanished has come back.

It reminds me of these mirrors that lined the walls of the now famous rest stop off the freeway between Lansing and Brighton. It's where I used to go before the police sting operation about four years ago. They set up hidden cameras inside the men's bathroom because it was known to be a gathering place for sex. Then they arrested almost fifty men for lewd conduct and printed their names in the *Lansing State Journal*, or "State Urinal", as Alf calls it. Important businessmen, doctors, politicians, and two priests were listed. I wasn't there that night, even though it'd be no big scandal if my name was in the newspaper under a headline naming local perverts. Alf was so mad that she wrote all week on her customers' checks, "You who are without sin cast the first stone. Alf." We're supposed to write, "Come again," or, "Have a nice day," but Alf's always writing down quotations from the stuff she's reading.

The funniest thing about the rest stop were those mirrors. They puckered out so that everybody was distorted, big and bulgy, like those trick mirrors at circuses. I liked it cuz it's not like you want a good look at who you're with anyway; that's the point, it's ruined if you really see each other face to face. So the mirrors kind of worked, because you couldn't really get a look at yourself, I mean what you really looked like. I used to go on Saturday nights, to pass time when I was horny, or when I was lonely, or when Ginn and Alf were working, and there was nothing to watch on TV.

If I were to stand in front of one of those mirrors now, it would look like I have four heads. I've got three tumors the size of golf balls. One is at the top of my head, one above my right ear, and one at the base of my neck. We joke about it, Ginn and me. Ginn will swing an invisible club in the air, like Johnny Carson, and yell, "Fore!" They are only going to get bigger, like lemons, oranges, then grapefruits. The doctor said that all the problems I'm having, like the seizures, memory loss, hallucinations, temporary blindness, result from the tumors pressing on my brain, squeezing different parts. Alf described all of the brain functions to me and how it was happening. Knowledge is power, is what she said, like I'd be less afraid if I knew the facts. She reads to me all the time. I like the sound of Alf's voice. It's low and gentle and, with my eyes closed, I imagine curling up on top of her, like a cat, with my face pressed against her chest. I don't tell Alf that most of the time now I can't make out a word of what she's saying. I'm afraid she'd stop reading to me then.

My sister Doreen used to read to me when I was little; she's two years older, and we were really close. She knew about me, too; when I started high school and Mom kept asking why I didn't have a girlfriend, Dor would tell Mom to shut up and leave me alone. Then Dor's best friend, Candy, started going to this church where they speak in tongues, so Dor goes too, and then we weren't close anymore. You know that feeling when something's over, like a movie, the screen goes dark and you leave and pretty soon it's like you'd never gone to that movie at all. You were laughing or crying and forgetting your troubles and then, there you are, right inside those troubles all over again. That feeling reminds me of Dor now.

I've been having these dreams a lot lately, except I'm awake when it happens, and it's like you're a car and you're speeding toward a brick wall and nobody's driving, cuz you're the car. Usually I scream and the sound of it splits my head in two, and a nurse or Ginn or Alf will be staring down holding my face between their hands. I told Ginn that when this happens, I'm always disappointed that I scream because I really want to hit the wall. Then Ginn got real close to my ear, cuz the visiting nurse was in the room, and whispered:

"Y'know, Teddy, I feel like a car too sometimes. Not my Mustang, more like a Ford Pinto, you know the ones that can explode. My heartbeat just thumps like a tire over speed bumps on some endless freeway. My eyes are headlights, and all I can see ahead of me is a straight yellow fucking line broken up into pieces, and deep inside I'm just waiting for a nail to puncture the air out of me, send me flying off the road in some other goddamned direction."

I knew then that someone finally understood about my dream, and what it meant. Even if she made it up about wanting to explode. She was grinding her teeth, I could hear it, and she pressed her lips against my ear and a couple of tears ran inside my eardrum, which tickled, and I started laughing and told her to be careful, she was watering my tumor.

4. During the process that follows, the patient's breathing should be monitored. Breathing will become slow and shallow. Put a mirror in front of the nose or mouth to detect breath.

It was weeks ago when I drove to this little bookstore across from Michigan State. It's dark inside and crowded with stacks of books. I went up and down the crammed aisles scanning the slips of paper taped to the shelves. I found a section called Death and Grieving, but the book wasn't there. I kept replaying Ginnie's voice in my head saying, "Don't be afraid, Alf, we have to do it." I finally mustered up the courage to ask the clerk who was behind the counter typing into his computer. I tried to sound light and cheerful when I asked: "Do you have the book *Final Exit* by Humphrey?"

He didn't even look up from the screen and said, "The practicalities of self-deliverance and assisted suicide for the dying. Yes. In the self-help section toward the back."

After I paid for it, he smiled and said, "Have a good day." When I left the store, I accidently knocked into a group of five chanting teenagers on the sidewalk, clad in oversized T-shirts and huge, baggy jeans that seemed to spill onto the pavement. They were unfazed by me and my quivering apologies, and just kept walking, clapping, and rhythmically rapping, "If you don't give a shit, like I don't give a shit, then wave your motherfuckin' hands in the air." I watched them for a while as they parted the sea of oncoming pedestrians like a boat. I crossed the street and decided to walk onto the campus and find a bench under a tree, maybe near the river where the ducks are.

After I graduated high school, I used to come on campus all the time to read. I'd drive all the way here from Grand Ledge just to sit among the old brick buildings while students walked with books tucked under their arms, and professors strolled together absorbed in serious conversations. I used to think people at colleges were deeper thinkers, more thoughtful than the people in Grand Ledge who came into Victor's.

After I met Teddy, I stopped coming to read on campus. He dropped out of hotel/motel management at MSU and came to work at the restaurant, and I found out that he was tied up by some guys in his dorm who gagged him and put him underneath the library in these underground tunnels that run like a maze from building to building. And they urinated on him and did all sorts of terrible things and left him there. The guys who did it weren't even disciplined or anything because they were on the football team. Teddy was moved to another dorm.

The day I got the book, though, I sat on a bench, I thought about those tunnels that have now been boarded up because two students died there mysteriously while playing Dungeons and Dragons, and I thought about Teddy being down there, gagging on the smell of boy-piss, terrified like I was with my brothers. I opened the book and the first thing I read was, "Be sure you are in a hopeless position." I was wishing I had brought Ginnie with me because she would have suggested we go for a beer or shoot some pool, play pinball or something. She would have probably walked out of the bookstore with me and joined those teenagers who didn't give a shit. For the first time in my life, I didn't want to keep reading. I closed the book, put it back in the sack, and left.

I drove straight to Victor's and sat at the counter through the rest of Ginnie's dinner shift. She kept coming up to me, taking drags off my cigarette, leaving the stain of her lipstick for me to taste. She brought me a piece of pecan pie with vanilla ice cream. Victor said, "Who's gonna pay for that?" Ginnie told him to put a lid on it. Then Victor said, "I oughtta fire both of you," then winked at me.

At one point Ginnie came up from behind and brushed herself against my back, real lightly, like a cat, then leaned into me. When she did that, she was telling me that we'd go back to my place and go right to bed. That's exactly what I wanted, but I'd never ask.

5. The extremities will cool, but this is a sign of reduced blood pressure, not necessarily evidence of death.

I don't care if they pump Teddy's stomach and find my goddamned fingerprints on each pill. That's what I told Alf when she read the part about only the dying person should mix the sleeping pills with the ice cream. Then it said don't unplug the phone or answering machine because if someone tries to call and no one answers it could alert them that something is wrong. I say, something is fucking wrong because nobody calls Teddy. His family lives three miles from his apartment and not one of them is the least bit interested that he is dying. Why should it be different, why should it change now? That's what Alf kept saying. They weren't interested in his living, why would they be interested in his dying?

Teddy's sister, Mrs Doreen Born-Again, had the balls to come into Victor's. She must have heard that Teddy wasn't working any more. She dragged in her four snot-nosed brats last Wednesday night and Victor tried to put them on a four-top with a child seat, but she insisted on sitting in a booth. I've got booths on Wednesdays, and she ordered four fried chicken baskets for the runts and a dinner salad for herself. She knows who I am but acted like the Queen of fucking Sheba. After I bring them all of their food, I say, "Can I get you anything else?" I said it three times. But she doesn't answer because they're all holding hands with their heads bowed, praying. I slam their ticket down and say, "If you want anything, ask Jesus for it," and walk away. Then she starts banging her glass with a knife, getting everybody's attention, and she says, "Oh, miss, miss, this spoon is dirty, this glass is chipped, you didn't bring enough honey for the biscuits." Shit like that. Clarise at the counter saved my ass from being fired. She swooped up behind me and said, "You're on break, sweetie." Clarise belongs to the same church Doreen does, but at least Clarise asks how Teddy is and says she's praying for him.

I was driving over to Teddy's to relieve Alf and I caught a glimpse of my face in the rearview mirror and my eyes were all pinched and my mouth was twisted and tight and I've got Bruce

Springsteen blaring "it's a death trap, it's a suicide rap," and I purposely slide the car to the left, right over the speed bumps, and I want it to be over, I want Teddy to die, I can't stand it any more.

I watch Alf with him, you know, all soft and cleaning out the shit in his nose and combing back his hair the way Teddy likes, like the picture of George Michael on Teddy's wall. I just can't be that way; I joke around all the time, keep Teddy laughing, act out these stupid scenes with him from his favorite movies, like *The Way We Were* and *Out of Africa,* and I have to be Robert Redford. Teddy says I'm a cross between Cher and Geena Davis and Alf is a mousier version of Meryl Streep. I play along; it used to be funny, but it's not any more. Sometimes I want to scream at Teddy, wake up goddammit, your fucking life is over, it's gone. I want to slice off this part of me because it swells up and makes my face twisted and my eyes throb and then it feels like nails are being pounded into my forehead. It only stops when I'm with Alf, when I lie down and I'm breathing hard and it's like hot steam is shooting from my mouth, bouncing off her back, and she draws it in as if her skin is a sponge.

Alf and I tried to explain to Teddy what was going to happen, and after hours, I just couldn't talk. It's impossible to know what goes on inside Teddy's head. He kept saying he didn't want to be here anymore. Then, when we asked if he understood what we were going to do, he said, "Yes, when I wake up, I'll be dead, right?" He has to completely understand. Finally, he says, "Just like you're the end of a movie." Alf said, "That's exactly it, Teddy."

He fell asleep then and Alf and I sat in his kitchen and drank beers. Sometimes Alf gets real quiet, and we're sitting at the table and our legs are touching, and she's staring at her beer can, reading the ingredients, and I know she's upset and probably wondering why I'm so angry. I'm on my third beer; she's still sipping the first, and we're passing a cigarette back and forth and I hotbox it cuz I take in a huge drag and hand it back to Alf and the burning ash falls into her lap and we both jump up and I pour beer onto the chair but it's already melted a hole in the green plastic cover. She's still not saying anything. She dries her

chair off and sits back down. So I barely say sorry, and she slips
her leg in between mine. We're just staring at each other and I'm
waiting for her to say something and instead she lit another cigarette and out of her mouth she blew a whole bunch of tiny,
perfect smoke rings, like balloons they rose to the ceiling and we
followed them with our eyes. Then we both started laughing and
I did the strangest thing, I plunged my whole body into her lap
and I push my head down between her legs and my mouth
opens and I just chew and chew and the skin on my face is on
fire, like burning your knees on carpet, until I can smell her and
the crotch of her jeans is wet and we forget completely that
Teddy's in the next room sleeping.

**6. Be absolutely sure that death has occurred. Test pupil
contraction by shining a bright flashlight in the eye.**

The name of the game was where does it hurt the most. Alf's
brothers would get on top of her and hold her down and then
pinch her all over to see where it hurt the most. She told me
about it after I told her about what happened to me on campus.
We were behind Victor's smoking a joint waiting for Ginn to
finish cleaning her area. Allen, the night cook, came back and
took a few hits and said, "Where are you sweethearts going
tonight?" He's such an asshole.

When Ginn finished, we drove out to the Ledges and climbed
up to this spot above the river where all these caves are that the
Indians used to live in. Ginn is using a red marker and changing
the names written on the rocks. Like if it says, Paul and Tammy
Forever, she adds an "ette" onto Paul, or maybe she put an "o"
in Tammy. I can't remember. Alf and I were pretty high and
Ginn is drinking a beer and Alf starts saying that they have the
remains of an Indian girl who was buried up here in one of the
museums at Michigan State. They have clothes on her and put
these things that look like marbles in her eye sockets. It says she
died of unknown causes although there were indications that
she had a concussion or something, like an indent in her skull.
Alf said it was really sad and that they'd never unbury someone

at a cemetery and put them on display like that. She complained to the person in charge and wrote a letter to the "State Urinal", but they never published it.

We were all quiet after that story and I kept thinking about Alf getting pinched and then I said, "So, where did it hurt the most?" Alf looked at me and smiled but didn't answer. I felt kind of bad, like I shouldn't have asked. Then Ginn stands up on a rock and screams, "Fuck this place!" Her voice kept echoing for a while and then I stood up like Robert De Niro in *The Deer Hunter* and yelled, "Okay!" over and over, just like him. Ginn did it too, but not Alf. I've never heard Alf yell. She was laughing, though, but at one point I looked down and I think she was remembering that Indian girl because she looked so sad.

That was so long ago, way before I knew I was sick. These things keep coming back to me, stuff I thought I'd forgotten because when I remember it's like suddenly having someone else's memories. It's hard to explain but they don't seem like mine anymore, like old photos of yourself and you don't recall looking like that at all. The one picture I have next to my bed is me, Mom, and Dor. Mom and Dor look like themselves but I don't. We're up at Mackinaw Island and I'm probably ten and I have these shorts on and my legs look like stiff pencils. I'm not wearing a shirt so I'm sunburned and I remember standing there with them and I'm shivering cuz I just got out of the lake. My dad keeps yelling at me to stand still cuz I'm shaking and the louder he yells the more I shake. And Dor's saying, "Stop yelling at him," and then he takes the picture. The only one smiling is Mom.

The worst part is going home and I'm sitting behind my dad who's driving and his neck is red from the sun and we have to stay quiet the whole way because he can't stand noise when he drives. Dor and I are faking, like we are talking to each other using our lips and faces and mouthing the words. My dad looks back at me through the mirror and he's staring at me like he has something rotten in his mouth. I know it's because I am acting silly and maybe he can see I'm pretending to be a girl.

I keep that picture, though, because it reminds me of swimming in the lake and I made two friends up there, Todd and Brad, they were twins my age. We're swimming together and dunking and splashing and watching each other piss in the water. They're both taller than me so I get up on their shoulders and they hold my legs and I squeeze my thighs around their heads and it's the most fun I've had with guys my age. When we shower in the public bathroom we stare at each other's peckers and our eyes swell up as they get bigger and then Todd keeps watch while Brad plays with mine. We take turns. When my family's leaving I almost start crying saying bye to them and we swear to come back the same time next summer. All year I bug my dad about where we are going for summer vacation and then my dad got laid off from Olds and we never had another vacation after that.

All these things keep coming back to me and it's like opening a door and there you are. I like it too, because I forget my body then, the burning and this needle I think someone stuck in my back and left there.

You know, it's like you forget you're here and where it hurts the most.

7. After death has been confirmed, make sure all medications are put away. Be sure to wash the dishes. Wait at least an hour, then call the police. Tell them the patient had a terminal illness.

I read in *Science* magazine about Albert Einstein being on his deathbed, and his doctor told him that there was an operation they could try that might save him, but it was very risky. Einstein said no, for everyone there is a time to die; it is my time. There was a moment tonight when Teddy said almost the exact same thing and I wondered what happens in the brain or maybe the spirit that leads somebody to know this so clearly. I didn't see that terrified look in Teddy's eyes at all, like somehow death wasn't a fist anymore, it was more like a cup of warm milk, at least that's what I'd want it to be like, a warmth that eases into your pores and lulls you to sleep.

It didn't take long for Teddy to stop breathing, just a few hours. Ginnie and I sat next to him and just talked to him, then when he was asleep Ginnie kept talking, going scene by scene through *The Way We Were*. When she got to the end where Robert Redford and Barbra Streisand part for the last time, both of us were crying. Then we were quiet for a while and just watched Teddy's chest going up and down and up and down and I fell asleep for a minute because I started breathing like Teddy. I was jolted awake when my book slipped out of my hand and hit the floor with a loud thump. It's a huge, thick book of great poems that Ginnie gave me years ago. She said she found it, but I could see that the paper pocket for the library card had been ripped out. I've been reading to Teddy from this book for the last few months. Mostly because I knew he couldn't follow a story or an article anymore, and I thought that at least with the poems he could listen to the words, he didn't have to know what they meant, all he had to do was listen. When I reached down for the book, Ginnie stroked my back and said, "He's gone, Alf."

After Teddy died, Ginnie carried the dinner dishes into the kitchen. There was a small amount of melted strawberry ice cream left in Teddy's bowl and she scooped it up with her tongue. The police came first and then the coroner. I was surprised how routine everything was. The worst part for me was when they put Teddy in the black plastic body bag. I was sitting next to Ginnie on the couch clutching my book when they zipped it up. The sound was so loud and jarring, and as if she read my mind, Ginnie pressed her palms over my ears. It shouldn't be that way at all. It should be real quiet, like sealing an envelope or closing a book.

I'm driving us back to my place because, by the time everyone left, Ginnie was feeling real drowsy from Teddy's ice cream. In the car she starts talking about giving Victor our notice, selling her Mustang, and how we would use the money to get to California. Then she asks me to slow down and just drive over the speed bumps on the road. She closes her eyes, leans her head back, puts her hand on my leg, and falls fast asleep. Every so often her muscles twitch as if she's got an electric current running through her and when she twitches some of that current is released.

It seems like it's only Ginnie and me driving under the moon tonight. When I glance at her sleeping, she reminds me of a night flower, the ones I read about in the California desert that bloom when the sun sets. She opens outward and whatever's clamped down inside just unfolds. Most people think Ginnie's a harsh person, but she's not, really; Teddy and I know that. Right now, in the car, I can feel that stiffness in her body drop off and she's soft and yielding like an old pillow, just like a pillow you can burrow into and you feel sort of sad when it's time to wake up and lift your face to the day.

I wrap my hand around her wrist and feel the rhythm of her pulse as it navigates us toward home. When we get there, I'm going to press my body real close to her as she sleeps. Then I'm going to talk to Teddy, tell him about flowers that bloom in the night desert, until my words start running into each other, just like those bugs that swarm under a lighted porch before it goes dark.

PAST TIMES

Past Times

Writers on lesbian themes have always had to answer the unspoken question: *isn't this just a phase?* "This" meaning the entirety of lesbian culture, which is often portrayed in the media as a frail young offshoot of the sexual revolution of the 1970s. And so lesbian fiction from its earliest days has reappropriated two genres – historical fantasy and historical fiction – to imagine and make real for itself a lesbian past. I have not distinguished between the two forms in this section, because lesbian fiction is always aware that history is a matter of fantasy-driven interpretation, of filling in the gaps, of strategically retelling a story that has been told against us.

Elizabeth A. Lynn's "The Woman Who Loved the Moon" is set in an imaginary place where exceptional women can be warriors, but borrows imagery of medieval life such as sorcerers, page-boys, and armoured warriors on horseback. It's a vivid example of lesbian fable-making, its unusual content shaped by the most traditional of structural elements: the three sisters, the series of duels, the impossible love between human and immortal. Part of what makes Lynn's story so satisfying is the way its imagery draws on ancient associations between lesbian sensibility and the moon as Diana, the virgin goddess with her band of women. Given its genre, "The Woman Who Loved the Moon" is surprisingly tough and unsentimental in its delineation of love between women – between sisters as well as between lovers. Yet it is stirringly romantic in its central quest: "Long have I searched for you, by whose hand perished the two people most dear to me."

My own story, "The Tale of the Kiss", takes part in a recent literature of re-imaginings of traditional European fairy tales. The best known are reworkings of heterosexual relationships, particularly by Angela Carter, but increasingly lesbian themes are being teased out, for instance in the work of Olga Broumas, Bryony Lavery, and Jeanette Winterson. "The Tale of the Kiss" is set in that pre-industrial Brothers Grimm world of poverty and magic; part of what feels so liberating about writing fairy tales is precisely not having to be true to a particular time and place. The story draws on traditional folktale elements and structure, but deviates sharply in having a first-person narrator and an open ending. It is a fairy tale in the sense of being about a transformation: "She who takes a kiss can also die of it, can wake into something unimaginable, having turned herself into some new species."

History and fairy tale overlap in the figure of the witch. Sara Maitland's "The Burning Times", one of many remarkable historical stories by this author, tackles head-on one of the most painful times in history, the centuries of persecution of so-called witches. Instead of choosing a particular case to fictionalize, Maitland offers a rootless, haunting story that could have happened any time, anywhere, during this long nightmare; its universality is its horror.

> "Dance, for God's sake dance," said the old parish priest, who I think meant well by us always, "dance and smile or they will burn you too."

Many a lesbian novel has presented witches as brave isolated herbal healers, persecuted out of sheer misogyny. What makes Maitland's story more dynamic and ethically complex is that the accuser in this case in a girl, caught in the crucible of adolescent sexuality, pulled between love and rage.

Some of our best historical fiction comes out of our worst trials. Quite literally, in the case of Ingrid MacDonald's "The Catherine Trilogy", three pieces about the case of the two women called Catherine who were tried in early eighteenth-century Germany for their "fraudulent" marriage. Though her source is a set of legal records, MacDonald manages never to get bogged down in detail, but lets the Catherines' intertwined lives take on their own momentum. The lyricism and theatricality of this text, which the author has also adapted for the stage, is remarkable.

Both women get to tell their own very different version of events, and a piece from the point of view of their troubled judges is driven like a wedge between the two. Like Sara Maitland, rather than emphasizing the innocence of the lovers and the evil of their accusers, MacDonald complicates things wonderfully, in this case by introducing grotesque fairytale images and a heady blend of gender-bending, religion and magic. "Seven miracles are given to each soul in a lifetime," says the wife, "and many people cheat their souls and never even use one."

Sigrid Nielsen's story is a sample of a more satirical kind of lesbian historical fiction. It's about two Edinburghs: the 1990s cosmopolis, where Catriona Gough works as a waitress, tears up love-letters unsent and struggles with her novel, and the dirty city of two hundred years before, where the elegant Jean de Vaubrun has escaped from the French Revolution. Nielsen perfectly captures the pedestrian difficulties of being a historical novelist:

> Dark flakes of snow tumbled past the candlelit windows of the Countess of Ratho's townhouse in Charlotte Square ... [Except that it wasn't snowing, because this has to have been November. Because Jean was fleeing from the September Massacres. Unless they didn't actually happen in September. The book's away to the library. Oh, who cares.]

She also manages to poke fun at the conventions of lesbian historical romances while simultaneously tracing a very modern and moving love triangle.

Historical fiction with lesbian themes is thriving as a genre, and as historians dig up more and more evidence of women who loved women in "past times", writers are getting bolder and more experimental both in their choice of settings and in what they dare to hypothesize. What historical fiction offers us, though, is not confirmation of some timeless lesbian identity uniting Joan of Arc to Martina Navratilova, but instead a sense of startling difference-within-sameness: the passions and flavours of lives not our own.

The Woman Who Loved the Moon

Elizabeth A. Lynn

They tell this story in the Middle Counties of Ryoka, and especially in the county of Issho, the home of the Talvela family. In Issho they know that the name of the woman who loved the moon was Kai Talvela, one of the three warrior sisters of Issho. Though the trees round the Talvela house grow taller now than they did in Kai Talvela's time, her people have not forgotten her. But outside of Issho and in the cities they know her only as the Mirror Ghost.

Kai Talvela was the daughter of Roko Talvela, at a time when the domain of the Talvelai was smaller than it is now. Certainly it was smaller than Roko Talvela liked. He rode out often to skirmish at the borders of his land, and the men of the Talvelai went with him. The hills of Issho county resounded to their shouts. While he was gone the folk of the household went about their business, for the Talvela lands were famous then as they are now for their fine orchards and the fine dappled horses they breed. They were well protected, despite the dearth of soldiery, for Lia Talvela was a sorcerer, and Kai and her sisters Tei and Alin guarded the house. The sisters were a formidable enemy, for they had learned to ride and to fight. The Talvela armorer had fashioned for them fine light mail that glittered as if carved from gems. At dawn and dusk the three sisters rode across the estate. Alin wore a blue-dyed plume on her peaked helmet, and Tei wore a gold one on hers. Kai wore a feather dyed red as blood. In the dusk their armor gleamed, and when it caught the starlight it glittered like the rising Moon.

Kai was the oldest of the sisters; Alin the youngest. In looks and in affection the three were very close. They were – as Talvela women are even in our day – tall and slim, with coal-black hair. Tei was the proudest of the three, and Alin was the most laughing and gay. Kai, the oldest, was quietest, and while Tei frowned often and Alin laughed, Kai's look was grave, direct, and serene. They were all of an age to be wed, and Roko Talvela had tried to find husbands for them. But Kai, Tei, and Alin had agreed that they would take no lover and wed no man who could not match their skills in combat. Few men wished to meet the warrior sisters. Even the bravest found themselves oddly unnerved when they faced Tei's long barbed spear and grim smile, or Alin's laughing eyes as she spun her oaken horn-tipped cudgel. It whirled like a live thing in her palms. And none desired to meet Kai's great curved blade. It sang when she swung it, a thin clear sound, purer than the note of the winter thrush. Because of that sound Kai named her blade *Song*. She kept it sharp, sharp as a shadow in the full moon's light. She had a jeweled scabbard made to hold it, and to honor it, she caused a great ruby to be fixed in the hilt of the sword.

One day in the late afternoon, the sisters rode, as was their custom, to inspect the fences and guardposts of the estate, making sure that the men Roko Talvela had left under their command were vigilant in their job. Their page went with them. He was a boy from Nakasé county, and like many of the folk of Nakasé he was a musician. He carried a horn which, when sounded, would summon the small company of guards, and his stringed lute from Ujo. He also carried a long-necked pipe, which he was just learning how to play. It was autumn. The leaves were rusty on the trees. In the dry sad air they rattled in the breeze as if they had been made of brass. A red sun sat on the horizon, and overhead swung the great silver face of the full Moon.

The page had been playing a children's song on the pipe. He took his lips from it and spoke. The storytellers of Ujo, in Nakasé county, when they tell this tale, insist that he was in love with one of the sisters, or perhaps with all three. There is no way to know, of course, if that is true. Certainly they had all, even proud Tei, been very kind to him. But he gazed upon the sisters in the rising moonlight, and his eyes worshipped. Stammering, he said, "O my ladies, each of you is beautiful, and together you rival even the moon!"

Alin laughed, and swung her hair. Like water against diamond it brushed her armor. Even Tei smiled. But Kai was troubled. "Don't say that," she said gently. "It's not lucky, and it isn't true."

"But everyone says it, Lady," said the page.

Suddenly Tei exclaimed, "Look!" Kai and Alin wheeled their horses. A warrior was riding slowly toward them, across the blue hills. His steed was black, black as obsidian, black as a starless night, and the feather on his helmet was blacker than a raven's wing. His bridle and saddle and reins and his armour were silver as the mail of the Talvela women. He bore across his lap a black-thorn cudgel, tipped with ivory, and beside it lay a great barbed spear. At his side bobbed a black sheath and the protruding hilt of a silver sword. Silently he rode up the hill, and the darkness thickened at his back. The hooves of the black horse made no sound on the pebbly road.

As the rider came closer, he lifted his head and gazed at the Talvelai, and they could all see that the person they had thought a man was in fact a woman. Her hair was white as snow, and her eyes gray as ash. The page lifted the horn to his lips to sound a warning. But Alin caught his wrist with her warm strong fingers. "Wait," she said. "I think she is alone. Let us see what she wants." Behind the oncoming rider darkness thickened. A night bird called *Whooo?*

Tei said, "I did not know there was another woman warrior in the Middle Counties."

The warrior halted below the summit of the hill. Her voice was clear and cold as the winter wind blowing off the northern moors. "It is as they sing; you are indeed fair. Yet not so fair, I think, as the shining moon."

Uneasily, the women of Issho gazed at this enigmatic stranger. Finally, Kai said, "You seem to know who we are. But we do not know you. Who are you, and from where do you come? Your armour bears no device. Are you from the Middle Counties?"

"No," said the stranger, "my home is far away." A smile like light flickered on her lips. "My name is – Sedi."

Kai's dark brows drew together, and Tei frowned, for Sedi's armor was unmarred by dirt or stain, and her horse looked fresh and unwearied. Kai thought, what if she is an illusion, sent by Roko Talvela's enemies? She said, "You are chary of your answers."

But Alin laughed. "O, my sister, you are too suspicious," she said. She pointed to the staff across the stranger's knees. "Can you use that pretty stick?"

"In my land," Sedi said, "I am matchless." She ran her hand down the black cudgel's grain.

"Then I challenge you!" said Alin promptly. She smiled at her sisters. "Do not look so sour. It has been so long since there has been anyone who could fight with me!" Faced with her teasing smile, even Tei smiled in return, for neither of the two older sisters could refuse Alin anything.

"I accept," said Sedi sweetly. Kai thought, an illusion cannot fight. Surely this woman is real? Alin and Sedi dismounted their steeds. Sedi wore silks with silver and black markings beneath her shining mail. Kai looked at them and thought, I have seen those marks before. Yet as she stared at them she saw no discernible pattern. Under her armour, Alin wore blue silk. She had woven it herself, and it was the colour of a summer sky at dawn when the crickets are singing. She took her white cudgel in her hands, and made it spin in two great circles, so swiftly that it blurred in the air. Then she walked to the top of the hill, where the red sunlight and the pale moonlight lingered.

"Let us begin," she said.

Sedi moved opposite her. Her boots were black kid, and they made no sound as she stepped through the stubby grass. Kai felt a flower of fear wake in her heart. She almost turned to tell the page to wind his horn. But Alin set her staff to whirling, and it was too late. It spun and then with dizzying speed thrust toward Sedi's belly. Sedi parried the thrust, moving with flowing grace. Back and forth they struck and circled on the rise. Alin was laughing.

"This one is indeed a master, O, my sisters," she called. "I have not been so tested in months!"

Suddenly the hard horn tip of Sedi's staff thrust toward Alin's face. She lifted her staff to deflect the blow. Quick as light, the black staff struck at her belly. Kai cried out. The head blow had been a feint. Alin gasped and fell, her arms folding over her stomach. Her lovely face was twisted with pain and white as moonlight on a lake. Blood bubbled from the corner of her mouth. Daintily, Sedi stepped away from her. Kai and Tei leaped from their horses. Kai unlaced her breastplate and lifted her helmet from her face.

"O," said Alin softly. "It hurts."

Tei whirled, reaching for her spear.

But Alin caught her arm with surprising strength. "No!" she said. "It was a fair fight, and I am fairly beaten."

Lightly, Sedi mounted her horse. "Thy beauty is less than it was, women of Issho," she said. Noiselessly she guided her steed into the white mist coiling up the hill, and disappeared in its thick folds.

"Ride to the house," Kai said to the frightened page. "Bring aid and a litter. Hurry." She laid a palm on Alin's cheek. It was icy. Gently, she began to chafe her sister's hands. The page raced away. Soon the men came from the house. They carried Alin Talvela to her bed, where her mother the sorcerer and healer waited to tend her.

But, despite her mother's skills, Alin grew slowly more weak and wan. Lia Talvela said, "She bleeds within. I cannot staunch the wound." As Kai and Tei sat by the bed, Alin sank into a chill silence from which nothing, not even their loving touch, roused her. She died with the dawn. The folk of the household covered her with azure silk and laid her oaken staff at her hand. They coaxed Kai and Tei to their beds and gave them each a poppy potion, that they might sleep a dreamless sleep, undisturbed even by grief.

Word went to Roko Talvela to tell him of his daughter's death. Calling truce to his wars, he returned at once to Issho. All Issho county, and lords from the neighboring counties of Chuyo, Ippa, and Nakasé, came to the funeral. Kai and Tei Talvela rode at the head of the sad procession that brought the body of their sister to burial. The folk who lined the road pointed them out to each other, marvelling at their beauty. But the more discerning saw that their faces were cold as if they had been frost-touched, like flowers in spring caught by a sudden wayward chill.

Autumn passed to winter. Snow fell, covering the hills and valleys of Issho. Issho households put away their silks and linens and wrapped themselves in wool. Fires blazed in the manor of the Talvelai. The warrior sisters of Issho put aside their armour and busied themselves in women's work. And it seemed to all who knew them that Kai had grown more silent and serious, and that proud Tei had grown more grim. The page tried to cheer them with his music. He played war songs, and drinking songs, and bawdy songs. But none of these tunes pleased the sisters. One day in desperation he said, "O, my ladies, what would you hear?"

Frowning, Tei shook her head. "Nothing," she said.

But Kai said, "Do you know 'The Riddle Song'?" naming a children's tune. The page nodded. "Play it." He played it. After it he played "Dancing Bear" and "The Happy Hunter" and all the songs of childhood he could think of. And it seemed to him that Tei's hard mouth softened as she listened.

In spring Roko Talvela returned to his wars. Kai and Tei re-donned their armour. At dawn and at dusk they rode the perimeter of the domain, keeping up their custom, accompanied by the page. Spring gave way to summer, and summer to autumn. The farmers burned leaves in the dusk, covering the hills with a blue haze.

And one soft afternoon a figure in silver on a coal-black horse came out of the haze.

The pale face of the full moon gleamed at her back. "It's she!" cried the page. He reached for his horn.

Tei said, "Wait." Her voice was harsh with pain. She touched the long spear across her knees, and her eyes glittered.

"O, my sister, let us not wait," said Kai softly. But Tei seemed not to hear. Sedi approached in silence. Kai lifted her voice. "Stay, traveller. There is no welcome for you in Issho."

The white-haired woman smiled a crooked smile. "I did not come for welcome, O daughters of the Talvelai."

"What brought you here, then?" said Kai.

The warrior woman made no answer. But her gray eyes beneath her pale brows looked at Kai with startling eloquence. They seemed to say, patience. You will see.

Tei said, "She comes to gloat, O my sister, that we are two, and lonely, who once were three."

"I do not think –" Kai began.

Tei interrupted her. "Evil woman," she said, with passion. "Alin was all that is trusting and fair, and you struck her without warning." Dismounting from her dappled mare, she took in hand her long barbed spear. "Come, Sedi. Come and fight *me*."

"As you will," said Sedi. She leaped from her horse, spear in hand, and strode to the spot where Tei waited for her, spear ready. They fought. They thrust and parried and lunged. Slowly the autumn chill settled over the countryside. The spears flashed in the moonlight. Kai sat her horse, fingering the worked setting of the ruby on her sword. Sometimes it seemed to her that Sedi was stronger than Tei, and at other times Tei seemed stronger than Sedi. The polish on their silver armour shone like flame in the darkness.

At last, Tei tired. She breathed heavily, and her feet slipped in the nubby grass.

Kai had been waiting for this moment. She drew *Song* from the sheath and made ready to step between them. "Cease this!" she called. Sedi glanced at her.

"No!" cried Tei. She lunged. The tip of her spear sliced Sedi's arm. "I shall win!" she said.

Sedi grimaced. A cloud passed across the Moon. In the dimness, Sedi lunged forward. Her thrust slid under Tei's guard. The black-haired woman crumpled into the grass. Kai sprang to her sister's side. Blood poured from Tei's breast. "Tei!" Kai cried. Tei's eyes closed. Kai groaned. She knew death when she saw it. Raging, she called to the page, "Sound the horn!"

The sweet sound echoed over the valley. In the distance came the answering calls from the Talvela men. Kai looked at Sedi, seated on her black steed. "Do you hear those horns, O murderous stranger? The Talvela soldiers come. You will not escape."

Sedi smiled. "I am not caught so easily," she said. At that moment, Tei shook in Kai's arms, and life passed from her. The ground thrummed with the passage of horses. "Do you wish me caught, you must come seek me, Kai Talvela." Light flashed on her armour. Then the night rang with voices shouting.

The captain of the guard bent over Kai. "O my lady, who has done this thing?"

Kai started to point to the white-haired warrior. But among the dappled horses there was no black steed, and no sign of Sedi.

In vain the men of the Talvelai searched for her. In great sadness they brought the body of Tei Talvela home, and readied her for burial. Once more a procession rode the highway to the burial ground of the Talvelai. All Issho mourned.

But Kai Talvela did not weep. After the burial, she went to her mother's chambers, and knelt at the sorcerer's knee. "O, my mother, listen to me." And she told her mother everything she could remember of her sisters' meetings with the warrior who called herself Sedi.

Lia Talvela stroked her daughter's fine black hair. She listened, and her face grew pale. At last Kai ended. She waited for her mother to speak. "O my daughter," Lia Talvela said sadly, "I wish you had come to me when this Sedi first appeared. I could have told you then that she was no ordinary warrior. *Sedi* in the enchanter's tongue means moon, and the woman you describe is one of the shades of that Lady. Her armour is impervious as the moonlight, and her steed is not a horse at all but Night itself taking animal shape. I fear that she heard the songs men sang praising the beauty of the women warriors of the Talvelai, and they made her angry. She came to earth to punish you."

"It was cruel," said Kai. "Are we responsible for what fools say and sing?"

"The elementals are often cruel," said Lia Talvela.

That night, Kai Talvela lay in her bed, unable to rest. Her bed seemed cold and strange to her. She reached to the left and then to the right, feeling the depressions in the great quilts where Alin and Tei had been used to sleep. She pictured herself growing older and older until she was old, the warrior woman of Issho, alone and lonely until the day she died and they buried her beside her sisters. The Talvelai are a long-lived folk.

And it seemed to her that she would have preferred her sisters' fate.

The following spring travellers on the highways of Ryoka were treated to a strange apparition – a black-haired woman on a dappled horse riding slowly east.

She wore silver armour and carried a great curved sword, fashioned in the manner of the smiths of the Middle Counties. She moved from town to town. At the inns she would ask, "Where is the home of the nearest witch or wizard?" And, when shown the way to the appropriate cottage or house or hollow or cave, she would go that way.

Of the wisefolk she asked always the same thing: "I look for the Lady who is sometimes known as Sedi." And the great among them gravely shook their heads, while the small grew frightened, and shrank away without response. Courteously she thanked them and returned to the road. When she came to the border of the Middle Counties, she did not hesitate, but continued into the Eastern Counties, where folk carry straight, double-edged blades, and the language they speak is strange.

At last she came to the hills that rise on the eastern edge of Ryoka. She was very weary. Her armour was encrusted with the grime of her journey. She drew her horse up the slope of a hill. It was twilight. The darkness out of the east seemed to sap the dappled stallion's strength, so that it plodded like a ploughhorse. She was discouraged as well as weary, for in all her months of traveling she had heard no word of Sedi. I shall go home, she thought, and live in the Talvela manor, and wither. She gained the summit of the hill. There she halted. She looked down across the land, bones and heart aching. Beyond the dark shadows lay a line of silver like a silken ribbon in the dusk. And she knew that she could go no farther. That silver line marked the edge of the world. She lifted her head and smelled the heavy salt scent of the open sea.

The silver sea grew brighter. Kai Talvela watched. Slowly the full moon rose, dripping out of the water.

So this is where the moon lives, thought the woman warrior. She leaned on her horse. She was no fish, to chase the moon into the ocean. But the thought of returning to Issho made her shiver. She raised her arms to the violet night. "O Moon, see me," she cried. "My armour is filth-covered. My horse is worn to a skeleton. I am no longer beautiful. O jealous one, cease your anger. Out of your pity, let me join my sisters. Release me!"

She waited for an answer. None came. Suddenly she grew very sleepy. She turned the horse about and led it back down the slope to a hollow where she had seen the feathery shape of a willow silhouetted against the dusk, and heard the music of a stream. Taking off her armour, she wrapped herself in her red woollen cloak. Then she curled into the long soft grass and fell instantly asleep.

She woke to warmth and the smell of food. Rubbing her eyes, she lifted on an elbow. It was dawn. White-haired, cloaked in black, Sedi knelt beside a fire, turning a spit on which broiled three small fish. She looked across the wispy flames and smiled, eyes gray as ash. Her voice was clear and soft as the summer wind. "Come and eat."

It was chilly by the sea. Kai stretched her hands to the fire, rubbing her fingers. Sedi gave her the spit. She nibbled the fish. They were real, no shadow or illusion. Little bones crunched beneath her teeth. She sat up and ate all three fish. Sedi watched her and did not speak.

When she had done, Kai Talvela laid the spit in the fire. Kneeling by the stream, she drank and washed her face. She returned to the place where she had slept, and lifted from the sheath her great curved blade. She saluted Sedi. "O moon," she said, "or shade of the moon, or whatever you may be, long have I searched for you, by whose hand perished the two people most dear to me. Without them I no longer wish to live. Yet I am a daughter of the Talvelai, and a warrior, and I would die in battle. O Sedi, will you fight?"

"I will," said the white-haired woman. She drew her own sword from its sheath.

They circled and cut and parried and cut again, while light deepened in the eastern sky. Neither was wearing armour, and so each stroke was double-deadly. Sedi's face was serene as the lambent moon as she cut and thrust, weaving the tip of her blade in a deadly tapestry. I have only to drop my guard, Kai Talvela thought, and she will kill me. Yet something held her back. Sweat rolled down her sides. The blood pounded in her temples. The salty wind kissed her cheeks. In the swaying willow a bird was singing. She heard the song over the clash of the meeting blades. It came to her that life was sweet. I do not want to die, she thought. I am Kai Talvela, the warrior woman of Issho. I am strong. I will live.

Aloud she panted, "Sedi, I will kill you." The white-haired woman's face did not change, but the speed of her attack increased. She is strong, Kai Talvela thought, but I am stronger. Her palms grew slippery with sweat. Her lungs ached. Still she did not weaken. It was Sedi who slowed, tiring. Kai Talvela shouted with triumph. She swept Sedi's blade to one side and thrust in.

Song's sharp tip came to rest a finger's breadth from Sedi's naked throat. Kai Talvela said, "Now, sister-killer, I have you."

Across the shining sword, Sedi smiled. Kai waited for her to beg for life. She said nothing, only smiled like flickering moonlight. Her hair shone like pearl, and her eyes seemed depthless as the sea. Kai's hands trembled. She let her sword fall. "You are too beautiful, O Sedi."

With cool, white fingers Sedi took *Song* from Kai's hands. She brought her to the fire, and gave her water to drink in her cupped palms. She stroked Kai's black hair and laid her cool lips on Kai's flushed cheek. Then she took Kai's hand in her own, and pointed at the hillside. The skin of the earth shivered, like a horse shaking off a fly. A great rent appeared in the hill. Straight as a shaft of moonlight, a path cut through earth to the water's smooth edge. Sedi said, "Come with me."

And so Kai Talvela followed the moon to her cave beneath the ocean. Time is different there than it is beneath the light of the sun, and it seemed to her that no time passed at all. She slept by day, and rose at night to ride with the moon across the dark sky's face, to race the wolves across the plains and watch the dolphins playing in the burnished sea. She drank cool water from beneath the earth. She did not seem to need to eat. Whenever she grew sad or thoughtful, Sedi would laugh and shake her long bright hair, and say, "O, my love, why so sombre?"

And the touch of her fingers drove all complaint from Kai's mind and lips.

But one sleep she dreamed of an old woman standing by a window, calling her name. There was something familiar and beloved in the crone's wrinkled face. Three times she dreamed that dream. The old voice woke in her a longing to see sunlight and shadow, green grass and the flowers on the trees. The longing grew strong. She thought, something has happened to me.

Returning to the cave at dawn, she said to Sedi, "O my friend and lover, let us sit awhile on land. I would watch the sunrise." Sedi consented. They sat at the foot of an immense willow beside a broad stream. A bird sang in the willow. Kai watched the grass color with the sunrise, turning from grey to rose, and from rose to green. And her memories awoke.

She said, "O, my love, dear to me is the time I have spent with you beneath the sea. Yet I yearn for the country of my birth, for the sound of familiar voices, for the taste of wine and the smell of bread and meat. Sedi, let me go to my place."

Sedi rose from the grass. She stretched out both hands. "Truly, do you wish to leave me?" she said. There were tears in her grey eyes. Kai trembled. She almost stepped forward to take the white-haired woman in her arms and kiss the tears away.

"I do."

The form of Sedi shuddered, and changed. It grew until it towered in silver majesty above Kai's head, terrible, draped in light, eyes dark as night, a blazing giantess. Soft and awful as death, the moon said, "Dare you say so, child of earth?"

Kai swallowed. Her voice remained steady. "I do."

The giantess dissolved into the form of Sedi. She regarded Kai. Her eyes were both sad and amused. "I cannot keep you. For in compelling you to love me I have learned to love you. I can no more coerce you than I can myself. But you must know, Kai Talvela, that much human time has passed since you entered the cave of the Moon. Roko Talvela is dead. Your cousin, Edan, is chief of the Talvelai. Your mother is alive but very old. The very steed that brought you here has long since turned to dust."

"I will walk home," said Kai. And she knew that the old woman of her dream had been her mother, the sorcerer Lia.

Sedi sighed. "You do not have to do that. I love you so well that I will even help you leave me. Clothes I will give you, and armour, and a sword." She gestured. Silk and steel rose up from the earth and wrapped themselves about Kai's waist. The weight of a sword dragged at her belt. A horse trotted to her. It was black, and its eyes were pale. "This steed will bring you to Issho in less than a day."

Kai fingered the hilt of the sword, feeling there the faceted lump of a gem. She pulled it upward to look at it and saw a ruby embedded within it. She lifted off her helmet. A red plume nodded in the wind. She lifted her hands to the smooth skin of her face.

"You have not aged," said Sedi. "Do you wish to see?" A silver mirror appeared in her hands. Kai stared at the image of the warrior woman. She looked the same as the day she left Issho.

She looked at the moon, feeling within her heart for the compulsion that had made her follow Sedi under the sea. She could not feel it. She held out her hands. "Sedi, I love you," she said. They embraced. Kai felt the moon's cold tears on her cheek.

Sedi pressed the mirror into Kai's hands. "Take this. And on the nights when the moon is full, do this." She whispered in Kai's ear.

Kai put the mirror between her breasts and mounted the black horse. "Farewell," she called. Sedi waved. The black horse bugled, and shook its ebony mane, and leaped. When Kai looked back, she could not see the willow. She bowed her head. Her hair whipped her face. Beneath the silent hooves of Night, the earth unrolled like a great brown mat. Kai sighed, remembering the laughter and the loving, and the nightly rides. Never again would she race the wolves across the plains, or watch the dolphins playing in the moonlit sea.

The black horse travelled so fast that Kai had no chance to observe the ways in which the world beneath her had changed. But when it halted, she stared in puzzlement at the place it had brought her. Surely this was not her home? The trees were different. The house was too big. Yet the token of the Talvelai family gleamed on the tall front gate.

Seeing this lone warrior, the Talvela guards came from the gatehouse. "Who are you?" they demanded. "What is your business here?"

"I am Kai Talvela," she said.

They scowled at her. "That is impossible. Kai Talvela disappeared fifty years ago!" And they barred her way to the house.

But she laughed at them; she who had fought and loved the moon. She ripped her sword from its sheath, and it sang in the air with a deadly note. "I am Kai Talvela, and I want to see my mother. I would not suggest that any of you try to stop me." She dismounted. Patting the horse, she said, "Thank you, O swift one. Now return to Sedi." The horse blew in her ear and vanished like smoke. The soldiers of the Talvelai froze in fear.

Kai Talvela found her mother in her bedroom, sitting by the window. She was ancient, tiny, a white-haired wrinkled woman dressed in lavender silk. Kai crossed the room and knelt by her mother's chair. "Mother," she said.

An elderly man, standing at the foot of the bed, opened his mouth to gape. He held a polished wooden flute. "Lady!"

Lia Talvela caressed her daughter's unaged cheek. "I have missed you," she said. "I called and called. Strong was the spell that held you. Where have you been?"

"In the cave of the moon," Kai Talvela said. She put off her helmet, sword, and mail. Curled like a child against her mother's knee, she told the sorcerer everything. The old flute player started to leave the room. A gesture of Lia Talvela's stopped him. When she finished, Kai Talvela lifted her mother's hands to her lips. "I will never leave Issho again," she said.

Lia Talvela stroked her child's hair and said no more. Her hands stilled. When Kai looked up, her mother's eyes had closed. She was dead.

It took a little time before the Talvelai believed that this strange woman was truly Kai Talvela, returned from her journey, no older than the day she left Issho. Edan Talvela was especially loth to believe it. Truthfully, he was somewhat nervous of this fierce young woman. He could not understand why she would not tell them all where she had been for fifty years. "Who is to say she is not enchanted?" he said. But the flute master, who had been the sisters' page, recognized her, and said so steadfastly. Edan Talvela grew less nervous when Kai told him that she had no quarrel with his lordship of the Talvelai. She wished merely to live at peace on the Issho estate. He had a house built for her behind the orchard, near the place of her sisters' and her mother's graves. During the day she sewed and spun, and walked through the orchard. It gave her great pleasure to be able to walk beneath the sun and smell the growing things of earth. In the evening she sat beside her doorway, watching night descend. Sometimes the old musician came to visit with her. He alone knew where she had been for fifty years. His knowledge did not trouble her, for she knew that her mother had trusted him. He played the songs that once she had asked him to play: "The Riddle Song" and other songs of childhood. He had grown to be both courtly and wise, and she liked to talk with him. She grew to be quite fond of him, and she blessed her mother's wisdom.

In the autumn after her return, the old musician caught a cold, and died. The night after his funeral, Kai Talvela wept into her pillow. She loved Issho. But now there was no one to talk to, no one who knew her. The other Talvelai avoided her, and their children scurried from her path as if she were a ghost. Her proper life had been taken away.

For the first time she thought, I should not have come home. I should have stayed with Sedi. The full moon shining through her window seemed to mock her pain.

Suddenly she recalled Sedi's hands cupped around a mirror, and her whispered instructions. Kai ran to her chest and dug beneath the silks. The mirror was still there. Holding it carefully, she took it to the window and positioned it till the moonlight filled its silver face. She said the words Sedi had told her to say. The mirror grew. The moon swelled within it. It grew till it was tall as Kai. Then it trembled, like still water when a pebble strikes it. Out from the ripples of light stepped Sedi. The moon smiled, and held out her arms. "Have you missed me?" she said. They embraced.

That night Kai's bed was warm. But at dawn, Sedi left. "Will you come back?" Kai said.

"I will come when you call me," promised the elemental. Every month on the night of the full moon, Kai held the mirror to the light, and said the words. And every month Sedi returned.

But elementals are fickle, and they are not human, though they may take human shape. One night, Sedi did not come. Kai Talvela waited long hours by the window. Years had passed since her return to Issho. She was no longer the woman of twenty who had emerged like a butterfly from the Moon's cave. Yet she was still beautiful, and her spirit was strong as it had ever been. When at last the sunlight came, she rose from her chair. Picking up the mirror from its place, she broke it over her knee.

It seemed to the Talvelai then that she grew old swiftly, ageing a year in the space of a day. But her back did not bend, nor did her hair whiten. It remained as black as it had been in her youth. The storytellers say that she never spoke to anyone of her journey. But she must have broken silence one time, or else we would not know this story. Perhaps she spoke as she lay dying. She died on the night of the full moon, in spring. At dawn some of her vigour returned, and she insisted that her attendants carry her to the window, and dress her in red silk, and lay her sword across her lap. She wore around her neck a piece of broken mirror on a silver chain. And the tale goes on to say that, as she died, her face brightened to near youthful beauty, and she lifted her arms to the light and cried, "Sedi!"

They buried Kai Talvela beside her mother and her sisters, and then forgot her. Fickleness is also a human trait. But some years later there was war in Issho county. The soldiers of the Talvelai were outnumbered. Doggedly they struggled, as the orchards burned around them. Their enemies backed them as far as the manor gate. It was dusk. They were losing. Suddenly a horn blew, and a woman in bright armour rode from out of nowhere, her mount a black stallion. She swung a shining sword in one fist. "Talvela soldiers, follow me!" she called. At her indomitable manner, the enemy was struck with terror. They dropped their swords and fled into the night. Those soldiers who were closest to the apparition swore that the woman was tall and raven-haired, as the women of the Talvelai are still. They swore also that the sword, as it cut the air, hummed a note so pure that you could almost say it sang.

That was the first appearance of Kai Talvela's shade. Sometimes she comes unarmoured, dressed in red silk, gliding through the halls of the Issho estate. When she comes in this guise, she wears a pendant: a broken mirror on a silver chain. When she appears she brings courage to the Talvelai, and fear to their enemies. In the farms and the cities they call her the Mirror Ghost, because of the mirror pendant and because of her brilliant armor. But the folk of the estate know her by name. She is Kai Talvela, the warrior woman of Issho, who loved and fought the moon, and was loved by her in return.

The daughters of the Talvelai never tire of the story. They ask for it again and again.

The Tale of the Kiss

Emma Donoghue

I know what they say about me: the gulls bring me all the gossip. Knowing what they say about you is the first step to power. Contrary to what you might half believe, I am no monster under my skirts. I grew up in a place much like this one, though half a year away. When I was the age that you are now, I was a girl like you, though not quite as stupid.

There was another difference: my bleeding was meagre, when it came, and by the time the cough carried off my mother, I no longer bled at all. This gave me reason to think about my future. As far as my people were concerned, women like me had no future. I knew what they thought of women past bearing; unless they had sons to honour them and daughters to clean them, they were old rags tossed in the corner. A barren woman was hated even more; the way they saw it, she had never earned a bite of bread.

But I was not going to become an old rag, when every hair I had was still red as a lobster in the pot.

I could of course have lied and smiled, got myself a sturdy husband. The men had started lurking near our door as soon as my mother was taken bad. I could have sunk my nails into one, girded him to me and kept him hoping and cursing year after year, even pointed the finger at some other woman for looking crossways at me and hexing my belly. But I wouldn't stoop to that. So after they buried my mother, I packed up all the herbs in her store and came away.

I found myself a cave on a headland, above a village like this one. It's three months' hard walk from here, but they fish and spin and make up lies just like your folk. The cave had been lived in before; there was an old blanket, and a water bag, and a dip in the floor hollowed by many small fires. I had rock to my back and the sea to my face, driftwood to burn and the odd fish to fry. I had time to wonder now, to unpick the knotted ropes of my thoughts. I could taste freedom like salt on the breeze. There was no one to nurse, no one to feed, no one to listen to but my own self. I thought no one would ever bother me again and I could live out my life like a gull, like a weed, like a drop of water.

What I found instead was power. I never sought it; it was left out for me to stumble over. Only a matter of weeks had gone by before I began to find presents left outside my cave. The first was a clutch of eggs; I thought for a moment some extraordinary chicken had flown up to bring me dinner. Next came a thick slice of meat, wrapped in a cloth to keep the birds off. The villagers left their offerings at first light, before I stirred out of my cave.

I thought such goodness had never been known in the whole world. I thought these were presents freely given to keep a stranger from starving. How was I to know that they were payments in advance?

It was a small boy who gave me the first hint. He threw seaweed into my cave until I came out with a big stick. He screamed when he saw me and ran until he fell over, then got up and ran again.

When he came back the next day, he was braver. He asked, "What happened to the old one?"

"The old what?"

"Witch. Have you got her locked up in her cave or did you boil her in her pot?"

"This is my cave now," I told him sternly. "There's no one here but me."

So it was a witch they were wanting. I laughed to myself, that first day, as the little boy ran down the headland, but soon enough I learned how to be what they needed.

It was not an arduous job. Mostly they left me alone with my herbs and my thoughts, but every few months one of the villagers would creep up the headland after sunset and call out, "Are you there?"

Are you there? the cave would echo back at them.

"Will you help me?" The voice more strangled now, the echo shaking. "I've brought something for you . . ."

And only then, when they were sweating cold as dew, would I emerge, step by slow step, a black scarf over my head to hide the fact of my youth. Not that they ever looked at me properly: they seemed to think my eyes would scald them. They stared at the muddy ground while they poured out their stories of sickness, envy, grief and hunger. I never said a word until they were sobbing.

Sometimes what they needed was simple enough. To the sick, I gave potions that could do them no harm and might make them well if they wanted it enough. To the grieving, I gave words of comfort and a drink to make them sleep. To girls with terrible secrets, I gave herbs to make them whole again.

As for the guilty, spilling their burdens of malice and shame outside my cave, I thought at first that they were asking for forgiveness, but I soon found it made them uncomfortable. Punishment suited them better. They liked me to curse them. May weeds spring up where you walk! May a tail grow in the middle of your chin!

There was a woman who'd never said a kind word to her husband since she woke up the day after her wedding. I flayed her with my tongue until she burst into tears and ran home to make his breakfast. There was a man who'd not slept for ten years for thinking of what he had done to his own daughter. I told him to sell every animal he had to make up her dowry. Once there was a stranger who half smiled as he told me the worst thing he had done in his life, and then something worse than that, and then something even worse. I let him talk all night; I never said a word of judgement. His eyes flickered on my face as he talked, as if searching for something. The sky lightened and I was still watching him. My eyes moved nearer to the cliff edge, and just as the sun was coming up the stranger let himself fall into the pointed waves.

I was a little shaken that day. It was the first time I felt the reach of my power. Power that came not from my own thin body or my own taut mind, but was invested in me by a village.

Power I had to learn how to pick up without getting burnt, how to shape it and conceal it and flaunt it and use it, and when to use it, and when to still my breath and do nothing at all. Power these scaly-fingered fishwives and their wiry husbands could have used themselves, if they'd only known how, but instead they told themselves how helpless they were, and came and laid power at my feet. As well as eggs, of course, and new-baked bread, and even gold coins if I judged that it would take a terrible price to make them believe in their cure.

And so the years passed, leaving little mark on me except the first grey fingerprints on my bright head. When the occasional petitioner came up the headland, I answered their questions with my eyes closed. I preferred the days when I was alone. I could recognize the cry of each kind of bird; they never changed. All that was different about me was that every year my needs were fewer. My bones grew hard as iron. I tried out every herb I found, till nothing could surprise my stomach. I got so used to sleeping on stone that it no longer seemed hard to me. I rolled up in half a dozen blankets and wrapped my arms round my ribs like pet snakes. Nothing touched me in the night except the occasional spider. I was complete.

I should have known. You can't live on a cliff for that long without risking a fall.

One morning a woman climbed up to my cave before dawn. I could hear her feet scrabbling outside. The sun was high in the sky before I rewarded her patience by standing in the entrance. Her narrowed eyes distinguished me from the shadows, and she jerked back.

"You want something," I told her, a little hoarsely; my voice was out of practice.

She looked behind her for her basket.

"I don't fancy butter," I said.

It was a lucky guess. She flinched. "Then what will you have?"

"The truth," I told her.

Her hands fought like crabs. "I have a daughter," she began. "A good strong red-haired daughter, but she is a trouble and a trial to me. Before sunrise, she's roaming the hills. I have a terrible fear she's lovesick. She gets a strange look in her eyes. When we're working I catch her singing songs I've never heard before, and where could she have got them?"

I yawned, to hurry her up.

"If you saw her, you'd understand," the woman went on in a rush. "She's no fool, nor idle; it's only this restlessness. She could be the best of daughters, if she'd only quiet down."

"And her sisters?"

"All gone. This one's my last, you see," said the woman, her voice subsiding. "I'm not getting any younger. I need to know for sure that she'll stay with me."

I turned my face away. "I will consult the oracles," I told her; that always stunned them into silence. "Come back at moonrise on the third day and you will have your answer."

That evening, at sunset, I was sitting in front of my cave, consulting the only oracle I knew, the orange sky, when a man climbed up the headland. He seemed too tired to be afraid. He stood a little distance from me.

"You want something," I said, without moving my head.

"Yes."

"Is that a fresh trout in your hand?"

"It is."

"Toss it over the cliff," I said, just to amuse myself.

He paused a moment before unwrapping it and throwing it towards the setting sun. A gull caught it with an incredulous shriek.

"Out with the truth, now," I said.

His foot dug into the chalky grass. "I have a daughter," he began. "A fine tall red-haired daughter, but she is a trial and a trouble to me. Half the evening, she walks along the beach by moonlight. She gathers seashells like a little child. There's a friend of mine has an eye for her, but whenever he comes courting she's behind her mother's skirts in the kitchen. I have a terrible fear she'll end up an old maid."

My eyes were wandering.

"If you saw her, you'd understand," he went on furiously. "She's no fright, nor feared of men; it's only this restlessness.

She'd make my friend a fine wife, if she'd only settle down, and then he says he'd give me half shares in his big boat."

"Why not one of her sisters?"

"All married. This one's my last, you see," said the man, his voice beginning to crackle. "I'm not getting any younger. I need to know for sure that she'll do what I say."

I stared at the soundless gulls. "I will consult the oracles," I told him. "Come back at moonset on the third day and you will have your answer."

The next morning I woke with my head full of scrag-ends of dreams. I doused it in sea water. Today I would need all my wits. Between the mother and the father, I had to pick my way carefully. I knew what happened to meddlers who came between man and wife. I knew there were some in the village below who, after strong liquor, talked of blocking up my cave in the night.

By midday rain had covered the headland. I sat in my cave, trying to persuade my little fire to stay alight. At least bad weather kept me private, shielded me from the village below with all its wearisome tribulations.

Or so I thought, until she appeared in the mouth of my cave, between curtains of rain, the girl herself, unmistakable, her blood-red hair glued to her wet throat.

It was the first time in all those years that I let another human being step across the threshold. I even lent her a blanket to stop the shivering. To make up for this softness, I unsheathed the blade of my tongue. "If you're the girl I think you are," I began, staring into the struggling fire, "I hear you're nothing but trouble."

She nodded as if I had remarked on the weather, and continued combing out the red ropes of her hair with a bit of old comb I'd found her.

"You're not child enough for your mother nor woman enough for your father. You don't work or play or think as they would have you work and play and think."

She smiled at me with teeth like quartz.

"What are you good at?"

"I don't know yet," said the girl, staring into the fire. Faint steam was rising from her.

"What is it you want?"

"Nothing," she said, half laughing.

"There is no creature under the sky that does not want," I told her severely.

"Only what I've got, then," she said.

"That's lucky."

"And time to think about what I want next."

I nodded judiciously.

"And time to just think."

"There's plenty of that up here," I remarked.

She stared round the cave. "There must be all the time in the world here," she said wonderingly.

My heart was beginning to thud.

"And time to not think, I need that too," she added.

I had one more question. "What do you love?"

She took a deep breath, as if her list was long, then she let it out in a sigh. "Everything," she said.

"Everything?" My voice was a squeaking bat. "How can you love everything before you know anything, you idiotic girl?"

"I don't know," she said seriously. "It seems to leak out of me. It's like a cup spilling over." She turned to look into my eyes; they narrowed against her. "How can you not?" she asked.

"What?"

"You're wise. You're the witch. How can you look at everything and know everything without love?"

My heart was pulling on my ribs. "Go now," I said. "The rain's eased."

She turned her open face to me. "But will –"

"Girls like you always get what they want."

Her full-throated laugh filled the cave for several minutes after she'd gone.

That night, I didn't sleep at all. The blankets were heavy with damp; the wind seemed to whine at the cave mouth. No matter which way I lay, stones poked me awake.

If I took a fever and lay tossing here till I died, I realized, no one would ever know. The villagers would still leave the odd bit of food outside, but it would be eaten clean by the birds. Only the wind would hear their petitions, and perhaps its answers would be wiser than mine.

Before the sun rose, I hauled myself up off the floor. As long as I had my health, the power was mine. I threw rosemary on the fire and breathed in its clarifying air. By moonrise, I had concocted my answers. To the mother I said: "The oracles tell me that because of your own faults, a terrible curse has been visited upon your daughter. If you ever order her to stay at home with you, she will turn into a hare and run off up the mountain."

Dumbstruck inside her shawl, the woman whispered, "Is there any cure for this curse?"

"Only time will wear it out," I told her.

I would take no payment. I watched her scurry down the headland. I sat there as the moon tracked its way across the sky and began to fall.

To the father I said: "The oracles tell me that because of your own sins, a dreadful fate has fallen upon your daughter. If you ever order her to marry, her husband will turn into a wolf and devour her on their wedding night."

Flinching from the words, the father said, "Is there any way of lifting this fate?"

"Only time will tell," I told him.

I would take no payment. I watched him stride home. And then all was quiet. I told myself that the job was well done.

Over the next few days I went about my business, but something was wrong. Everything I cooked tasted bitter. My daily tasks seemed long, and yet when I sat by the fire to rest in the evenings, the time hung heavy on my hands. I could make no sense of what the gulls were saying.

The girl came back one day. I hadn't realized it was her I was waiting for. I almost wished it was raining again. In sunlight she glowed as if her hair had caught fire. I stood in the mouth of my cave, and all at once I couldn't think of anything to say.

She put down her basket and crossed her arms a little nervously. "I wish I knew where you get your power," she remarked. "This past week my mother and father have let me work, sleep and wander as I please. They make no complaint or prediction, cast neither my past nor my future in my face."

I allowed a small smile to twist my mouth.

"Have you put them under a spell?" she asked.

"An easy one; you could learn it yourself."

She remembered her basket. "I brought you something."

"No need."

"It's only butter. I made it myself."

"I don't want butter. It gives me a rash," I said, the lie coming easily to my lips.

"What'll you have, then?" she said. "Because I owe you."

"A kiss."

I think I asked it just to shame her. I would have liked to see that calm face furrow up for a moment. But the girl laughed.

Anger began to clamp my teeth shut.

Her laugh rippled on. "Is that all?" she asked. "Why are they all so afraid of you, when your price is so easy to pay?"

Even then I didn't believe she would do it. Kissing a witch is a perilous business. Everybody knows it's ten times as dangerous as letting her touch your hand, or cut your hair, or steal your shoes. What simpler way is there than a kiss to give power a way into your heart?

She stepped up to me and her hair swung around us like a veil.

It was a bad idea, that kiss I asked for. Not that it did the girl any harm. She walked off across the hills as if she had just embraced a cat or a sparrow. Once she looked behind her and waved.

On the whole, I am inclined to think that a witch should not kiss. Perhaps it is the not being kissed that makes her a witch; perhaps the source of her power is the breath of loneliness around her. She who takes a kiss can also die of it, can wake into something unimaginable, having turned herself into some new species.

Days passed, somehow. There was a long red hair on my shawl that was too bright to be mine. I tried to get on with my life. I did all the same things I had done day by day for years on end, but I couldn't remember why I had ever done them, or indeed what had brought me here to live alone in a cave like a wild animal. I tried not to think about all that. I tried not to think.

I woke one night. The moon was full, filling the mouth of the cave. All at once I knew I needed that girl like meat needs salt.

What could I do? Could I bring myself to follow her down into the village? Could I lower myself so far, to let the little children throw sand at me? Would she be gone away by the time I came down? Would they tell me where she had gone? Would I be able to find her?

And if I did, I swore to myself, swore on the perfect disc of the moon, then I would not let pride stop up my mouth. I would ask her to come live in my cave and learn all I knew and teach me all I didn't. I would give her my heart in a bag and let her do with it what she pleased. I would say the word love.

And what happened next, you ask? Never you mind. There are some tales not for telling, whether because they are too long, too precious, too laughable, too painful, too easy to need telling or too hard to explain. After all, after years and travels, my secrets are all I have left to chew on in the night.

This is the story you asked for. I leave it in your mouth.

The Burning Times

Sara Maitland

"All witchcraft comes from carnal lust which is in women insatiable."

> Kramer and Sprenger, *Malleus Malificarum*, 1486.

In the long evenings of winter the house becomes intolerable. It is too close, too smoky and too full of them, my men, my husband and my sons. Their limbs seem immense; once I looked at one of the boy's legs, spreading out it seemed suddenly half across the room, and I thought that they were once folded up and inside me, and I felt sick. When I start having thoughts like this, I have to go out.

Usually I walk to the church. Tonight it is cold going through the village, with evil little winds that turn and bite at my ankles. But the cold makes precise every surface of my skin, so I can feel the edges, the limits of my body and so be alone.

Inside the church it is still. The huge rood, the suffering, broken Jesus suspended high over the chancel steps is lost in the dark, his agony mercifully not visible. There are, though, two sources of light. Far away, high on the altar the light in front of the tabernacle flickers; he is always there, watching, waiting, listening, and we cannot get away from him. Down here, much nearer, is the Virgin, the lady crowned with the sun, aglow with the light from the candles lit by women like me. I kneel beneath her feet. "Mother, mother, Holy Mary Mother of God, help me, please, mother." But as I say the words the tears come, and when I look up at her through the tears and through the candle flames, she seems to be on fire, the flames licking round her bare feet. She is burning, smiling, burning and I scream.

Aloud. Dear mother, let no one have heard. But she will not listen to my prayers, because I burned my own mother. I betrayed her and they burned her and I danced around her pyre. She saw me and she understood and she forgave me. So I cannot forgive myself.

And I cannot confess this sin, because they will burn me too. They will torture and break me as they did her. Then they will burn me.

The church is empty, this time. There are only her and me here. Mother and daughter. Like before.

The statue of the Virgin is in painted wood. She holds her son somewhat clumsily I feel, having held three of my own. A chance lurch of that serene head and he will fall out of her arms; she should bring him lower so that he straddles her hip, as my mother-in-law showed me, as every mother learns. I try to concentrate on that, on the dangerous way in which she is holding the Son of God; and how easy it is for a child to fall out of even the most loving arms. But the scream does not go away, and while apparently locked in prayer I am crying and remembering.

It was a long way south of here, in an altogether pleasanter valley. Afterwards I came north. My old parish priest helped me find a new place; I worked for his friend, who is priest here, at first. It seemed like a sensible idea. Of course, no one knew what I had done, but probably they would have been pleased even if they had. But our parish priest wanted me to come away because the daughter of a witch is always in danger. In a small village, they remember well. The next time it can be you.

I do not want to remember these things; nor do I want to remember the smoke-filled cottage, those enormous and demanding men, and the sense of being always a stranger in a strange land. There is very little in my life that I want to remember, but though I concentrate on the precariously balanced child and the repeated chain of prayers, I cannot forget that I thought she was burning, I thought I saw the flames of the bonfire and I thought that her eyes were my mother's eyes.

I used sometimes to try and justify what I did to her. What she did was an abomination to the Lord God. It was the final sin – so dreadful that it was not even named in church, where every sin imaginable and unimaginable was named. So grave a sin that I did not even know it was a sin. God would have wanted her burned. But I do not justify myself any more, because even if that were true, it was not why I did it, not for the greater glory of God. No, not at all.

I blot it out, you see, but it comes back. It comes back when I least expect it, when I think I am safe, like here praying in church, most piously, and I look up and I see the flames and my own mother burning.

She often seemed on fire, my mother. There was something wild in her. She laughed at everyone and at herself. Her hair was a great mass of tangled curls, and she would not smooth them down. She was a widow woman, they said, though as a child I heard other things, as children will. She did not come from that village, but from another further west, towards the mountains. She never spoke of her childhood, or of what and where she had been before. She was a lace-maker; a very skilful lace-maker, and she loved the work. Our cottage was not kept very clean; she was not interested in that, my mother – not like me, who wrestles with the smoke and the long muddy legs and the tight cluttered space to keep my home clean, who stays up through the night, despite my husband's calling me to bed, to shine and polish and scrub. I need the house to be clean and orderly, but not my mother, who picked up pretty things like a child and left them around to grow dusty and muddled. There was just one corner of the room that was clean and that was where her work was kept: her lace pillow with its hundreds of tiny pins bright as jewels and around them the flax threads bleached white and tied into knots that were spiders' webs and flowers and wreaths and pictures that grew magically out of nowhere; hanging down from the pillow were the bright nuts and shining stones and polished bone bobbins. A beautiful thing, a well-used lace-pillow is, and she was far the best lace-maker I have ever known. Up here they do not make much lace; one of the few things I brought with me, because I knew she would hate it to be lost, was the veil she made me for my first communion. It was the envy of the village, with the sacred host and roses and apple blossom and little violets. Perhaps it was the beginning of our troubles, for it was then that people began to say that it was not right that a poor widow woman, if she was a widow woman indeed, should flaunt her daughter in lace like a lady's in front of the whole village. The women did not like her because she did not care what they said and seldom gossiped with them. Some evenings men would come round to our cottage, wanting either to kiss her or to marry her and take her lovely lace-pillow and the money she earned home to their own houses. But she would have none of that, but would laugh at them to their faces. The men did not like her, either, because she laughed at them and did not care.

To make lace you have to have very good light; so that she did not work for many hours of the day, though there was spinning and washing and flax-gathering, of course, but as I grew older I did much of that. But when she was not working, in the early morning and the dusks, we would go out singing through the fields, and the people thought that wanton, because they had to work those fields daily. Now I know what hard work it is to be a farming family, but then of course I did not, I knew only that we went singing and laughing while others worked and grumbled.

She could tell stories, my mother. I remember that. When I tried to tell them to my sons, they came out lumpish and heavy. I do not know where I went wrong, except that for her they were a joy to tell. She told them for her own joy and for mine if I wanted to share hers, whereas I told them to hush the boys when I could stand their bawling no longer; it is probably different to tell them in joyful love. Sometimes when I was small and she was telling stories, the other children would come and listen too, and on sunny evenings between hay-making and harvest even the grownup folk would come and she would sing and tell stories. They would even forget for a while that they did not like her, because they liked her stories so well.

Perhaps I make her sound like a soft and easy woman. She was not. She was all I have said, but hard and fierce too. By the time I was about eight, I was spinning for her and she would not tolerate even the tiniest flaw in the threads; she said it was an insult to her, to the work and to me myself. Spinning flax hurts your fingers, not like spinning wool, which I do now easily and without thought, as I go about my work. I have never spun flax since she . . . died.

In my own head I come to it with such reluctance, so slowly. Only the thought of how close and loud it will be in the cottage, and how one of them will be wanting something of me, keeps me here at all. They cannot interrupt prayer. It is the only place for peace. But here, beneath the feet of the Mother, I cannot help remembering and all the memories pull towards the same point, the leaping of the flames and me dancing. "Dance, for God's sake, dance," said the old parish priest, who I think meant well by us always, "dance and smile or they will burn you too." He did not know what I had done, but I think that he held my mother in true respect; protecting me as best he could was for her. And "dance", he urged me with his eyes and his hand, the one on the furthest side from them. I looked at my mother and all the heat and hate was gone and I knew that she knew and understood and wanted me to dance and smile and not be burned.

I was coming to woman-years. When we swam in the pools of the stream, my mother would tease my new body, not harshly, with affection, but children of that age should not be teased. Even my sons I protected from their father's teasing and from each other's at that age. My mother and I were together all the time. Because the village was unsure about her, because she did not belong to them, they were unsure of me too. So I was cut off a little, slightly distant and did not have a friend. But I did not think this either a need or a loss because I had her, my mother, and she made me happy.

Then Margaret came. She trudged into the village along the road from the West, carrying a sack over her shoulder. They say she paused in the village square and sniffed the air like a dog. They say she turned three circles and marked the ground with her left foot. They say she stared at old Simon with her right eye closed. But this was afterwards, when they would have said anything. And, after all, she went to the priest's house and knocked politely on the door, and he came out to her and spoke civilly with her, everyone agrees. So directed, it seems fair to assume by him and not by any other power, she walked back across the square, right through the shadow of the church tower and came down the lane to our home. It was a warm late summer afternoon, and my mother sat at the doorway to work in the soft sunshine, and her hands were like butterflies on her lace-pillow. I was beside the cottage, turning the drying flax, and we were singing together as we so often did. And quite suddenly my mother's singing stopped and she gave a little shriek. When I turned round, there was her lace-pillow rolling in the earth, the threads unwinding, the bobbins tangling with each other and the pins bent crooked in the dirty soiled lace. My mother was running up the lane and embracing a strange woman.

They came back to the cottage together, their arms around each other, and together they went into the house. Silenced, I gathered up the lace-pillow, tried to sort out the muddle and then, slowly, I followed them into the cottage. They were standing there, quite quiet, not talking, their hands on each other's shoulders and smiling. I was forgotten.

I stood in the doorway, uneasy. They turned at last, my mother with her eyes all wild and shiny and Margaret, a friend they said from my mother's homeplace and childhood. Margaret pulled back her hood and the curious reddish curls that grew quite short on her forehead sprang up uncontrolled, as they always did. She smiled at me with a sweetness like sunshine, and my confusion began.

Here in the hushed church, the cold and quiet of it, I truly cannot remember the wildness of those few months. It is this cold stillness that I want now, not that mad, fevered, triumphant, terrible time. My mother made no lace, but was up at dawn and singing, singing. She made me do my work, but never paid me any attention. Or so it seemed to me. The harvest time came and I, as every year, went out as hired help in exchange for the grain we did not grow ourselves. I hated to go out in the pale light of the morning leaving them together, but I did not know what it was I hated. I wanted my mother back, but that was not all because Margaret ... oh Margaret, Margaret. The joy, the delight of her for me then. She had high round breasts and between them a valley deep and filled with promises I did not even guess at. She was not like my mother and I, small quick women; she was tall, big, but not heavy with it; when she walked, and especially when she used a broom, I would watch the rhythm of her whole body and not know what it was that seemed so perfectly pleasing. She would sing with my mother and my own singing seemed childish squeaking. She would pick up the little pretty things that my mother would bring into the house, flowers, stones, old feathers, and just by her calm looking would transform them from pretty into beautiful. I wanted her to go away and leave us in our old closeness and comfort. I wanted her to stay, to stay near me. During the day, I would follow her like a puppy-dog and she treated me like one too with casual pats and tender gestures, but laughing and happy to have me amuse her. At night the big bed seemed too small for the three of us; if my leg touched hers, or even her ruckled night-shift, I would be instantly awake and aware of every inch of my skin; and yet I did not know why this was or if it was something I liked or hated. I stopped sleeping in the big bed, creeping out to lie by the hearth, but I slept no better there, straining through the night to hear her every movement, fearful and excited. She and my mother shared a secret joke that made them laugh and it drove me crazy that I did not know what it was.

So I ached and dozed and giggled and sulked and longed with longings that I had no name for. I thought they treated me like a child when I was not one. I yearned to be a child, to climb into their laps, either or both their laps, and be fondled and patted and stroked as children are. When we swam together, I would watch my mother covertly, wanting her not to touch Margaret's wet, smooth body. Wanting Margaret not to follow my mother's fishlike swiftness with her eyes, wanting them both to look at me. But if they did, I was ashamed of my own body which seemed ugly, gawky, childish, but which was disturbing my sleep and confusing my heart. But it was not a sad time, it was golden and laughing and joyful and I was confused.

After the harvest, the lace-man came, as always. He would buy my mother's lace, and look at the work of other lace makers in the district. The prices were agreed between her and the lace-man in the presence of the parish priest, and usually my mother would come home with a glow of pride and pleasure. The lace-man would bring with him news from the world outside the village and my mother would be full of new stories and good humour. But this time my mother came back from the selling looking anxious. I thought it was because she had not done much work since Margaret came, but it was not that. She had got a good price for what she had done and had been asked for more. I pretended to sleep because I knew that my mother and Margaret would talk; I shut my eyes and lay and listened.

The Inquisitors were coming again.

They had not been to our village in my lifetime. I thought like a child that it sounded exciting, with bonfires and savage hunt-ing, to the glory of Jesus Christ. I peeked through slitted eyes, waiting for more.

But my mother and Margaret looked like old women, hunched over the fire muttering, made small by the darkness and shadows, diminished by fear.

"We can go," said Margaret.

"Not again," said my mother, "not again, I can't bear it."

"I'll go," said Margaret, and I wanted to cry out and stop her. "You'll be alright if I go."

"I don't know, I don't know."

I shut my eyes. I did not want to see. My mother plaintive, defeated, afraid.

The days afterwards seemed darkened. Margaret did not go. She did not speak of going again, but some light had gone out of them both, and out of me. I wanted them to tell me what was happening. I wanted them to notice how their shadow had fallen on me, but they looked always at each other and with stricken eyes. I wanted to make them safe and smiling again and I could not.

The Inquisitors came. We were all summoned to Mass and a beautiful man with a white and passionate face preached to us of the dangers of hell and the perils of witchcraft, pleading with us to give up our witches, purify our community, glorify the Lord Jesus, and give the angels new tongues of praise. I remember thinking that I wished I knew a witch so that I could hand her over to him and be blessed with his smile and God's joy. And after the Mass, we had a feast for our Lord Bishop's Inquisitors, who gave up their safe city lives for our protection, and who took to the dangerous highways in order to drive out the forces of Satan. It was a good feast and when Margaret and my mother went home I stayed in the square.

There was a small bonfire, and we danced around it, the young people of the village, excited by the sermon we had heard, and by the presence of strangers. At first, I did not notice that something was different. Then I felt it; when I went to speak to groups of chatting people, people I had known all my life, they moved away. There was a silence where I came and it alarmed me. Then the parish priest came and took my hand and talked with me, and I thought the whole village was listening to us, and the rich clerics on their dais as well. The priest talked strangely, loudly, and with unusual affection. And suddenly I was very afraid.

When he let me go, I turned to leave the square because I wanted now to be home. The people parted for me to walk past, and when I reached the corner where our lane came out into the square I heard a disembodied voice, no one's voice, call out "Devil's brat", and I ran.

I ran down the lane, frightened. I ran down the lane as fast as I could because I wanted my mother. I ran into the house seeking her arms. My mother was lying on our bed with Margaret and they had no clothes on and their legs, bodies, arms, faces were entangled with each other in movement, intense and intensely beautiful. When I saw Margaret's buttocks in the light from the doorway, saw them lift and plunge, saw my mother's strong small butterfly hand reach across them, spread out, holding her, then I knew what I had longed for. When I heard my mother moan softly, I knew what I had wanted. I wanted to touch Margaret like that. I wanted to moan like that. I had wanted and known for months without knowing what I wanted. I crouched down, clasping my own stomach in a craziness of desire. I watched them to the glorious end, Margaret triumphant kneeling over my mother, and my mother moaning and laughing, legs kicking free and abandoned, and her arms reaching up round Margaret's neck to pull her proud head down onto the breasts where I thought only I had ever lain. They had stolen this from me. Margaret had stolen my mother from me, my mother had stolen Margaret from me. Under my very eyes, laughing at me, in the face of my longing which they had laughed at. Or had not laughed at because they had not noticed, in the heat of their love for each other. On hands and knees, I crept away from the door out into the lane, and they, wrapped in their own beauty and passion, did not even hear my coming and going.

I lay for a while curled up, reaching with my own fingers as they had reached for each other, not sure what I was looking for and finding it and hating it and loving it and hating them and hating them and hating them.

Then I got up, hating myself for that lust, hating them for raising it in me, and I smoothed down my skirts and arranged my snarling hatred into a modest smile, and I walked back up the lane, burning, burning with the sight of their excitement and my exclusion from it. I walked across the square and the fiddler stopped playing and then in the silence, before all the people, I denounced my mother for a witch.

The white-faced Inquisitor said I was a good girl.

When they went to hunt them up out of the cottage, Margaret was gone. So they had to make do with just my mother.

They burned her.

They tortured her too and raped her and broke her. Through the next two nights, we could hear her screaming. And I was afraid. I was afraid that she would denounce me, and I would burn. I was afraid that she would not and I would have to live. When they brought her out at last, you could see what they had done to her. She told them that she and Margaret flew out the window at night and fucked with the Devil. She said that she and Margaret kissed the Devil's anus, and that they used his excrement to make men impotent. She said that Margaret had been made invisible by spells to escape her just punishment. She even said that the Devil made her lace for her, a web to catch Christian souls and that she transfixed the souls with her pins and weighted them down with her bobbins, the souls of babies who had just been baptized, that all her lace-making was a glamour and illusion. At the end she could not stand up, but she would not denounce me, though they wanted her to. She said I was innocent. And when they lit the fire and flames leapt up and our parish priest told me to dance and I danced, she smiled at me. She kept smilling at me until she started screaming. Only two people were smiling, though the village square was full: my mother and the chief Inquisitor, whose pale face was glowing with a radiant joy.

That time they burned three other women too, from the district. I did not know them, I did not smile. I had betrayed my mother, because my evil desires had betrayed me. But on the bed, my mother's hand on Margaret's buttock, reaching across, fingers spread out, that had not been evil. It had been beautiful.

Nothing else in my life has been beautiful. The parish priest arranged for me to come here. Afterwards I had a strange time and I could not look at fires. He was worried that they would come back for me. So I came here and I worked for his friend until my husband wanted to marry me. He is a good straightforward man, well respected. It seemed the safest thing to do; it seemed like a safe place, as far as possible from all flames. He does not worry about my occasional nightmares. He never asks any questions. So long as I do all my duties, I do not think he cares.

I have three sons, but I am glad I have no daughters. I might have loved a daughter.

They say it is better to marry than to burn, but only just I think, only just.

The Catherine Trilogy

Ingrid MacDonald

Part I – Catherine, Catherine

Being the last and accurate confession
of Catherine Margarethe Linck
alias Cornelius Caspar Brewer
alias Peter Lagrantinius
alias Anastasius Rosenstengel
convicted of sodomy, desertion, multiple baptisms
and many other serious crimes
in Halberstadt, Prussia,
the year of our Lord 1721

I fester in this prison, waiting for God to tell his mercy to me and show me the way to escape this condemnation. The magistrate wants to put me to death for all I have done to undo the womanly nature of me, and I have begged him not to, for I have done nothing that cannot be fully forgiven.

From my birth, I have rebelled against my flesh and wanted to live as a man, for a woman is forever spoken to by life and forever forbidden to respond, but the magistrate has no sympathy for me. He has forgotten me here, a wretched creature with eleven steps from the piss-pot to the locked door to the pallet bed, and my feet are cold as clay inside boots, and my arms as thin as whipping canes.

I was born to a peasant family in Gehowen in 1694 and we ate heavy bread every day. The bread was barely enough and I waited for something to happen that might change my circumstance, all the while watching my beloved mother carry stones and grow crops, humiliated by the dryness of the unyielding earth. I saw how my life would emulate hers, with its meagre harvest, and how sorrow would echo through my face into the faces of my children.

I remained chaste, working beside my mother in the fields and sitting near her feet at night. The day my mensus first made a stain between my legs, I hid my face in my mother's skirt and poured out all the grief in my heart, for I longed for heaven to swallow me and take away my womanness and spit me back out on the earth, spit me out even as the lowliest man in Prussia, for there is more freedom in a wretched man's life than there is in the entire lives of five strong women.

"I shall find a kind husband for you," my mother said.

Unconsoled, I told her how the fanciest woman I know, Mrs Krauter, the Lutheran wife of the burgher, must lower her eyes and keep them set upon the shoes of her husband's feet.

"Be careful which wish you wish," my mother sighed and said, "it might come true."

That October, a big white tent appeared in the first field east of the village and the Prussian flag flew from a tall pole. The news that recruiting officers had come to call men to serve Frederick William our king spread through the whole county, and my father and several other men who worked the fields and wanted to make the harvest ran into the woods and hid.

Frans Erbst who played the organ maimed one of his eyes and Hans Fruling who had just married put an axe through his foot, so as to seem unable. Max Kunst our neighbour offered a bribe so large it ruined his whole family of everything they owned, and even then the officers saw fit to take the money out of fingers they had bent back and broken.

Only I wanted to give myself to the military's wooden table inside the white tent and longed to wear the buttons of a Prussian soldier's coat and knew those would belong to me if I had a man's name and a set of men's clothes to enlist in. I begged my mother for something to wear, and she slapped my face, so certain she was that the recruiters would kill me the instant they saw me. But I argued with her that I was tall and could style my hair and lower my voice and convince them to take me. We fought all night in bitter tears. In the morning, there was a set of clothes laid out for me, and I bound my breasts and stood tall, and the men at the table in the tent hardly looked up at me. There was no uniform either, and I began my career with a long and irksome march north, frozen and stiff at night by my freedom and following the barking voice of an officer who spared no cruelty when he told us where to stand and where to sleep and not to speak and not to think.

Soon I carried a musket, was given a buttoned jacket and knew my commands, practising and drilling but never seeing any battles, for an army was what the king wanted all of Prussia to become for the sake of his fancy. Sixty battalions of infantry and one hundred cavalry squadrons and sixty thousand garrison troops were recruited from the fields and yet there was not a single battle to fight. My life drained from me like an untilled field and grew sluggish with shouted commands, constant drills, the threat of punishment, the mouldy bread and the wet ground that served often as our bed. I served Frederick William for three years, when a letter came telling me my mother was gravely ill.

Wearing my buttoned jacket, I went to my captain's tent and begged to be set free. He looked up from a lighted table full of maps and explained how I could not go free, as the king wholly owned me.

"Then give me a leave to see my dying mother," I said.

"I know your type," he said. "If I let you go, you'll never come back."

"Please, sir," I said.

And he said, "Stop asking now or I'll have you disciplined."

I was so angry that night. I left my buttoned jacket on the ground and stole away from the troops and took to the forest and ran, all the while jabbing my palms with brambles and thistles, and didn't stop running until I could lean down and wash my eyes in the waters of the Rhine.

I walked along the banks and saw a ship at mooring. Not far away, underneath a windmill, sat a red-eyed merchant marine. He was very drunk and welcomed me with a fierce grip of his hand on my arm. I asked for some drink and, as I can tell quite a tale if there's something strong under my tongue, I passed myself as a sailor to him and told him of my mother and asked if he were southward bound on the river. He grew fond of me and invited me along. At dawn, I went to board the *Maria Magdalena,* the mist covering her seven sails. I held my arms open for her to carry me south to my mother. But there, on the wooden dock, was the Eighteenth Infantry Unit of Frederick William's military garrison, waiting for me, full uniforms, muskets cocked.

I was flogged and would have been killed that day, had I not begged for confession with a Catholic priest. I wanted mercy for my soul, for the sake of my dying mother's peace. The ancient priest held my hand gravely. "Concern yourself now with your soul, my boy, and forswear the corruption of the flesh." I poured my heart to him and told him my true nature, but he only shook his head. "It is not for a country priest to oppose the will of Frederick William," he said, leading me to the noose.

For the sake of my mother, I begged him to tell the regiment command of my nature, but he refused, shaking his sad head. When the noose was lowered onto my neck and I began to weep unrestrained tears, I saw the priest whisper to the presiding captain, and then they argued between them for a minute until the captain called halt. The captain took the hangman aside, who in turn took his hood off and gripped my face in his giant hands, crushing my cheeks, certain he was being tricked out of his day's work.

In the end I walked away free, though fiercely abused and forced in the clothes of a woman by the captain and assigned papers naming me Maria Schmidt. The captain invented this name when I refused to call myself by any name other than Anastasius Rosenstengel, the name I enlisted under. The hateful clothes of Maria Schmidt I wore all the way back to the village where I was born, only to have the neighbours point me towards the city, where my mother had gone to hospital. Then I wore those clothes into Halle.

Halle was a city of twenty thousand people, one gate, a fever epidemic, and a maze of narrow lanes eternally criss-crossing.

The laneways wandered and turned like the wedges on a sundial that shift as the day lengthens. I asked at the shrine of the virgin, at the apothecary, at the water well, at the buttermarket, and then again, always moving inward on a spiral, I asked at the miller, at the butcher, at the weavers, coming into a place where I saw fewer and fewer persons in the streets until at last there were no people, only a tiny wooden door that held the sign of the Jesuit hospital.

Drying plant-stalks hung between windows in the narrow lane. A thin cat brushed against the back of my legs. The sound of my knocking and the door opening.

"You can't come in!" A monk opened the door slightly and held it shut. He resisted me with all his might and would have kept me out, if his arms hadn't collapsed. His eyes rolled upwards as he fell to the floor. His arms were ragged as hemp, red pocks marked his body, his lips were cracked dry, and his skin was yellow as wax.

I called my mother's name and followed a faint reply, past empty beds and up a ladder. My heart welled with sorrow when I saw her, for she was the last being left alive, and even then she was barely a cadaver with a small bit of voice in her. Her long hair had fallen out in clumps, making a nest around her. Her teeth were gone, the skin covering her nose had rotted away, and her eyes seemed not to recognize me.

"Do you know who I am?" I asked. The yellow smoke of fire smouldered in one corner.

"I knew you would come one day."

"You need to drink water." I lifted a bucket, only to hear hammers striking upon the door. I ran to the shuttered window and saw a physician in his heavy cloak, wearing a full headed mask, the head of a bird with glass beads for eyes, hammering nails into the door, locking it shut. The monk lay at his feet, his face covered by a black cloth.

My mother's soul must have known what the terrible hammering meant, for she fell dead in that moment. With smoke smudging my eyes, I wept. I longed to tell my mother so many things, of my soldier's life and the ways of the king who loved a military more than gold but hated weakness more than death.

Now death nailed her ears shut and left me alive inside. I cried out to God, for I had tried to live my life chastely and honour my mother and had met only shame and hardship.

Through the yellow smoke, an angel appeared to me and took my hand and showed me a cupboard with the clothes of men who once took beds in this hospital, and I put breeches and a jacket and a hat upon my person. They were poor clothes but amounted to as much of a man's dress as I needed to conceal my nature from the eyes of men. Then I took a sheet and lifted my mother. She was skin and bones, small as an unnurtured bird that has fallen from a nest. I took the leg of a chair and held it in the fire until it grew bright as a flaming pillar, and I set it upon the wooden door and let the fire open the door with its red hands.

It was night by then and I waited at a bridge until a man came with a cart. I asked him to take us to the burying acre. On the acre I lowered my mother gently into a newly dug part of the ground and settled with the driver of the cart. He was a nervous fellow who held a rag up to his nose against the stench, and I gave him a little piece of metal my mother carried in her purse. It wasn't a coin, but it might be worth something. So many citizens had died from the fever, the ground was a fierce sight, churned and steaming, like when the butcher throws a pail of offal into the ditch. I waved goodbye to the cart driver, though I did not know him at all, but there was no one left I wanted to say goodbye to.

I walked in the direction south, away from the city of Halle, leaving behind its encircling streets and hammered shut doors and the swarm of its fever that sets upon the body like wasps into a grey paper nest. At daybreak I ladled water from a trough for my thirst and looked back towards the acre. I imagined how each corpse was a brick and how so many bricks make a wall and how so many walls make a pavilion and how a great pavilion is being built underground, a huge fantastic building where half of the kingdom, and she who was all my family, now live. I was thinking of something else, but I couldn't remember what that was, oh yes, a name. The name, the right new name for myself.

★   ★   ★

Nightfall had come on by the time I had walked through seven villages in the clothes of a man, and I was ailing with hunger for I had taken but a mouthful of alesop in the midday. I feared the thought of going to houses abegging. It is known how hostile men are to strangers, especially if they suspect you've come from the cities, for they have it they will catch sickness from the mere sight of us. Afar in a field, I saw the lamps of ramblers and reckoned they'd be kinder than settled folk and went to ask for comfort from them even if it would be only to sleep near them and not be afeared of the night.

Coming near them, I found them not ramblers at all but a group of religious inspirants. They parleyed among themselves with great vigour about the intentions of God and the defiant ways of men. Chief among them was a woman with one black tooth, and she gave me first a stew of boiled roots and a rasher of pig and then a learning in the spiritual way.

She told me her name was Eva and asked me mine. "I have no name at all, for what is it to be named by those who never saw thee as thyself," I said. Eva thought there was wisdom in that and declared that I should have a new name, but first she concerned herself with the more urgent task of purifying me and described how she saw in me a multitude of demons that must be banished.

Thus she learned me the utterances of holy words spoke directly to God himself without the nuisance of the priest in between. Just as if God sat in the chair near yours was how I learned to speak. Although I could not discern whether this religion or bewitching be, on account of my soul's salvation I followed her ways and most powerfully her blessing appeared to me.

She asked me if I could be holy and freed my ears to hear by blessing them and speaking many things to me. I learnt a prayer spontaneously, and Eva took me away from the others, to the middle of the harvested oat field, and there among the stubble and stem she lifted up her kirtle and peed into a small cup and took the warm yellow drink and blessed me by pouring it into my hair. "Out, out all besetting demons," she called afore me and then gave me the name by which she always called me, Peter of Lagrantinius, for we were near the village of Langrantus.

My tongue was freed for prophecy, and I travelled with these inspirants by day and slept on the blanket beside Eva at night. I pined for her and might have touched her sweetly but she laughed at my every approach, saying she was abstinent for the sake of the spirit, and I should be as well. The deeper my religion went, the harsher my love for her felt, and I often gave myself the bittermost penances, wearing nothing but a coarse blanket and ashes for the sake of her love. I gladly starved my flesh for Eva's distant eyes and secretly took blood from my arm and drank it through a sieve made of her hair, in the hope of gaining her heart.

Our work as prophets in the world was not easy. Coming into towns and hamlets, we met with hostility; the folk were routinely savage and called us scourge. Yet among the people there were those blessed by the spirit, hungry for our news, and my task was to seek these out. I had a gift for seeing angels perched on the shoulders of several men or women in a crowd, and I would choose which of these would open their hearts to us. These ones with angels I declared publicly how they were named by God, and they provided us with our sausages and cabbage, our beer and bread.

For my deeds in procuring food through prophecy, I was greatly favoured by Eva and remained her chief prophet, speaking always after her on the scriptures and of the peril of man's path in the world, and though she would not take me and let me touch her, I was at least her favoured companion, and we lived as brother and sister chastely.

All was well until one Percy came, wanting baptism and to join us in our travellings. Percy was a former seaman, a former importer of spices, a former horse-groomer, a former most everything of any manly appeal. He was physically strong and handsome with a moustache, and I trusted him not and so took Eva aside and told her how I saw an evil demon looking out of Percy's eyes. Only Eva chided me for speaking against him, for she said he was a gift to her from God, a gift she had waited so long to receive. I did not fully understand her words until I saw the shadows of them under the stars of a field, embracing in a flagrant pose, and I could not believe how Eva could defile her flesh to lay on her back with that man above her. Didn't she see demons covered Percy, pestilent as fleas? In the morning I was sullen and criticized her with a comment about her unkempt hair. She laughed and called me jealous and kissed me once on the lips, just to tease me. Forever I rued that moment, for Percy's infestation spread to me, and a demon of lust jumped inside me, and my loins burned in shame and desire.

Soon we went to Cologne, where I saw angels on the head of one rat-catcher named Heinrich, and this Heinrich had great wealth in the town, for his business had prospered during the infestations while all others ailed, and I prophesied that this Heinrich could walk on the Rhine as the Lord had walked on the sea of Galilee. Only Percy took Heinrich aside and spoke ill of me and spoilt the rat-catcher's faith so that when he went to step on the river he sank directly and nearly drowned and had to bc hauled up on ropes.

This rat-catcher was a braggart, too – at any time, he carried six rats tied by their tails to his belt – so to his miracle he had invited the burghers and all the town to come watch. When he floundered, the crowd saw me as evil and turned against me and set upon me. I called out to Eva to defend me, but she knew well the depth of our peril, and away she ran with Percy close behind, leaving me alone with a mob encircling. I tried to flee but they set their dogs onto me and took me, intending to kill me with bare hands for the rat-catcher's ruined faith and my failed prophesy.

In sport, they cut my man's clothes from me, and when they saw my original nature all the louder did they call for my neck to be hung from a tree. One among them saw a ghost like a shadow in me and declared I was pregnant with evil seed and proposed to the others that the demon-child be cut out of me and spilled on the ground, for a demon-child not properly killed is quick to return, to haunt and bring ruin to the lives of his assailants. Away I was taken to a leather-aproned blacksmith who sharpened his axe against a stone.

Hand and foot they threw me into the smith's hut, and as he sharpened they shouted, "Cut the devil from her," in terrible voices out front. The blacksmith never raised his eyes to meet mine, so shamed I think he was of my nakedness. I feared for my life, and the pain of a knife terrified me until I saw an evanescence in the air around the smith's shoulders.

"Take yourself through the small door out to the back," a voice instructed and then, with force, "Run, child!" Only my feet wouldn't obey, and I tottered. I felt a firm push from behind that thrust me through a small door, through a passageway and away.

Tired and wretched though I was, I did not dare to stop until I had run for some hours and hidden myself in a dark woods. I was so tired I could have slept where I fell on the ground but the murmurings of wild beasts gave me fear – for what is it to escape the blacksmith's knife, only to be devoured by an animal's tooth? I devised that I would have to beg for mercy from some person and approached a cottage where I wailed in a low voice and hid myself so that my nakedness could not be seen.

A man came quickly to the door, and in the light of his lamp I saw how his whiskers stuck out of his face, the way hairs poke from the crackled rind of a roasting pork back. I marvelled how his doorway suited him as much as a pulpit, for he hardly had the door opened before he began to preach. He described only the evil of the poor who know not how to work and call damnation upon themselves with their stink and poverty, for no one in his esteem could be poor or ill without the Lord having assigned misery unto them, and what is misery if not the due penalty for sins? He preached, stoking the hot hell-fires of his mouth until he had expended all the miserable creatures of the world with his perceptions, and then he shut his door again, leaving not a scrap for me to put in my belly nor a rag for me to wear on my naked back.

I was in greater misery than when I had first cried out, and tears came quick for I hated my wretchedness. I tried to quell my tears as soft footsteps came near me, and amazed I was to see a woman whose countenance I had never before seen, for she was dark brown in her whole figure, with broad features for her face and hair that softly shaped around her head. I hid my naked person in the hedge, regarding not the pain of the brambles. She spoke with a tongue as fine as any good lady could ever possess, and I took her as the mistress of the property come to expel me, until she described herself, and then I realized she laboured for this preaching man. Sharp words had she for his miserly ways, "What nature of man is this who spouts pious concern and then breaks the Lord's first rule with his very sermon?" She said, "Come near, Poor Tom, whoever thou be."

"I cannot come near, for I am naked," I cried and hid myself further from her.

"Then you shall have clothes," she said and went away to bring breeches and doublet well-used, although finer in their aged state than my father ever had, and a bowl of warm groats that she set down where I might take it. "When God asks of you, report that it was Sabina's kindness you received tonight. I shall pray for the relief of your misery as well," she said, and I gladly took what she left for me and slept that night secretly behind her small cottage, at last to sleep in the comfort of the merciful.

From there I took to wandering in lanes and streets and would have made a career of begging, had the Polish forces not come that way towards Berlin with their grievances against the French king. I had no grief against His French Majesty, but the purse they offered a man who could fire a musket to join their side suited me.

The first time I joined the forces, I wanted only a soldier to be, thinking soldiers were free. But even they have a bitter existence. A soldier is only free to follow commands, and I wanted more from God than the privilege of marching about with a rifle. So I studied manhood itself and let my desire teach me, and the forces are training ground enough, and the manners of men with their lewdness and shit-stained breeches are not difficult to emulate. Our duties were arduous, with great distances to walk, but never so foul as the time we ruined the cathedral at Liege. The commonest of things cause the common man to rise up, and a cathedral is a difficult thing to take away, for it is owned by all, and it is harder to move a single stone from a man's sacred place than it is to cut out his heart.

The streets were full of persons who fought against us, and the women and the religious the worst among them, shouting names at us, pouring water out windows, smacking us with brooms. We soldiers had to hit them, men and women alike, and break the colourful glass of the cathedral and ruin the glass faces of the apostles and show nothing in our eyes.

All the while I was among the Polish army, I concealed my person carefully and was reputed to be shy, for I held my piss and shit until I could dump it in private, although shyness among men is fecklessness, as far as they were concerned. While I had none of the membrum of men, I did have the hands of a woman and clever hands, too, and still I longed for another way to be. So I took some leather and sewed a long sausage of it and filled it with dried peas and to it added the bladder of a sheep that hung from the bottom of the sausage and fastened the piece onto me with a leather strap that went between my buttocks and around my waist. To this I added a sheep horn, born through with a hole that allowed me to piss from a height as my fellows do, and my membrum virile woggled proudly in my breeches as a clapper dangles in a bell.

Near to Brussels we fought a battle that left the ground a sight to sicken the strongest. I came upon a man named Caspar, a young man I had known and loved, who was very proud of a set of playing cards that he carried in his pack. Face down he was, clotted like clay to the soil, his blood turning the earth black around him in a pool. I wanted a decent grave but we were being hurried on and told not to worry about burials, and I argued with my captain and blamed his stupidity for Caspar's death, and when he disciplined me I struck him back across the face and cursed him. He said I was to run the gauntlet, and I saw the other men preparing to beat me with swords, but I did not give them the chance. I was gone into the woods of night, and they could not follow, for they would have to break from their battle to find me.

I travelled secretly, hiding in forests and walking the roads at night, discarding the parts of my clothes that described me as a soldier. On the morning of the third day, when I was weak and hungry, I spied a maiden tending her fields. She was alone, and I prayed in my heart she would help me.

She was Catherine, she told me, and lived in a humble cottage with her mother, her father having long since died. I gave my name as Cornelius, thinking it an attractive name, and amused her with tales I had learned from soldiers. Perhaps I deceived her, although without unkind intentions, when I told her my father was a wealthy weaver in Nuremburg. I never intended to ail her when I described myself as one who imports fabric from the New East for it interested her so much, and I could not foresee how it would bring grief. In turn, she delighted me, and we went into a cow shed together, and I tickled her with my substitute, and this she greatly fancied.

Presently, we went to her mother to have her agree and then to the parish for the askings. All the while, her mother looked at me askance. I knew she took Catherine aside and instructed her how she must touch me just so, here and here, and report precisely what she feels. But no amount of touching would come to any advantage, for I have never had much of a woman's chest, and whenever Catherine stroked my pants my membrum would be there in full virility, erect with its bulge underneath, such that Catherine would have had to blush to describe to her mother how the manness of me held constant vigilance.

The mother had little case to refuse us, and soon it was arranged that she should sleep in her own small bed in the corner while Catherine and I took up the bigger bed in the house that now properly belonged to me. The mother never eased her contempt for me. She was scurrilous as a dog whenever she caught smell of me, and soon I saw the reason for it. In the late afternoon, she stood with the afternoon light behind her, and I could see them all there, more pestilent than Percy's, a thousand demons covering her, setting her soul against me.

Catherine's mother's demons always looked through windows at me. Though I did my best to treat Catherine as my wife, it was no use. I entered her with my leather member often and frequently, no matter now it tired me in the effort, for I would not have her complain to the other wives that I had no courage in me. But the soldier's life had ruined me. I worked not, and my tales of weaving and importing proved untrue. I took my business to the public house and drank ale all hours. When I had no coins left for paying, I went to the house and took some such thing, linens or clothes or what-have-yous, as they all were now rightly mine, and sold it to one man or another for the price of a drink.

Catherine turned a shrew and called me abbeylubber and scolded and complained bitterly how she hadn't any eggs, for I had sold everything, even the biddies that scratched in the yard. In return I abused her and clapped her ears with my hand and yelled how her mother poisoned her thoughts and set her against me. When I was home with her, she would sit in woeful tears until I went off again to the public house.

So it was, until the night when her hateful mother came after me and sought me in the public house and in front of all present and with her rotten teeth shouted of the womanized nature of me, making a tittle of my affairs. I approached the spiteful woman with my sheephorn in place and pissed a full pint of piss onto her while the other men jeered and laughed. "That will learn you for womanizing me," I said, and the carpenter clapped me on the back and gave me his jug. But when I left off my aleing that night, I knew how much ruin was upon me, and I shunned my home for ever and took to wandering in the roads to the southeast.

Thus abegging did I feel the full breath of wretchedness, for I had become a creature without society, hated by men and women, not at ease in nature either, for I found no peace in the form I was born with. Yet, in my mannish state, what had I wrought but grief? If I have ever woven anything, it was a tale of misery, neither man nor woman and neither able to be.

I slept in cow barns and ditches and asked passers by for a bit of caudle to eat. They called me hateful baggage until a vision of a woman came to me as round as a milkmaid and wearing fifteen rags for her skirts. She recognized me where I lay sleeping and spake easily to me, and called me Cornelius.

This was my own Catherine, returned to me, relating the full tale of her mother's havoc, and she, not wishing to be eternally leashed to so wicked a thing as her mother's tongue, did set after me to rightfully be my wife. Together, we carried our hunger and begged with hands outstretched.

After we travelled for many days, Catherine woke with a sickness in her that inclined her to vomit, though she had scarce eaten, and greatly weak she became for she spat up the very blood and bile of her. She was so badly that we went to a parish and described ourselves as Lutherans and begged sincerely for a bed to lay her in and, after a day of waiting, for God watches even the smallest sparrow fall, a room was given us in an alms house.

Catherine stayed in that bed for near to a week, and I did sit with her, and never did we argue. I pitched the phlegm from her spitting pan daily and held her hand. We needed money for making our way, and once she had some strength returned I went about asking in the streets, but the smallest coin made me only think of ale, and when a cleric in a brown robe pressed a coin worth two Reichstalers into my palm, I had no strength to resist.

I went to a house where a fleshly woman named Miss Hilde spread her legs and let me please her for the price of the first Reichstaler. The second Reichstaler bought me a whole jug of red wine. Filled with wine and bringing my member inside Miss Hilde's legs made me happier than anything in the Frederick William's palace ever could, for everything about her person, her hair, her face, her legs, were opened to me, and I was not wretched in any part of my person, but my legs tingled and my arms sang.

I stayed away the whole day, and when I returned, drunk as Davey's sow, to Catherine, she put the devil upon me with her tongue, for her strength had returned enough to ballyrag me for taking up my old drunken ways and being a wretch who cares not whether his wife breathes or dies, and this riled me for I was full of pride.

Being drunk, I had to piss and fumbled with my sheephorn and, while standing above the chamber pot, dribbled onto my shoes. "Other men piss without wetting their shoes. What is it in you that you can't even piss like other men?" she mocked me.

I threatened her with my fist, only to fall drunk asleep before my hand was fully raised. Catherine took a candle then and lit it near me and unfastened my clothing, first my doublets and then my breeches, and felt the soft of my skin and discovered the inanimate nature of my membrum. She was greatly amazed and afraid, for she discovered our natures were identical in every way. Then she took a knife and cut my membrum free and concealed it.

In the morning, when I woke, I saw clearly what was gone from me, and yet I did not want Catherine to suspect any wrong, so I feigned to have lost a coin in the bed and searched in vain. Soon desperation set upon me, for I found nothing.

Then Catherine looked at me from where she stood and confronted me with my travesty and told me how she burned my hateful member in the fire. "Can't you smell the stink of evil burning?" she asked me. I knew that I was ruined and begged her to kill me at once, for I feared a riled mob would come to make mockery of my flesh. For that is what they did with the old couple at the workhouse in Halle who were said to be witches. First they tied the thumbs of the woman to her big toes and flung her in the river and, once the wife was drowned, they tied the husband to her corpse until he also was drowned, and the chief tormenter among them collected money for showing the town such sport.

Except Catherine spoke easily to me and called not for my blood. She would abide with me if I mended my ways to live in decency, which I then promised, and this promise I have always kept, and not from fear of exposure either, but upon my honour.

Once Catherine had shown mercy to me, I felt a covenant more binding than with any Lord. Even the Lord who sits beside you in his chair cannot compare with the mercifulness of my Catherine. Of my truer nature, we made a pact of secrecy, for I still wore my mannish garb and her husband proclaimed to be, and in our lives, where fear might have wrought evil, only kindness reigned. We stayed at the alms house and kept intimate company, and one time Catherine asked me what my name was from birth, but it eluded me and would not come in my thoughts. So Catherine, being learned of most of the alphabet, penned a letter to the parish clerk of Halle, where I was born of my mother, and described me in such a way as I was when I was very young and inquired what the Christian name of this child might be.

We exchanged work for food at the parsonage, and Catherine took sewing that needed to be done for gentle ladies. As I had no

tasks myself and being learned by nun's servants of such delicate things, I would sit and sew with Catherine. Soon she gained
a reputation for excellent needlework done in half the time that
any other woman could do it in. Some days Catherine would
feel an itch in her, and we had our intimate ways together again,
and I would pleasure her with my hands and freely caress her
teats and lie athwart her and bring her thrill on.

One day, in the peak of her pleasure, Catherine reached under
the bed and returned my membrum to me, for she had never
destroyed it as she said, but put it away, thinking she hated it, only
to be in the swell of her passion and wish for it once again. So I
wore my membrum and mounted her and entered her repeatedly
until she shouted with the greatest pleasure imagined.

Then she undressed mc, and for the first time I willingly let
Catherine take my clothes from me. I stood wearing only the
membrum I had fashioned so carefully, and I wondered what it
is to be a man, to have arms and legs and a membrum, and what
it is to be a woman, to have hands that can express so much.
Then Catherine moved gently and knelt before me and fondled
my teats to rush my blood and kissed my thighs with her soft
lips, only to set her lips upon my membrum and take it deep in
her mouth. Then the fullest passion swept me such that I could
barely stand.

Thereafter I kept my membrum, wearing it always and
frequently pleasuring Catherine with it. Soon a letter came from
the old parish, and we learned that my name was Catherine, the
same as she, and there we were, two Catherines, only I was
Cornelius compelled to be.

On Saint Boniface's feast day, we woke to a scuffling in our
room and discovered a rat the size of a badger thrashing. When
Catherine stood to shove it with a broom, the rat leapt at her and
bit her foot and caused her to bleed. She let out a terrible scream,
and I took a stick and brunted the hateful beast to its death, only
to see its gut run yellow and its blood run green, and both of us
were chilled with fears of the worst. Soon Catherine took all
ampery and lay with a fever on the bed.

I sought out preparations to help her but without money
could not procure any, so I arranged for some travelling

marketers to convey Catherine to her mother's home, where she would have money to fetch the physician to her.

A day behind, I followed on foot, begging all the way for what I could, crying out of my wife's misery and our great misfortune. I collected a smoked ham and a pot of treacle and was glad to have some nourishment to bring to Catherine, but when I came to her mother's door it was barred against me. Her mother was enraged and stood behind the door, calling me scourge and proclaiming the womanly nature of me.

Yet I prevailed against her madness and shouted how I had brought food to she who was the rightful wife of me. Beset as she was by so many demons, the mother stank most foul and laughed at my efforts to bang down her door. Her laughter caused me to push all the harder, and soon a crowd gathered to watch our dispute. I banged and shouted, and then all of a sudden she opened her door and said, "Amends, amends, enter."

I should have known that demons make only a mockery of promises, for as soon as I entered she fell upon me with her carvery knife and gashed my thigh and tore open my breeches and seized my masculine emblem from me. She raised it high for all those gathered to see and rushed into the street with it, shrieking to fetch the bailie.

In her frenzy, she left me unattended and free to run away, but I did not run. For it would be only a rabbit's freedom, as a rabbit runs free until the tooth of the hound pierces her, and I had no want for such freedom. I longed to see my Catherine and found her in the back room feeling greatly relieved from her ailments. I called out, "Catherine, Catherine, it is me, the one who loves you who comes near." And she called me to her, and together we amended our grief and gave our promise to each other. We kissed and vowed that all that was ever intimate between us be forgotten from Catherine's memory, and our joy as much as our grief be lapsed from her thoughts. The true nature of me, we confirmed for her future and safety, was never by my Catherine known.

Part II – True Natures

Halberstadt
October 5, 1721

Dear Gregorius,

Shadows of cloud passing before the sun streak my desk. I study them, engrossed by their quiet changing and gaze long outside, until interrupted by a servant's knock. The scent of lemon oil in the heavy wood of my desk, the crucifix above me on a plain wall, my own hand emerging from a sleeve holding an inked feather, the yew trees through the window are surrendered to the servant's presence, telling me this infuriating woman is there again.

"She's been at the gate all morning, shouting she was robbed of her pots and linens. Shouting she wants the Linck woman hung."

I gave instruction to chase her away by the dogs. "Make sure she won't return! Tell her I will have her arrested and flogged if she ever comes near here again."

It infuriates me. Is this what the law has come to mean, Gregory? A tit-for-tat that gratifies a hateful old woman's vengeance against her daughter and another woman who have stolen her pots and pans?

I have the case of the Linck woman before me. I read and reread the argument for prosecution. The charge of sodomy is strange, but I keep returning to it.

This woman masqueraded her whole life as a man. She mocked the king when she served in the Prussian forces as a musketeer. She performed abominations with a masculine member made by her own hands. She wore this instrument strapped onto her person, even devised a way to urinate from it. She married a woman, the screaming woman's daughter, and had sexual relations with her, using the hateful substitute every time. She took pots and linens from the house of her mother-in-law and sold them for money. The preliminary court may have been fascinated to a fault by the evidence of her *membrum virile*, but I do not feel they have made an error in naming this sodomy. If it is not sodomy when two women come together and mock the order of the world, then what is?

Women are strange. They dwell outside the grace of laws and without peace. These two on trial and the mother that screams at my gate, even my own mother who is not in any way like these others, all live without peace. Mother tries to be devout but falls into despondency so quickly and becomes irritable and weak. She argues with me and bemoans her suffering, for she has so many ailments. When I answer that we could call the physician in, she disregards me, pretending deafness. Her eyes slitted shut, and her tiny fists angrily wrapped around a spoon, confound me.

But this is not why I am writing to you, Gregory. Forgive me this ageing man's grief over his aged mother.

I have had a terrible argument with three ministers, and this argument has left me deeply disturbed. We were discussing the penalty for Catherine Linck, who I want condemned and beheaded. But these three men (you know at least one of them well, but I fear writing their names in a letter, lest the military intercept), who are the wisest of men and all confidantes to the king, consider her blameless. While we were in session, I became so enraged that they would forgive this woman's abomination only because she is a woman and does not properly fit into the definition of the law, that I banged my fist on the table. I shouted at them for their stupidity. They sat passively looking at me through spectacles. Then I became distressed that I might be losing perspective and I took myself away from the table to gather my thoughts.

I fear these ministers, for they might say something to Frederick William about me and, as you know, it has been so difficult since his ascent. He wants to see every trifling that issues from a court. At first I mocked his intentions, thinking no prince in all of Prussia has ever cared for a day's work. But Frederick William is insatiable and reads long into the night, remembering names and details. And he is cruel with those who displease him. I heard how a magistrate named Wolken, from Magdeburg, criticized Frederick William for harvesting so many peasants into the army that the crops were left to rot in the fields, and there was no grain for Prussian bread. That very night, when Wolken, who lectures at the university, walked with a young student, a troop of cavalry confronted him. They shamed him and trampled them both so fiercely that the student lost his life. And Wolken has lost his post at the university.

In truth, all Frederick William cares for is his military, and it is well known how Prussia suffers while he collects his tall soldiers, which he loves more than anything. He sends his recruiters to Denmark and France to find tall men. There isn't a circus in all of Europe with a giant left in it, for they have all been bought and now wear the uniforms of the king's guard. As much as I fear the king, I do not want to let this sodomy charge be reduced to petty theft.

I apologized to the three ministers, asking them to forgive my outburst, saying my kidney stone torments me and the pain of it alters my temperament. Then I excused myself to walk outside and went to the place of the punishments. You know well how it is out there, Gregory, but this was the first time in many years that I looked with any interest, for I am distanced by the duties of court and never witness the end result of our work.

I came first to a man who lay on a rack, hands tied behind his back, while the handles of the mechanism disfigured his skeleton. Two men poured a jug of water into him such that he gulped to swallow and could not cry out, and his belly became as bloated as a corpse found after three days in the well. Another man knelt with a crucifix held in his roped hands. Above him the sword suspended in the arms of a hooded executioner waited while the kneeling man wept his mother's name.

I walked to the forest where trees are stripped of branches and crowned at the top with a wheel. On a wheel, alone and high above the ground, a man sleeplessly gripped the rungs. He seemed familiar to me, but I could not place it at the time. Now I realize how much this one man, in his shape and height and colour and age, resembled myself.

Repelled by horror, yet unable to take my eyes from what I saw, on the wheel and all about me, I saw the terrible truth at the heart of man. What a profound experience suffering is! Gregory, man is, because man suffers!

In the distance I saw the flames of a burning, its dark incense billowing up to heaven. Souls are flying up to God in that smoke, flawed and contaminated flesh returned by the process of justice to the spirit. We are God's gatekeepers here, giving back to God what we cannot tolerate on earth, and the greater judgment waits us all, in heaven or hell.

I returned to the court deepened by the sense of suffering and searched for my ministers, but they had gone without leaving a word. So this business of the Linck woman has been left overnight. I could not sleep, and a terrible dream came to me that in my absence they let the woman go. The king pursues me with the hateful mother-in-law close behind, screaming of her stolen pots. Frederick William is the age of a mere boy but mighty on horseback and dressed in his full military uniform. He is furious with me for failing to punish the Linck woman properly. He takes his sword to cut my tongue out. I woke just as he pushed his knife into my opened mouth.

If only these ministers weren't so literal in their reading of the law! Gregory, this is the trouble with Prussia today, for the military mind has taken over and left no room for the interpretation. They wish to command the courts like troops in drill and do not know how law must be always read with new eyes.

One smokes his pipe and draws his stained finger-tips through his beard and argues that the absence of semen, which cannot have been spilled or ejaculated from the Linck woman's leather member, does not follow reasoning for a charge of sodomy. "By pressing a lifeless leather object into the vulva of another woman, no penis is abused, no semen spilled and no fleshly union perpetrated." He rolls his eyes impatiently. "Sodomy requires a penis."

The pious man of them, a priest who infuriates me by speaking always in a whisper, says he has consulted his superiors. "Although the Holy Scriptures expressly forbid sodomy between men, nowhere do they explicitly discuss such an abomination between women. In Leviticus, it is mentioned that women are forbidden to pervert their flesh in union with animals."

I rallied against him. "In the Scriptures it is described how the Sodomites turned away angels who visited their city. The Linck woman's crimes are not comparable to some schoolboys playing itch-buttocks in a shed. Her sodomy let her very soul be corrupted by desire. Sodomy carried her into the streets wearing a dead man's clothes, to steal and prophesize and corrupt other women, changing them into puppets of their lust. The imagination of the Sodomites was so evil that God rained fire and brimstone and devoured whole cities because of them. The prescribed penalty in the Scriptures for perversion between women and animals is death. It would not be too unlikely to use the Scriptures in an analogous condemnation."

But he was smug. "What God did not write, God did not intend."

The third of them, who studied in France where they care more about decorating their mouths with clever expressions than with saying anything intelligent, began, "Perhaps you have heard of women in the far eastern plains, who are born with large clitorises. Among these women, penetration and fleshly union can be experienced, and here it could be argued that, analogous to the male experience, sodomy is perpetrated. The flesh has been contaminated with sin. But this is hardly comparable to a leather sock filled with sand and tied to a sheep's liver."

I could tell he was mocking me, but I described how the Linck woman had been examined, and no physical deviation was found. The city physician Dr Borne and a surgeon, Dr Roper, examined the Linck woman. They brought in a midwife to examine the defendant's genitalia, for they did not want to look upon that part of her, but the midwife found nothing masculine nor hermaphroditic about her. She has breasts and a large womb. Her vulva is fully proportioned and feminine. The midwife described a disfiguration present on the vulva that is the result of abuse during her years vagabonding. But she was born naturally as a woman, they all agree.

The real obstacle with these ministers is that they do not wish the king to know a woman served in his beloved forces. "If the royal monarch were to learn that a woman was recruited and carried a musket for Prussia for three years, he would be enraged."

"Frederick William's guard has been defiled."

"But that is not the essence of the crime!" I argued. "This woman has made a mockery of the designs of nature and the laws of God! Can a correlation not be made," I argued, "between the explicit sodomy of men and that implicit of women? St Protius of Basilius has expounded on the teachings of Paul, and he would have it that the punishable sin amounts to the same. She has openly confessed to her crimes. I want her burned alive."

"In our country," the priest whispered, "we allow the convicted person to be killed by the sword first, and then burned. To alleviate despair."

"Then kill her with a sword," I said bitterly.

A platter of fruit and cheese was brought in, and we eased our argument for a moment. Then the first minister, holding an apple in his hand, his long yellow stained nails like claws around the fruit, cleared his throat and said, "And for the wife, Catherine Muhlhahn, you have asked for second-degree torture?"

"She requires a severer process of justice," I defended. "While Catherine Linck has confessed freely and fully, the alleged wife is sullen and suspicious. The truth has yet to be arrived at, in her case."

He clucked his tongue. "The process of justice should not be harsher than the penalty for any crime."

The priest whispered, "She denies any knowledge of the nature of this woman."

The arrogant one added, "Surely she is a simple woman who has been seduced into depravity."

I could not admit to them how Catherine Muhlhahn is an enigma to me. When I was speaking with the midwife I asked if, in her opinion, it would be possible for a woman to marry another and not detect that the sexual member was inanimate.

She gave me a discouraging response. "Sir, I am so amazed at the ignorance of country people that I truly wonder how they manage to reproduce themselves at all, for they hardly know what part of their anatomy the babes come from, that it must be trial and error and a great deal of lust that gets their members in there in the first place."

The priest folded his hands as he must in the confessional, when he sighs and gives absolutions. "Are you aware that the wife has asked for full acquittal on the basis of suffering she has already endured? Both in the squalour of prison during the term of the trial and the severe melancholy caused her by not being able to come to the aid of the defendent during that time."

This argument provokes me! "The woman has claimed melancholy, but when Dr Borne was sent to perform an examination on her spirits, she was hostile and vulgar with him. She spat upon him. He saw no signs of melancholy."

The third minister held a green pear in the air, waving it as if it were an actor's prop. "The co-defendent pleads she was unaware of her alleged husband's nature. She reports that her husband's member was always warm and full. She also says that once, when she fondled his chest, which was covered by a shirt, she commented on the size of his breasts. He replied that many men have such chests. As an ignorant girl, how would she otherwise know?"

"It is apparent that Catherine Muhlhahn is simpleminded. However, her own mother says she told her frequently that she doubted her husband's nature, and nonetheless the girl perpetuated her marital arrangement and continued to perform sexual acts with this so-called man."

"She argues that she only followed her marital vow to honour her husband. Clearly we can not condemn a woman for honouring her husband."

I banged my fist on the table again. "Why did she never feel the strap that secured the woman's leather member to her body?"

"She says she was never able to feel it! Because it was kept between his legs, and he always wore his clothes!" the third minister shouted.

"Furthermore the alleged husband was given to demonstrative bursts of violence, and as he beat her often, Catherine Muhlhahn lived in fear of her husband's retributions."

The bearded minister lit his pipe. "During the process of trial, has Catherine Muhlhahn been flogged?"

"Yes. Fourteen or fifteen times."

I ordered every one of those floggings myself, so determined I was to get the truth out of this lying young woman. Her will is so difficult to break! I asked the soldier who I sent each time, if there was a confession yet.

"She's some kind of demon, Sir."

"How so?" I asked.

"Doesn't say a word at the beginning or end, Sir. And when I whipped harder, like you told me to, not a sound. It's eerie. Doesn't even flinch."

I didn't tell the ministers that.

But they all looked at me. "Fifteen times and no contradiction evoked?"

I was reduced, but determined. "Catherine Muhlhahn has been known to steal an entire season's harvest for her gluttony – her own mother denounced her!"

The ministers shook their heads, and the bearded one smirked at me. They don't recognize how deeply God's law is imbedded in this world and underestimate me. They don't know that I will go to Fredrick William on my own. He will hear me!

For do you not agree, Gregory, that sodomists are not merely those who misuse flesh for perversions? They are those who reject their true natures given by God.

And this Linck woman is so preposterous. So bold! "Why punish me," she says, "when there are so many more like me?" I try to imagine if she is authentic when she says this, and I think of every man or woman I know and scrutinize them in my mind. The men seem like men, and the women like women, and the differences are clearly defined. The worst of it is that she knows no remorse and explains her every sin in terms of herself.

"Because you do not learn," I said to her, "I shall use your death as a lesson to others and start with you and continue one by one until I have you all."

The Linck woman's case is as strange and wretched as I have seen. To her, I want to award the harshest penalty. Perhaps in the case of the so-called wife, her ignorance can be considered, and some clemency given. But as for Catherine Linck, I will not let her go. I write to you in confidence now, that you might counsel me, for I want to send a letter to Frederick William quickly and supplicate to him and petition his support. In my heart I know this woman is guilty of the worst of sins, but counsel me my friend, has she commited sodomy?

My honour rests with you,
Hans-Josef

Halle
8 October 1721

Dear Hans-Josef,
    I am moved by your argument and write to you in haste. My brother, I feel you are being called by God to do His will in the world, and I counsel you to act quickly. Your ministers are cowards. They care more about their comfort under the king's rule than they care for God's will on earth. Your instincts, Hans-Josef, are astute and correct, and this is truly a case of sodomy, for the defiance and the sinfulness of this woman is flagrant and unforgiveable.

It is not merely a matter of forbidding women to wear a set of clothes, for clothes alone are not reason for sin. We know how some of the female saints were given to wearing men's clothes. Though the truth has been embellished, we can look to the life of St Marina, whose father became a monk and smuggled her into the monastery as a boy, to keep her with him. After his death, she stayed at the monastery. She was expiated for five years after a controversy, when she was accused of fathering the child of an innkeeper's daughter. Upon her death, her sex and her innocence were discovered. It also appears to have been true, that a woman entered the monastery at Schönau and lived as a monk undetected until her death. She is quite popular among devout Prussian women who pray to her as St Hildegung, though of course she is not an authentic saint.

But the wearing of men's clothes for the purpose of devotion and the wearing of clothes for the sake of perversion cannot be compared. Halberstadt must not become the new Sodom with every crazed woman going about as she pleases, bearing arms and preaching, marrying women and flagrantly taking the places of men at tables and in bed.

This woman is a horror, for she even amended the flesh God gave to her with a mockery of a male member. This is what true sodomy is, for what does the Devil himself do, but parody the work of our Lord?

I hear a terrible uttering in the world, Hans-Josef. The din deafens me! Women are building a tower of Babel for their kind, using their flesh and tongues and hair as brick and mortar, taking the devil as their architect, and soon they will want to run the whole world according to their designs.

Prosecute them as hard as you can. Letting one go free allows her to make a doorway in the world where others will follow.

I leave you in God's good care,
Gregorius

Part III – Seven Miracles

*Being the full relation
of the life of Catherine Margarethe Muhlhahn,
alleged wife of Catherine Margarethe Linck*

Come sit and listen to me now, you angels. You know nothing of the sorrows of women but I will give you some satisfaction to drink and tell you how it is I came to be so angry with God.

When I was a child, I was the smallest maiden in our whole county. I was constantly mistaken for a hedgehog when I crawled under the strawberry leaves to gather hidden berries. In blackberry season, I needed a rope to hoist myself up the trellis, and as I could pick more than I could carry, I taught the dog to hold steady with a basket. I never liked harvesting after dusk for moths are as large as ravens to me, with ancient, sorrowful faces that sweep at small torches giving me sadness and fright.

I lived with my mother in a house next door to Colleen, who lived with her mother and father in a big family. Colleen is younger than me but she grew so big by the age of her menses she needed two stools, one for each buttock, to milk the morning cows. When it was too hard to walk, she wrapped me in her apron and carried me home from the fields. I could have taught the dog this too, but her coat is coarse as cat whisker and sharp as scythed hay. Besides, I liked when Colleen carried me.

All the lads ran after her when she carried the mop and pail at Frau Durden's, and Colleen had stories only a large maid could tell. Her arms are like rising loaves of bread, and the lads ate as much of her as they wanted and still had plenty for next time. Colleen's mother is from the east near Poland, and she laughs in the evening, and Colleen's father gets mocked because he puts salt on oats for the cows to lick. But where did parents like that get her? She still lives next door, but in the married way now, with a pack of children and a ne'er-do-well for her man.

My father died when I was young, and my mother is from the north where the New Laws made a scarcity that caused a famine for food and also for kindness. The crowned prince forbade the people to eat deer. So the people were driven out and forced to eat what the deer ate, green bark of trees, soup made of pond water and handfuls of red berries when they could be found.

My mother married my father, moved south where fish leap from brooks and there are enough woven blankets for everyone to have their own at night, but she brought with her the spirit of her people. When people from the north have too much food, their instinct is to bury it, letting it spoil, before giving extra to a neighbour. People complain about them, that they are stingy and their dialect is harsh-sounding. In the south, folk are not accustomed to the way women from the north sharpen the knives of their tongues on another's skin.

I have always lived with my mother, and under the vigilant scraping of her voice the part of me that was me grew small, small and hard as a grey flint. And when I reached the age that other girls married, I was more like a sharpening stone than a woman, and no husband could be found for me, as no one wanted a wife the size of a doll and without any flesh.

My mother forbade dancing in front of the hay-harvest fires, where other girls learned how to fondle a man's legs. She taught me never to parade under the maypole with a foolish gleam in my eye for a lad. When Carnival came, my mother stayed us both inside, gave me something sweet on bread, and then we mended our stockings. The only congregating we did was in church on Sundays or on the feast days of saints, when we'd make a pilgrimage.

One November, on my name day, the feast of St Catherine of Alexandria, the harvesting finished, we put our best wooden shoes on and walked all the way to town. In one gate, through the whole town and out the other gate. Me looking all the while at the splendid buttercakes, the dripped wax candles, the bolts of cloth, and my mother's hand pulling me tightly forward. Night came. The sky glowed yellow like metal on a sword. We walked outside the village walls, past the monastery fields, to the gallows.

We arrived in time to watch a young man, with a thick beard and a few fingers missing from his left hand, swing. All about us were torches and drunkery, men fallen down in the mud, men singing. My mother's eyes stayed fixed on the gallows. "It's always a man up there," she pointed with her rosary. "Don't you see, Catherine? The flesh of men is weak."

I thought of St Catherine impaled on her wheel of spikes, for I had seen her death portrayed on the sepulchre wall and, if men are put to death for sin, I was certain that women were put to death for holiness, because women's holiness is not by others understood.

Men remained strangers to me. The sight of a thief tugged by a rope until his neck breaks and then left hung has a chilling effect on the smallest soul. I never watched a cock fight, or placed a gamble on a dog race, and I'd never seen a deck of playing cards, though I had heard of all these things from Colleen.

And I heard about them from the parish priest who took young women aside and reminded us how unchristian playing cards are, as they entice men to sin. The Devil's alphabet is of pictures and not words made, as words are the property of God. In the beginning there was the Word, but the Devil was also alive then, a young and a handsome man, and God loved him. Then the serpent came and tempted the Devil to eat the fruit of the tree that would let him see the shadows under all creatures, shadows that only God can see. The Devil felt desire and ate the apple the snake had given him.

When God walked in the garden, he knew something was ill for the Devil gazed in delight at the ground under God's feet. God became angry, for he saw how the Devil had made himself like a god. God summoned the serpent and cut his arms and legs from him, that he would forever crawl on his belly eating dust. God banished the Devil from the garden forever and forbade him to use words to tell what he saw. So it is that the Devil uses pictures in his book. Then God wept because he found himself alone in a beautiful place, and the garden was empty. So God took a clot of earth in his hands, spat some spittle and made man in his own image.

The following spring, after the frost unchained itself from the ground, but before the wood thrushes mated, I was near my twenty-second birthday and pruning the blackberries at the far edge of the eastern field. Colleen was bleeding the bed red, awaiting the birth of an infant, and I worked alone. I devised a web of ropes to skivvy myself about, but had to cover all of me in a heavy cloaking, for the rope rubs and burns the skin. I was more concealed than a novitiate at the Carmelites, my only sight through an unpatched hole in my hood, when I was startled by the presence of a young man.

Though I could not imagine what he thought of me in my hood and gear, I observed him keenly. He was tall, but slight of build, and had such nervous gangly limbs that I could not discern if he be friend or foe. He ceaselessly hastened the air about him, rifling a pocket, churning the wind. He ran his fingers through his hair and now and then let his eyes look directly into my own. He had a soft urgency in him that I suspected, maybe I hoped, was passion. I know now it is only the look of a hunted man. That look of naked terror, as the fleeing soul presses your eyes closed with the garments of romance, is easily mistaken for love.

While I was still entwined in my pulley, he opened his knapsack, unwrapped a cloth package, and for the first time I saw how handsome a thing a set of playing cards can be. He offered to play me a hand. But I knew he was a mongrel with a flourishing manner, his clothes and gear were muddy, and in my mind I heard the voice of my mother rattling in my ear.

"You've stolen those, haven't you?" I said.

"Nay, I won them in a duel and chose to take the man's cards rather than his life."

I thought of my mother. "Nay yourself. I'm not interested."

"But you are." He smiled in a way that brought my cloaking off and soon the grass was pressed down, and he taught me cards so well I soon won a hand. Just as I laid down the Jack of hearts, who should arrive scolding, but my mother. It caused me to shudder that this man should see what age and ill fortune would reduce me to in time. But he was trained in the military way and bowed so contritely that my mother turned of a sudden and asked him his name.

"My name?" he said, admiring the tangle of blackberry vines with a gesture that let me notice his delicate hands, "My name. Is Cornelius. Cornelius Caspar Brewer."

I watched my mother walk away. As soon as she dwindled to a speck the size of a sparrow on the thistle path that leads home,

I threw down the Queen in my hand and pulled Cornelius towards a tree that Colleen had described to me as having large branches and soft grass underneath. He was not so large a man, this Cornelius Brewer, yet I feared my feminine parts might be as small and tight as the rest of me. I had my menses so I was wet between my legs, and we found a way for him to slip inside me. So pleased was I with his smooth skin and this wonderful pushing-tugging deep inside me that we kissed until the evening's soup and bread. Then, all twittering, I took Cornelius to our house and announced to my mother our intentions to marry. She made the sign of the cross against her breast, but otherwise said not a word.

We three went to the priest to ask for the banns, and my mother wouldn't remove her curious eyes from Cornelius. She stood with her head cranked when he spoke, as if she had never before witnessed a man pronouncing words. When the banns were called in the square, one man, Johannes Fleischer, who is a lout and near to a vagabond, scandalized how Cornelius was father to a child and husband to a wife in a village north of ours by thirty miles. A letter had to be gotten from there, and the parish priest testified no Cornelius Brewer had ever there been married or baptized, and a fortnight later, with Colleen and one of her daughters throwing the corn, we married. I have always wondered whether my mother didn't put an oath in Johannes Fleischer's ear for him to say such a thing. It would not be beyond her to pass a pence or a pint to someone like Johannes, if it meant delaying the moment that Cornelius would join us as the man of the house.

For the first time I was happy. Cornelius and I lived in union, and shortly thereafter my first miracle came.

My mother had taken sick. She spent many days rasping for breath in a cot near the cooking fire, and perhaps I was more prayerful at that time because I requested her healing, but in the time it took for my mother to become well, God had shown his mercy to me. I grew large.

All my life I had felt myself a smudge on my mother's face, a blemish she constantly rubbed at with her thumb, and this is how I had known the world. When Cornelius came to me with his deck of cards, his tales of fabric-spinning and his years in the forces, my spindliness could no longer hold me. The concave chest I wore all my youth melted and two breasts, large and raging as untempered horses, emerged. My legs and arms grew long, my belly round, and I grew invincibly hungry.

My mother rose from her bed, amazed at the size of me. She peered at my figure wrapped in a cloth that could cover a bed. "What are you doing?"

A bowl of cooked oats and barley malt nested in my hands. "Eating."

"Did God put you on earth only to eat five times your share?"

"I'm hungry."

"Learn to pray." She tugged my bowl from me, "Only prayer quenches hunger, and only prayer quenches lust." She made a disgusting sound, imitating the noises I made at night when I took Cornelius into me, for she moved her bed since she was ill, and we all slept in one room, and I was as hungry for Cornelius as I was for food.

Cornelius came in and looked about the cupboards. He took linen out and put it in his pack and then whistled with pleasure when he found a pair of leather shoes. He put the shoes on his feet. They fit loosely, but he looked pleased.

My mother gasped. "Take those from your feet!"

My father had been dead since before I ever put a thread through a needle. I could not put a face to his name, but I knew my mother revered him as a saint, and these were his Sunday shoes.

Cornelius snorted and took a place at table and thumped the back of a spoon on the wood. My mother threw herself on the floor, pulling at the shoes on Cornelius' feet.

He stamped on her fingers. "Everything in this house belongs to a living man now and not to the ghost of a man!"

I held my breath and prayed for the Virgin to show me how to love them both, for I loved Cornelius but feared my mother. My duty was to serve him, but my fear compelled me and, when they quarrelled, I was certain I would perish. That night I ladled Cornelius the largest bowl of stew while my mother glared and would not herself eat. In contriteness, I did not eat myself but then I was so hungry that I stole oats from the larder, replacing them with stockings filled with stones, hidden at the bottom of the barrels.

In time, when my legs were the size of satchels on the back of a Royal Post horse, the second miracle happened.

Milk flowed from my breasts.

Milk poured out of me, and Cornelius could hardly drink all there was of it, though he sucked me long after dark. In the morning, I woke to find the bed soaked through. As my mother began to stir, I ran next door to Colleen and let her four babies suck me. I was still full and in pain. Colleen put her milking gloves on and pulled two buckets from nipples as large and sturdy as two thumbs. In return for the milk, she cooked a sack of barley. I ate the whole thing out of a washing tub so big it could have once been my bed.

I used the empty sack to tie my breasts up on me and stopped by the chicken house to bring eggs. Where once I moved freely, gazing out the little chicken windows, reaching up to pull out a broody egg, I now crouched with my body filling the whole aisle and only my hands able to freely move. The smelly heat overwhelmed me, the straw bedding dusted the air, and I became dizzy, almost faint. In the tight coop where the biddies clucked, I felt my belly swell under a deep rumble swim. A great joy leapt to my lips, for I never imagined life could come through me. The basket of eggs clattering, I ran to Cornelius, and flung myself into his lap.

The third miracle had come. I was pregnant with a little life inside me.

Cornelius' face coloured, and he grew cross. "Then you've been playing the whore again, have you?" I denied it truthfully, saying that I'd been to the neighbour woman, exchanging grain for milk, but Cornelius raged. He cried out to God. He pulled his hairs on his chin, brunted his hands against his own arms and hit his fists against his own legs.

My mother came upon our quarrel and said, "What have you made of yourselves?"

I said, "I am with child."

Cornelius said, "You are NOT! You are NOT!" Then he left the house, staying away until supper the next day. All night I swept the floor with my long hair and wept as an infant weeps for its mother because I loved Cornelius, and I had a little life inside me and feared he would never come back.

Cornelius returned the next night, remorsefully and carrying a gift for me, the only one I ever received from someone other than God.

Where he found it I don't know, but he gave to me a mirror, with a glass clouded and so obscured that I would have better admired myself on the side of a scrubbed kettle. Cornelius held me close and described how the clouding was caused by its properties of magic.

Looking in, especially after a time, I saw my own face reflected in beauty, and the parts where I had to imagine some aspect of my cheek or eye or lips doubly beautiful. I gazed into that blurry realm until I saw not only my face clearly, but Cornelius' as well, and the room around us, then the house, then all the thatched houses in our town and the fields outside the ring of walls all the way out to the gallows. At the gallows I met a young woman weeping. I asked her why she wept.

"Because no one can see or hear me."

And I said, "But I see you."

I've known miracles in my life. Seven miracles are given to each soul in a lifetime, and many people cheat their souls and never even use one, but a miracle is a gift from God and different than magic. Magic does not come from God the father, nor even from Mary the mother who hears the cries of those in despair, but from a person's heart. A heart is a deeply woven thing, woven upon itself as a labyrinth is, and seems tangled and dark until magic lets you see your heart as clearly as a path found in the woods.

My mother came upon me. "Frederick William's own daughter aren't you imagining yourself to be?" I feared she would take my mirror and secured it in the folds of my skirt only to hear that she had another plan for me. She described how she suspected Cornelius a woman to be.

I was amazed.

"Cornelius shuns intimate company and never shows his parts, though he must have to piss like any other man. His beard is feeble, his person slight."

Then she questioned me in vulgar terms, about how warm or wide his member felt when he took himself into me. I thought her mad, and when Cornelius came to table that night I mocked my mother openly.

"My mother is so jealous and perverse that she wants your male member to see."

"I will never wave my blessed cock in your depraved face," he said.

And she answered, "Because you haven't one."

Outside, the sky had a few streaks of yellow and green light left as evening was almost fallen, and Cornelius arranged that my mother should stand across the garden from him, with the hedges blocking the light behind him. He undid his leggings.

"But it's all black!" my mother sneered.

"That's how it is with men," Cornelius told her. "When boys are small, their members are pink, but they darken with age."

In the morning, my mother still scorned Cornelius, calling him thief for every morsel put in his mouth. I thought only that jealousy had made her lose her perceptions, such that all the world seemed an enemy to her. She interrupted the affairs Cornelius and I began, such that we had to have our sexual relations long into the night and quietly without a gasp.

Just before Easter, my mother went to the oat barrel and found a dusting of oats over a barrel of stockings filled with rocks. Cornelius and I were still asleep in the early morning when her rage came towards me, and for once I raged back, for I had come to know my hunger as a part of me that I could no longer diminish. My mother was beyond reason and took my mirror from my things and smashed it over Cornelius' head. Blood poured from his forehead, and I cursed her. Only Cornelius was hardly hurt and proved invincible, and the two of them began hitting and fought bitterly.

My mother called him "Woman! Woman!" and grabbed a knife and aimed to pierce Cornelius between his legs, but Cornelius was stronger and beat her with his hands and put her outside the house and bolted the doors. She screeched so loud she could be heard all the way to the cathedral, damning Cornelius, cursing me. She raged all day and, when it was dark, she finally quieted with exhaustion and then slept in the workshed that night for none of the neighbours wanted her in that state.

If Luther had given me an axe, I would have put it through her skull that day, so angry was I with her for always trying to take away. I wish now I'd done it and changed the course of these events, for she took my dreams from me, wanting me to live without the eyes of another in friendship or passion. To live without dreams is to have a stump of wood instead of a tree for a heart, and this is what she wanted for me.

Long into the night, Cornelius paced in the house. Like a trapped wolf he moved restlessly, staring at the shuttered windows, unable to sit in his chair for longer than a moment, muttering to himself. I went to him, his arms leaning on the wooden table, an exhausted soldier on vigil duty. I stood in a doorway; a single candle lit the dark between us.

"Cornelius. Are you a woman?" I asked.

He shrugged. "What choice do I have now?"

In his eyes I saw hunted exhaustion. Those eyes spoke a truth that made the whole world shift underneath us, as if the earth itself were rising on a wave. There was a terrible quiet as the plates of heaven creaked the stars to new positions. My heart knew the truth then. That Cornelius was a woman, and I understood clearly who I was then and what that meant for both of us.

"Come to bed now, my man." I put out the candle. In bed, I held him close, though he lay stiff for hours, with his back turned, and when I woke in the morning the bed was empty.

I was in great pain. A clot of blood the size of a goose egg passed from me, and I hated having Cornelius gone. I bled heavily, no longer pregnant. On the path out front, I heard that Cornelius had been seen in the ale-house, but I knew in my heart he was truly gone.

I longed for Cornelius and suffered my mother who restored herself to the command of the house. I suffered the pain of not knowing what to do. From my corner of the room, I saw how small a being she was, little and scrawny, but anger burned in her with the intense heat of a harvest field set alight. From her, a charcoal cumulus rose upward. I dreamed of a walled garden where two terrible dragons lived, and I had to kill one, but only one to save my life. If I killed the wrong dragon I would myself die, and both were so fierce I could not know which dragon to kill and which one to let live.

With the vengeance of a murdered queen, my mother governed me. She locked the larder that I might not eat of it and took Cornelius' place beside me in the bed at night. Throughout the days she ordered me with a stick, and hit me if I wavered or tarried. She gave me broth of boiled bones to eat and on Pentecost Sunday, as a solemn procession walked, their decanters of incense swaying, she dragged me before the priests and the nuns with their covered heads and pulled me to my knees by my hair. "This is my daughter. She's so holy she found herself a woman and married her!"

From next door, over a little fence, Colleen saw how I declined. She took me in quietly and gave me food to eat. "You could move away," she said suckling a babe with one arm and stirring a stew with another.

"How could I do that?" I said.

"You could change your name, find a sensible man to marry. Stay away from trouble."

"She would come after me," I said of my mother.

"People find a way," Colleen said, looking long outside. I wondered how much she knew about my life with Cornelius, but I was afraid to say more. We talked of other things, and soon I had to go before I was noticed missing.

Though my mother tried to starve me and likewise I tried to shrink myself out of her sight, and though I worked ceaselessly in the fields and felt hunger so real it became another of my limbs, I did not grow small.

That was the wonder of it. I stayed big when there was no food feeding me, and then the fourth miracle came. The Blessed Virgin Mary, mother of God, who intercedes for those who have recourse to her, appeared in a dream. She lifted her mantle and out of her sacred vulva produced an egg. On the egg was a compass and the Queen of Heaven carefully showed me how the needle of the compass pointed east.

I woke. Without waiting for dawn, I climbed over my mother's snoring, pinched body and took the road from the village that leads east.

After a fortnight, I found Cornelius, slumped in a ditch outside the west gate of an unfamiliar town. A terrible funk rose from a few open sores on him but our time apart had softened his heart, and he kissed my hand and turned his hat upside down on his head as a clown in a pageant would.

"Madam, come you searching for your king?"

"Aye. But my king is a humbled man."

"Indeed he is. And may his soul prosper from it, for no other part of him has."

I laughed, and it had been raining, and we were both truly wretched.

Begging supported us. We planned to walk to France and begin a new life there. All the begging day we talked of our life there, learning new words for the names of things. But a dampness got into my chest, and I coughed ceaselessly, braying like a donkey. Soon I coughed blood, and we had to ask for a bed, for I needed to rest.

While I slept, Cornelius went out to beg some food, and I felt our troubles were behind us, for I thought they were my mother's doings. Only Cornelius came home to me much too late that night, smelling of womanly perfume under his drunkenness. We quarrelled bitterly. I scolded him as harshly as I could, and when he fell drunk asleep I despaired that there would be no end to this suffering between us.

So I took the knife that hangs from my skirt, carefully undid his leggings and opened his shirt. I took off as many of his clothes as I dared without waking him, and I examined in wonder the instrument she had made – the member which she had carefully sewn and the ingenious piece of horn. I cut it from her and concealed it. I hid these despairing things of hers and returned to Cornelius, to touch her skin with my light fingers and kiss her and press my cheek against her soft chest and rest myself between her breasts in contentment.

In the morning, fear visited us both. Cornelius made me so angry because she wanted to squander falsehoods and lie and lie even when it was obvious that I knew her true nature. "What is known is known!" I shouted.

"By everyone?" she said in great trepidation.

"By me! You stupid woman!" I shouted, and then something in Cornelius changed. She knelt and took my hands and said she was sorry to me, for all the pain she had given me, and repented her wretched ways, and asked my forgiveness for treating me as the most wretched of men would. This was the fifth miracle given to me, for thereafter Cornelius changed her ways, as if born from one life to the next in a single moment. She touched me and loved me deeper than God.

Though we were often intimate, and Cornelius showed herself to me as my beloved, she always forbade me to see the feminine parts of herself. In the bed one day, with much softness, I kissed her skin and asked to see that part of her. She did not want me to, but I gently insisted until she agreed, and when I saw it, I understood her deepest sorrow.

She told me softly, "I served under the name Anastasius Rosenstengel and fought for several months in a force, but soon learned I could not bear to always march about in fear of the king. I deserted on a night without moon and followed the glow of a fire across a field, only to find a gang of robbers warming their hands. I wanted to have a drink of spirits and feel free but drank of the wrong man's mug. Soon I found myself in a quarrel with a brute twice my size. I fought as well as I could, but I hadn't eaten much in days and was weak. Then he wanted my buttoned jacket as a trophy and claimed it with force, only to discover the feminine nature of me.

"There was much cavorting and howling. The largest of them held me down and took fire-hot needles and tattooed my vulva with one of the few words they could spell, WOMAN."

The imagination of cruelty is unrelenting, and I kissed that part of Cornelius to send away the misery those needles had pierced into her and, as I did, a sound came from her that was like the crying of a babe when it is young.

"I was so devastated by their violence that I returned myself to my regiment and confessed to desertion. My penalty was fifty lashes of the whip on a bare back, which I endured all the while holding my shirt to my front, lest anyone see my breasts."

After that, Cornelius served two and a half more years, only to desert again. Thereafter she wandered and found her way to the village where my mother had come from the north so many years before, where I have always lived.

Once I felt better from my illness, Cornelius liked to please me with her stories and I took in sewing for wages, and Cornelius, who had been a girl in her youth and whose mother loved her, had an excellent hand for reweaving delicate threads in a fabric. We kept Cornelius a man, and the women I did work for were impressed with my speed, and the quality was good, so I charged a *pfennig* or two more. Cornelius would put her hands all around my big belly and her mouth on my teats and her fingers down between my legs where she would bring me towards pleasure until I gushed my waters.

On a day when the sun got dark early, we were having our ways, and I gave Cornelius the leather member back. When I first took it from her, I thought it the source of all our troubles. But as God and the angels move through the world without bodies, only the spirit can change the flesh. Her heart was with me, whether she was a woman or a man, whether she had a leather member hanging from her belt or not. I gave her that member back because it was a part of who she had made herself to be in the world, and I felt my love for her, deep inside me.

I never learned what our life would have been like if the wheel of our fortune had not swung and taken me ill again. Without money, we imagined I would be better in the house of my mother, where some medicine could be brought. So I went seeking medicine and found only poison when everything was taken from us, at the house that had been our own.

I am older now, and our lives have never left my imagination. I talk our lives to God when I draw the water. Although God has blessed me with seven miracles, I have not forgiven Him for what He let happen to Cornelius.

When my mother returned to the house after trying to fetch the bailie, she arrived with Frau Peterson, the Catholic wife of the carpenter, and in the time that the bailie took to come, they separated me and Cornelius. I was locked in one room, where I beat my fists to blood on the door, and Cornelius was taken into the other room. These women hit Cornelius' head and kicked her so brutally that, when the bailie came, Colleen's man from next door had to be called to come. He was needed to carry Cornelius, which he did gently.

Then the bailie said, "The wife will have to come, too."

"Of course, as a witness," my mother offered.

"The evil of the one is the evil of the other, in the law's eyes."

My mother unbolted my door, found me on the floor weeping and said, "Here she is. The Devil's whore."

And all I can say is how language is an empty and useless affair, if that is the only name there is for me. I was brought to prison but separated from Cornelius, though we were both women by then. Nails were put under my skin and my back beaten until God brought me the sixth miracle. I shrank in size. I became quite small again. That helped. There was less of me to torture, less of me to feel pain.

Now I know how everything real is called by a name. In prison, they had names for what Cornelius and I did that I never imagined. I can be with Colleen who is older now too and has some trouble walking. We'll be coming the long way home, and we can say every word we know, including the new ones that have come from France and the north, and I still have nothing to call myself but a woman and a wife and sometimes Catherine.

The knife hanging from the belt on my kirtle is called a keeper. The mud that catches under the wooden heel of my shoe is called a clot. The straw roofs on our houses are called thatches. A day's work is called a measure. A nipple is called a teat. A dog, a mongrel. You angels are called by the names God gave to each of you before He made the world in his own likeness. The Devil is called by so many names that we each choose our own to speak of him. When I speak of the Devil, I use my second husband's first name, which is Simon.

Simon is a disciplined and a stupid man, a jailer whose first wife drowned herself in the east pond of the village. Now he is my second husband, this Devil Simon. He has thick arms and considers himself my first husband, and that is as much as we have discussed of what happened between Cornelius and me. I cook and work four fields for my second husband, and in return he pierces my backside until I bleed.

He and I met when Cornelius was taken up the hill. It is the court's custom to have other prisoners brought to watch their fellows perish. They call these things outings, as if they are pleasant rovings in the woods, but they are meant to put fear in the sinful, who witness an ordeal so soon to be their own. For my outing, I was placed in chains and fixed in a cart drawn by an ox and driven by him, this jailer I did not yet know but later married. Everyone from our village, including my mother, was there. Colleen came running to me and held a mug up to my lips and there were tears in her eyes, "Poor baby, look at you! Drink this," and sweet wine was in the cup.

Others that knew me averted their eyes and tugged on their children's ears to keep them from me. Those who knew me not called me filth, and a group of boys scooped the steaming clots of the ox and smeared it on my fettered arms and face. My jailer giddy-upped the ox and said, "At least this will learn you right."

Before I saw Cornelius brought to the block, I wanted the last miracle to be for her, that it would be over quickly, and she should not feel pain, that she would not know despair. The driver stopped the cart some distance down the hill, and I was glad to be faraway, where I could avert my eyes. But one glimpse of Cornelius, with ropes binding her arms and bruises disfiguring her face, brought fire to my mouth and a shout shouting, "No! No! NO!" I didn't care that all the plain and miserable heads of the village turned towards me. I screamed, "Woman, you are my love!"

Hearing me, Cornelius woke, as if from a morning's sleep. She resisted the grip of her handlers and struggled. She cursed the souls of her executors and called on her God, and the axe had to be brought down many times before her head was severed, and blood spattered everywhere, and her screaming was more terrible than the most frightening dream.

I had already become small, but in my fetters the vision of Cornelius so mistreated melted my hands until they were tiny hands, tiny as the claws of a small bird. My vision fell away and darkened, sound receded to a muffled drum in my ears, and when I woke I was on the floor of my cell. Soon the magistrate came to me with his ring of keys and heralded the seventh miracle.

The court had decided I could go free.

"The process of justice should not be harsher than the punishment for a particular crime," he said. And I had been in that forgotten cellar for longer than a year, with Cornelius separated from me, my body whipped every fortnight to coax some confession out of my mouth, and in that time not once did I understand the methods of justice.

"The court also strongly endorses the proposal of marriage from Simon the widowed jailer," and I said, "What proposal is that?"

"The one I am telling you of now."

"Is this a condition of my release?" I asked.

"Not exactly," he said, looking around the cellar, a handkerchief raised to his nose, "but it is strongly recommended. To prevent future problems."

I looked at that cellar. I could taste my own vomit before I could imagine another breath inhaled in there. I took the offer, not knowing I had even seen this man.

"Go and sin no more, my daughter," he said.

I wish my last miracle had been a cold blue sword from a rebel angel so I could have chopped his soap-smelling hands from his arms.

When Cornelius was taken up, with her went all her words for things, and I never bothered to gaze in a mirror any more either, though we have better mirrors now that show every eyelash in detail, only I get no pleasure in seeing in my face what I have become. When I feel my emptiness down there, where Cornelius' hands used to be, her silken tongue, I swear by Mary the mother of God I don't know what prevents me from lighting the broom and setting fire to every thatch in this village, beginning with the thatches over my second husband's head and ending with my mother's house.

I do not know what prevents me.

Colleen, perhaps. How the prophet begged God: if there is one holy among them, would God spare the whole village? I could spare the one holy among them, spare Colleen and her brood of children and her man who carried Cornelius, pass over all of them, as the angels did in Egypt, for Colleen's mantel is painted with the mark I recognize, the blood of women whose holiness is not understood. Yes. Come with me now, you angels. I will divert my heart no longer. Yes. Here is my broom, and here is the fire.

The Woman She Came to Seek

Sigrid Nielsen

Jean de Vaubrun rode to Edinburgh from France in the autumn of 1792 [or possibly 1793], never pausing in his search for the woman he loved. Here I shall find you, Céline, soul of my soul, he told the summits of Arthur's Seat as they rose into view over the flats of Dunbar.

[How far away could you really see bloody Arthur's Seat? On the train journey, it came up somewhere near the Prestonpans Power Station, but it was no use trying to mention that.]

His horsemanship was superb. His clothes clung to his tall, slender frame, though they were slightly mussed after being slept in for a week. He had shared a bed in the mean inns along the way and preferred not to let anyone know he was a woman. He took out his watch in its battered silver case with Liberté, Égalité, Fraternité engraved inside the cover, framing Céline's perfect features and commanding dark eyes ...

"D'you go out in the evening?" asked Patrice McKechnie.

Catriona started to say, "Not a lot," in a sort of hard, youth-of-today voice. She used it with people who didn't know her very well. Now, however, it struck her that she'd better not give Patrice an opening, though she wasn't quite sure why.

"I work on my novel," she said.

"Oh," said Patrice.

"It's about the French Revolution."

"You're no bad-looking," said Patrice.

"Ta very much," said Catriona, deadpan.

"I mean it."

Catriona's brain was jamming. "Red hair," said Patrice, taking a hank of Catriona's very long and kinky hair in her hand. "Means you're passionate." She grinned. "Ooh, there's my order up. Can you give that lot on 2b coffee, hen? The table in the corner. Ta. If you're no busy."

"I'm no busy," said Catriona.

Dark flakes of snow tumbled past the candlelit windows of the Countess of Ratho's townhouse in Charlotte Square. The granite steps and the pillared doorcase were new and unmarked by the city's dirty air. Jean, elegant in his cloak and three-cornered hat, strode up and put his hand on the cold brass door-knocker ...

[Except that it wasn't snowing, because this has to have been November. Because Jean was fleeing from the September Massacres. Unless they didn't actually happen in September. The book's away to the library. Oh, who cares.]

"I've been waiting for you," said the Countess. She had a soirée known as the Cercle Republicain. *Jean handed his cloak to the liveried servant, who bowed. His gaze met the intelligent green eyes of the Countess, eyes whose expression had all the warmth and silent wilfulness of her native land. Jean looked at her a moment too long, then forced himself to gaze over her shoulder to the well-tailored figures among the candelabra. It was not going to be simple, finding Céline ...*

"It's my cousin," said Patrice.

"I see," said Catriona.

"He's a mate of my husband's. You'd like him. He's doing the business course at Stevenson College. We're all going out on Saturday night –"

Even when you knew you were going to blush, thought Catriona, you could never do anything about it. And it was one thing to lie, and another to blush. Blushing suggested you weren't just lying, but that you had something to hide. What Catriona had to hide was that she hated turning down any gift from Patrice, who was the best waitress in the place, as well as the nicest. Catriona liked having someone to trade silly remarks with at the staff table, and to say "safe home" when she walked back to her bedsit after the evening shift. Patrice was an impulsive, on-or-off sort of person. She wouldn't ask twice.

Have to visit my mum at the weekend, thought Catriona. An honest lie, not one of your wee slippery round-the-corner-from-the-truth excuses with nervous grins on their faces.

"Catriona," said Rose-Marie, "that's your turkey cérise on the counter for the last five minutes." Rose-Marie, part owner of the Right and Wrong Restaurant, was a former model from Toulon in the south of France. Napoleon had fought one of his early battles at Toulon, but Rose-Marie hadn't realised this until Catriona pointed it out.

"This is a going concern!" said Rose-Marie. "We're not here for glamour."

"Sorry," said Catriona.

Patrice pretended not to have heard. "What about –" she began, but Catriona grabbed the moment to escape to the kitchen with an amiably wretched smile on her face.

"Patreese," said Rose-Marie, "there's a new girl coming in tonight. I want you to show her the ropes. She has a lot of energy, uh-huh? I know she'll work out and be very, very good. Not like some of these slack people. The Scottish aren't lazy like the English. I don't care what anybody says."

Dear Anne,

I've had a job now for about a month. It's in the High Street in a restaurant that's named after the old Right and Wrong Club in Edinburgh. The point of the Right and Wrong Club was to see if you could get guttered six nights a week and not a lot has changed. All the doors have fanlights even though they are in the basement. We do crêpes Flambées and lobster thermidor. The menu says the lobster is flown in every day from South Africa.

I write every afternoon between shifts. The story is getting quite exciting. Céline has escaped from the Marquis de Pierre-Noire and fled to Edinburgh. I plan to be finished in eighteen months or so. The only problem is that I'm tired sometimes and write more or less whatever comes into my head. I still can't make up my mind what exactly to do about trying to get a university place or something like it, and I would feel better, I think, if we could talk about what you said when I visited you. I'm sorry I haven't written since then, but I've felt very confused about some things that happened with us and you didn't seem to want to say any more. I mean, that may have been the right impression, and I don't want to force you to say more than you want to, or really anything, but I'd like to know if you still want to write to me, possibly just about books, or if you wanted to –

> *"When I met you in Paris," said Mme de Ratho, "I wanted to say –"*
>
> *"Citizen Vaubrun!"*
>
> *It was a familiar voice, but not, Jean realized with a start, the voice he thought he had heard. With a shock of disappointment he recognized Livée de St-Orages, another republican refugee like himself, whose background was no longer humble enough for the government. Livée played the spinet and was one of the few women in France to have mastered the analytical geometry of René Descartes.*
>
> *"Livée, perhaps you can be of some help to Citizen Vaubrun," said Mme de Ratho pointedly. "He is searching for another refugee. Perhaps you have heard of her?"*
>
> *"Edinburgh is packed with refugees these days."*
>
> *"He is looking for Mademoiselle Céline de Mont-Mercure."*
>
> *"Surely not . . . the Duchesse de Mont-Mercure?"*
>
> *"She has renounced her title," said Jean firmly. He had no sense of telling a lie; after all, Céline must surely have realized that she was forfeiting her title by fleeing to Scotland.*
>
> *"Alas! I have not heard of her," said Livée wistfully. "I fear I cannot help you. I am desolated."*
>
> *"Come, Citizen Vaubrun," said Mme de Ratho, "there is someone over here I want you to meet . . ."*

Dear Anne,

How is your course going? I'm sure I know the answer to that anyway. I saw your mum when I was visiting my parents in Greylaw, a couple of months ago. She said you were interning with a stockbroker and it was a special summer programme, so all the best and all the rest everyone else has already said to you. Your mum said you weren't liking the Smoke much better but that it was alright. So here I am in Edinburgh, same old place, thinking I might as well write and say hi ya ...

Catriona didn't send that letter either.

"There's someone over here I want you to meet," said Patrice.

Catriona's eyes raked the room for the cousin, but the bar and the more downmarket tables were empty.

"No over there, over here. The new lass."

"Oh."

"Sarah Donahue."

"Hullo," said Catriona, hoping she didn't sound too relieved. But she did. She realized she sounded elated.

Sarah was shorter than Catriona, and she had straight reddish hair, not the wild and curly type. Her eyes were a washed-out blue with a level gaze. She wore no make-up and no rings on her freckly hands.

"Hi," she said.

"Sarah's from America," said Patrice.

"I'm just here for the summer," said Sarah.

"It's spring," said Catriona stupidly.

"It's almost summer," said Sarah, obviously not put off.

"Catriona's a writer," said Patrice.

"I usedta know some writers," said Sarah, leaving no doubt she could handle the experience.

Later, at the staff table, Sarah told Catriona and Patrice that she was from New York and that she and her mother were travelling around Europe. Her mother was doing a study of unemployment for an American government department.

"She'll be with us yet awhile, then," said Patrice with a sour laugh.

Sarah lit up a fag. Catriona decided not to mention that she hated cigarette smoke. Somebody left a half carafe of house red, probably with good reason, but they all downed it while Rose-Marie was in the kitchen arguing with her husband.

"Thought you hated wine, Kate," said Dougie the table-clearer.

"I hate being called Kate," said Catriona in Jean's accent, flicking her fingers and pouting, which inspired a rash of imitations of Rose-Marie and the French in general. They all had to

wipe the smiles off their faces when she came striding through
the door.

> *Great longing, thought Jean, has its uses. Great longing sets the*
> *mind free of concern for trivialities. Great longing leaves the soul*
> *free to feel clearly and spurs the imagination to create what is*
> *most truly desired.*
>
> *In the short space of time it took him to walk across the*
> *room arm-in-arm with Mme de Ratho, he thought he saw . . .*
> *Could it be? She stood in the doorway with her hand on her*
> *hip as she always did when she was angry. Her dark hair fell*
> *loose in ringlets, in the fashion of the time. She was dressed in*
> *brilliant white, in a simple gown and satin slippers. A fichu of*
> *the finest Valenciennes lace covered her neck and shoulders.*
> *"Jean," she cried, her eyes blazing, "why in God's name didn't*
> *you write?"*
>
> *At the sound of her voice, Jean started forward. "Is something*
> *wrong?" asked Mme de Ratho.*
>
> *His heart pounding, Jean looked at the door. A different*
> *woman stood there, a meagre little woman of twenty-eight or*
> *nine or even older. His imagination had created it all. How*
> *powerful I am, he thought. How powerful! How helpless!*

"This way," said Sarah.

"Where?"

"If I don't have a smoke, I'll crack."

"Isn't that Rose-Marie's garden?"

Sarah sniffed, or laughed, it was hard to tell which. She ran
down the stairs and opened the glass door, and Catriona
followed. They sat on a patch of wizened grass at the foot of a
three-storey-high rose-bush.

"Whoo. Jesus. That's better."

"What if she comes out here?"

"She and greasy Guy are doing an inventory on the wines."

The garden wall and the towering backs of the High Street
tenements were catching the sun. It was almost warm: Edinburgh
was having its two weeks of summer. It would be mid-June soon.
Anne would be finishing her term.

"Besides," said Sarah, "didn't you notice her eyes? She may take quite a while adding up the wine list."

"She did tell me she has sensitive eyes. That's why she always wears tinted spectacles."

"Looks like pot. But it might be coke."

Catriona had already laughed when she realised it wasn't a joke.

"I suppose you're very experienced," she said apologetically, but Sarah took it as a question.

"Well, at my age, I ought to be."

"At your age?"

"Thirty." Sarah held her ringless hand up to take another drag.

"You're really thirty," said Catriona, trying to sound as if she were pretending she didn't believe it.

"And I'm not married," said Sarah. "Isn't that the next question?"

"No – I mean –"

"I was engaged. But he gave me a hard time. So one day I poured a cup of coffee over his head. I think he took it personally." She grinned.

Catriona's mind was spinning. She felt she ought to write Sarah a very simple and sincere and official letter of thanks for not being married. She had never known any woman who had survived to the age of thirty unmarried without developing a severe case of flower-patterned blouses and low-heeled blue-grey shoes.

She looked at Sarah's face. Sarah didn't seem to mind. Sarah's skin might be thirty (except that Catriona had never tried to judge the age of anyone's skin before). But it made no difference. Sarah's face was young.

It was not until a long time afterwards that Catriona thought she understood the reason Sarah seemed young, which was simple: she looked directly at everyone and let them look back at her. She even let the school-leavers who washed the dishes and cleared the tables look straight into her eyes. Most older people never invited such a thing; most younger people never dared to do it.

That day, however, Catriona thought it was Sarah's eyes and her mouth which were young. She noticed Sarah's chapped lips.

Sarah's face was bony (as well as freckly), but her lips were rather full. She had a nice mouth, almost a kind mouth.

Sarah stubbed out her cigarette at the foot of Rose-Marie's rose-bush, stood up, and studied the round black mark with satisfaction.

"Who could've put that there? Did you see anything?"

"No," said Catriona.

"My oldest friend," said Mme de Ratho. "You must meet her.

We shared a room at convent school. We were lonely together. We suffered the barbarities of the school regime and swore to live free for the rest of our lives!"

Jean swept a graceful but careless bow. Sarah van Williamsburgh, of the new American republic, smiled as she took in his fiery hair, strong regular features, and green eyes.

"I'm glad to see that the cause of freedom has acquired such energetic support in Edinburgh," she said.

Jean took a deep breath. In the course of filling his lungs he felt as if he were rising a few inches off the ground. He also remembered that he had a secret, though, at that moment, he could not quite recall what it was.

"Look at this," said Sarah, the next day.

They were together in the big cupboard behind the staff room, refilling the sugar bowls. It was the magical hour after the lunch shift, when everyone had gone away and there was no sound louder than the hoover.

"Present from Alan behind the bar," said Sarah, drawing out the glass she had been holding behind the frilly apron the waitresses at the Right and Wrong had to wear.

Catriona took a look at the brown liquid and thought, I'm nineteen years old, I've failed all my O-grades, and I'm a disgrace to my family. I think I can just about manage whisky. She took the glass from Sarah.

"It's cognac."

"The kind Napoleon liked," said Catriona, wiping her eyes and pulling a face.

"Stop exaggerating. It's not that bad."

"No, no, fine, fine," said Catriona, faking a cough.

"Always sending yourself up. Innocent Scots lassie meets the big bad world."

Catriona grinned. It was a painful grin. She had never heard anyone make this kind of remark to another person's face before. It wasn't a compliment. But the fact that Sarah had said it at all seemed to mean she thought they were very close friends. Or was she just trying to make Catriona angry? Sarah seemed to have a special liking for angry gestures, even when she had provoked them herself.

"I expect you have to know someone quite well to say things like that," said Catriona solemnly.

Sarah ignored her. "Somebody should give you practice drinking your own whisky. I'm going to Mather's Bar on Friday night. You know where that is?"

"Yes, it's right on my way home."

"Good. I don't know this place. You're going to have to get me there."

Another flash was going off in Catriona's mind. A minute before, she had hated bars and drinking and what people called "going out"; now she felt pleased and flattered, just as if Sarah had invited her to do something interesting. It was very odd. They finished filling the sugar bowls and Catriona left for the afternoon. She could taste the cognac all the way down the Mound.

Dear Mum,

I tried ringing, but you were out, and I can't ring in the evenings because I'm working. I expect I didn't get your message because people in the other bedsits sometimes forget to pass them on. Or they put them under the wrong door. Unfortunately, there is nothing to be done about this. I'm afraid I won't be able to make it back to Greylaw this weekend because I have promised to go out with the cousin of a friend. He is studying business management. He seems very nice. I think it would be rude to try to put him off now.

I hope you and Dad are well. The garden must be looking very nice. I expect you're busy with the ladies' altar guild and the old people's picnic. I will try to arrange things better another time.

Love,
Catriona

The clock chimed in the hall; as it stopped, Jean heard the faint sound of the bells drifting across the Old Town. He never noticed the hour. Mlle van Williamsburgh was sitting beside him in a corner of the study, by the fire. Far away across the room, her mother was deep in conversation with a handsome young advocate; they were discussing the merits of a written constitution.

"I fell in love with her, the first time I saw her," Jean was saying.

He was surprised to find himself speaking about Céline to Miss van Williamsburgh; but not deeply surprised. Ordinarily he would not have spoken of one woman to another, but Miss van Williamsburgh was so straightforward, so unaffected, and Céline was always so near the surface of his thoughts.

"You fell in love with her. And did she fall in love with you?"

"Yes," said Jean. "And we swore a pledge."

"And what happened then?"

"Oh, quite a lot," said Jean, who found it rather hard to explain the number of duels, pursuits on horseback, quick changes of identity and narrow escapes from the authorities he had experienced by the age of twenty-four. "Her grandmother married her to a very royalist nobleman, and she ran away from him to Edinburgh."

"And she sent you a message asking you to join her?"

"I would find her, wherever she was. No matter what effort it might take."

"But did she ask you to come here?"

"I'm not sure what you mean," said Jean.

"She is a lady of means," said Miss van Williamsburgh gently, "and, from what you say, a lady of strong character."

"Absolutely!" said Jean, whose lips and fingers tingled slightly at the opportunity to say as much.

"For such a person, finding a protector might not be so difficult, even in Edinburgh."

Jean smiled. He might have known that even someone as sensible as Miss van Williamsburgh would try to make a play of this sort. It was hard for most people to understand the quality of Céline's love.

"Surely," said Miss Williamsburgh, "the poor lady has the right to organize her own rescue at her leisure? I detest being rescued myself, unless I have specifically requested it."

Jean never doubted himself. But, at the moment, it did strike him that he ought to have thought more about Céline's situation. Perhaps it wouldn't be such a bad idea to be slightly more circumspect about looking for her. He studied Miss van Williamsburgh's unpretentious gown and simply done reddish hair. She was a truly republican woman, the type of a new age. Her strength lay in her innocence, he thought. A servant came by with a tray of bottles.

"More wine?" said Jean.

"I'll have whisky," said Miss van Williamsburgh. "Go on. What were you saying?"

"Lime and lager," said Catriona.

"One lime and lager," repeated Sarah.

"I think that's lager and lime," said Myrtle, and laughed like a mynah bird. Catriona had never seen anyone like her. She wasn't much over five feet tall and had dead white skin, pipes-tem arms and a broad grin like a cartoon character. "And then they painted the walls of his office with a chemical that made him lose his mind," she was saying to her brother Phil, who was sitting next to her. Catriona gathered that Myrtle was a soap opera fan.

"You could meet anyone in this bar," said the young man on Catriona's other side. She hadn't caught his name. It sounded like Forgue. The bar was very noisy. "I've met so many people in our local," said Forgue. "I can imagine that," said Catriona, and she saw the local, dark and quiet and fairly empty, and Forgue in his donkey jacket and tartan scarf listening to an old man talk about mining in Calgary.

Sarah squeezed in beside her. "This's all right, I would say." She handed Catriona her glass.

"How did you meet so many people?" asked Catriona.

"My mother met Myrtle at the jazz club," said Sarah. "Myrtle plays sax."

"I don't know much about jazz," said Catriona.

"I don't know anything," said Sarah. "You'll have to come along sometime."

"But would you hope to marry her?" asked Miss van Williamsburgh.

"We could never be respectable, in the eyes of the world," said Jean, "but that hardly matters."

"A lady of her background . . . so closely involved with the old régimes –"

"I believe in the perfectability of man," said Jean, with great feeling.

"Forgive me, Citizen Vaubrun. I claim the privilege of age. Perfection is not for the making, or for the keeping, only for the finding. And it is only found in the most unlikely places. One needs to take it while it's there."

She placed her honest, angular hand on the table, palm up. Jean was unable to resist the impulse to return her smile.

The pubs were shut. The chippies were filling up. In the daytime, it was mostly older people you saw on the streets of Edinburgh, but late at night everyone was young. They wore black, with make-up, spiky hair, and eerie cheap jewellery. And here was Catriona in the crowd, watching the last of the twilight in York Place.

"You look pretty sober for someone who's just started on whisky," said Sarah as they walked towards the bus stop.

"I think I'm old enough to be young now," said Catriona.

"Good. What are you doing?"

"Your friends are really nice. You know?"

"Yeah. Really hospitable. You going anywhere just now?"

"All the way home."

"Why don't you come back with me?"

"Oh. Well. But this is the last bus."

"I've got lots of space. And I'll need somebody to wake me up for work tomorrow."

"You're not that drunk."

"Not now. But there's more booze at home."

Catriona laughed. Most people didn't try wit or persuasion on her, drunk or sober. What would Anne think of this? Not very much, one way or the other. Where was it all leading? Too many questions, too many questions, I'm not going to ask any more questions.

"What if we *both* get too drunk to get up for work tomorrow?" she asked as they climbed aboard the bus and put their money in the ticket machine.

"Then my mom will make us coffee," said Sarah.

"She wasn't the woman I came to seek," said Catriona aloud. She was walking up the Mound to do the lunch shift at the Right and Wrong. It was another close, hazy day, warm enough to wear her Georgian waitress uniform without even a sweater and carry her raincoat under her arm.

She couldn't remember where the verse came from. "She wasn't the woman I came to seek." And something about how she did not speak the French of France because she was from Martinique, and how she wasn't rich and she wasn't chic. The verse wasn't about Sarah, of course (she wasn't even from Martinique), but it was just right for her somehow. It was adventurous and yet a bit modest and down-to-earth. Catriona was picturing a series of film-preview shots of Sarah wearing a velvet dress and cape, looking cool and alert but everyday.

She supposed the story would be more *realistic* with someone like Sarah in it, who wasn't glamorous or the love of Jean's life. More mature. Then she thought, hard and suddenly as if it were someone else's thought, I'm in love with someone who's not Anne.

So? she answered herself. It's just a story. Nothing's going to happen.

I don't want to think about it, she went on. It's a nice day. I'm not even dreading work.

Still, she said as she turned the corner of the High Street. I suppose it won't do to let things drift.

Who's letting things drift? she argued. There *isn't* anything to drift.

But it's not, well, responsible to think about it that way.

She was late to the Right and Wrong. Rose-Marie glided up in her clinging black lunch frock, raised her finger and said, as she'd already said several times that day, "Catreeona, this is your last warning."

Dear Anne,

I'm sorry I didn't write to you before. It's not easy for me to do. I don't know how much you want to hear about anything in particular. But I've thought about it and what's most important to me is being your friend. If that makes a difference to you, I hope you'll write to me.

Catriona wrote her new address and the Right and Wrong's phone number at the bottom. She stood the envelope up on the mantel. I really will post it tomorrow, she thought.

It was another lunchtime at the Right and Wrong. There were two separate rushes and someone tried to walk out without paying one of Sarah's tickets. A huge party from the City Chambers arrived without reservations and they had to shove three tables together, and right after that, in came fourteen Japanese tourists.

At two-thirty, Patrice, Sarah, Catriona and the boys were just starting to tackle the clearing-up. They were all tired, though a little richer. Catriona wiped down the last of her tables and suddenly realised that the conversation around her had stopped.

"I think there's somebody here to see you, Catriona," said one of the boys.

She stood in the doorway with her hand on her hip as she always did when she was angry. Her dark hair stood up in gelled planes, in the fashion of the time. She was dressed in brilliant white, in a jacket with padded shoulders, Palm Beach trousers, and thick-soled shoes. A shawl from Oxfam in Morningside covered her neck and shoulders.

"Catriona Gough," she said, her eyes blazing, "why the fuck didn't you ever write?"

POSSIBILITIES

Possibilities

The six stories gathered in this final section have little in common except a certain quality of strangeness. They each depart, in one way or another, in style or substance or both, from the conventions of naturalistic fiction. I offer them as signposts to some of the places lesbian fiction is heading.

Patricia Duncker's brief "Aria Nova", like the kind of song for which it is named, refuses to produce a plot. Impossible to summarize, it is about a change of clothes, a change of mood. Combining highly specific details (a sinister lavatory bowl in Paris, for instance) and existential questions, it manages to catch an ephemeral moment, a vision of universal rejoicing on the platform of a train station.

> Dancing contains the force of the great green wind, which will be the destruction and salvation of the world. So take your partner in your arms and dance.

Rebecca Brown's suitably titled "The Dark House", by contrast, draws us into an extraordinary landscape where the details may come from everyday life (a conference, sash windows, a coffee-cart) but the whole has the feel and pace of a nightmare: the repetition, the flight, the waiting, the segue from one setting to another. All the things Brown doesn't tell us (who and where are these characters? what is the conference really about? is the river literal or metaphorical?) hover around us. This is an unnerving world in which we never know quite what's going on, but at its centre is an obsession anyone can understand: a lover's desperate complaint. One way of reading "The Dark House" is as an allegory of life in the closet, with all its confusion, self-abnegation and betrayal. Like Mary Dorcey's story, it is written from "I" to "you"; the tone is not tender, this time, however, but accusatory.

> Never, you said, don't waste your time waiting. Then you looked at me and asked, your lower lip pouting, coy, Don't you believe me? I was the only one to whom you spoke about any of this. I brought it out of you. When you said, Never, I thought, You never have, but you will with me if I wait.

Aileen La Tourette's "A Triangular Eye: 1, 2, 3" is composed of the first three of a set of six pieces. A surreal wedding day is told from contrasting points of view: the reluctant bride, the betrayed lover, and the photographer who is doomed to live behind her lens, excluded from the picture. A story of masks, wedding superstitions, mythic and fairytale roles, "The Triangular Eye" also catches the hallucinatory quality of pre-menstrual tension.

> Like doing a round in the ring with an invisible opponent. Shadow-boxing. Like hearing the sharp sweet pipes of Pan in the forest at night. Derivation of panic.

Anne Cameron, known for her realistic novels and her collections of fantastical myths, combines the two sides of her writing in such stories as "Did'ja Ever Hear of a Goolieguy?". Like its title, this story is both colloquial and magical. Cameron offers a fresh take on a theme which was very popular in the 1970s: the feminist utopian impulse, seeking out a world in which women can be at home with the rest of nature. But what saves her story from cuteness is the gravity of the pain it explores: the narrator's terrible family secrets, the agonies of the gooliguys. This powerful piece is as much about Vancouver Island's loss of its forests as about the narrator's loss of her lover.

Christine Crow's mad, scholarly fantasia, "If Pigs Could Fly", has three epigraphs and a plethora of mocking and serious references to critical theory. It wryly proclaims itself to be "that queer kind of writing where Fiction and Gender Theory take each other to task, so to speak". Throughout, Crow quotes and rethinks Christina Rossetti's poem of strange love between sisters, "Goblin Market". What holds this riot of wordplay and free association together is the polymorphous vitality of the central image, the pig: "Your child, your frog-prince, your naked, cloven-hoof lover, your precious, rumple-trumble what-you-will self."

This section ends with an outstanding example of science fiction. Tanith Lee's "Love Alters" is a classic reversed-world scenario with a highly original theme. Like Michelene Wandor, Lee investigates what happens if a lesbian falls for a man, but the story is quite different when it takes place in a future society where same-sex bonds are the only "normal" ones. At first Lee produces great comedy from the idea of a world where a mother keeps trying to set her daughter up with "the boyish rangey sort of girl". But soon the note of autumnal melancholy is sounded; the conventions of this new society are just as constricting as the old. This powerful story will force straight readers to see what being the "queer" ones might feel like, but it also asks lesbian and gay readers to confront their own prejudices. The sorrowful narrator finds herself in a dilemma that could happen in any place or era. "Everything is always changing. Seasons, weather, time. So why not the climate of love?"

Aria Nova

Patricia Duncker

Let me tell you about the briefest and most extraordinary love affair I ever had. Everything about the incident was original, peculiar, bizarre. It was so unexpected. I was not looking for trouble, so to speak. Indeed, I was on my way home after an interview for a university post, and I was in a state of panic because I had accepted the job. I was also quite convinced that I had made a terrible mistake. But it was too late to withdraw my consent. A bleak mountainous future, lost in the northern provinces, stretched before me. I sat on the train thinking about driving rain, damp mornings in congealed mist, morose colleagues going through horrific divorce proceedings and depressed, debt-ridden students. I hardly noticed the summer fields dancing past. The train reached Paris at midday.

I have good friends in Paris. I have the keys to their flat. I let myself into the dark, shuttered space: tiny galley kitchen, a bathroom narrow as a dagger's blade, a soft interior full of technology and opulent plants. I took off my shoes and burst into tears, facing a precipice of unavoidable disaster. Every evil is much worse imagined. I am cursed with a vivid imagination. Wailing gave way to sniffing gulps in due course and I began to take note of the sounds outside pigeons on the window sill, shitting among the geraniums, the sound of smashing glass in the bottle bank, a quarrel in Arabic. I shuffled sideways into the bathroom and washed my face. My friends have one of those idiotic theatrical mirrors surrounded by a string of white bulbs, vicious as parsnips, which add ten years to your age. I put my tongue out at my own reflection. Then I rammed half the Kleenex box down the lavatory. No matter how conscientious they are about cleaning that sinister yellow bowl, it always smells of urine and disease. They have a barrage of ozone-friendly aerosols positioned suggestively on the edge of the shower. None of them are effective. I watched the Kleenex vanish. My tears swirled away into the Paris sewers. I sat down to take stock of my progress so far.

All right, so the future was not promising. But at least it was going to be paid for by a state institution. Money is a great consolation in times of sorrow. So I thought about money. Solitary nights on a lonely mountain were not immediately appetizing either, but I would buy a video and watch homoerotic forties war films where the men fall into one another's arms, declare themselves and then die. There was one film I remembered, set on a very slowly sinking battleship full of gaping holes, in which the entire cast, their shirts unbuttoned to the waist, died one by one, moaning against the captain's manly chest. I'm surprised it got past the British Board of Film Censors with a "U" certificate. I've seen it three times. So the winter evenings were more or less taken care of, or at least, their terrifying length was halved. Reading books, writing lectures, and marking essays would fill up the rest of the time. I turned my thoughts to food. If you have lived in France for years, the prospect of being separated from your favourite restaurant and your friends' kitchens is harrowing. The vision of the British supermarket and pre-packaged, chemically enhanced pizzas, accompanied by wizened roots, unfolded before me. Once more I was very near to tears. Then it struck me as odd that food was clearly so much more important than sex in my shaping of this atrocious northern world. Well, it would be too cold to take your clothes off, ever. A montage of erotic scenarios therefore faded away with fife and drum into the distance. I tried thinking hard about the money. And for a while, this worked.

I had a shower and then sat dripping on my friends' postmodern rug, while I pulled every single, filthy garment out of my travelling bag. The only thing left that was crushed but clean was my interview suit. I had worn that for a terrible thirty-five minutes, then run straight back from the chamber of confrontations to the bed-and-breakfast where I was a refugee on the third floor. The suit was scrunched into the bottom of the bag and I re-emerged, booted and spurred, ready for flight.

I peered dubiously at my smart high heels, the fraudulent woman's complete disguise, and decided against them. There I stood, thirty-eight minutes later, in lush dark green, ironed white shirt, Wyatt Earp tie, tiny gold studs and Doc Martens, laced up my calves, with steel discs on the toes and heels, in case I needed to rupture someone's spleen. I looked back into the mirror and saw myself, impeccable, extraordinary, bryllcreemed, murderous.

"Go forth and conquer," I leered at my reflection.

The phone rang. It was one of the friends who owned the flat. "F-E-L-I-C-I-T-A-T-I-O-N-S!" she shrieked.

"*Tu parles*," I laughed, very pleased, and danced a two-step with the phone in my arms.

My boots always give me confidence. I thudded aggressively down the Metro steps and took up two seats' worth of space on the train to Montparnasse. I crossed my legs, pulling my full skirts wide around me. I was a great ship on her maiden voyage, my bows still sticky with champagne. I was a 757 touching 40,000 feet. I was a catamaran, winning the Fastnet. I was travelling again. Without the suit or the boots, my shoulder bag was much lighter and so I bounded up the escalators into the huge, glass-frosted dome of Montparnasse. I was turning the corner on the last flight when I heard the music.

It was the "Blue Danube" waltz, played by full string orchestra with woodwind and percussion, a mass of wonderful, echoing, cascading strings. I reached the top stair and stopped, amazed. For there in the centre of the great concourse, traversed by rushing crowds, surreal and magnificent, flanked by the computer-assisted ticket-dispensing machines, was an orchestra, a perfect orchestra, glamorous in evening dress, creating around them, stucco, pink cupids, chandeliers, bare-breasted women in great masses of taffeta, shining parquet floors, and the shiver of diamonds. Someone pushed past me. I gazed open-mouthed at the phenomenon. There was no conductor, for they were a dance orchestra and followed the first violin.

As the waltz hurtled towards its triumphant close, I heard the roar of applause, rushing out of the girders, cracking the glass, splitting the concrete at my feet. I cried Bravo, Bravo, possessed by uncanny joy. The orchestra rose, turned towards me, an eerie mass of black and white, and bowed. As they seated themselves once more, I was certain that the leader nodded and winked. They began the "Emperor's Waltz". I held my breath.

All around the life of the great station continued. There was someone buying squeezed oranges, ignoring the cellos, a man grappling with the ticket dispenser, which had swallowed his credit card, a group of schoolchildren jostling each others' slogan-covered sacks. The vast, red panels high above us announcing the arrivals and departures continued to click, glitter and change. In the distance, above the tidal surge of the dancing waltz, I heard the hiss of the TGV on the *Grandes Lignes*. Nothing ceased, paused or changed. Everything was touched by the music. The whole world had begun to dance. Then I noticed that someone was standing beside me.

Who is the other who stands beside you? Sometimes, when you look directly, there is no one there. You are simply aware of a mass, a breath, a presence. I was aware of someone in white tie and tails. But I decided not to look. This was probably a colleague collecting money for the orchestra. Yet no importunate top hat appeared before me. What do you want? What are you waiting to hear? Puzzled, I turned to look directly at the apparition, who was now clearly expecting to be acknowledged. Who is the other who stands beside you? Uncanny, familiar, disconcerting beloved and unknown. I looked into a face I had never seen before and had seen every day through all the years. The slick hair, smooth olive skin, the tilt of the chin, the grey eyes; this was the face in the mirror, glimpsed in the night, the face waiting by the open door, the face in which I knew every line of the smile, the face I had never seen. We knew one another. We had never met.

"May I have the pleasure of the dance?"

I had heard the voice a thousand times. I had never heard that voice before. Who is the other who stands beside you? Who is the angel who waits for your greeting? Who is the other who asks you to dance? I put down my bag and held out my arms in a huge open gesture of liberating joy.

Dancing touches the pulse in the veins, in the lips, in the heart, breaks down dams, explodes bombs, rocks dictatorships into catastrophe. Dancing ends wars, heals wounds and sets the captives free. Dancing lights the stones, the trees, the stars with flame, fills the glasses with wine, breaks the pearls from the chain. Dancing fires the churches and the courts, smashes bank doors apart, scatters the sands in the deserts, melts the polar flows. Philosophy is best done dancing. Without dancing, dancing, dancing, no revolution will ever be complete. Dancing is making love. Dancing contains the force of that great green wind, which will be the destruction and the salvation of the world. So take your partner in your arms and dance.

I heard the steel discs on my boots crashing against the floor. All around me the commuting crowds waltzed into eternity, clasped in one another's arms. I caught my train with only seconds to spare. The great red eyes of the electric brain were alight. The footplates were ready to fold quietly back into the body of the long silver creature which was waiting, waiting to dance away down the lines.

See where the angel waits, elegant, loving, fastidious – with outstretched arms.

The Dark House

Rebecca Brown

Never, you said, not me. Don't waste your time waiting.

But after a while you said, Well possibly.

Then after a longer while you said, Well maybe. But that whatever you might do, if you did anything, you'd certainly make no promises and one would be wrong to assume or expect. Then you cocked your head just a little and said that if anything were perhaps to happen it would take a long, long time. But if one were around anyway and felt like it, one might wait.

This was your way of saying Someday. Of telling me to wait.

You said you couldn't even begin to think about it until after the conference. The conference was held every year. The job of hosting the conference rotated every year. You had been the hostess twice before. Once ages ago before me, then once when I first came to you, then now.

Yours was a good place to have it. Yours was a big and well kept place of honey-coloured stone. Mostly it was a long wide block like a country estate with wings on either end. There was a row of big sash windows with thick heavy curtains which you liked to keep drawn completely so, you said, the furniture wouldn't get faded. In the back was a courtyard with round, smooth white or grey stones, so perfect they seemed to have been washed in a machine, not just plucked from a river. There was a river past the courtyard, way past it, on the other side of the huge expansive yard of clipped green grass. The river, though you could hardly see it from your place, was wide and green-blue and rushing with water as thick as oil. Though whether the water felt oily you could only guess, if you cared to, having never been in the water. The river was not mentioned in your introductory tour of the grounds. All that was lush and rich and unmapped and untaxed, what you said you had no interest in, lay beyond the river.

From whence I had come.

Never, you said, not me.

You said you could never leave. You said you couldn't, you just couldn't.

Then wouldn't. Because you didn't have any interest. Because it was all right enough here and familiar. Then because we could scratch out a niche right here if we were discreet enough. Then because we ought to see how it went for a while anyway. Then because we seemed to be managing all right right here with all the nooks and crannies and hidden out-of-the-way places where we could rendezvous. (After a while one of those places was recognized as most convenient for our appointed rendezvous.) Then because of other reasons, reasons bigger than both of us. You said:

I don't have the papers.

You don't need any papers.

I haven't had the shots.

You don't need shots.

You ignored me.

More reasons:

You hadn't studied the maps (implying there were no maps). You needed to work up until retirement, you'd invested so much.

Then, what if you went but when you got there you didn't like it?

Well, just come back.

Or what if you got sick or injured or tired out there, you continued, ignoring me.

But what would make you sick, I knew, was sticking around here forever.

Never, you said, don't waste your time waiting. Then you looked at me and asked, your lower lip pouting, coy, Don't you believe me?

I was the only one to whom you spoke about any of this. I brought it out of you. When you said, Never, I thought, You never have, but you will with me if I wait.

After I'd waited a long time, you sighed and said, Well, maybe. We'll have to see. Wait.

So I did. I was good at waiting. I could wait a long time.

This year was your turn to be hostess of the conference. I was glad. Always before I had missed you when you had gone, and when you had come back you were always so distant I had to wait for you to be with me again.

Every year it was the same people or at least the same kinds of people in the same positions. Though you said you didn't like any of them particularly, there was a kind of comfort in the familiarity. Every year the host or hostess had to plan, organize, arrange, order the same things. You were good at it; you liked it. Actually, what you liked was how everyone praised you and congratulated you and said how marvellous you were for organizing so well and how dedicated you were. (You thought they thought, but didn't say as it would not be polite, that your whole life was dedicated to your work, you had no personal life; you liked that appearance.) In fact, though, as you told me with a dismissive sweep of your arm, you didn't like the conference. All the petty politics and run-of-the-mill repetitions made you sick and tired. And frankly you thought most of them were pretty stupid and boring, and certainly "intellectual cowards" (your phrase). You said you didn't participate because you liked to or got much out of it but because you had to.

The first time you said this to me, ages ago, I said, Why do you have to, you don't have to. You looked at me like I'd just said, Where? when the tour guide was pointing to the Nile. Ooops, I thought, but didn't say. I tried very hard to understand, to sympathize with you.

I also thought to myself that if you were going to get sick and tired, truly sick and tired, of what you said you didn't like, that I would stay and wait for that. Then I'd carry you away.

*   *   *

The same people, or people just like them only with different names, came every year. Whosoever's turn it was to be host or hostess had a big job. I didn't deny that. I agreed it was important and time-consuming and took concentration. I never disparaged or belittled what you did. On the contrary, I offered to help. I'd do anything, I said. Could I help with the mailings or flyers? Accommodations? Leisure time activities? Meet anyone at the train station? Arrange things with the caterer? Sit at the welcome booth and say Welcome? Or at the information book and say Two doors down on your right? Or meet you at night for our traditional appointed rendezvous and do what you asked?

But, you said, with your coy smile that was usually reserved for our traditional appointed rendezvous, and always reserved for me, my presence would distract you.

I said OK.

You lifted your chin slightly, trying to look noble and sad, and said that you had never had anyone before to do those things, you were used to doing them alone. Also you found it more efficient.

I said OK.

You said, Wait, when it's over everything will be different.

I said OK. I looked at you.

In a couple of seconds, you said, very sweetly, I'll be different.

I hoped so. I'd waited for it.

Then you cocked your head and said, Well, maybe I'll find something for you to do.

I didn't say, because I didn't need to, because you knew, that I'd do anything.

You knew that, though I didn't want to, I would have pretended for them, for you, that I was just another helpful civic-minded volunteer and not your one and only.

The conference went on a long time. Lectures, papers, seminars, discussion groups, morning coffees, evening sightseeing tours (optional), and lots of cocktail parties.

Given your organizational role, you weren't expected to come up with anything original, the way you would have if you were just a participant. You didn't have to be alone to think. Nor did you have to work so hard pre-planning. There were committees and volunteers and interns. You could have delegated, but you didn't. Some of the junk you did was busy-work. You wanted everyone to say, My, she certainly works hard, doesn't she. Or, Look how much beyond the call, how marvellous she is.

I also think you wanted to overwork, to tire yourself.

When you and I met secretly, for our special rendezvous, you said to me, brushing your hand across your brow, your voice a shadow of its former self, that you were getting tired.

You don't have to do so much, I said.

You ignored me.

Are you not going to be well enough when it's time to go? I said.

Can't you see how tired I am, you pouted.

I saw you were tired of the stupid work. Everyone saw. But I'd given up trying to tell you to do less. I also saw you were sick, and more tired still, of pretending. Not only that you liked what you did, which you told me you didn't, but also about you and me.

I said, Look, if you think you're going to fall, at least let me be near enough to catch you and hold you up.

You didn't want anyone to see you, especially to see the way you were with me. I should have said, Stop lying.

You found something for me to do at the conference. You made me the coffee-cart girl. My job was to deliver the coffee, tea, doughnuts and cakes. When there was no immediate coffee or tea need, I was clean-up girl. With these jobs I could always manage to be in the vicinity of you so I could know if you needed me, but far enough away so, as you insisted, no one would suspect. I also emptied trash cans, ashtrays, greasepots in the kitchen, glasses with residue of red or white or mineral water. I washed floors and did windows.

When you passed me in the hall where I was scrubbing on my hands and knees, making your floor the cleanest anyone had ever seen it, though you didn't appear to notice, I bowed my head and muttered, Ma'am. You muttered nothing to me.

I did all this because I understood, not only your "predicament" (your word) but also things about you no one else did, even you. When you said, Wait, you've got to understand, I said OK. I stuck by what I said.

You said that to me quietly so no one else could hear. Though no one else had ever been near when you spoke to me. You spoke to me when we were private and secret on our rendezvous, with hands and tongue and teeth and with – when it was open, it was very dark – your mouth.

Yes, I said breathlessly, I could hardly say no when you had me like that, I'll wait.

I willed myself to wait. You were the one who didn't.

The convention had been going on for days. You had been so busy and had done so much work that you and I had not had time for our traditional appointed rendezvous activity. Though we had met. But when we'd met, we'd worked on organizing. Together we solved the little problems that arose each day about the conference. After a while, when the organizational kinks had been worked out so we could have started our traditional appointed rendezvous activity again, you said to table our meetings for a while because you were tired and needed some time alone. You didn't want to get too tired, you said. I said, OK, I'd wait.

After the conference had gone on quite some time, you started getting bored. We hadn't met in a while, at least, not close-up. Though I had seen you every day, sailing from room to room, nodding your approval, clapping politely at others' findings or engaging in stimulating conversation, and generally holding forth until something even more important and/or interesting called you away. You always slipped away graciously. You didn't act tired at all.

I was with my coffee cart. My cart had two large pots – one with brewed coffee and one with hot water for those who prefer tea (we offered a selection of black and herbal varieties) or decaf.

The cart had four boxes of one dozen mixed doughnuts each (glazed, twists, chocolate covered, plain cake, cream-and jam-(blueberry, cherry, lemon) filled, and maple bars). I was wearing my white apron over my black dress, dark tights, sensible shoes, and a small white cap, which actually looked more like a doily. I was pushing my cart down the empty hall to Seminar Room West 1B. I was passing the elevator.

I didn't hear someone sneak up behind me, but I felt someone slap their hands over my mouth so I couldn't scream, and push me and my cart into the empty elevator. When the elevator door closed behind us the hands came off my mouth and turned me around so I could see who had abducted me: you. It had been so long since we had met for our rendezvous that I didn't recognize your hands. It was awful to have forgotten the touch of your hands.

We were in the elevator on the first floor, where my coffee was headed. You pushed the button to the fourth floor. The elevator door had a small window in it which people could see out of or into when the elevator was passing by a floor. But between each floor there was a space of about six feet where no one could see out or in. As the elevator went between the first and second floors, you yanked me towards you and kissed me on the mouth. Between the second and third floors you stuck your tongue down my throat and squeezed me hard through my uniform. I tried to touch you, but the window of the elevator was starting to show above the third floor.

Wait, you said.

You took a step away from me and dropped your hands to your sides. I looked at them. You looked at the buttons that lit up the floors the way strangers do on elevators.

When the door opened on the third floor, you stepped out without a glance at me. I looked at your retreating back while I tried to catch my breath and straighten the rumples you'd made in my uniform. As the doors closed in front of me, I saw, through the increasingly small slit between the panels of the door, and then through the window, you shake hands firmly with a couple of your colleagues. I waved to you but the elevator was going up so I didn't see if you waved to me.

But I told myself that you had waved, and that it was a secret sign for me: A little longer only, Wait.

It was so lovely what I saw, and so much what I wanted, that I closed my eyes between the floors and saw the sight of your hand waving in to me.

You were very concerned about doing things right.

But it was right, I said, what I wanted us to do. It was not new or wild or unique. On the contrary, it was common. We were going to be part of a fine and lovely and long and true tradition. Not the greatest, granted, nor the best endowed, but a noble one in its own way nonetheless. Perhaps more accurately a heritage.

I knew this. But for you, in my time off, the time that any other time I would have met you for our rendezvous, I researched the history to show you that what I wanted us to do was right. Granted, the old pre-war encyclopaedias didn't give much space to what I was looking for, and what they did say was inaccurate, but all modern scholarship supported it. Even the new edition of the *Children's Book of Knowledge Encyclopaedia* had an article, a sweet one. There was a precedent.

But I'm not like that, you said.

Yes, you are, I said. I showed you an article.

But I'm not like that, you repeated.

How 'bout this, I said, pointing at a picture. Right here –

I am not like that, you interrupted. How do you know that's not a lie?

I didn't say anything. I had photographs and documentary footage and tapes and records and videos and maps and I had come from there.

Besides, you said, even if you're not lying, that's not like me. I'm not like that. I'll never be like that. I'll never be like – You looked away from me, snapped your chin up and said with disdain – any of you coffee-cart girls.

I should have slapped you. I should have done you with a power drill, but I just sat there.

You had made me the coffee-cart girl.

★   ★   ★

Why did I keep waiting? Why did I keep believing that someday you would come around and stop lying? Was it only because I had waited so long already?

Partly. But mostly I'd gotten so used to hearing what you said the way I wanted to that I couldn't tell what you really said. I wanted, when you had said to me, I'm not, I'll never, for you to have been lying. I wanted someday for you to stop lying and be with me.

One afternoon I was pushing my tea and coffee and cakes cart (cakes rather than doughnuts, as it was afternoon) through the hall and I heard your voice coming from outside one of the rooms. I stopped the cart outside the room to listen. You were delivering a paper, nothing new or original, simply a recitation of some old stuff, the kind of thing any child or lazy undergrad could have copped from an encyclopaedia. It wasn't your language. As I listened, I recognized phrases from the *Children's Book of Knowledge Encyclopaedia*, the outdated version you'd grown up with. I could almost see, as you read out words which weren't your own, those old retouched black-and-white photo "reconstructions", edges blurred, of low-life hoodlums in rough, dirty clothes lurking around in menacing creepy places. I think you really didn't realize that what you were reading from was not only obsolete and ridiculous, but wrong. I was embarrassed for you.

I set the wheel lock on my coffee cart and tiptoed over to look in the room. You were standing at the podium. I could see your profile from the back, lit up by the little podium light shining on your text. I looked out at the people watching you. They were shuffling in their seats and glancing at one another out of the corners of their eyes or over the rims of their glasses. Some of them sadly shook their heads. Some of their lips moved, whispering. They all saw through you.

There was one place where you departed from the *Children's Book of Knowledge Encyclopaedia* article you'd copped. Everyone looked up from their laps when they heard you stutter. They were afraid you'd collapse – what if you were so tired you had a heart attack right then and there! I almost barged in to carry you away. But you caught your breath and continued your lecture. You said the words you'd stuttered over: coffee-cart girls.

I pressed my face to the glass and stared at you. You cleared your throat and adjusted your glasses and looked down your nose as if you were not quite used to talking about such things in company, other than clinically. You described the black skirt and white cap and sensible shoes I wore. You said the way one handled the coffee carts, the way one lifted the doughnuts from the tray, the movement of one's wrists and neck and shoulders when one poured coffee made it quite obvious what one was.

What should have been obvious to me, was what you'd made me.

You were recounting, once again, the age-old questions: what makes one turn into a coffee-cart girl? Heredity or Environment? Dominant-submissive or submissive-dominant? Childhood clothing and games? How long one is breast fed? Or simply something very, very wicked? Then you launched into How to Deal with Them. Are they to be pitied or reviled? Are they to be treated as criminals, disturbed or handicapped?

Everyone who was listening to you was polite. They shifted in their seats, stopped taking notes of what you said and started doodling to make it look like they were still taking notes, and also so they wouldn't have to meet your eyes if you looked out at them. You spoke as if your interest was purely academic. Though nothing you have ever done was pure.

I wondered if you actually thought the people you were speaking to believed you. Because the fact is, the people you were lying to, the colleagues you said you didn't respect in the first place, had figured you out ages ago. Despite what you thought of them, they weren't dumb. And they couldn't have cared less about what you were lying about. However, they were puzzled. Why is she lying; they whispered, Why is she saying such dumb archaic stuff? They tolerated you, though, with the sweet sad sympathy of people who hoped they'd never be victim to the same self-delusion as you. They pretended they did not see through you. They felt embarrassment for you, they felt the pity felt for fools.

You'd always wondered what they'd say about you. What they were saying was, Poor dear, who does she think she's kidding, who's she lying for?

The person you were lying for was you.

At the end of the talk, there was polite applause, but no questions. They squirmed in their seats with embarrassment, hoping someone else would come up with some polite little comment or query for the discussion period. They all knew if they opened their mouths they'd only say, You don't really believe any of that stuff, do you? Or, Poor old dear, why can't you just admit it? They all were thinking, sadly, that they'd humour you as long as they had to put up with you. They knew, as I did not, that they didn't have much longer to wait.

That night there was a party in the big room. The room was supposed to be done up like a ballroom, but I couldn't keep my eyes off the things that had not been properly covered; the fold-up dining hall tables, the lunky cash registers at the ends of the self-serve cafeteria lines, the wrestling mats hanging on the south walls, the thick, heavy fire resistant curtain on the stage. This was not a ballroom but a thinly disguised cafeteria and sometime gym. Beneath the smell of this evening's catered canapés, I could smell years of boiled cabbage and boiled potatoes and steamed hotdogs and sweatsocks. Everybody made a good show of not being aghast at the shoddy décor. But I couldn't help thinking of those awful high school dances, or even junior high sock-hops, where everyone stood around nervous and sweaty and pimply under our Clearasil hoping we would, and praying we wouldn't, be asked to dance.

The lights were low in the room. There was no furniture out except at the sides, long tables for the bar and canapés, and at the back, one long table for coffee and tea. I stood by the table at the back in my black dress and white apron and doily cap and sensible shoes. I served people coffee in china cups and saucers and asked them if they'd like milk or sugar. For tonight, we had real milk and sugar, not the little packets. I pointed to the bright shiny silver pitcher of milk and the shiny silver bowl of granulated sugar. I had my standard two pots going – coffee and hot water for tea or decaf. From time to time I'd partly lift the pots to see if I was running out and would need to refill one. Only once did I have to unplug the coffee pot and go back to the kitchen and ask the guys to fill it again. I didn't like to leave my table unattended, and I hated having to tell people that I was temporarily out of coffee but would have a fresh pot in a few minutes. I gave each person a napkin with their cup and saucer, a bigger napkin than they got, which they only got on request, with their drinks from the alcoholic bar.

Someone knocked the milk pitcher over. I thought it was someone who had had an alcoholic drink too many. I was pouring coffee so I didn't see who it was. The milk spilled on the table, wilting and wetting the crisp white pseudo-cloth table cloth. The milk spilled over the back of the table too. I wiped the biggest spill off the table, then squatted down under the table to wipe the wall and floor. When I was under the table, my dress pulled tight against me, I felt someone pawing my butt. I spun around as quick as I could, which wasn't very quick beneath the table, to slap the person who had taken such liberty with me: you.

I hadn't recognized your hands.

It was awful to have forgotten the touch of your hands.

My hand was raised to strike you, but you didn't notice.

Do you know what this party is for? you whispered.

It's – it's just a party, isn't it? I stammered, lowering my hand.

You put your finger to your lips. No, you whispered. You leaned close to me. I smelled your breath; it wasn't coffee. This is my retirement party.

I was too excited to ask you why you hadn't told me before. I blurted out, Then we can leave tonight.

You smiled, but put your finger to your lips to silence me. You pressed your hands on my legs above my knees. I had to steady myself with my hands on the floor, but it was hard scrunched beneath the table.

Tonight – I whispered, unable to contain myself.

Wait, you said, like a bad joke was over between us. Your eyes were bright.

When I opened my mouth again to ask you where we'd meet and when and the arrangements, you covered my mouth with yours so I'd be quiet. You knew a kiss would always, every time, keep me from asking, you from telling.

Wait, you said. You squeezed my legs with your hands again then scooted out from under the table.

I sat under the table a couple seconds watching your feet, your calves and bottom of your skirt, walk briskly away. Then I shook off my daze of happiness and went back to work. I got back on my hands and knees and finished wiping up the milk. When I returned to pouring coffee, there was a sudden rush at the coffee table, like at an intermission. I worked hard and took care of everyone. I was so busy and so eager to be finished waiting that I barely noticed the people I served or heard what they were whispering about.

After the rush was over, the lights in the room began to dim. I heard the rattle of coffee cups against saucers. When I looked up everyone was adjusting their coffee on their laps, their bodies in their seats, more comfortably. There were rows of folding metal chairs with an aisle down the middle from front to back of the room. Someone had been very busy, perhaps as busy as I, when I'd been pouring coffee. In front of me, I saw a roomful of backs of heads. When the house lights were dimmed halfway, one of your colleagues in a dowdy grey suit with thick, black-rimmed coke-bottle glasses walked on to stage. She stood behind a podium and scratched the mic to see if it worked. The whole room crackled. She cleared her throat, leaning too close, then too far away from the mic. She said, Good evening, ahem, what a marvellous convention this has been. Then how well run and efficient, etc. and then how none of this would have been possible without the tireless efforts of one amongst us.

This time, for once, you hadn't seated yourself on stage or front and centre so everyone could see you. This time, rather, you sat at the back of the room, pretending you didn't expect to be called up for acknowledgement. You sat in the last row in the room, the humblest and lowliest, the one in front of the coffee table, in front of me. I stood at work, my hands clasped tidily over my white apron, ready in a moment to pour a cup of coffee or tea for anyone who asked.

From where I stood, I could see your perfectly straight back. Your back is strong and square and white. I knew exactly what every bit of it looked like. When your dowdy colleague said. All the way at the back of the room . . . the people you'd always said you didn't give a damn about, turned and looked at you and smiled. They couldn't see me standing behind you waiting in the dark. You bowed your head as if you were very humble and very touched and as if you hadn't ordered the chairs set out thus, as if you hadn't calculated where you'd sit. Everyone looking back at you started to applaud. Your colleague on stage clapped loudly, her hands above the mic. She was actually quite sweet. After a generous round of clapping, she asked, Banner lights, please, and a banner above the stage was illuminated. I saw a roomful of backs of heads turn simultaneously. The banner said THANK YOU and GOOD LUCK and then your name, Miss – That's the part I looked at most. Your colleague started reciting into the scratchy microphone the official version of your long career of selfless, tireless dedication. She said what an inspiration and what an example you were. I stood at attention, my back to, but not touching, the edge of the coffee table. Part of me thought, If they only knew. But another part of me also felt a secret pleasure in knowing I knew the secrets of you that they did not. Despite myself, I felt a smile forming on my face, for you. But I hid it. Also for you.

Then your colleague asked the house lights to be cut entirely. For a second, the room was completely dark. Though I couldn't see, I pretended I could, the back of your head, and that it turned around and looked at me. A spotlight was switched on above, to the right of your colleague. She cleared her throat as the light staggered over to her. She blinked into it, her coke-bottle glasses reflecting harshly. She fidgeted around in a flat grey purse she'd pulled from inside the podium. From the purse she removed a small package wrapped in festive, but sensible, shiny silver paper. About the size of a watch or a pair of pens.

I am most honoured, she said slowly, trying to sound solemn, on behalf of all of us, to make this very small presentation as a very small token of our very great esteem and gratitude and respect for a most deserving one amongst us.

Your colleague said, If we could possibly persuade our generous and tired and hard-working hostess of the past marvellous conference to let go her hard work for just a moment (knowing chuckles across the room), I should like to ask her to come forward. (Dramatic pause.) Miss –

I'd been so taken in by the theatrics of the darkness and the stage's single light, and of the long-windedness of the speaker, and of my eagerness to leave and of the practical business of leaving – is it too late to book a train? would I have time to pack a bag? how many pairs of shoes would you need? a regular or a traveller's size of toothpaste? – that I hadn't noticed anyone sneak up beside me.

But when your colleague called your name, Miss –, you grabbed me.

You grab my hand and pull me. On stage, as she expects you to make your slow, hand-shaking way up to the front of the room, your colleague departs from the official version to add something new: you're about to embark on the dream of a lifetime, what a lovely place you're going for your retirement. Because you've grabbed my hand, because you're dragging me out of the back, I don't hear the details.

Your free hand pushes the horizontal push bar on the door. The two big metal doors close behind us. We hurry out into the night.

It isn't easy to run in my tights and black skirt and apron. I tear my white doily cap off and drop my apron as we run across the back courtyard. The white-grey stones look like a million tiny moons, smooth and round, beneath us. You pull me across the courtyard to the clipped green grass. It's damp and my rubber soles squeak on it. I hear us breathing as we run, and behind us I hear puzzled shouts, Where is she, Where's she gone? Your moist hand, warmer as we run, is tight. It's tighter as you pull me to the river.

The land begins to slope down near the river. The ground gets slick with mud. You fling your arm around my back and we slip down the bank. Moonlight falls on the still river in a flat wide line. You push into the river, your body cutting the water into black triangular arrowheads. The black water climbs your calves and thighs. I stand at the edge of the water, wetness sucking around my ankles. The water is cold. I turn back to look at the big, light, well-kept place we've run away from. They've turned on the flood-lights. The lights look harsh, accusing, against the honey-coloured stones.

In the courtyard the conventioneers, your former colleagues, rush around looking for you. They open doors and windows. One of them picks up my apron and waves it, What's this? None of them notices I'm missing. A few of them have flashlights whose matchstick beams are weak against the sky. They look so small. Some of them run out to the grass. I wonder if someone will come to the edge of the river. They're so concerned for you. I feel sad for them. I almost want to shout to them that you're all right, don't worry. Why didn't you say something to them?

I want to ask you why but when I turn to you I see your back in front of me. Your hair and clothes are black. I almost can't see you against the black sky and the water. When you feel me looking at you, you turn around. Your face is white except for the black slit opening of your mouth.

Come on.

I hesitate.

What are you waiting for?

I turn back to the old place again.

Don't wait.

When I look at you, you've turned around again. You are heading deeper in the river.

Black water is up to your back. I hear water lap you as it climbs your shoulders. The back of your neck is a white line; everything else is black. I expect you to dive in the water and swim but you don't. Your head goes under, your hands splash up. You're waving frantically. Your voice gargles: I can't swim.

I run a few paces then take a breath and dive into the water. The water feels thick and oily, like my skin won't breathe. I open my eyes underwater but I can't see. My stomach tightens. I swim to where you went under but I can't see you. I swim below so long my lungs feel tight. Water starts coming in my mouth and nose. I need to swim up for air, but I feel something in my hands, your hair. I try to grab but it sways away like an underwater plant. I reach for your body though I can't see it. My hand finds your lips and eyelids. I cup my hand beneath your chin and pull you up towards the surface. When I go up my ears pop. I hadn't realized how deeply you'd sunk. When we break through the surface we gulp air.

You've got to carry me across, you say, I can't swim.

I turn on my side and pull you so your back is in front of me. Your body moves very easily through the water. I reach my arm over your neck, across your chest and hold you by the pit of your arm. The skin inside my upper arm and forearm feels you breathe. The back of your head is in front of my face, your hair stuck up like spiky grass. I smooth your hair down, pressing my palm to touch you. You don't say anything.

Your back is against my hips, your shoulders are against my breast. I feel the slight, regular shift of you, each stroke. I don't see your face.

But though we're close and though I'm pulling us, and though my skin is near you, there is some thing between us. The oily water coats us with a separating skin. What I touch isn't you, but what's between us.

The river is wide. We've stirred the water up. By the middle of the river, where the strongest current is, I'm tired. My head sinks. I sputter. You don't say anything. I don't know how long I can carry us.

When I feel the river bottom beneath my feet, I stumble.

We're across, I say. I hold you under my arm a moment longer than I need to before I say, We can walk the rest of the way. I start to take my hand from your neck.

I can't, you say. You hesitate. I can't walk. I sprained my ankle when I fell in the water. You look away from me. You'll have to carry me.

I squat back into the water and hoist you onto my back. You're much heavier than you were in the water. Your clothes drip on me.

I can't walk, you say again, as if I haven't believed you.

The bank rises up. It's a slippery climb into the woods. Tree branches scratch my face and arms. I trip over roots, in holes, but I don't drop you.

You don't say anything to me, but sometimes I hear you breathing as you sleep.

After a long time beneath your weight, I fall.

We've got to stop, I say, I'm tired, I've got to rest.

I start to put you down but you clutch my neck. You can't stop now, you say.

I'm tired, I need to rest.

Not here, you say, we're so exposed.

We are in the woods with nothing to cover us. But there's no place near, I say.

There's a house ahead.

I can't see anything in the dark.

You'll see it soon, you say. You tighten your arms and legs around my body.

I'm so tired. You'll have to tell me where, I sigh. I readjust your thighs on my hips.

You point your finger in front of us, through the trees. This way, you say.

You lead us to the dark house.

No clearing is around it. All of a sudden, right up against the back of the trees, there's a picket fence surrounding an overgrown yard. The yard is around a huge house. The turrets and gables and roof of the house are sharp, and blacker than the sky.

I hold you steady on my back with one hand while my free hand lifts the latch of the gate. Rust cakes on my skin as the gate creaks open. I carry you into the yard. My feet find the remains of a path through the spiky grass. I carry you up the swaybacked wooden steps. The paint on the porch is chipped. The front porch swing is broken, one chain snapped so half the chair lies on the porch, the other dangles like someone hung.

When I knock on the door, your hand tightens around my neck. I lift the heavy iron knocker against the door and drop it. You whisper something I can't hear.

I knock again. After a few seconds, I try the doorknob. The door gives. It hasn't been latched. I push it open. I carry you over the threshold. I blink to adjust to the darkness. When I reach my hand to find a light, you whisper, No –

But I can't see –

Sshh! You put your hand over my mouth. Put me down.

I can't see where to put you. I can't see anything.

There's a couch over there. You point.

I walk a few feet on the creaky floor. You put your hand over my mouth as if you can stop the floor from squeaking. Your palm is sweaty. I bump into something. I squint down and can barely make out a settee. We're in an alcove off the entry room.

Down, you motion with your hands.

I take you off my back and set you down. I'm about to sit down next to you, but your fingers against my chest stop me.

I need to put my feet up, you whisper, Get a stool. You point in the dark where I can't see.

I follow your directions and trip over the stool. I bring it back to you and put your feet up on it. I start to sit beside you, but you shake your head no. I look at your face; skin grey, lips black, the tops and bottoms of your teeth between your slightly open lips, white.

You don't say anything so I try to sit again. I put my hand on the back of the settee behind your shoulder. I hear something.

I look up. When my eyes adjust to the light, I see a banister, a second-storey hallway. From where I stand in the alcove, I can only see the bottom of the banister. The floor of the hallway is lit from the side, moonlight coming in through an upstairs window.

When I look at you, you're not looking up where the noise came from, you're looking at me.

There's a shuffling sound. I freeze. I'm afraid to whisper. I move my lips silently to you: There's someone in the house.

I hear the shuffling and look up again. I see a pair of slippers, the bottom of a dressing gown. I hold my breath not knowing if we should give ourselves away by asking mercy, we're only here for temporary shelter.

I look at you. You haven't looked up where the noise came from; you're still looking at me, apparently unafraid. I wonder if you haven't heard the noise.

There's someone in the house, I whisper.

You put your finger to your lips, Sshh.

The slippers upstairs shuffle again.

Get out of the house, you whisper to me.

I look at you, not believing you want me to abandon you.

I – I can't run, you whisper, pointing to your feet on the stool. You've got to go.

I'm so happy you want me to escape. You're thinking of me. This is a sign that shows me that you love me. Now that we're away from where we used to be, you can.

I won't leave you, I whisper earnestly. I close my eyes and reach for your hand.

I'll be all right, you mumble, pulling your hand away.

When I open my eyes, I see you less; the darkness of the room has gotten darker. When I look up, the figure upstairs is blocking the moonlight in the hall.

Get out.

I'm about to declare all my undying – when the person upstairs clears their throat. I gasp, then try to hide my fear. I look at you.

Your face betrays no fear.

The voice from upstairs says, Is that you?

Your face shows no surprise. Go, you whisper to me.

I look upstairs again. The slippers are facing us like this person is trying to see where we are. I start to pick you up and carry you away. Your arms are strong when they push me off.

Is that you?

You open your mouth in a way you never have for me.

That's when I realize it is not me that you're about to answer.

I grab your chin and turn your face to me. Whose house is this?

You lower your face.

I yank it up again. Whose house did you make me carry you to?

You close your eyes.

Tell me, goddammit.

I don't hold you hard enough so you can't get away, but you don't pull away. You want me to ask you again. You want me to think I could get it out of you.

Tell me.

You open your mouth as if you're about to answer me. Instead you tell me, Kiss me.

I hesitate.

Quick, you say, Don't wait.

You know I will. Your holding out that kiss to me is making me make a choice which is no choice. I know there isn't time for both, an answer and a kiss. The mouth closed with the mouth won't tell. And you know I will kiss you, and in doing so, I'll let you get away with never telling.

I kiss you. A quick one on the lips; your mouth remains unopened.

Your hands push me away from you.

The steps creak upstairs. I look up between the banister legs and see the bottom of the housecoat, the slippers, moving. You turn me around by my hips and point my body towards the door I carried you through.

When I don't move, you stand up and push me. I gasp when I see you stand, your ankle cured miraculously.

Disarmed by your apparent cure, I can't resist. When you push me towards the door, I go.

Behind me I hear your voices.

Is that you?

Yes, I'm just coming.

You close the door behind me.

I stand outside the closed door of the house. Inside I hear a miracle – you walking.

I step off the porch. I look at the dewy grass and close my eyes. I imagine I see the legs that you said couldn't walk, walk. I imagine I see you walking up the stairs, then down the upstairs hallway, through the door, into the room. I imagine you being inside the room. I open my eyes and look back at the house. It's dark.

But then, in the window of the upstairs room, the one I have imagined, a light flicks on, then slowly burns brighter; a candle. The light wavers, gold and slight, so I can see the shadows on the ceiling of the room. The shadows are of yourself and of the person of the house. They're moving. I watch the moving shadows of the two of you together. Suddenly they break apart. One of the shadows stays still while the other, yours, moves towards the window.

Your hand reaches up to the curtain. Your hand pulls the curtain partway closed, then hesitates as if it knows, because it knows, I'm watching. I wave to the hand but it does not wave back. But it leaves a small, thin opening where someone could wave through. I close my eyes and imagine your hand waving out to me. You leave that opening for me, a sign for me, a way of saying, Someday, if I wait.

The Triangular Eye

Aileen La Tourette

The Triangular Eye: 1

I would be premenstrual on my wedding day.

You would, echo her sisters, the bridesmaids, in the mirror.

"I could be pregnant," she says aloud.

"So could I," they giggle, each in her turn.

"Yes. But for you it would mean something different."

"A trip to the Marie Stopes," one says crudely.

"I mean," she says with dignity, taking up her hairbrush, "it would mean terror and change. For me it would mean routine and predictability. That's why I'm not."

"That's why we're not, too," they give it back to her, like throwing the bridal bouquet back in her face, she feels. She waves her hairbrush.

"Get out of here, will you, please? I want to be alone."

Madame Butterfly, her mother, floats in, handsome in crimson slashed with indigo. She palms a glass of champagne. Her palm is luckily cool and will not smear the chilled glass.

She sets it down.

"She wants to be alone," one of the sisters explains.

"Do you know what Garbo did on her wedding day?" another hesitates in the doorway to enquire.

"Climbed out the window," she nods in the mirror. "Goodbye."

"See you later, alligator," another says affectionately.

She manages a crocodile smile.

Madame Butterfly mouths a kiss in the mirror and turns on her delicate heel.

"I'll leave you to your thoughts, darling," she murmurs. She, too, turns around in the doorway. "It's a good idea to have a quiet little moment before the onslaught," she says, more or less to her own reflection. Her eyes flicker to the bride's. They hold for a second like duellists' eyes behind their masks. Then she's gone, the door softly closed behind her.

"Have you ever slammed a door in your life, Mother?" the bride asks in a stage whisper. "Have I?"

Now, there's a question. She picks at a cuticle. Is it a sin to deprive the unconceived of life? If they're there in preconception, might they not have souls?

She leans towards the mirror. Madame Butterfly's mask was perfectly applied. A reproach to a face which is still just a face. Fingers reach for the little jar of foundation. Her fingers are hot. She curls them around the champagne glass to cool them, then lifts it to her lips.

In a minute she'll send a posse. It's too quiet, she'll think, as she thought when I was a child playing alone, absorbed and happy. Something had to interrupt such perfect concentration.

Funny, our species makes king butterflies of the women. The men are mourning doves today. What can come of the mating of a butterfly and a mourning dove? A poor ungainly bird with useless gauzy wings like a thalidomide child's arms.

Jesus *Christ*.

So she said, aged ten, confronted with a front-page story of thalidomide horrors, graphically illustrated, intended to shock, intended to sell the rag that had printed it.

Exploitation, she wrote, spelling the word out in her head. Addressed it to The Editor and sent it off; but it wasn't really the crassness of the newspaper she was protesting against. It was the crassness of the cosmos in which such a thing could happen.

She raises her head and looks at herself.

Wonder when will it come? Roll on the red sea, not back. PMT means swarms of memories, associations and feelings, especially feelings. None of them specially welcome. It's like being shaken by the scruff of the neck, once a month. Knocks you awake. Like doing a round in the ring with an invisible opponent. Shadow-boxing. Like hearing the sharp sweet pipes of Pan in the forest at night. Derivation of panic. Like: panic.

"Don't panic," she says to her reflection, rubbing in foundation. "You can always – you can always . . ."

Get a divorce? Run away? Commit suicide?

Sleep.

But you won't sleep, or if you do you'll wake up once a month at least. There's the rub.

But I'm not planning to sleep.

Oh, no?

White dress like snow under which you'll grow numb, my dear.

Don't be stupid.

She takes out the compact with the blue enamel design on top, wedding present from MB. The necessary somethings blue and new, MB determined to make this work.

Snow blurs lines, blots out distinctions. Only while it falls, only while the veil hangs in the air, everyone a bride. Then it shapes and sharpens everything again, emphasizes singularly with shadows.

Blush.

Why do we like red cheeks? As if the colour rose from the heart.

From the heart! From the plastic case.

My heart is a blood-red sun. Who said that? No one, probably.

Red sky in the morning, sailors take warning.

I'm getting tired of my mind.

She slurps the rest of the champagne, deliberately piggish.

Pearls before swine, as she clasps them on.

The moon's doing, my mind. PMT. Dismiss it. Biology. Deny, deny. A perversion of truth. A distortion of reality. Once a month the veil lifts, and we shudder, to see the shadows.

Eyeshadow. More blue, on the lid. Borrowed from Kate. A plethora of blues, all shades, this a good healthy aquamarine, nothing brooding.

Eyeliner. Never got it close enough to the actual rim of the lid, not unless you worked at it.

She works at it.

Who am I so angry at? The moon?

Mascara wand. Black, mystic.

A soft tap at the door.

"Shall I help you with your veil, dear?" She's not leaving anything to chance.

"In a minute, Mummy."

Don't overplay your hand.

There's ever so little time left to think of Paul.

There's all the time in the world to think of Paul. And why "ever so"?

Because he says it. It's starting already. Buried in snow-drifts. It does blur, it does. Shadows are negatives. They name only types, they lose features, erase every distinguishing mark, every detail. And yet snowflakes are mortal, individual, like us, each one different. Like thumbprints. Used to identify the guilty.

But snowflakes? Used to whitewash.

I'm a negative. This is a guilty party, a festival of whitewash. Will there be whispers?

"You know she had that –"

"No. I didn't. Know she was like that."

"She isn't now."

Another soft tap at the door, as if she can read the drift of my thoughts. It's not a drift, it's a rip-tide to drag me away from here, it's a whirlpool to pull me down like a ballerina in quick pirouettes.

But I was down before. When I was pretending. The mask is set, but the eyes flicker in the mirror. They'll flicker behind the veil but no one will see.

Unless Jane comes.

MB doesn't know I sent her an invitation. Didn't put her on the list, of course. Anyway, she won't come. She'd toss it into the bin, embossed paper and all. She'd heave it down the plughole. And love. And me.

She'd bury her love in the snow, keep me alive suspended in nitrogen whatever-it-is. Not snow, not for Jane: dry ice. The scorcher, the preserver.

Another tap, louder. Come along, please.

Paul, I must think of Paul.

For ever.

Tap-*tap*.

"Mother, I'll let you know when I'm ready."

"All right, dear."

Nose for rage like a pig for truffles.

Enough of that individual nonsense, time to be gathered and harvested, time to be snowed into your veil, walled into your eyes. Like an icon. They're all the same face. Huge sad eyes, but all the same eyes.

How about an icon with furious eyes? With red eyes from weeping too much wine changed to salt water? How about a madonna screaming?

Jane would love it! How about one sticking her tongue out? How about ...

Jane.

The thought had come. The inspiration, to break the mould.

Now I can go through with it. Let the cock crow three times for me, now ...

"Mother?"

Snowfall without flakes, every circle the same. She adjusts with cool fingers, then lifts the froth for a Judas kiss, cheek to cheek. She's in the lipstick generation.

She knows whose name is on my lips.

Down the stairs to the mounting music. Is it better or worse to be married at home? Not even home is safe. For better or for worse, here I stand at the foot of the stairs, with a smiling man. A bouquet magically in my arms like a wind-borne baby.

Head cold and empty as a snowball under its double masks. Triple: two layers of veil and the make-up.

Oh moon, oh mother. The ritual might freeze but it might also thaw. Masks were once used for healing.

Yes, but they weren't pretty.

Goddess with perfect pitch, make this ring true.

Make me be utterly here, just this once. All present and accounted for. A quorum of my own contradictions so that I can make a valid decision.

"Candles look funny in daylight," she sniffed. "Not worth it."

"If I close the curtains, she'll wonder why."

"I know what." She took the quilt from my bed with one majestic heave. "C'mon. You can blow them out: it's your birthday."

I was ten. Everyone else had gone home. We filled our pockets with candles and scrambled upstairs as we're now scrambling down. She led me, with an enquiring look, into the seldom-used formal parlour. Cold, as they kept them in Irish families, for wakes. We didn't have wakes, but we still kept the parlour cold.

"No one comes in here, do they?" she whispered.

I shook my head.

She threw the blanket over the piano to make a tent and then we sat inside it with the candles. I'd brought a plant to stick them in the dirt. I couldn't think of anything else. She seemed to approve, smiling, with an arm around my shoulders.

"We'll get married," she said confidently. "When we're twelve."

"How can we?"

"Oh, they let you get married younger if you marry a girl."

"They do?"

"Of course they do!"

It must be another example of what my mother called Common Sense. I could never figure out what it was or how it worked. I was glad she knew. It made me feel good about marrying her.

"Know what they'll ask you tomorrow?"

"What?"

"How it feels to be ten. Isn't that a stupid question?" It is. And they got what they wanted: a stupid answer.

The Triangular Eye: 2

In some countries you can get off murder for PMT.

That's what I said to myself as I got ready. Plead insanity if you have to plead.

Then I thought, shit no. That and being a lesbian'll finish me. Life in some loony bin where the masks don't come off.

As I fitted the mask on.

What made me think of it? Old mythologies of healing. You imitate the thing you fear, or the thing you desire. Sympathetic magic. I could've gone dressed as a bride but I didn't fancy it.

So I went as a crone. I thought if I could take that shrivelled-up self and put her outside instead of carrying her around inside me like an ancient foetus grown old without delivery, maybe then I'd be delivered.

Guts, they said.

Nerve, they said.

Cheek, they said.

Sounds like an autopsy, I thought.

Of all the gall, someone said.

I liked that one best. It rhymed.

At first they thought I was a sidekick of the groom's, pulling a practical joke. As they came out of the house towards the marquee on the lawn, I stationed myself at the entrance, the tent flap thing. I wanted to see her walk towards me in that get-up.

Then they thought I was some leftover girlfriend of his. That really annoyed me. I had to take care that they got the idea. But first I had to find a quiet place to scowl at them from, like Quasimodo from the belfry.

There was one woman alone. All the rest were couples, or sisters or brothers or cousins or something avuncular. Why isn't there a word like that for aunts? It just goes to show.

Just remembering it makes me grind my teeth like an old cranky lady. That seemed to me to be about the most objectionable thing I could do from behind a mask, apart from just being there.

There was even one person who was something or other once removed.

"Wish they'd remove him again," I said to someone at my elbow, who turned out to be a camera. Most sympathetic eye I'd seen all day. Objective. I'd tell her my story, as I'd come to play the Ancient Mariner. She was the woman alone.

"Let's sit down. I'm through for the moment."

She didn't seem particularly fazed by my outfit, though she, too, had made the absurd assumption that I was something to do with him in the monkey suit. I quickly put her right, and she smiled.

One picture's worth a thousand words. She didn't have to tell me. Knowing we were comrades-in-arms gave me confidence. I plunged right in and told her all about Frances, first I told her not to judge by appearances, that she was no rent-a-bride. I should know. Told her the places we'd been together, till she decided I was a phase.

She kept getting up to take pictures and whenever she stood up I got a clear view of the High Table, or whatever they call it, with Frances in the middle like Lady Macbeth.

She couldn't see my face, behind the mask. With all that make-up on I could hardly see hers.

"Maybe this is twisting her arm." I defended myself to Evelyn, the photographer, as she sat down. "But it hurts me more than it does her. It's an act of survival, not terrorism."

"Maybe sometimes they're the same."

I wasn't really listening. We painted ourselves once, all over, with flowers and faces and signs. Then we washed it all off and stayed in our colourful bath till the water got cold and we had to run for the bedroom. The sheets were left the shade of a bruise when it's starting to heal and it gets that bright yellow in it and looks worse than ever. I kept them.

"She says I'm not sentimental. She says I don't understand about things like this because I'm not fucking sentimental. Would I have done that? Kept it? Unwashed? Even slept on it sometimes? Actually, it's filthy now. Actually." I had to confess, Evelyn looked so sympathetic I felt a fraud. "It got so bad I had to let the dog sleep on it. Does that mean she's right?"

She smiled.

"Unsentimental people don't even have dogs," I adjudicated for myself. "So there. I wouldn't've given those sheets to any old dog anyway. Just this one. She slept with us, too, sometimes. So it seemed sort of appropriate."

She nodded.

"What about you?"

"Parties are my religion," she said with another smile like a flashbulb. "I follow the crowd, in a literal sense."

"But always stay a little bit apart," I reminded her. Her face was better than you thought, at first. Frances wanted her face to rape, on impact. But this face kind of lights the lamps and waits.

"Weddings are my least favourite parties."

"Mine too. Especially this one."

We drank. I'm getting a wee bit maudlin on the champagne. Must do something, hit and run before I crumble.

"I was in two weddings as a child," she said softly. "I knew then I never wanted one of my own. It seemed wonderful to be a bride, but what then?"

"Anticlimax."

She nodded. "I never made any one of my own great state occasions," she grinned. "First Communion, got measles. Confirmation, mumps. Birthday parties, I was always about to get my period, so I was there but not, you know?"

"I know. I'm like that today."

"Me too." She grimaced. "Weddings do it every time. And of course, there was never any question of a wedding," she made a dismissive gesture, "once I knew. But even if I'd been straight I'm not sure I'd have had one. It's like preferring Easter to Christmas, because it's a moveable feast. It goes according to the moon."

"Christmas goes according to the sun."

"Yes, but the sun is fixed. I prefer moons."

"I know," I grinned at her as flirtatiously as I could. I could see Frances watching us, and her mask slipped just a little over one eye, enough to reveal a greenish flare. "So do I."

Eating smoked salmon behind the mask was a funny sensation. Almost intravenous. I was pigging away nervously when it occurred to me to ask myself why I was nervous. Hadn't I had my big moment by the flap of the tepee? Was there anything else for me to do, anything public and difficult, that is?

Are they the same? Evelyn asked. "Public and difficult?"

"I can't very well make a small intimate gesture under these circumstances," I snapped. She'd definitely struck a nerve. If I'd known her better, I'd have inserted an "of course" after that thought.

"You could try," she said blandly, lighting a cigarette. "I should think the only thing you have to fear –"

"Is fear itself?"

"Is the danger that she might think you only wanted revenge."

"I do want revenge."

"I was under the impression there was something else you wanted."

"Yes, but I can't have that!"

"If you're that convinced, then you must've come here looking for revenge."

I could've bashed her with her camera. As if she knew, she picked it up and started snapping away.

"Listen," I said to her, as she came back to the table to reload. "You know what?"

"What?"

"You're the terrorist, that's what. You try and steal their souls, don't you? Like the old superstition? Capture them?" I was pretty well loaded myself, by then.

"I try to capture a moment in time," she replied. "That's all. Not to steal anything. People think that because they feel exposed. Or because they want to forget. But I don't believe in forgetting."

"Neither do I."

"Most people seem to feel pictures confirm them in some way. Their pictures or something. Rather than detract from them. It's seeing yourself on the other side of the mirror that's odd."

"Like in somebody's eyes. Like love. But then when it's over – the moment – you have to lapse back into yourself again."

"But that's part of the process. Like going back to the darkroom and developing them. You can't be with someone all the time. You have to go and develop your memories – or something. You have to sleep, for Christ's sake!" She laughed a rich champagne chuckle.

Frances was staring again.

"It's all part of the process," she finished. "My whole life is bound up with the process – and so is yours."

"Different processes."

"Maybe. Maybe just different methods."

"I have an idea. If I ask her to dance, will you take pictures?"

"Join the methods."

"Well?"

"Of course I will."

"Better not wait." I stand up on the two sticks I'd hobbled up in, to complete the part. They gave me a terrible feeling of frailty, as if I really needed them. The room seemed to hush slightly as I wobbled over towards Frances. With all that champagne inside me, I did need them.

"What the hell do you think you're doing?" she whispered furiously. "Trying to humiliate me?"

Upstage her, did she mean? Evelyn was right; this could backfire. I could drop down on my knees in front of her, but that'd be over the top.

"Frances," I threw my sticks away in sheer bravado, as if I anticipated acceptance. I anticipated having to play pick-up-sticks in about a minute. "Would you like to dance?"

She looked at me hard. I'd have taken off the mask but I sensed she wanted it left on, for effect. So I just held her eyes through the mask, and she held mine through hers.

Then she stood up, and held out her hand.

The Triangular Eye: 3

Back to the darkroom. Home!

My rabbit hutch. Not cramped, though; room to stretch. I stretch. Every movement in here makes you aware of the walls, not crowding you, just there. I never feel lost in here.

Deep breath. My favourite perfume; sharp, chemical. A constant rain of fluids keeps the air rinsed and fresh, despite the haze from my cigarettes. There's a strong whiff of coffee in the blend, too.

This room used to be a larder. The door leads to the main house through the kitchen. I commute from here to the coffee pot, hardly noticing my to-ings and fro-ings.

There's a bottle of Scotch strategically placed on a shelf. If I've worked a good solid day, I have a whisky and soda at five. Used to make it six, but I'd waste the last hour fretting and fumbling. Funny how hard it was to trust my own sense of time enough to move the drinking hour forward. Felt like the first step down the path towards having a splash of Scotch on waking; but it wasn't, of course. Why do I still have that stubborn idea of linear progressions when everything tells me it doesn't work like that? I set my own pace, my own discipline. I'm ready at five. I emerge at five.

Occasionally, if I'm going out in the evening, I make it a little earlier or a little later. I never skip my ceremony of re-entry into the world. If I do I arrive undeveloped, still in the negative stage. Living alone, working alone, you need your rituals no less than couples or families do, to negotiate the crossing from inner to outer. You have to build your bridges.

I hear voices and motors distantly, as if across water. Sometimes I listen for minutes at a time, crouched over on my stool or standing, transfixed, without a thought in my head. My process in the darkroom is silent. I love the silence, and I am grateful for the sounds.

Today I want to get on with it. It's been a week since the wedding. As I close myself in with my steaming mug of coffee and light a cigarette, I'm aware of an uncomfortable feeling I've fended off for that week. It's hard to fend things off in here. Bit of a confessional. I was afraid to develop these pictures before, afraid I'd be jealous.

That's better. Now it's out of the bag and I can see its green cat's eyes gleaming in the dark. A big cat, a tiger. I've seen it before. You see a lot of things, in the dark; but only what you bring in with you.

My tiger's the photo of a dream, developed over some ten years. Successive dreams, successive negatives dipped in some nameless fluid to become a memory. I always wake up richer from the dream.

A woman sits at an easel, in the middle of a marsh. The clouds are dark but the sun is shining. Cat tails rise around her. The pools of water are gold on the marsh, from the sun. She wears a black dress with gold buttons and a black turban. Shadows are black, reflections gold; they thatch the spongy ground.

She's painting a tiger. The picture is extremely clear, like a photograph. The sun behind her acts as a sort of lens; the dark clouds help develop the picture. Sometimes the woman falls asleep in the sun, and the tiger springs down from the easel to circle her, faster and faster, a ring of fire or gold wedding band to warm and protect her. Sometimes the tiger stalks off across the marsh, light as a bird, dipping his head to sip from the golden pools. He's always back on the paper when she wakes up.

I sleep in here sometimes, fitfully. A wake, I never see the woman, only the tiger. She's too much me to need seeing. Her age changes. Sometimes she's very old, sometimes a child. The tiger's age is constant.

Today there's a green glow of envy in his face, a certain sulky cast to his posture. What is it, my beauty? Proud and sleek, but a little fantastic, and always alone?

Yes, my sullen familiar, you are the golden stranger at the feast. Usually you have no appetite for what's served up along with the canapés. You purr like a motor travelling between their clusters, refreshed by the shutter's click against the blurred murmur of voices, the prevaricating laughter.

But not this time. Oh, I wanted to put the camera down and be there. I did; I was. Not just as an eye, but a heart and a mind and a cunt: a woman. I fancied the bride. Fair enough, that happens. Shrug, feel a little macho as I snap her picture, remind myself that smile isn't for me, it's for the album and the grand-children. Claim it anyway, secretly. I fall a little bit in love with all of them, at their big moment.

So far, so good. Nothing to erase your feline smile, Cheshire one. This bride gave off a whiff of something blue, all right, and not in the traditional shade. Not to my nostrils anyway. Not that that's a first, either. But this was fresh and recent, unresigned. There was a moment just before she said her soft "I do" when she seemed lost in a kind of mist under her veil. The pause became embarrassing, attacked but not quite punctured with coughs and throat-clearings.

The best photos are the ones you don't take. I began to assemble myself for a shot of what promised to be an event, but by the time I got there it was over, whatever it was. I wanted the expression I could just read, or so I thought, through the grating of her veil. She was somewhere else. Wool-gathering, as they say;

gathering courage, I thought, to fracture the uneasy silence with a firm "no", a *non serviam* that would surpass Lucifer's.

It was my damnable pride that ended the dream. I snapped the picture and the next moment I heard her low assent. I won't know what that expression was until I develop the picture; maybe not even then.

I trailed after the bridal procession despondently. It was all over. I was all wrong. I went to stand by the entrance to the marquee to snap them as they came towards me, smiling those ritual smiles. A child stood next to me. Then a real child screamed, and I looked again. The person next to me was leaning on sticks. Two halves of a broomstick, I identified. The face was hidden behind the mask of an ancient woman, skin craggy and lined, only the eyes her own. I knew she was a woman, though the whisper had gone up, by then, that the strange dwarfed thing was a friend of the groom's, playing a prank.

She wore a trenchcoat, an old gabardine one, backwards. Then the whisper changed. I heard the rumours around me like waves in the background. She was a woman scorned come to play spectre at the feast, a cast-off girlfriend of the groom's.

It was eminently possible. But what did Aristotle say? A probable impossibility is a better bet for drama than an improbable possibility. It was the probable impossibility I was interested in. It connected with that pregnant pause in the ceremony, with the look I thought I had seen on the bride's face.

It's you, I told myself sternly. Your tool is a camera, not a projector, so stop projecting. Don't get caught up in it. Take the pictures.

I was caught up, but I did take the pictures. She was always there in the corner of my eye. I saw her search the room as if for an ally. I felt her choose me, drawing me into the action. Shattering my neutrality. What neutrality?

We sat down and she proved to be probable and impossible, just as I'd thought. A glimpse behind the mask showed a young, tense face. The love story she told me was old as the hills, old as Demeter and Persephone, old as the news that kinder, kirche and kitchen always win out in the end. She was losing her anger, dissolving it in the champagne, dissipating her energy. I didn't want her to accept defeat. I didn't want her magnificent stand to be mere sniping, her courage to be just revenge. I thought she should go one step further and give it one last shot. Her best shot. Gather her grace and her guts and go over to Hermione, or whatever the hell the bride's name was. By now I felt quite hostile to *her*.

Frances. That's her name. The other one's Jane. She drank a little more and then she stood up on her sticks and pogo'd across the dance floor. I wished her well with all my heart, and made myself watch. I quailed for her. I couldn't just watch, but I didn't hide my head either, though I felt suddenly alone in a theatre with the terrible climax about to come. I picked up my camera. I got it all.

She trod lightly across the floor, clearing a path through the couples who rolled back for her obediently like the Red Sea for Moses. She smiled when she got close to Frances, I could see the smile under her mask and I hoped it showed in her eyes. Then she held out her hand to escort her to the dance floor, and Frances took it.

I got it; the smile, perceptible or not, the hand, the long walk to the dance floor while the band played on, oblivious. Probably thinking the bride was dancing with her grandmother. Her own mother looked livid, a red and blue dragon.

They danced the next three dances, talking all the time. Even the band began scratching their heads. They kept playing fast feverish music as if to forestall a scandal. Then the bride and crone danced over to the bandstand to make a request. It was a long, slow, smoochy number. After it, they left.

I wanted to follow them, I wanted to run upstairs where I could hear them, in my mind's ear, giggling and kissing as they changed, both discarding their disguises. They didn't take long. I was tempted to go and say a word to the groom, who sat stroking his chin solemnly, blinking like a drunken owl. I felt a welling-up of compassion for him, but that was projection, I informed myself; because he was left out, too.

"Evelyn," a laughing whisper came from the entrance and I followed it. Maybe it was wishful thinking; had they called me? Someone had summoned me. A picture had summoned me. It was the last picture, of the two of them leaning over the banisters with the bridal bouquet. Two kids in jeans, that's all they were, setting out together. I didn't have to wish them anything. They had it all.

I snapped, and Frances leaned over the banisters with clear intent. Then the huge great thing trailing ribbons like a jellyfish landed with a soft plop on the carpet. There wasn't time to put the camera down so I could catch it.

Jane handed it to me with a wink as they went out the door. I heard the motor, dully, bereft. It seemed more like a funeral suddenly. Who was I but a caretaker of memories, what was I undertaking with my arms clamped around a camera, instead of reaching for the magic bouquet?

An undertaker, not a caretaker. But I heard them roar away with a smile, thinking of the precious photographs I had. Thinking of the precious afternoon I'd just witnessed. That's what I was, when you came right down to it. A witness.

"We'll be in touch," Frances had said. They would. Will they be a couple then, each singularly unavailable? Remains to be seen. I doubt that's their way.

I've been asleep, hunched here over the sink, my arm on a pile of equipment including the camera. I lift my arm; it's striped from the stuff I was lying on. So's my cheek. I can feel the grooves as I touch it. Funny how I love recording change. That's what I'm after. Yet I can't change my own stripes, even if I want to, sometimes. Solitary confinement in here, middle-aged dyke in love with a darkroom. Think I'll go get some fresh coffee before I start.

Did'ja Ever Hear of a Goolieguy?

Anne Cameron

The final straw is so often nothing at all. You go through years of daily give-and-take, each trying to adapt to the moods of the other, making adjustments of minor or major proportions and then, there you are, part of you knowing it's no big deal and part of you numb with fatalistic horror, watching the third, external part of yourself, fiercely packing, stern, unyielding, stubborn as a terrier. And she is just as stern, unyielding, stubborn, getting ready for work as if nothing at all was happening, as if your life together wasn't in jeopardy.

And I knew nothing was going to make any difference. This wasn't happening for any of the reasons we might say. It had a life of its own, and we were both observers as well as players, caught in some damn thing for reasons we probably would never understand.

Carol left for work. I hauled out clothes from drawers and closets, stuffed them in black garbage bags, knotted the tops shut and hauled them, two at a time, to the pickup truck, heaved them in the back, under the canopy.

Then I whistled for Bess, opened the door of the pickup truck and patted the seat. She was there in an instant, wagging her stub tail, her tongue lolling in that spaniel grin that could usually make me laugh. I slammed the door, moved to the other side, got in and started the engine. Then I drove away from the place that had meant Home for those days, weeks, and years.

The angry part of me drove to the gas station, filled the tank, topped the oil, checked the tyres, handed over the credit card and waited until the attendant fussed with the form. Then I signed my name, took my receipt, put it and my plastic card in my wallet, stuffed that in my pocket and drove to the bank. I got some cash and headed out, pretending I didn't know where I was going.

But we always run home, don't we? We always run back to that first place, that place where we got hurt worse than anywhere else, that place where we were so scarred by what they told us was love and family that any hurt afterward seems small in comparison.

Three days of steady driving, three nights in forgettable motels, a ride on the ferry and there I was, back where I hadn't been for more than half my lifetime.

I had memories of huge fir trees swaying gently in the summer breeze, of miles and miles and miles of road winding through forests of evergreen, dogwood and arbutus. I looked for the net racks and sheds full of crab traps, I looked for the small trollers with names like *Barbara Anne* and *Margaret Joyce*, and what I found were four-lane highways, golden arches, two-storey painted ice-cream cones and a foreshore lined with motels boasting ridiculous names.

The hotel the old man had built decades earlier looked the same on the outside, but any hint of individuality inside had been very carefully either painted over or covered with that ghastly red carpet they seem to think is compulsory.

It was easier just to check in like any other befuddled tourist than to bother with the phone calls and verifications. I signed the register and the clerk didn't even check my signature, let alone react to the name.

I went up to my room, had a shower, changed my clothes, then went down to the dining-room for supper. It was strange sitting at a table by the window, looking out on the harbour, remembering other times, when the harbour wasn't a place for sea planes to land, wasn't constantly crisscrossed by one power boat or another. The meal was exactly what you would have had every right in the world to expect for what they were charging. Good, but not great.

In the morning I went to see the lawyer. I think the reception-ist thought I was some country housewife wandering in to ask about divorce proceedings; she was aloof and a bit off-putting until I told her who I was and why I was there. Then she was polite, efficient and smiling so widely you'd have thought I was her long-lost cousin. Who knows, considering the way some of the men in the family had behaved, maybe I was.

The lawyer came from the same mould all lawyers on that Island seem to come from: the one with the very expensive suit, the shoes treated to look shined at all times, the expensive shirt and tie, the hair carefully combed over the growing bald patch, the flabby little pot belly already starting to spread and burgeon. This blond had been pulling in a good yearly retainer for most of his working life, ever since the old one had offed himself with too much alcohol, and this was the first time anyone had come to see him face to face. He wasn't quite sweating, but then, he hadn't known I was going to drop by his office.

He was burning with curiosity, but I wasn't interested in giving him any details. All I really wanted to know was if the old place was rented out to anyone or if it was, again, empty.

"There hasn't been anyone in it since, uh, the, uh, late spring of, uh, last, uhm, year," he managed, quickly moving pieces of paper around on his desk, checking the file as he spoke, trying to cover the fact he hadn't really been doing much about earning his money.

"Fine." I gave him the frosty smile they had taught me in private school, the one almost guaranteed to make anyone except the royal family suddenly feel diminished. "Please remove it from the listings: I'll be staying there myself for a while."

"Oh!" he blurted, blushed, fussed with the papers a bit. "Well, uh, if you could, uh, give me a day or two to, uh, have the place, uhm, well, prepared for your arrival . . . yard cleanup, house-cleaning, the usual thing after a place has been empty for, uh, almost a year."

"That's okay." I gave him the cheerful, we're-just-folks grin I learned from my aunt who was, in fact, just-folks and not at all anyone the family could accept. But she'd been nice to me, and had given the grisly bastards a good run for their money until Uncle Tony caved in under the constant disapproval and patronizing and started to rot his brain and liver with the finest of Glenfiddich. That grin, learned from her, coming close on the heels of the private school frost-face smile, always throws the Philistines off balance. "I'll just contact the Blue-Collar Army." He probably wasn't going to be too happy about that; it would give me a chance to find out first-hand what those organized handymen really charged, and compare that with what this beagle had said they charged. I was willing to bet everything had been inflated and he had pocketed the difference himself. You have to expect that if you choose, as I did for so long, to pay as little attention as possible to any of the details.

I declined his offer to take me up there himself. I knew if he was given any control over anything, he'd find a way to delay the visit until someone had been up there and started doing what probably ought to have been done months ago.

When I was young, the mucketymucks had their summer cabins up Nanaimo Lakes Road, and the family had finally put in a gate to keep these upwardly aspiring trespassers from coming to the old place to visit as if we were all really neighbours in the accepted sense of the word. For the most part, those mucketymucks worked for the logging company, which had grown only after the mines had begun to decline. They seemed to think we would have things in common, although I can't imagine what they thought those things would be, and now that the trees were gone and the slopes ruined, the logging company had moved on, the mucketymucks were gone and the summer cabins and cottages they built were becoming derelict shacks, used by the locals for hunting shelters and fishing shacks.

The logging had scarred the hillsides. What had been a solid cover of stately evergreen was a stubby cover of trash wood; alder, wild cherry, several kinds of maple – what they call "non-commercial deciduous" – and the lake was not what I remembered at all. I suppose someone must have signed whatever permission paper was necessary to allow the butchers onto the family land, but I knew it wasn't me, and I wasn't interested in finding out which of the idiot uncles was responsible.

My four-times great-grandfather came out from Scotland with nothing more than a change of clothes and a head full of schemes. He smiled and joked and made friends until he was trusted to the limit by everyone who knew him here, and then he went into partnership with someone who knew something about mining and between them they laid out claims and proved up a seam of rich anthracite coal. They started mining with three or four trusting men who worked for shares, and while those men worked digging coal, my four-times great-grandfather kept looking around, laying claims and then, suddenly, my great-great-great-great grandfather owned the whole thing, what the natives here call the whole shiterooni. His partner got a grave-stone, a marble marker, after they brought his body up out of the cave-in which crushed him and two other men. The surviving men who had started working for shares with the old man had either gone back to Scotland, been given the title of supervisor or just somehow seemed to disappear off the face of the earth. The scheming heatherhopper wound up a millionaire so many times over that, even when the bottom fell out of coal, even when miners were out of work and starving, even when the shafts had been sealed shut, even when other fortunes were lost, none of us had to worry. Not even with those ridiculous uncles involved, not even with those lawyers the children of those ridiculous uncles hired and put in charge.

That old crook had three wives and buried each of them, he had a dozen children who married and had children, all of whom married and had children, but there is only me and my Uncle Tony left, and Tony has been living in a rubber room since he realized he lost more than his wife when he gave in to the pressure the family put on him.

It was my aunt who had the old place fixed up. Maybe she hoped she could get Tony to live there with her, miles from the rest of them. The main part of the old place was built by my grandfather, when he was a young man and hadn't yet started to turn into what he eventually became. He took it into his head to return to the place the old crook had built when the first mine was in production up there in the hills. He tore down the rotting cabin and brought in a crew of Chinese to flatten a big section of hillside, and on that flat piece he had them build a rectangular house of peeled fir logs. By the time my aunt saw it, the big log house was a neglected mess. She had it all fixed up and had a porch added along the front and the south-facing wall. The old roof was replaced and extended out over the porch so you could sit out there, even on a rainy day, and look down to the lake.

She had a studio built there, too, separate from the house, a place where she would go by herself and write her poems and books, paint her pictures, make her figures carved from wood, her strange sculptures of rock and bone, even of feather and moss. All of which the family used to prove she just was not the kind of person Uncle Tony should have married.

Even after he'd caved in and she'd left him, she tried to help the sodden fool. She was the one got him out of the drunk tank and took him up to the old place, even moved a piano in for him in the hope he'd dry out and go back to the music she had once thought he would play for the world. He dried out all right, but sat on the porch and wept until the family smartened up enough to figure out where he might be and sent someone out to collect him. Six months later they took him off to the funny farm.

The peeled logs had been treated with some kind of preservative. It darkened the wood, made the place look more solid than I remembered it, more firmly entrenched in the landscape. A tin roof had been put on it, and that was a shock; I had expected cedar shakes, weathered to a dull silver. The small sheds were ramshackle and the chimney looked as if it badly needed attention – the mortar was missing and some of the bricks slipped to crazy angles or were absent completely. But no crisscross of fallen branches or rotting logs, no slash or mess, no English ivy gone mad and crowding out the grass. No trashy elderberry tangle or salmonberry thicket, and the meadow of knee-high grass was brightly spotted with foxglove, lupin, columbine and dahlias gone wild and escaped from what had once been flower-beds. Small arbutus and maple, none of them more than twelve feet tall, had moved into the clearing, but not among the dozen large fruit trees.

Bess was whining nervously, trembling and sticking to me like adhesive tape, but I ignored her. She'd been too many days in a car, sitting so close as to almost be on my knee. She needed to get back to being a dog instead of my security blanket.

I looked at the studio first, because it had been my aunt's place, and a refuge for me at a time when I badly needed to be away from the family. For a minute I thought I'd gone crazy. Then I decided the former tenant was the one had gone goofy. The front door was open, and it was obvious birds of all kinds had been flying in and out at will, building their nests inside the studio, shitting over everything. The enormous front windows were filthy, smeared with mess, festooned with cobwebs. The beautiful big wood-and-glass built-in storage buffet was piled with old magazines; the expensive enameled woodstove from Ireland was covered with bits of metal, rusted heaps of nails, nuts, bolts; the built-in double bed was hidden by bits of broken board, lengths of damp warped plywood; and the floor was littered with stove wood, heaps of it, stacks of it, piles of it, all the way to the gigantic counter-weighted door, propped open by dropped wood.

And someone had nailed sheet metal all around the edge of the door and around the frame. It made no sense. The window-sills outside were sheeted with metal, nailed with big-headed nails every three inches, as if there was some reason the metal had to be put there and kept there until after the crack of Doomsday.

The big house was incredible. Not in the sense of crystal chandeliers or gold-leaf paint; just incredible in the sense of "who'd'a thunk it". Someone had left this place in exactly the same way I'd just left a place. Grab the clothes that come to hand and never come back for the other stuff.

Except for the thick layer of dust and cobwebs, you'd have thought someone was due home any minute.

Big windows looked out over the covered porch, over and past the studio, down the slope to the lake. From the north window, in the corner by the sink, you could look out and down to a year-round stream feeding into the shallow end of the copper-coloured water at the foot of the hill. A hint of what might once have been a fenced-in enclosure around one section of the stream and a small hoochie made of plywood, but no sign of the ducks which might have lived there, unless they had been turned loose to become part of the flock down on the lake.

A large combination kitchen-living room was the original part of the house, and behind that room there were two bedrooms, once accessible from the kitchen itself. But when the porch had been added, the old house had been extended, and now you stepped up two small stairs to the addition: a small room, barely big enough for a double bed, opening into a larger room so spectacular I knew that was where I was putting a sound system, a collection of books and comfortable chairs to sit in at twilight and watch the colours of the lake change as the sun slipped behind the mountains.

The hallway to the back rooms had an old sideboard in excellent condition and a large table, similar to the one in the studio, but this one, thank God, was unmarked by bird shit. Windows in this strange cross between a dining-room and a hallway looked out over the porch to the south slope and the thicket of maple, alder and arbutus, past that to the blue-green mountains rising on the other side of the lake. I knew why my aunt had put the porch around this side, had the old wall removed, the addition put on, but I didn't know why whoever had left so suddenly had abandoned the furniture.

The back bedrooms were creepy. The windows were covered with plywood, the sills sheathed in sheet metal, like the metal around the door and on the sills of the studio. Metal like the metal laid on the threshold of the studio door, on the stairs leading up to the porch of the main house, even on the threshold of the door to the house.

The back bedrooms were dark. They were also damp, musty and faintly foul-smelling, that heavy, sick smell that means mould and fungi are moving into the corners and under the furniture.

Outside, the oddness continued. I knew the windowsills would be sheathed with metal; I hadn't expected to trip over a railroad spike driven into the path. It had heaved partway up in the winter freeze, otherwise I might never have noticed it. But having found it, I soon found others, and I almost giggled at the thought of some supreme lunatic trying to nail the topsoil to the earth. Maybe the former tenant hadn't gone away at all. Maybe he'd been taken away in a jacket that fastened his arms to his sides and closed at the back.

Some things I just don't bother thinking about until I absolutely have no choice. Carol used to tell me I needed to learn how to deal with things. I told her not dealing with them was my way of dealing with them. Things are either internal or external. Even problems and troubles are either caused by something inside yourself or by something outside. If it's something inside, there probably isn't much you can do about it; even clinical depression either wears off or doesn't. If it wears off, you don't have to do anything about it because it's gone; if it doesn't wear off, you still don't have to do anything because they'll put you away and feed you funny things to combat it. If your problems and troubles are caused by something outside yourself, what can you do about it? Force someone to love you? Stop the war? Insist the world run the way you want it to run? Demand everybody be nice to you so you can be happy?

The puzzles about the old house and the former tenant were things I wasn't ready to even try to think about, let alone solve. I knew that sooner or later they'd stop puzzling me, or I'd stumble over the reason and they wouldn't be puzzles anymore. I had other things to do.

I made arrangements for the Blue-Collar Army to come out and start fixing up the place so I could move into it. Three men in a pickup truck full of tool boxes, ladders, scaffolding boards and an assortment of brushes and chains put ladders up to the roof, climbed up, cleaned the chimney from top to bottom and started replacing bricks and mortar. They took the stove apart and scrubbed the inside of it, cleaned out all the years and years' accumulation of caked soot and baked creosote, then put the stove back together again. They hauled the plywood off the back windows, they put new stovepipe from the stove to the chimney, they chinked around the windows and doors, they winterproofed the place as if we were living in the barren lands of the far north and they never spoke to me. They spoke messages to the left of my head and messages to the right of my head, they grunted responses and talked over my head, but their eyes slid away from mine and they seemed so uneasy I wondered if there was a big secret none of them wanted me to find out – like maybe none of them knew what they were doing.

The linoleum in the kitchen was awful, and I had them rip that up, but when I said I wanted the metal sheeting over the threshold of the door removed, they hesitated and looked at each other, then looked past me to the bush, then looked at each other again. They looked at the bush and the lake, they looked at the studio and the woodsheds, they looked everywhere and then looked away, but they wouldn't look at me.

"Is something wrong?" I asked, impatient and getting angry. "Is there something wrong? Like maybe a big hole in the floor or dry rot in the joists, or . . . ?"

"Foundation's solid," the young one blurted, "joists is fine. You want that taken up, I'll take it up, but . . ." he darted a shame-faced look at the other two, "what about the goolieguy?"

"I beg your pardon?" I said carefully.

"The goolieguy," he repeated stubbornly.

I didn't want to laugh, vowed to myself that, whatever else I did or said, I wouldn't laugh. It wasn't their fault. They're ignorant and under-educated to the point of being functionally illiterate, but they didn't ask to be born on an Island which has been abused, mistreated, exploited and ruined by companies exactly like the one started by my four-times great-grandfather. People with smooth-tongued skill talked of blue sky and free land, of the chance to own your own place, of brand new coal mines with the best of working conditions, of top wages working in seven- and eight-foot shafts, not the miserably low-roofed shafts where men had to work with their heads and shoulders bowed, their backs bent and aching. Clean streams, they were told, and nobody with the authority to refuse you the right to fish for free food.

And so they came. And found most of what they had been told they would find. But generations later, their descendants were chronically under-employed or unemployed, and the land they had been promised was still controlled by people who lived elsewhere.

"Tell me about the goolieguy," I suggested. The poor, superstitious fool looked miserable, and the other two weren't about to do or say anything to let him off the hook. I just waited and finally he nodded and stuffed his hands in his pockets. "The guy who left here took off because of the goolieguy." He seemed to feel an incredible relief, once he started to talk, and the other two, although they in no way relaxed their disapproval of his indiscretion, seemed glad the cat was out of the bag. "He was okay as long as his missus was alive, but after she died, well, he started to get . . . goofy." He took his hands out of his pockets, started to reach for the round can of snuff in his back pocket, then blushed and reached instead for the papers and tobacco in his shirt pocket and began to roll himself a cigarette. "He was just about on a par with your average outhouse rat inside of about a month of her dying. I guess he nailed up the metal before she died, but he got lots worse real fast."

"What are we talking here?" I probed.

"Goolieguy," he repeated. "Lives in the bush most of the time. Or in old sheds and barns."

"Are we talking roof rats?" I asked carefully. "Or pack rats or . . ."

"No, we ain't!" he said stubbornly, insulted by my questions. "We're talkin' goolieguy. I suppose," he said, as if excusing me for something I couldn't control. "I suppose you're not Welsh."

"No," I admitted.

"You related to that bunch as owns this place? Or did. They're pretty well all dead. Or locked in the bin, I suppose."

"I am," I admitted, and then I laughed, and it didn't insult them because they knew, or at least intuited, why I was laughing. I wished with all my heart that the entire sanctimonious collection of them could hear themselves described as "that bunch". Dismissed as a crackpot collection instead of being revered, as they had revered themselves, as some kind of superior form of life.

"Well, even so," he grumbled, "you ought to know goolieguy. That bunch was Scots and so was my gran, and she knew goolieguy."

"I'm sorry." I gave him the friendly grin. "I've been off-Island most of my life. I'm not very . . . clued in."

"Well, we all figured as much," he admitted, the corner of his mouth twitching in what could pass for a grin among this dour bunch. "A goolieguy –" he had his cigarette rolled and in his mouth, and lit it with a big wooden match he ignited by drawing it quickly across the rough denim of his jeans "– came from the old country with the first people who came here. They brought people to work the pits at White Rapids Coal and Coking Company, and the goolieguys hid." He was serious, as serious as any teacher in a classroom. "They hid in the big wooden boxes they shipped the blankets and bedding in, and maybe some of them hid in with the sheep and cattle the people brought over with them. My gran's gran on my mother's side told my gran, and my gran told me, a goolieguy attaches herself to you or to your family, and they stick to you, no matter where you go. They'll die rather than ... abandon you."

"They're brown," the oldest worker said sternly, "brown-skinned and brown-haired, brown-eyed and kinda hairy. Real long thin brown fingers'n'toes. Even their nails are brown. Live where they can, in the bush or in the hayloft of the barn or under the house." He looked at the place at the edge of the porch where the boards were splintered away and the ground flat and bare, the place where Bess wouldn't go but sat watching, whining softly. "The only way to get rid of 'em is to use iron on'em. It burns them," he finished, glaring at me and defying me to contradict him or deny what he was saying.

"My gran said –" the young man rose, stubbing his cigarette out by pinching it between his fingers, then scuffing a small hole in the dirt, dropping in his butt and covering it with dirt "– the goolieguy used to live with us, but when we started using metal they had to back off from us. Couldn't stand bein' around the metal, you see. My gran says they never abandoned us, we abandoned them, and when they moved us off the crofts and moved on the machines, the goolieguys had to go further away. She says it was said that what had been the ruination of the goolieguys would be the ruination of us. Machines. Industry." He looked out at the clear-cut slopes, shook his head gently, and looked as if only good manners kept him from spitting.

"And what do they do that is ... bad?" I was careful about my tone of voice, the expression on my face. I didn't want these workmen taking insult and walking off the job before it was done. Poor ignorant bastards, I thought, reminded of my uncles and their lucky rings made from horseshoe nails, or their endless other superstitions.

"Nothing," the young man admitted, "but most people go kind of . . . wingy." He was suddenly very uneasy again, looking over his shoulder at the bush, stuffing his hands in his pockets and removing them again hurriedly. "Can't stand being watched by something they don't believe they can see. Goolieguy likes to look in your windows and such. You hear them on the roof, warming their hands at the chimney. Under the house at night. But if you want that metal sheeting taken offa the doorstep," he said quickly, obviously wanting to terminate the conversation, "I'll take'er up. But without that metal . . . goolieguy could get into your kitchen. Pull the soft middle out of your bread, leave nothing but the crust. Drink your cream, you wake up in the morning and there's no cream for your coffee. Eat your cheese."

The whole thing sounded more like mice to me than some kind of hairy brown spook smuggled in from Scotland. A good mouser cat would probably keep the goolieguy away a lot better than any amount of nails or sheet metal. Still, had I known any of this before I asked them to remove the metal, I wouldn't have decided to have it taken up, but I wasn't going to back down now in front of these three ignorant louts. "Well, I think we might as well take up the metal sheeting," I said, trying to sound casual. "After all, if the goolieguy doesn't really hurt anything . . ." All three of them looked at me as if I was absolutely insane. But the tension between us was gone and, who knows, maybe those people know they themselves are crazier than the proverbial outhouse rats and can afford to be relaxed and friendly with lunatics. The metal came up off the kitchen floor, and I drove into town to rent a sander for the boards exposed when the linoleum was removed.

While they were busy working on the main house, I busied myself in the smaller one, the one I had thought of as a studio. I heaved the stove wood outside, making no effort at all to stack in neatly, just heaving it out onto the grass. Then I wrestled the big square table to the doorway and got it outside in the light where I could have a good look at it. Even with chicken shit, bird shit and pigeon shit smeared on it, it was beautiful, and anyone would have been proud to have it in their home. I knew I could wash it clean, and if the dried droppings had stained or damaged it, a good refinisher could have it like new in only a couple of days.

The Blue-Collar Army worked on the main house for a week and I worked on the studio, sweeping, scrubbing and doing a lot of cursing. It just isn't right to treat a place like that, as if what you'd really rather do is just burn it down, but first you want it to suffer. I had the metal removed from the doorway and sanded the floor, then rented a propane heater and boiled linseed oil. Just before the oil was hot enough to burst into flame. I turned off the propane and started dippering out the boiling oil, spreading it on the boards liberally, literally frying the wood. It was something my grandfather had always done with his floors. He said you could use ordinary fir for the flooring, and by the time the boiling oil fried and hardened the fir, you had a floor better than the most expensive hardwood. What he didn't tell me was how much hard work it was, spreading it liberally but not unevenly, scrubbing it into cracks with a long-handled brush. While it was still wet, I took a big, rented, commercial floor-polisher to it. Why spend all that time getting blisters if there's a machine to do the worst of it?

And when the floor was finally dry, it didn't shine like it would if it had been varathaned or varnished, but it glowed rich golden and looked the way I remembered floors looking. By then I had the various kinds of guano off the table and the youngest workie had it sanded smooth, Danish-oiled and polished. He helped me move it back into the studio and set it up in front of the big window at the front, and even if there weren't any matching chairs, it looked gorgeous. The stove was cleaned, the new stovepipes carefully and properly wired and metal-screwed in place, the chimney cleaned and the walls and cupboards scrubbed. Of course I had no need or use of the place, but all this tidying and elbow greasing kept my mind off all those things I knew I wasn't ready to try to sort out, explain or even decide.

The main house looked even more wonderful than the studio did. Nothing fancy, nothing your average millionaire would covet, but everything was clean, in good repair and all the cracks were chinked and sealed; it could turn winter tomorrow and the house wouldn't care. The junk and garbage was heaved into the two pickup trucks and driven off to the festering mess that is the local garbage dump, and none of us had made any mention at all of the supposed resident goolieguy. But that part of the skirting at the far end of the porch was left unrepaired, and I was the one that had to go under the house to check and repair the insulation.

They did as much as they could from outside, but not one of them would come under the house. I knew I could offer them ten times their hourly rate and they would just stand there, pretending they had suddenly been struck deaf, blind and mute. So I got them to explain what it was I was supposed to be doing and I went under the house with a trouble light.

They moved the big, lightweight, fibreglass batts where I could get them easily and called advice from outside, but I was the one had to lie on my back, push the fibreglass up between the joists and stuff it in place. I was the one had to run the heating tape along the pipes and drains and pass it out to them to finish off at the plug-in box. I was the one looking for chinks of light showing from outside, and I was the one stuffing wadding into them. I was also the one stapled polyfilm vapour barrier over the insulation. It took two days and let me tell you, I know of no other job so goddamned miserable.

And after all that insulating against winter draughts and winds, we all of us ignored the place where the skirting was fractured and the wind could blow in at will.

They left, finally, and by then the phone was installed and I had a new big woodshed. There was still enough work left to be done to keep me half occupied for the rest of the summer, but nothing pressing. I wrote them a cheque and we all shook hands and then they left, and not one of us had said a word about the stove wood I'd thrown out of the studio onto the grass. The stove wood was stacked in the old woodshed the next morning, when I woke up to find most of my coffee cream had vanished.

Once the workmen were gone, I went back under the house with the trouble light, back to that horrible thing I had found while I was under there with the insulation. Now that I didn't have to try to appear to be at least partways normal, I could admit to what I was seeing. The old bastard! Evil old bastard! No wonder the goolieguy had driven him off the place!

It was a big metal box, like a tool chest or a steamer trunk, about two feet long, a foot wide, and a foot high. Metal sides, metal top, metal snap-lock, metal handle for carrying it. I opened it, as I had the day I was under there swearing at the fibreglass.

It was hard to tell how big it had been; it was withered and dried like a little brown mummy. Curled up on its side with its tiny knees against its baby chest, its skeleton hands up by its face, and I was sure it had been crying and sucking its thumb when it died. A rotted piece of rope around its waist, like a lasso.

Just like the first time I opened the box and saw the goolieguy baby, I had a fantasy image of a little kid toddling in the field, picking foxglove flowers for momma, and then the Thing coming from the Place, whirling a rope, yelling, running faster than baby legs could run, and then something around the baby's waist, catching it, and big rough hands grabbing and stuffing the baby into this awful, burning thing, this metal monster, this burning, burning, burning, and the lid closing, and burning, burning, burning.

He hid the box with the baby in it, hid it under the house where his wife wouldn't see, she who had sat crippled by arthritis, watching from the window as the goolieguy moved with her baby, moved hidden in the bush when He was at home; moved openly around the clearing when He was away to town. Away to town to buy more nails to put where a goolieguy might get burned, to buy more metal to keep the goolieguy out of the buildings. Away to town to buy a metal box to hold a baby goolieguy until it died of burning and suffocation, its mother frantic enough to rip the skirting from the porch and try to get to her dying infant.

I could see her as if I had been there, sitting with her knees jack-knifed almost in front of her face, rocking and mourning, reaching out to try to open the box and release her baby, her fingers blistered and bleeding, unable to grasp the metal, unable to open the lid, unable to do anything but go nine-tenths mad knowing the goddamned metal held her child.

And the pain, the terrible pain, rising through the floor-boards, flooding the back rooms of the house, poisoning every-thing until the woman moaned and the prescription was changed, the medicine made stronger and stronger, and still the goolieguy's pain mounted, until the woman's heart stopped.

I took the box out from under the house and carried it to the front yard, and then went into the house and got a clean, fluffy blanket. I lifted the desiccated little mummy-shape from the metal box and laid it on the blanket, and didn't know if I wanted to cry or swear. I didn't know if the goolieguys buried their dead or put them in trees the way Indians used to do or what, so I finally figured the best I could do was do what I'd have done if it had been Bess or even my own kid. I got a shovel and started to dig the hole.

I was crying and digging and sniffling, and then this skinny, long-fingered, brown hand reached from behind me and wrapped around the wooden handle of the shovel. I let go of the shovel and the goolieguy took it from me, walked a few steps and laid the shovel on the grass. Then she moved to the hole, knelt and started to dig with her bare hands. She winced at first, winced every time her hands touched soil that had been dug with the metal shovel, but once past that, everything happened very quickly. Goolieguys have amazing fingernails, about the same shade of brown as the shiny shell of a horse chestnut, about as wide as ours, but probably a hundred times tougher, and, just like a dog can dig up a rat hole quicker than a person can dig with a shovel, a goolieguy can get a two-foot-deep hole done in no time at all. Two feet deep, two feet long, about a foot wide.

She lifted the goolieguy baby, blanket and all, and put it in the grave, then covered its face with a corner of the blanket. I could understand that; it gives me the shivers to think of sleeping forever with dirt in your face. And she moaned a bit, her big, round, dark brown eyes flooded with tears, then she filled in the hole and patted the earth flat again.

The goolieguy is maybe five-foot-two or five-foot-three inches tall, and very slender. Most of her height is in her legs, and her arms hang down – her hands are below her knees when she's standing upright. Long, thin arms and long, thin fingers, nicely shaped, with fine, downy hair on her body and limbs. She's got a face just like you or me or anyone else – not as round, maybe, as most of us, but nothing you'd call animal-like. Little pug of a snub nose, high cheekbones, wide, delicately shaped mouth, and teeth like ours. I'm not a dentist, and I don't know any more about tooth and jaw structure than anyone else knows, but I'd bet you could look at a goolieguy skull and not really know for sure you weren't looking at a person's skull. You might know that person wasn't exactly caucasian, but you'd know you weren't looking at any animal. The goolieguy has lips like ours, except for the colour. Not exactly purple, not exactly blue, but if you've ever seen a kid who has just spent most of the past three hours pigging out on blackberries or blueberries, you've seen the colour of the goolieguy's lips. And when they cry, their bottom lip trembles, just like ours. And their eyes flood tears down their dark brown faces. When a goolieguy kisses you on the cheek, it's like being kissed by any gentle person, and I don't think they hug or cuddle the way we do. I think they pat gently, because that's what the goolieguy did to me; she patted my shoulder repeatedly. Then she left, running graceful as a deer across the clearing, disappearing into the alder and wild cherry scrub.

I took the goddamned metal box to the dump and heaved it in with all the other slime and mud, then stopped at the store on my way back and stocked up on different kinds of cheese and plenty of French bread, a couple of pints of whipping cream and two quarts of half-and-half coffee cream.

In the morning, I wakened to the sound of hummingbirds zizzing at the feeder, quarreling with each other. A small rufous was so busy fighting with the others, so busy darting and threatening, she had no time to push her beak into the spigot and drink. She could wind up winning the power struggle and starving herself to death.

I put water on to boil for coffee, put the plastic cone on the porcelain coffee pot, put a paper filter in the cone, measured coffee and stared out the side window at the woodshed, at the clearing, at the brush beyond, and thought of her, swollen and cramped with the agony of arthritis, hurting even when he was being incredibly gentle, unable even to cuddle him without feeling pain, unable to be held and comforted, and I wondered at his frustration. What must he have felt when he discovered that the goolieguy could come into the house and sit quietly on the floor beside the aching woman, sit quietly and, for a while, take the pain and pass it on to some other place, so the woman could sleep without medication, could even hold in her contorted hands a cup of fragrant tea, sip its soothing warmth and relax. What must he have felt on realizing that the goolieguy could reach out with her abnormally long-fingered hands and touch lightly, so lightly that even the most inflamed tissue felt no pain, only comfort and love. What he could not give, the goolieguy gave, what he could not convey, the goolieguy could, and in his own house, to his own wife, until he couldn't stand it any more and went for the first lengths of sheet metal to protect what was his, to claim his own territory, to piss on all his own fence-posts like a dog become vicious.

I sat on the front porch, looking down past the studio to the lake. The ducks were feeding in the shallows, bums up more often than their heads. Off beyond the peaks of the mountains, a small dark cloud was creeping eastward, towards the sea. It looked almost lonely in a pale blue sky, where high, thin, white, cirrus clouds streaked gracefully. One small storm looking for a place to happen, too far from here to cause even two seconds worry.

Families have storms too, some of them large, some of them small, most of them kept hidden from the sight and gossiping tongues of outsiders. My mother had been a tempest the crazy bunch had first tried to absorb, then tried to hide and eventually erased.

All the anger was gone, and most of the regret as well. I had no memories of her, no faded photographs, no souvenirs, no keepsakes. I didn't even have any stories given me by someone who had known her. I never learned who she was or where she came from before she met my father. They'd done a good job of erasing her. I had always felt they were trying to erase me, too, so that all sign of her ever having drawn breath would be gone. I had no idea how tall or short she had been, whether she had been beautiful or merely pretty, whether she was quiet or bubbling with laughter. Nothing. Any question I had ever asked had been ignored. What I knew about my father, you could have poked under your eyelid and not felt discomfort. The oldest son of the oldest son of the oldest son. All the best schools. His first sign of rebellion was his decision to go to university here instead of to a "good" one in Britain. Instinctive genius for business, he pulled the loose ends of a fraying fortune together, guaranteed everyone's continuing comfort, then met and married my mother, and the year after I was born, they both were gone. Died, I supposed.

The family used the money he had protected to hire nursemaids and what they insisted on calling nannies. As soon as I was old enough, they shipped me off to private school. Summer holidays in camps with names I always remembered as Wanna PeePee. Young women I did not know who suddenly appeared at my school to escort me on ten-day Easter holiday tours of the cathedrals of Europe.

And then one summer holiday, it wasn't some adenoidal companion who a few years earlier would have been called nanny; it was my aunt, in jeans and a loose shirt, cotton socks and sneakers, and before the headmistress had time to rally her wits, we were gone, heading off in an improperly racy bright green sports car.

"My God," my aunt said as soon as we were away from the ivy and brick, "we've got to get you some decent clothes!"

I'd lived in school tunics for so many years, it hadn't occurred to me I could wear anything else. I knew, of course, that other people wore other clothes. Somehow they had taught me that was fine for Other People, but not for me.

The first time I saw myself wearing jeans, cotton shirt, white tennis socks and leather sneakers, I felt as if the clothes were wearing me. The second look I took, I recognized myself for the first time in memory. When I sat on a rock on the shore of the lake and felt the sharp blades of my aunt's big paper shears slice off the heavy mane of hair they had taught me to wind in a thick, heavy bun at the nape of my neck, I felt as if my brain was being unwrapped, taken from a thick layer of shit and exposed for the first time in my life to sunshine and fresh breezes. I wept, but not because I felt sorry my hair was being cut.

Actually, I didn't weep at all. I bawled and howled, snoffled and sobbed, and didn't even want to look at my long hair, cut loose from my head. My aunt took it and I have no idea what she did with it. Nor do I care.

Uncle Tony was still functional then. Still laughing, still joking. He played the piano, thundering complex chords that rolled across the lake and came back to us from the opposite hills. He played the guitar, sitting on a stool on the porch, the individual notes almost visible in the air.

I didn't go back to school in Britain. Uncle Tony and my aunt forced them to enrol me in a school on the Island. I still had to wear a tunic, I still had to troop around wearing the school tie, I still didn't live a normal life with normal people, but how could I have done that with the anything-but-normal family I'd inherited? My uncles, in various states of debauchery, dressed to the nines, working overtime to develop cirrhosis. And each of them, for all their stuffy insistence on things of culture and class, wearing rings made out of bent horseshoe nails, for luck.

I would have liked to have known if my mother had ever seen this place, if there was one particular part of it she had liked, some place she went to when being alone was important. If I knew even that much about her, she would be real to me and I could mourn her death, celebrate her life and my own.

I asked my aunt about my parents. Not immediately, but later, when I felt we knew each other a bit. She shook her head, shrugged almost apologetically, and said she knew almost nothing. "Car crash, I heard."

"Nobody tells me anything," I confessed. "I ask and ask, but . . ."

"Then you have every right to invent the mother you want." She patted my hand.

"No," I argued. "I can't invent her back alive, and that's what I want: a live mother!"

My aunt was like a mother – for a while. Then she disappeared, too. It made headlines for a day or two. Local Artist Vanishes, Police Lack Clues. The headlines withered, the articles got smaller, eventually the mystery diminished to a half-inch filler toward the back of the local rag. Search parties stopped going out into the bush, eventually the Reward For Information posters faded and were taken down in the bus, train and ferry depots, and the only one who seemed aware of the fact something had obviously happened was Uncle Tony, but nobody had listened to him for years. Every time one of his brothers went to visit him, Uncle Tony screamed and raged, and only his canvas restraint jacket held his arms at his sides, kept him from ripping out throats.

They disappeared in a hurry then. It took less than eight years and the whole lot of them went. A suspicious number of Death By Misadventure verdicts, a few Probable Suicide decisions, and some of them incredibly inventive and awful. One seems to have gone to the time and trouble to pry open the gelatin capsules containing his allergy medicine, replacing the medicinal compound with ordinary Drano which, of course, ate holes in his stomach. He'd had an ulcer for years, most drunks develop them, so nobody paid attention to his bellyache until he was bleeding internally so badly even waterglass doses of gin couldn't stop the pain. An ambulance was called, he was taken to hospital screaming and died before they could diagnose anything. The truly bizarre part was, nobody seemed to find it at all odd that the man had put Drano in more capsules than he swallowed. There were four others in the bottle, but nobody discovered that until months later, when another member of the family checked out the same way. That one was deemed an accident, however, because how could he have known how the other had done himself in?

Powerful automobiles wrapped around hydro poles; a speedboat hit a deadhead and five people drowned because they were too drunk to survive, had been too stupid to wear lifejackets. Mostly, though, it was suicide of one sort or another, the self-destructive impulses of generations of alcoholics bubbling suddenly to the surface, demanding something faster than genteel soddenness.

And now there was me and Uncle Tony, and he might as well have been dead. Tony, who went from music to money because the family demanded it, who went by way of the London School of Economics and the World Bank to a rubber room, where he sits reading the Dow Jones Index and muttering spells like some kind of sorcerer. The last coherent thing he said to me was that the International Monetary Fund is a game of Monopoly, and it only matters because so many people continue to pretend it matters.

I put my coffee cup in the house and walked down to the lake. A duck was swimming, with a flotilla of yellow ducklings accompanying her. She was like no wild duck I'd ever seen. She was a light chocolate colour, lighter than a Khaki Campbell domestic duck, bigger than one too, with dark bronze markings in the pattern of a mallard.

I heard something whispering in the bush. I didn't turn to look – you seldom get to see a goolieguy, unless she wants to be seen – but the movie began to unroll behind my eyes again; tame ducks, virtually helpless on their own, left to survive or perish by a grief-crazed fool who did nothing more for them than grab the enclosure fencing and rip it open to allow them to wander. And they had; they had wandered down to the lake, propelled by hunger. Small-bodied, unable to fly, they copied what they saw the wild ducks doing, ate what they saw the wild ducks eating, and eventually mated with the mallard drakes, and their offspring, neither wild nor tame, stayed when the others left for the winter. They probably thought the lake was theirs, now.

I had a vision of millet seed, and didn't know it was millet seed until I remembered a canary my aunt had kept here, a stalk of millet hanging in its cage. It could be planted around the rim of the lake; the ducks would feed on it all winter.

I turned to go back to the house, and for a moment I thought I saw my Uncle Tony sitting on the porch, sobbing, unable to play music because he had betrayed his gift, betrayed it by dabbling in the cesspool of family approval, betrayed it by turning his genius to the gathering of money, betrayed it by letting those soulless bastards convince him their standards were the ones that mattered. She would have done better than merely

forgiving him, she would have done better than merely understanding why he had done it. She would have loved him. He
could have lived here with her, and if he had never again been
able to play as well as he once had, well enough to fill concert
halls and bring people to their feet crying and cheering, he
would have been able to play, play for her, play for himself, play
for the goolieguy. But they had taught him not to believe in or
trust in love, and because he didn't believe, it wasn't there for
him, and he wept, knowing he had thrown away the only salvation possible for any of us.

They did something to her, too. My aunt, I mean. She wasn't
one to kill herself, or leave because they'd taken Tony to an
asylum. She would have been getting ready to fight them, to
bypass the hired beagles and get a decent lawyer, maybe storm
into court with writs of *habeas corpus* or whatever, get Tony out
of the quiet, aseptic place where they put coloured pills in your
custard and jabbed needles into the slack flesh of your flaccid
arm.

But she vanished. In rolling hills, honey-combed with mine
shafts; in valleys where ventilation tunnels dropped straight
down for two hundred feet, covered by heavy metal plates to
keep half the world from falling in. It wouldn't take much. A
bump on the head. One burly creep to pick her up and walk off
with her, unconscious, until he got to the shaft, pulled aside the
big metal plate and tossed her inside, into the dark and the air
foul with rat-shit and bat-droppings. Then put the metal plate
back in place and leave. Those shafts are full of gases of one kind
or another, most of them poisonous. And the poor goolicguy
digging, digging, digging, unable to get past the crisscross of
railroad tracks, the shafts with the metal coal cars still standing,
waiting, the winches and machinery slowly rusting in the dripping dampness. A goolieguy whose fingers were seared to the
bone, whose poor hands dripped blood as red as our own, trying
to dig in a place throbbing with metal, digging and howling like
the mad winds of autumn, trying to free the woman who had
been kind, who had left bowls of cream, who had bought frozen
yogurt and left it where a goolieguy would find it on a hot
summer day.

She vanished because she knew something they didn't want anyone else in the family to know. She knew it wasn't necessary to worry about the big game of Monopoly, to turn yourself into something like my four-times great-grandfather, who was willing to bury people for stuff that doesn't really exist or matter. Maybe they'd done in my mother, too. Maybe they didn't trust a man who had the talent to accumulate the invisible and non-existent, but who preferred to turn his energy to other things. Maybe the only reason they hadn't done me in was they thought they could bring me up to be like them, and, after all, I was family, and crazy people get bent out of shape by little things like that.

There was no sense looking for the place the goolieguy had nearly killed herself fighting the metal. The rain forest can cover anything in three years, and it had been far more than three years since she had vanished into thin air. The sword fern, elder-berry, salmonberry, alder and evergreen can cover the black scars of forest fire, the abomination of bad logging practices, the ripped-out and vile refuse of mining; they can cover sin, they can cover love. I knew what I knew and that's all I needed. It's all any of us need.

Back at the house again, I tidied up, thinking about gardens. About rows of peas held upright by small sticks, of tomatoes ripe and musty-smelling in the sunshine. Curly kale and swiss chard, collard greens and red leaf lettuce, broccoli and cabbage, cauliflower and eggplant and the magic of bright pumpkins in dark soil. Rows and rows of corn, beets, and beds of green onions and garlic. I'd never had a garden, not really. A few flow-ers if they wanted to grow, a lawn that needed cutting, but not a real garden.

I whistled to Bess. We went into town to the feed store and I got packages of seed at reduced price because it was several weeks past the time to plant. "Might not get a good crop," the clerk warned, "it's a bit late in the season."

"Better late than never," I quoted, and he grinned as if I'd come up with something original, amusing, and very intelligent. I almost bought a roto-tiller, too, but turned away from it. There was no rational reason why I turned away, but the goolieguy doesn't like machinery.

When we got home, the place where I'd envisioned the garden, the place which had been grass and clover when I left, was dug and ready, the clods of earth broken into fine soil. Instead of daring to intrude, I put the seed packets on the grass and left a small blue cardboard container of imported hothouse cherry tomatoes beside them.

Several miles from the flatland city where I had spent so many years of my life being a fool, there was a roadside stand where farmers had taken their produce and left it to be sold by sun-tanned and smiling teen-agers, out of school for the summer. We would go there on weekends and buy far more of whatever was in season than we needed, and Carol always got cherry tomatoes. She ate them one after the other, the way some people eat grapes. She never put them in the fridge, she left them out so they would be warm; she said chilling them took the sunshine taste out of them.

She had loved me so completely and unquestioningly. I moved to a flat, dry, yellow place, not because I loved her, but because I needed the love I knew she had for me. Every love affair, every relationship is uneven. There is always one person loves stronger, more, better, more completely, and the one who loves the most, gives the most, and gets less in return. And maybe that is what love is, the giving without thought of what might come back in return. It can't be easy to try to hold something with an open hand.

She loved me so much she did not get custody of her daughter, and saw her only at intervals, for part of Easter and summer holidays. And not at all at Christmas. When her daughter arrived, I always found a perfectly good reason to go somewhere else within a couple of days. Gwen would bring silly chatter and clattering feet, would get Bess wound up like a hysterical mutt; mealtimes became clattering of knives and forks and jokes like, "How do you know if there's an elephant sleeping in bed with you? Because he's got a big picture of a peanut on his pyjama shirt." Carol would laugh happily and I would try to smile as if I meant it, but it didn't seem funny to me, it seemed ridiculous. And so, within two or three days, I would absolutely have to go somewhere for some absolutely legitimate reason, and by the time I got back, Gwen would have returned to her father's apartment, three hundred miles away, where the "stepmother" figure changed every year or so.

We were supposed to take a vacation together, everything was planned, and then the phone call from the ex-husband and everything got changed. Instead of coming in August, Gwen would come as soon as school let out; instead of staying a month, Gwen would stay six weeks. My whole summer turned inside out because one unofficial stepmother was leaving to make room for another, and it would be best all round if the new one was given a period of time to adapt without having Gwen there because it seemed Gwen was showing signs of being upset and disturbed; the school marks had not been up to expectations; there had even been, perish the thought, arguments and visits to the school counsellor.

And who had thought to ask me how I felt about it? Too many people had, for too long, had too much control over my life. And no more! Carol wouldn't argue about it, she wouldn't even talk about it, she just quietly made arrangements to have her holiday time rescheduled to accommodate the kid's arrival.

I left before the kid got there. Left, and discovered within minutes that what I had taken so lightly for so long had become such a part of me that just knowing it was over was pain. I'd been away from Carol before for days, even weeks, and not felt this cold, burning hole in my stomach. I knew she'd be there when I went back. But two blocks from the house, knowing I was not going to go back, never going to be held by her again, never going to hear her soft laughter in the lilac dusk of our bedroom, something started to burn and every day it took more and more of my energy to not confront what I had done, not look at what it was going to mean.

I heard a chittering, high-pitched, half melody, and turned to see the goolieguy standing by the corner of the house, beckoning with her long-fingered hand. I went to see what it was she wanted, and she was standing with the blue cardboard carton in one hand, picking little tomatoes one at a time with her other hand, putting them carefully in her mouth, and eating them slowly. The garden was planted, straight rows, spaced maybe eighteen inches apart, marked by little sticks at each end.

I would have sworn I could taste the slightly acid tang of tomato in my own mouth, and I understood why the goolieguy was trembling with joy. So many years without the taste of tomato. Think of it. An ordinary thing like that, but it had been denied her because, in the time she should have been tending a garden, she was insane with pain, trying to help a woman who had dared to show the family the power of love. And the garden died, and with it the seeds the goolieguy might have saved and planted for herself. Years and years without the tang of tomato, without the crunch of green onion or the delicate wonder of fresh green peas.

And Uncle Tony had let them do it. Hell, he had helped them do it! And he knew it. Knew it and sat blubbering when what he ought to have done was come down off the porch, run across the grass to the door of the studio, and yell I Love You! She would have stopped what she was doing, she would have put aside whatever it was and gone to him and taken his hand and laughed up and said I Know You Do, and they could have gone down to the lake together and had a life.

"Hi," I said into the phone, "is your mother there?"

"She's at work," Gwen said cheerfully. "Where are you?"

"When will she be home?" I avoided the kid's question. If you answer one, she's got six more waiting in the wings, and I wasn't up to it.

"She'll be back in about an hour. Where are you?" she repeated.

"When are you going back to your dad's place?" I countered.

"I asked first," she said, in that cheeky tone that means she isn't going to back off until she gets her answer.

"I've been busy," I evaded.

"Yeah? Doing what?"

"Insulating my new house, among other things. If it's any of your business."

"It's my business," she said angrily. "Of course it's my business! What new house?"

"When are you going back to your dad's place?" I repeated. "I answered, now it's your turn."

"You never answered. I asked where you were, you talk about a new house. You don't say where it is, so I don't know where you are!"

"That's a secret." I said. "Maybe a surprise. Stretch yourself, you brat, trust me."

There was a long silence. What reason did she have to trust me? She hardly knew me. I was a signature on birthday cards Carol bought.

"I don't want to go back to my dad's place," she said, her voice trembling. "I think I'll run away if they try to make me."

"They who?"

"You know. Them. Custody people, I guess."

"Fuck 'em." I said, and was surprised at how much I meant it. "If I give you my phone number, will you make sure your mother calls me? Please?"

"Sure," she said easily. "What's your new house like?"

"Gorgeous." I said. "It's got a spook lives in the bush. Like an elf or a leprechaun, only taller."

"Oh, I just bet." She was laughing that high-pitched cackle that so often had annoyed me to the point of wanting to slap her. Now it sounded like the kind of laugh that makes it almost impossible not to join in and laugh along with her.

Carol phoned back two hours later, and I knew the kid was hanging around, trying to hear at least that half of the conversation. Ordinarily that would have enraged me, but it didn't seem to matter. The goolieguy was twittering around the side of the house, fussing with the rose bushes, and that didn't bother me; why should a human kid bother me? I told Carol where I was and I told her I was staying at the old place, wasted some time telling her about the repairs and such, and then asked, if I bought the plane tickets, would she come out for a visit. "Gwen is living with me now," she said, her voice carefully controlled, her tone neutral.

"I gathered as much from Gwen," I said, my tone as neutral as hers.

"She doesn't want to go back to her father's place."

"That's what she told me," I agreed stupidly. "Ask her how she feels about a lake and a creek and some hummingbirds." And I tried not to feel as if Carol's sigh of relief had knifed into my throat.

The goolieguy came to the window of the music room and stared in at the sound system, her eyes wide with longing. I watched her until she looked at me, twittered pleadingly, and then I beckoned for her to come inside. She isn't comfortable in the house, and has to watch where she's putting her long, thin, bare feet, because if she steps where there's a nail, even if the head of it is pounded down below the level of the surface of the board, it hurts her. She can't go near the stove, of course, and can only open the door of the fridge by using a stick to hook the handle on the door and pull it open, but I know she comes inside when she wants to, so there was no reason to think she wouldn't come in when invited.

I showed her how she could use a yardstick to push the button on the sound system and turn it on, how a second push could turn it off. I demonstrated several times, then handed her the yardstick and gestured. And then the music was playing and she was grinning happily. I opened the window to let the music outside, and the goolieguy jumped easily over the waist-high sill, onto the porch, then over the porch rail to the grass.

Some people laugh and say herons are ungainly, awkward, even clumsy, but I have always thought them graceful. And a goolieguy dancing in the sunlight reminds me of a heron walking slowly, proudly, in shallow water, lifting each leg deliberately, placing it exactly where she wants it to be, totally a part of her own world. The music was playing when I drove Carol and Gwen up to the house, and neither of them asked why I had left the sound system on, or why it was turned up so loud. Of course Gwen fell in love with the studio and wanted to sleep there instead of in the main house, and things between Carol and I were such that it seemed a good idea when she put her sleeping bag on the built-in bed next to Gwen's blue one. But on the fourth day, Carol brought her suitcase into the house and put it down on the floor in my bedroom. I know for a fact Bess slept on the bed in the studio, curled up beside Gwen, breaking half the rules of existence that night – or, at least, those rules imposed by me for reasons which no longer seemed the least bit important.

"I guess you weren't kidding," Gwen said softly, sitting cross-legged on the grass between Carol and me. "I guess there really is a spook in the bush here, eh?"

"Does she scare you?" I asked, not looking at the kid because I'm still not sure what it is I feel when I look at her. Amazement, maybe.

"No. Not scared. But . . . I bet if I told people, they'd think I was nuts."

"I'm not sure," I admitted. "People don't admit that they believe she exists but . . . there are a lot of people here who will deny she doesn't!"

"But not a leprechaun," Gwen said firmly. And so I told her what the youngest workie had told me, and some, not much, but some of what I had experienced myself in the time I had been here. And all the time, Carol stared at us as if she wasn't sure we shouldn't both be put in a jar and the lid screwed on tightly.

"What does she want?" the kid asked uneasily.

"Nothing," I said. "Everything," I amended.

"I think she likes me," Gwen blushed.

"I'm sure she does," I agreed. And I told her about ice cream cones and about tropical fruit, about coffee cream and soft bread, and she nodded. "If you tell people," I laughed, "they'll tell you that I'm as crazy as everyone else in my family, and they'll insist it's raccoons or cats eat the food."

"Are you?" Gwen asked. "Crazy, I mean?"

"Sure I am," I said, and it didn't hurt to admit it. "I'm absolutely insane. In a world like this one, a person would have to be a fool to want to be sane and normal and like everyone else." The kid began cackling wildly, and Carol was staring at me, laughing, but not at me. Never at me.

"The goolieguy," I said, tears pouring easily, "really believes in love, and all she wants is for some of us to be willing to defend love at least half as fiercely as we're willing to defend stupid stuff like private property and money. To put as much effort into learning how to love as we're willing to put into learning how to balance a chequebook." I knew both of them could see me crying, but they didn't take it as a sign of weakness or stupidity or of anything other than that I was crying, and we ought to be able to do that as easily and unselfconsciously as we laugh. Or argue. "I guess I have a long way to go," I admitted. "It isn't as easy as it sounds."

Even pot-bellied legal beagles can come in handy. You treat them like shaman's rattles and wave them in the face of the ones pestering you, and the bothersome interference backs off, leaves you alone.

The kid is as noisy as a Stellar's jay and as undisciplined as any supposed savage. There is no school tunic, no highly polished Oxford shoes, no boarding school; she lives here and every weekday morning Carol drives her down the Lakes Road to the highway to catch the bus to school.

There's a new building on the place now, out behind the orchard at the edge of the clearing. Brick and mortar and a fitted tile roof, with big windows for light and a stone fireplace where, on wet winter days, a bed of warm embers can keep the place warm. A thick, foam-stuffed mattress and some warm blankets, and the cheerful orange bowl in the middle of the table always has grapes or tangerines, apples, and even peaches in it. Cottage cheese and fresh fruit can make a goolieguy vibrate with pleasure.

The metal roof is gone from the main house, we leave the pickup parked halfway down the hill and all the metal pots and pans have been replaced with glass. The metal knives, forks and spoons are silver now, and Carol insisted on covering the floor with glazed pottery tiles, so that even an inexperienced baby goolieguy can come in the house without burning her toes on the fire from the nail heads in the flooring.

They aren't that different from us. All they want is a bit of room, a bit of acceptance, a chance to be what they are, to become what they are capable of becoming. A chance at a bit of love, and the freedom to love in return.

If Pigs Could Fly

Christine Crow

... The emergence of symbolic thought must have required
that women, like words, should be things that were
exchanged
(Lévi-Strauss, quoted by Judith Butler in *Gender Trouble,
Feminism and the Subversion of Identity*, 41)

... what if the goods got together
(Luce Irigaray)

Cheek to cheek and breast to breast
Locked together in one nest (. . .)
(. . .) Come buy! Come buy!
(Christina Rossetti, *Goblin Market*)

"... *Pigs!*" grunted our stepfather, his mouth full of bacon and
egg, designating with his usual vituperative intensity at this time
of morning the two middle-aged women who had recently come
to live in the farm on the hill. '... *Nothing but pigs! And if I ever
catch you or your sister ...*"

One of the women was a writer and one was a painter. Mother
had whispered nervously when further questioned. The painter
one wore corduroy trousers and a long, dirty shirt with paint
splashed all over it (but it would be, wouldn't it, I remember
thinking somewhat guiltily). And the other, the writer one, had
never been seen. That's all we knew, in those days. All we *ever*
really knew, in fact.

Suffering from an enlarged heart ever since the painfully complicated birth of my sister, Mother died about a year afterwards, when I was thirteen and my sister five and a half. The old house blew down in a storm a few years later (our stepfather had long since abandoned us to our own devices) and we moved our separate ways. Opposite corners of the globe, you might say.

He need not have worried. We never went to visit the farm on the hill.

More than anything else, her sister wanted a pig.

To *keep* a pig, you mean? To live in the country and do her painting? Such great fire in her loins still waiting to get out.

Perhaps. But something much more, it seemed. Something which, dear as happiness, dearer than desire itself ...

A pig. *Sus scrofa*. Omnivorous ungulate mammal. The eager, quivering snout with its wide, flattened nostrils. The thick, pink skin with its fringe of gold bristles. The small, knowing eyes with their long, bland lashes. The neat, vigorous trotters. The spritely, silk-purse ears with their long, white hairs. And, there where they had blindly aimed the drawing-pin at so many giggling, long-ago birthday parties (why not again now, in her near sixties?), the trusting pink behind with the curly, string tail.

Intelligent, too. Social cognition. Knowing when another is hiding food. Performative identity and all that.

Yes, prejudices of greed and uncleanliness apart (Leviticus?), there *was* something deeply compelling about a pig, she found herself thinking as she stared towards the cliff through the half open French windows (must get a wedge or something to stop that banging): something primitive, subversive, free ... *"I am a pig! Your heart's desire! I shall live by your side for ever and ever ... Your child, your frog-prince, your naked, cloven-hoof lover, your precious, rumple-trumple what-you-will self."*

A shower of blossom fluttered down from the apple tree on frail pink wings, to bob for an instant on the greenish waves and vanish below like a tiny lost ship.

A lump came to Laura's throat as she thought of Liz imprisoned far away there in the dark little city flat, alone, anorexic and devoured by her vast, secretive anger and pain (too far gone these days even to *think* of painting), her brave dreams of happiness still to come.

She would have done anything to give her sister a pig.

Unlike her younger sibling, defiantly single and childless, Laura herself was long since married "with children", as they say. Grown-up twin boys already left home who seemed to have been metamorphosized by Circe over night into tall, grey businessmen identical with their tall, grey, solicitor father . . . leaving her more alone now, she sometimes wryly reflected, than if those boneless gums had never once suckled (Lady Macbeth?) at her nowadays vast and shapeless breasts (you'd *expect* to put on weight after a hysterectomy, though, would you not?).

As she thought of the longed-for pig again, it began to take on an appealingly sensual, almost erotic note. A bit like a baby itself, in a way. Doubtless not for nothing was it known as the Womb Animal, emblem of Earth, not to mention a Mother Complex or something, didn't Jung say? As for the general notion of taboo such as saddled the poor creature's back . . .

(With time to kill now, as they say, Laura had begun to read greedily in the local library . . . including, nowadays, believe it or not, the bottom shelf near the door marked "Women's Studies" and – really no more than a battered old shoe-box – the subsection marked intriguingly "Gender Theory". One had to exercise the old brain cells, after all . . . know at least a little of what was going on in the cultural world. Not that she could understand much of the language they all seemed bent on getting their tongues round these days: "EXOGAMATIC HETEROSEXUALITY" or "THE HOMOEROTIC UNCONSCIOUS OF THE PHALLOGOCENTRIC ECONOMY" and the like . . . Monstrously seductive phrases which she carefully copied into a special pink spiral notebook, complete with would-be definitions usually no less obscure. "EXOGAMY", for example, was "*the exchange of women in marriage outside the tribe, often in the form of a certain number of pigs*" (sic, but this was in the days before the subject took hold). Otherwise, apparently, nothing but INCEST, HOMOSEXUALITY, CHAOS . . . the total destruction of the whole social pact! No wonder her stepfather had got himself in such a stew, thinking of the two strange women up at the farm! . . . Strange, though, all the same, to find the violent views of such an ogre coinciding with those of the great contemporary STRUCTURALISTS (see Lévi-Strauss), always assuming she hadn't missed something . . . So difficult to see which side anyone was on in these things. Why, for different reasons, even the LESBIANS themselves (asterisk, see later) seemed sometimes to be cutting off their noses . . . arguing against themselves. Not that you needed to be a Lesbian yourself, of course, to long to reveal the hidden menu feeding the bias of the said social norm. What you needed was some kind of modern Fairy Tale to bring it all home to roost in simple, graphic terms).

As for her sister herself . . . So much younger than Laura ("*the runt of the litter*", Liz had once referred to herself, half-jokingly), she had virtually been brought up by the older girl as her own baby . . . baby doll, more like it . . . ever since their poor Mother first took to her bed.

. . . Changing her nappies (giant safety-pins in those days, remember?), tucking her up in her bright patchwork blanket and reading bedtime stories (*The Three Little Pigs* had been a favourite, now she came to think of it), pushing her in the pram to the farm on the hill (it was before the two strange women moved there, needless to say), warming her bottle in the little green enamel saucepan – there it was still, up there on the dresser! – humping her over her shoulder as she had seen her school-friend's mother do with her new baby daughter . . . and, as if to restage some crucial step in human evolution, preparing her meals as she turned to solids later on. (All those dutiful maternal chores . . . can't think why it didn't put her off having children herself).

And what an appetite, too! . . . stopping at nothing in its voracious capacity and seeming, in hindsight, to have grown from some secret, insatiable LACK (see PSYCHOANALYSIS, if she could ever get round to filling it in).

"*Don't be such a pig*," Laura used to shout, smacking away the clamorous little hands, desperate for yoghurts, sweets, cakes, fruits (ah, fruits! fruits! come buy! come buy!) . . . always though, of course, for Liz's own good, apple as she was of her older sister's eye.

The relationship between the two was fraught, even nowadays, so many years later, with unspoken tension: a proverbial love-hate which both kept them apart and held them together in a grip of iron: Laura guilty of a crime of seniority and surrogate motherhood no mere kind word could ever quite expiate, and Liz permanently trying to assert herself in the face of it, – trapped in a kind of defensive aloofness from which she suffered self-critically in turn. As for which sister really had the upper hand (does there have to be one?): in such intimate family matters, how should I presume to know!

And the pig?

Ridiculous though it sounded, to feel oneself responsible for another's well-being (that rare breed of happiness can only spring, after all, from within one's own entrails), Laura, I repeat, would have given anything to answer her sister's desire, supply the fiery antidote to whatever poisonous thoughts devoured her so.

> *Lizzie, Lizzie, have you tasted*
> *For my sake the fruit forbidden.*
> *Must your light like mine be hidden (. . .)*
> *Thirsty, cankered, goblin-ridden?*

(*Goblin Market*. Sisters, sacrifice, Victorian forbidden fruits with a vengeance – the notebook stretched to the odd literary quotation. See EROTICISED TABOO.)

"To market, to market, to buy a fat pig . . ."
Liz's fiftieth birthday was rapidly approaching.

Amused at her own obsessive persistence, Laura found herself rooting mercilessly through the local shops in search of at least *something* pig-like to fit the bill. The once busy fishing-village where she and her husband had set up home on the edge of the cliff could at least be relied upon to put at her disposal a glut of plastic goblins, mermaids, gnomes and other such unwittingly libidinous wares designed to tempt the tourist purse.

Oh, the discrepancy between action and wish!

A birthday card depicting a gluttonous specimen, one neat, trotter in a trough of pink icing and "*Make a pig of yourself! It's your special day!*" issuing in a bubble from its glistening snout was the first porcine item to meet her eagle eye ... followed by a roughly carved "Old Salt Pork" by a fishing-boat, a mammoth book of Feminist Fairy Tales with a grey-suited pig on the cover (male chauvinist, predictably enough, not that Liz would read it anyway), a small pig door-stopper made of cast iron, a tartan porpoise breadbin (Porcus? the sea-hog? some secret connection?) and a blue porcelain piggy-bank fired, no doubt, in a local kiln.

She chose the latter. At least it seemed relevant, in an odd kind of way, not yet fully unearthed.

How horribly conscious Laura felt, meanwhile, that in reducing her impassioned quest to such paltry, substitutional icons, she was in a sense deflating and eviscerating the ambiguous reality of her sister's desire (the phrase had a pleasingly contemporary ring ... maybe all the theory she'd trustingly swallowed had started to impregnate her own thoughts at last), failing to satisfy, by placing it back so squarely in the land of METAPHOR (rash of asterisks), the genuine cry of need from which it sprang, always supposing *that* was not in some way a metaphor too.

... Failing, likewise, to satisfy her own mysterious EMPATHY! ... a quality strangely suspect nowadays, apparently, for confusing the Other's desire with one's own, if not for appropriating DIFFERENCE (see, alas, ENEMY and POLLUTION, not to mention, yet again, TABOO).

Indeed, any initial clation dwindling by the second, here she was now, trotting sadly back home with nothing more than the blue porcelain piggy-bank clutched in her bag like the proverbial pig in a poke (pig expressions had seemed legion, ever since starting her swinish mission), together with, for herself this time (the French windows), the little cast iron door-stopper.

(Iron! pig-iron? "*cauld iron*"! Her equally urgent researches in the "Myths and Superstition" section of the library had revealed, incidentally, that, for fear of bad luck – presumably in the form of some monstrous admonitory wrath from the

Deep – the local fishing-folk were loath even to that day to utter
the dread three-lettered word. "CurlyTail" was its name instead.
And, should such an ancient taboo be inadvertently broken,
hastened to touch "cauld iron" for all they were worth. Once,
when an unsuspecting Minister chose as text that well-known
passage about the Gadarene swine, a growing tap, tap, tapping
was heard throughout the church and the entire congregation
up and rushed for the door, leaving him preaching to thin air . . .
The Gadarene swine! Mark V, 1–20. Multiple voices of the
"unclean spirit" departing the sufferer and entering instead a
nearby herd of swine, who conveniently hurl themselves over
the cliff! For some reason the image had always haunted her.)

Symbols, symbols! Always symbols!

Pushing a book inside a pram!

Was there no way to GROUNDTHE INFINITE SLIPPAGE
OF DESIRE . . . ? and, come to that, no alternative economic
transaction (a secret smile now, towards the blue piggy-bank)
than exchanging women for the birth of words? What if the
goods got together after all?

"Nothing but pigs! . . . And if I ever catch you or your sister . . ."

Anything, it seemed, to kill two birds and make their stepfather eat his hat.

The theory notebook was indeed paying off.

It started slowly at first.

A slight heaviness in the abdomen, a feeling of tiredness, the
notorious morning sickness she remembered vaguely from
years ago . . .

And then, her belly soon hard and even more swollen than
usual, the unmistakeable realization she was pregnant . . . all the
more incredible in that, let alone the hysterectomy, she and her
husband slept in separate rooms . . . had done, in fact, for many
long years.

She was eating ravenously by now, wolfing down everything
that caught her eye. Dates, turnips, cabbages, apples, packets of
chocolate truffles, even, on one occasion – her usual vegetarian-
ism flown out of the window – eggs and bacon like long ago.
Raiding shops with open basket. Gobbling yoghurts, cakes,

vegetables, fruits . . . the taut, spiky skins of prickly pears or the round, succulent flanks of grapefruit and melons . . . with a kind of kind of greedy ecstasy almost poetic in its way.

An unexpected acquiesence, too. Quite unlike the horror of being invaded by an alien being she remembered before with the twins. And which made her feel . . .

Well, blissfully happy! In the pink! (see JOUISSANCE).

. . . Almost as if, never mind her fierce vindication of the integrity of the modern woman who had chosen like Liz herself not to have children (which is more selfish after all, to give birth to yourself or bring others into the world to live and suffer in turn?), she had found in this late procreation on behalf of another – for that is surely what it was – something like her true identity: something primitive, subversive, free . . . something which, far from guilty in its power of transgression, seemed to speak the voice of some deep new order, some . . .

But don't ask me, though. How should I know?

Thoughts of her sister still burning inside her, but somehow, now, not quite so particularized, almost as if she had other sisters, too . . . how many times, lying there wide awake in her lone bed (even through the wall, her husband still snored, as if driving pigs to market), she would run her hand secretly over the unknown yet somehow familiar shape growing hourly inside her . . . messianic shape, even . . . radiating it with warm, intense wishes, willing it safely towards the light of day!

No wonder the Ancients thought the mother's imagination to be capable of affecting the foetus in the womb . . . monstrous embryonic bifurcations and anomalies, springing directly from the fantasies of the hysterical, female brain. She must be careful where she let her thoughts wander, these days!

Careful what she read and copied into the spiral notebook, too! Gender Theory has powerful seeds and powerful goblin fruits to sell!

By now, Laura's belly had swollen to monstrous proportions: a heavy, low-slung shape which seemed to start in her groin and hog every inch of space available . . . right up past her ribcage into the base of her throat and even, or so it felt, higher and

higher, to the very abode of that lusty organ of desire, the tongue
. . . while, making her grunt and snort aloud every few seconds,
the determined off-spring in its turn was delivering regular kicks
far sharper and more vigorous (she thought of their poor
Mother) than she would have thought it possible to endure
without positively splitting in two.

Huffing and puffing, ham-strings taut with the extra weight,
she was waddling up and down now by the mirror every five
minutes or more, preoccupied, apart from the occasional
thought of her sister, with nothing more now than her own
obscenely splendid, sow-like form. Indeed, talk about Liz and
the distorted self-image of the anorexic! . . . her previous horror
at the size of her own body seemed miraculously to have
vanished through very excess. Painful or not, the experience of
labour was obviously acting as catharsis all round. A kind of
expurgatory diet in reverse, you might say.

Then, one fine morning just after breakfast (bacon and eggs
again), still strangely calm and smiling, off she set towards her
favourite sofa – an elegant, pre-Raphaelite affair inherited from a
kind, but prissy old aunt – and, a stream of fresh air from the now
safely secured French windows gently lifting the rose-pink curtains
(so much better than the trauma of the hospital!), with no one to
witness but her own small, knowing eyes in the mirror, proceeded
to deliver herself on its white cushions in an ecstatic rush of blood
and bristle and hoof . . . *cloven* hoof, dear ones, needless to say.

"And this little piggy . . ."

It was a pig, of course. Had she half-suspected, in a way?

A pig. *Sus scrofa.* Omnivorous ungulate mammal (see above).
The eager, quivering snout with its wide, flattened nostrils, etc,
etc (see above). The spritely, silk-purse ears with their long,
white hairs. And, there where they had blindly aimed the drawing-pin at so many giggling, long-ago birthday parties (yes, she
must reinstigate them, why not?), the trusting pink behind with
the curly, string tail.

British Saddleback?

No. They're black as well as pink, she knew from her library
researches.

The long, low-slung body with its short, thick legs and concave jowl like the one on the birthday card (*"Make a pig of yourself! It's your special day!"*) ... Must be a Large White instead.

Female, too, shall we say? If you must. But ... female, male, androgynous, what does it matter now that *psychic* not *gender* identity is at stake!

That jaunty row of incipient teats all the same, and, presumably a variant on those little brown spots said, like the cloven hoof, to be marks of the Devil (no doubt where the unclean spirits made their entrance?), a slight feathery extruberance on each of its fleshy, pink shoulder-blades. And, strangest of all, though, for such a pristine spirit, a small gold ring in the end of its nose.

She gazed at it tenderly a moment, guiding the hungry, restless snout to her once more purposefully swelling nipples (however cold and ticklish at first, the ring was reassuring, in an odd kind of way), her thoughts flying back at once to those little guzzling mouths of long ago. Further back, even. Further back still ...

Pig in clover? Pig in the middle? Another of Circe's conjuring-tricks to charm the menopausal brain?

Not on your life! This was for real!

No half-measures! The whole perfect hog!

It stared back at her a moment through its small, knowing eyes with their long, bland lashes (almost identical to her own eyes, she saw with a start now in the mirror), and, as she struggled to hump its warm, naked bulk over her shoulder (memories! memories! the green enamel saucepan!), grunted three times: *"Oink! Oink! Oink!"*, perfect trinity of sound. flesh and word. Well, so dear, so gay, so vulnerable, so fresh and comically eager and clean, so unlike all the abominable things pigs have always been made out to be, and filling her with a sense of such total, unsullied joy.

Tears came to her throat.

"Perhaps I'll keep you for myself alone," she whispered, bending to place her lips on the silky, white hairs, softly imbibing its special piglet scent, the scent of wish and rose and apple-blossom dream come true.

Touch cauld iron to make you not go away?

It was not hers to keep, however.

The self-appointed pledge to her sister intensified even more by the process of labour (EVERY SACRIFICE IS THE SITE OF REPRESSION), she knew all along it belonged to another:

For there is no friend like a sister

In calm or stormy weather;

To cheer one on the tedious way ... (see *Goblin Market*, yet again).

And as if it too knew the very same thing (social cognition skills, indeed!), the creature itself gave a further loud "*Oink!*" (four little pigs now! Mother, Father, Son and Holy Daughter, that's better!), jumped lightly off the sofa, leaving a ring of her own dark blood on the cushions and, stopping but a second to sniff its cast-iron double by the French windows (some ancient totemistic supersition, no doubt), trotted off across the springy turf towards the edge of the cliff (must have got wind of that passage about the Gadarene swine ... so susceptible to every shade and false division of language, these self-conscious cultural hybrids of wish, are they not?).

Out in the garden itself, a further shower of frail, pink blossom fluttered down slowly, falling, this time, part on the water, part on the grass.

And it was gone.

"*If only pigs could fly!*", she heard herself shout after it, expecting to hear a heavy splash as her brave, tender offspring plumped into the green, green waves below.

No splash. No monstrous wrath from the Deep. Perhaps after all they *could* fly, she told herself gently, reaching for her pen – or, rather, knowing my obsession with my own unconscious (all those unclean spirits trying not to get out), handing her pen to me instead, that queer kind of writing where Fiction and Gender Theory take each other to task, so to speak, neither gaining the upper hand, language turned on its own head and all the pennies rattling out.

How, otherwise, enter that unspoken land where a woman can father her sisters a pig? How, otherwise, reverse a negative into a positive without simply repeating in reverse? (see DESTABILIZED IDENTITY and all that). How, above all . . .?

I paused, listening now myself for the penny to drop.

Silence. Hogwash. Pearls after swine. Preaching like the Minister to thin air.

Then . . . tap, tap, tap. The idea slowly clambering out of the mire.

"Nothing but pigs! And if I ever catch you or your sister . . ."

What *I* had unwittingly brought to birth, thanks to the tale of procreation she had handed me, so to speak, on a plate (is there no end to these culinary idioms linking the stomach and the head?) was the perfect METAPHOR of the LESBIAN SHORT STORY (see above and below): that which both is and yet is not, because it can really only speak from seeing and losing where it should not need to go. A political animal must vanish, after all, when its truth is out. Gender identity is fiction, after all, LESBIAN IDENTITY AS MUCH AS THE REST!

All is movement. All is change. Friendship only is the cage through whose living, golden bars sails the phoenix of the sun.

I was one of the strange women in the farm on the hill, you see: the writer one who was never seen. Or, at least (for how, then, I ask myself, could I have been a child back there at breakfast with our stepfather?), I moved in later, shall we say, when the farm came up for sale again years later on. Or perhaps I was even an only child all along, and she and the pig were really me. Fiction's like that when it comes to the crunch. Performative identity. Saving its bacon to run free.

. . . Soaring, soaring, safely soaring, over the cliff edge, over the green, green waves of silence . . . God and the Devil left behind for ever and ever . . . where Mother Earth (sic) is but a forest . . . where the porpoise/mermaid waters cleave the all-embracing sky and the binary belovèd . . .

The spiral notebook was replete now at last, and even Gender Theory had begun to fade with the coming of dusk: the time of magic masquerade when all the farm animals we'd acquired needed feeding and everything safely penned down for the night, including, not to put too fine a point on it – perfect rose absent from all bouquets – the trusting pink Curly Tail I kept in the front yard myself by then.

> *Walking the silent streets alone*
> *bearing a stone for the birth of a baby*
> *in the bleak mid-Winter dusk*
> *where the chimneys lean and lean*
> *and the waves cry Nevermore*
>
> *I too gave birth, you understand.*
> *She isn't a stone, she can't be seen,*
> *she has your eyes, she has my pain,*
> *her hair is red as gingerbread.*
> *Wearing her body in my brain, I'll never know her like*
> > *again,*
>
> *this crazy love-child all my own,*
> *this Phoenix of the desert shore,*
> *this salamander fed on air.*
> *Born of the too late found too soon, her name is Tenderness,*
> > *I'm told.*

"*By the way, I've gone off pigs,*" announced my sister that evening cheerfully. "*What I really want …*"

But here the line went dead and she either dared not or could not say.

Perhaps she simply meant a pair of corduroy trousers and a long, blue shirt with paint spilled all over it. Well, it would be, wouldn't it, I thought with a laugh, mixing pigments for my next masterpiece. "*All that fire in her loins still waiting to get out …!*"

When I emptied the blue piggy-bank, it was full of gold sovereigns, by the way. Strange to think of saving up to give birth instead of being paid for unseen labour (see above. ALTERNATIVE ECONOMY). Strange to give birth at all, come to that.

Tiny foot, tiny hand,
under my skin a stone is breathing.
Pig in a poke, frog in a well, dragon of creative fire,
gold and frankincense and myrrh,
frankincense and myrrh and gold ...

For fear of pregnancy, no doubt, we never quite made love, though, Theory and I. Fiction is my deepest love, now I know that pigs can fly!

Love Alters

Tanith Lee

I had been married to Jenny for two whole years, when I fell in love with a man.

It happened in October. (The leaves were yellow.) I didn't know what was going on – and if that sounds coy, I can't help it. It wasn't like any emotion I'd ever experienced before, or it didn't seem to be. I thought at first it was anger, or autumn. Then one morning I walked out of the apartment and down the stairs, and along the Avenue, under those topaz trees, and I knew. It made me sick, physically nauseated. It disgusted me as much as I may now be disgusting you, telling you. But I *knew*. There was no going back.

Worse than everything, I felt there had never been any warning. Nothing. I was quite normal, I was like everybody else. Reasonably ambitious, quite talented, capable of happiness, and grief. And as for Jenny – well, I was envied Jenny. And there were plenty of times, even after three years together, when I wondered how I'd been so lucky as to find her, and to be loved by her.

When I was at college, I had made some mistakes in relationships. In a funny way, I'd virtually been pushed into picking the wrong ones, because everybody was so sure I ought to like the boyish rangey sort of girl, the kind you see in adverts for certain soaps, with one shallow breast bared, a bow in her slender tan hand, and a lean hunting dog at her side. Or else the big pushy type, who would "take care of" me. All that because I'm just the opposite. And I let myself be convinced. My God, both my mothers joined in. They'd bring the daughters of friends into the house, flat-chested, golden athletes, or older women who never wore a dress. I had a few affairs, not all bad. But I can be a bitch, and I got bitchy, and I did a lot of harm to women who never deserved it of me. I began to think that was the only scenario: a hopeful attempt, followed by protesting too much that this was great, followed by boredom and slight panic, and going for the throat. All affairs ended that way, didn't they? Slinging plates, slamming doors –

One winter morning, on the river bus, I saw Jenny. She was little, and she had beautiful hair like softly gilded ash, and her eyes were full of soft clear winter sunshine. We started to talk, and the grey river went by, and I thought: Damn, damn, why does the trip only take twenty-five minutes? But it was as if we'd talked to each other a lot already, known each other, lived next door, played in the garden as children – a slight mysterious gap in time, and now we had met again. And I thought, she can't possibly feel the same as I do. When we got to the Central Jetty, I asked her if she had seen the new three-screen movie at the National View. She would say, Yes. Or she'd say, No, I loathe that sort of film. Or she'd go red and freeze me with her gentle eyes. Or she'd say, I'm going tonight with my girlfriend. And then I'd drown myself in the bloody river. But actually she said, "If you're asking if I'll go and see it with you, I'd like that. But I'm free for lunch today, too, if you are."

To start with, when people saw us together, they assumed it was merely a friendship, the kind you might have with a man – or a sister, perhaps. My elder mother (Eleanor had been dead only eighteen months, and sometimes we still both cried about it), had some notion Jenny was a sort of crazy substitute for Eleanor, who had been that feminine, dulcet kind of woman, too. But Jenny was no substitute, and though she was my friend, it wasn't that either.

We decided to live together after five weeks. It caused more upset than when we married a year later. I remember a girl at Computer-Eyes, whom I'd once dated, and who came up to me and said, "Listen, you're making a big mistake." As if all the mistakes before, of which she had been one of the messiest, hadn't told me at last Jenny was right, was perfect.

There has been universally so much of this opposites attract rubbish. Friends now even said to me that Jenny and I looked wrong together, because we were physically alike, not in colouring, of course, but both being small, "curvaceous" – as some are pleased to call it – very feminine in appearance. To my mind, since I started growing up, this cult for a "masculine" or "feminine" divide in partners is the depths of idiocy. Jenny and I could swap clothes, and could buy lingerie for each other, which was both useful and amusing. Both of us without shoes, she was just one inch shorter than me. We wore our hair the same length.

I recollect very clearly, she once said to me, "But all that is finished with. I don't understand why everyone still has to pretend to be women and *men*."

But it was the general rule. The male staff at C-E, even friends of mine, conformed to this standard. There were the male men, and the female men. I'd more or less accepted it in men. With women, it had always vaguely annoyed me, especially when it seemed to be ruining my life. After I'd met Jenny, I found I could tolerate it less and less with my own sex. A woman was a woman, wasn't she?

As for Jenny, she never had a lover before me. She was so gentle, she didn't want to hurt them, the types she didn't want. She used to say she'd been waiting for me. She knew somehow one day we would meet. I used to love her saying that.

We got married in the summer of '85. My mother, Lin, wanted us to have a great big showy wedding, so we did it to make her happy. It was a lot of fun, in its way. Lin also wanted granddaughters, and she'd begun to think she would never see any. "One dark little girl for you," she said to me, while the champagne flowed, and Jenny laughed with a white rose and silver confetti in her hair, "and a blonde for Jennifer."

"Oh, why stop at two?" I said. "Let's make it a round dozen. And you can look after them, mother mine, because Jenny and I will be out working one week after we collect the brats from the baby-bank."

"Now, don't call it that," said my mother.

"You would prefer the five-mile-long technical name? Anyway, I don't like babies. Ghastly things. I used to be one, and I know."

But Jenny smiled at Lin, who loves her madly, and Jenny said, "In a year or two, it would be nice."

"I hate hospitals," I moaned on. "And it's a day off work, sometimes two."

"What nonsense," said Lin. "When Eleanor and I started you, it was ten minutes each. I wasn't even sore. We used to go to see you once every week, all through the seven months you were growing. Eleanor used to cry. She thought you were beautiful even when you were just a little curled-up embryo."

I was afraid Lin was going to cry herself, but she cheered up and only gave us a lecture on how easy it all was for women, because obviously the X chromosomes make girls automatically. ("Gosh, Mum. Do they *really*?" I said.)

The clever part is, of course, to make the eggs fertilize each other, and the sperms do likewise in the case of a male partnership that wants a son. There you need, too, the Y to show up in order to concoct the right mix with the X. I have never grasped the mechanics, and had no wish to at my wedding. Marco, whom I had known and worked for for years, then broke the lecture up by telling a very bawdy version of his experiences while he and Alex got their boy.

"Dear girls," said Marco, with his long fair hair trailing in the wine, "I just couldn't – I could *not* – I got sent home in disgrace three times. And then they discreetly trundled in this machine with rubber hands. I *ask* you –"

"Do you truly," I said to Jenny, hours after, when we were alone, "want children?"

"Isn't that the best reason for getting married?"

"No. The best reason is to grapple you to my soul with hoops of steel."

"Silly," said Jenny lovingly. "We'll make pretty daughters."

Three months later, Marco came up to me and apologized for telling That Story.

"What story?"

"God. You know. About the hand-job for the baby. Alex has been on at me for weeks to say I'm sorry."

"Well, when I remember, I'll let you know if I forgive you."

"Did I ever tell you," said Marco, stirring his cherry-flavour caffeine drink, "I knew a guy once who wanted to have a daughter."

"Nobody does that. I suppose it might be possible, if the Y got left out, which it never would. Isn't it illegal? The only case I ever heard of, which is doubtless a lie, it was a female birth with a Y added in. The women kidnapped the boy and drove off somewhere in the mountains. But they couldn't cope. Eventually he was abused, beaten, locked in cupboards, that sort of stuff, poor little kid –"

"You are so *intense*," said Marco. "Lord, I was only joking. Look, there's someone I want you to meet. You're going to be working with him on the *Magenta Dream* contract. He's some whizzo genius Alex was at college with. OK?"

But, being Marco, the contract hovered, and I didn't meet the whizzo genius for another twelve months. His name was Druse, and I disliked him instantly. The look of him, his manner, his way of speaking. We disagreed on everything. The layouts, the promotion, the packaging, the choice of models. Even the computer terminals waxed partisan. My personal console would give Druse nippy little electric shocks. When I had to feed into his board, it would block. Many times the repair team had to come in, with their black box and their friendly scowls.

Druse (I hated his name, too. Why did I have to work with a man who sounded as if he should be a mutant breakfast fruit?) was unattached. He had been living with a man in Springs, but the relationship fell through. All his relationships, according to Alex, did this. Druse had a tall, coordinated runner's body, and dark red hair I wished cheerfully to pluck with red-hot pincers. He was the *male*-type male. The firm's freelance girl-boys tended to haunt him. Druse took no notice except sometimes to be pretty cutting, and that didn't endear him to me either.

I became so angry all the time, I began to have migraine headaches, which hadn't happened to me since my adolescence. The medical Jenny made me take returned a verdict of stress. It prescribed homeopathic pills, and mooted a holiday.

"The remedy should have been," I said, "a strong poison to slip in that monster's midday caffeine."

"Surely he's not so bad," said Jenny. "He's clever, and he needs to work with people, but they make him uncomfortable. Then again, he hates being alone."

"He doesn't have to be."

"He doesn't know what he wants."

"Let's hope he discovers, and it turns out to be to jump from a sixtieth-floor window."

Jenny had met Druse in my company once or twice at C-E social events, and there had been an occasion when she came to meet me from work. They stood and talked quietly, as I finished off a rush piece of copy. I didn't do it very well, I was keeping an eye on him. But Jenny is Jenny, she seemed to have calmed him down. He even laughed once.

Next day he said to me, "You have a lovely wife. That makes two of you. Two beautiful girls."

And he looked at me, a long long look, out of his dark auburn eyes that burned. My impulse was to sling something sharp and heavy at him.

"Don't," I said, "try to get around me. I know I have a beautiful wife. I know what I look like. And I know you think I have the wits of a four-day-old soufflé. Which opinion, my friend, is mutual."

"Jesus," he said. And gave me the normal look again, contemptuous, cold, miles off and glad to be so.

"Marco says," I said, "we should try to finish this project together. So let's try. You try not to insult me, and I'll try not to murder *you*. How about it?"

"Stop shooting your mouth off," he said. "I know you have a brain. You just forget to use it all the time."

"You wouldn't know what a brain is if you found one on your in-tray."

"You act like a child," he said loudly.

"You act like a moron!" I shouted. "Why are you here? You should be on some desert island. You hate human beings."

"Then that lets you off the list," he said.

"Listen, Druse," I said. "I don't know why it is, but the moment we met, you and I, we took an instant dislike. Let's be adult. We can go to Marco now, and have ourselves reassigned.

The contract is going to slip, this way. We're making a mess of it."

Then he exploded. He went white and he came at me and I thought there was going to be a fight, and every fighter's hold I know came whipping into my mind, all ready for him. (It shames me, that. In or out of context. I might have killed him. He'd never learned those moves.)

"Don't you bloody throw this project down the drain because your damned stupid ego won't take any competition. *You* are the fly in this jam."

"For Christ's sake," I yelled at him. "Why don't you go and fuck someone and get it over with, and then you can go fuck yourself!"

And I slammed the switch down on my console.

Instead of shutting off, it shorted out. And instead of giving Druse a shock, it flung me five feet across the room.

I heard myself scream, like some heroine of long ago in those ancient movies, which now, through their all-pervasive hetero-sexual content, are mostly banned as objectionable. The scream hung in the air, and I heard it fade and sink and die.

I lay on the plush. I thought: I'm lying on the plush. Then I opened my eyes. Druse was kneeling by me, checking my pulse. He looked at me. "Don't move," he said.

"I don't think I could." I said.

"I've pressed the emergency bell," he said. "Someone's coming. You're going to be fine."

Suddenly I started to cry. I lay there with the tears running down into my hair. Reduced to infancy, I was sobbing, "I want Jenny. I want Jenny." I could hear myself, like the scream, and dispassionately my mind remarked to me, Oh, you are making such a fool of yourself.

But Druse held my hand, and he stroked away the tears and the hair and he said, "The moment someone comes, I'll call her. It's going to be all right."

His hands were warm and kind, strong but not harsh, not brash. He's got beautiful eyes, I thought. They remind me of Eleanor's eyes. He could be her son, only women never have sons, or brothers, or fathers, any more. Just the way a boy never has a mother, a sister, a daughter. Because now it's as it was always meant to be. Once birth and the continuance of the species ceased to rely on the function of a woman's womb, the impact of a man's semen, the pleasure-drive they used to call "sex" reverted to something more natural and fundamental: the recognition of one's own self in another. They say it took only twenty years for that to happen, and another twenty for humanity to face up to it, agree, relax. And twenty more, maybe, to see the other method the way we see it now, as stupid, uncouth, clownish. In fact, before the mechanics of progeniture had altered things, there had been plenty of men, and large numbers of women, who preferred to seek pleasure with those of their own gender, and could accept love in no other way. It was simply biological function that held the process up so long. The natural bodily urge was male–female, but the natural intellectual, spiritual *truthful* urge ran always in opposition. You see, I have read the books . . . But there are ethnic primitives still, who practise the old formula, who even carry their offspring physically to term. And there are perverts who *want* it. Men who want to sleep with women, and women who –

I sat up, and Druse grabbed me. "Keep still," he said. But he held me. I lay against him. I felt safe. *Safe!*

Before the C-E medic arrived, I fainted, and woke up in the firm's clinic, all expenses paid. They kept me in a day or so, but, as he had promised me, I was fine.

Oh, I was fine.

And then I had the holiday that check-up had suggested, and found in any event the electric shock had cured my migraines. It seemed to me I never thought so clearly in my life.

Jenny managed to get leave, too, and we went to Paradise Beach. We had a good time. The late September, early October sun was almost tropical, and the blue palms swept the earth. We ate pineapples, and danced to music under stars large as the great golden shells you find in the sand. I'd never loved her more. I used to go to sleep in her arms with a sense of utter peace. We didn't make love, not once. She never reproached me, or tried to persuade beyond the mildest limit. I was tired, wasn't I. I'd nearly been killed. I'd had a bad year. Yes, Jenny, be kind, be thoughtful.

Let me not, to the marriage of true minds, admit impediments. Love alters not when that it alteration finds, nor moves with the remover to remove ... He wrote all those sonnets to boys, Shakespeare, centuries ago. (All to boys. The other version surely isn't credible.)

Jenny, not altering. Sweet Jenny, under the palms, in her beach costume, smiling, sea colour in her eyes, and unalterable love shining.

When we arrived home, I made a joke about going back to the grind of work. I made jokes about Druse. And when I realized I was making them too often, I controlled myself and stopped. I didn't know, not consciously, even then. I thought I was ashamed. The autumn season had affected me. I'd have to be polite to him, too, since he'd held my hand.

The leaves had changed. The leaves were yellow.

I went out one morning, down the stairs, on to the Avenue, on my legitimate way to return to legitimate work and, as I walked among the topaz trees, I knew.

I wanted to bolt back to the apartment, and to hide. The people who passed me on the street, some of whom I knew, greeted me. But I had a notice pinned to my back, and branded on my forehead: the word *pervert*.

Coming to the East Jetty, I caught the river bus. I had met my wife on this bus, over three years ago. I'd thought, If she won't come out with me, I'll drown myself. And for Druse, what would I do?

I tried to imagine, cruelly, how it would be, if he had any feeling for me, to touch, to hold, to kiss, to make love – and finally I had to go down into the bus lavatories. I vomited. I vomited because when I had thought of making love with Druse, a tide of sexual desire had gone through me, as strong as – *stronger* than – any pleasure-lust I had ever felt for Jenny.

When I reached Computer-Eyes, I was trembling. Somehow I got up to my floor and found my space, and sat down before my console which was sparkling new. Marco had tied a bow around it, and there was a label: *Trust me. I won't shock you.* I smiled, since I ought to, as I took off the bow. As I was doing that, Druse came into the room. It's a large room, and there were other people there, and going in and out, and there was no reason I should know it was Druse, but I did know; and it was. He started to walk towards me. I seemed to freeze, but I froze with heat. I was burning alive. No escape.

"Hallo," he said.

I didn't look at him. I looked at the bow off the console as I tore it in small bits.

"Druse, I'm sorry, I can't work with you."

"That's okay," he said, very quietly. "The project was finished while you were away. Marco is supposed to have let you know. So, we're all on fresh contracts now. But I just came over to say, I'm glad you're all right. Welcome back."

I looked up at him. And once I began to look at him, I felt I could never look away. He met my gaze and returned it. Was it the same for him? There was something in his eyes, there always had been, something I never saw before in the eyes of any man.

"I have to talk to you," I heard myself say.

"Yes," he said. "When do you want to?"

"Now," I said. My hand shook so hard I could no longer even rip the paper bow. "I'll go out. Up to the Glass Garden. This time of day, it should be empty. Will you –?"

"I'll meet you there. Give me five minutes, to make it look good."

The Glass Garden runs around C-E's twentieth floor, a ballooning window-walk full of plants and little fountains splashing glassily in glass basins. Hardly anybody was about, except the girls on the soft-drink stand, and the automatic ice-cream vendor getting itself ready for the mid-morning break.

He wouldn't follow me. Or he'd want to, and something would prevent him. And when he got here, what would I say? And if I was able to say anything, and if he said anything in return, what then? Our society has no place for the kind of people we'd be. (Was it this that drove him out of Springs? The knowledge he was potentially a misfit?) No, of course it isn't illegal. Heterosexuality is merely – offensive. Or risible. There are even a few dirty jokes about it. It's the untidy ignorant thing we did, when we were animals tied to procreative functioning. Funny. And now, if he and I were to be the subject of that kind of humour, what? Leave our jobs. Go away somewhere. Pretend to be good friends, oh such good friends. And date girls, and date men, to sustain appearances. Invent wives and lovers elsewhere. And in the dark, in the shadow under the stone of convention, *couple*, make love – no, we couldn't call it that – screw, *do* it – and it was so alien, could I even bear to let him. *Could* I? But I wanted him. I wanted it. I didn't care how alien it was. *Wanted*.

And Jenny, where was Jenny in all this nightmare, this fire-shot blackness beneath the potted trees?

Druse stepped between the leaves and sat down beside me.

"I told them I'm taking the key for the *Tiger Light* project up to twenty-one. That gives me about twenty minutes before I need to do it for real."

"Druse," I said.

"I'm here."

I stared into his face again. He was very serious now. He looked vulnerable, and sad.

He knows. He's been seeing it all, the way I have. We're in the dark together, and we don't know each other.

"Why," I said.

"Why what? I know it's sticky," he said. "But let's talk it through. I don't object. Come on."

"Why did you leave Springs?"

"Why do you think I left?"

"To get away from a man."

"That's right," Druse said. "To get away. And, as you see, I got away and straight into something much worse. Didn't I?"

"Did you?"

He couldn't hear me. I couldn't breathe, and so had no breath to speak. I wanted him to hold me. I wanted not to have to talk about it after all. I wanted the world to be different.

"Look, kid," he said to me with such tenderness, "this hasn't been kind on you. I'm not saying it's been terrific for me either, but that doesn't matter now. I've given it some thought. I wasn't sure you – that you realized. But you did, you do. You know. So when I've taken this damned rubbish up to twenty-one, I'll go find Marco and see about a transfer out of here. Get out of town. Leave you in peace, the two of you."

I started to say, to try to say, I didn't want that, but the words wouldn't come. He shook his head at me and smiled. His eyes were bleak. You couldn't look into them any more. Their doors of sombre amber were fast shut.

"For God's sake," he said, "one thing you have to know. I only saw her twice. Yes, I engineered the meetings, but they were both in public places. And she – she didn't know. Well, I think she knew why, the second time, she knew why. But not that it would happen, that we'd meet. And I guess she never did tell you, but that was to protect you. Not any sort of subterfuge. Because there really was nothing. She loves you. You're the only one she'll ever love. The other thing – that just isn't in her, to be that way. And I should have accepted that straight off. It never could be that way, with her. Please don't ever have a second thought on that."

I found I was breathing again. Breathing was easy. It was being alive that was difficult.

"What are you telling me?" I said. "*Who*?"

"Jenny," he said. "Your Jenny, who loves you. Who'll never love anybody else. No woman. No man. Your Jenny that I wanted. Your Jenny, the one I – but you know all that."

My Jenny. My sweet Jenny. Ash-blonde gilded hair, eyes shining with sea-shimmer and love. Jenny, my Jenny, who loved only me. And that he loved.

I closed my eyes.

"I'll leave you now," he said. "I'm sorry. You're a nice lady. We should have got along better. Be happy, please, if only for her sake."

After he was gone, I sat alone in the Glass Garden until the mid-morning break, when the area began to fill with people, music and noise.

Then I went down through the building and out on the street, and I walked somewhere. And in the end, I came to a View, and went inside. They were featuring contemporary films, the *Romeo and Julio* whose doomed lovers are both male, and the *Julia-Juliet* where they are both girls of fourteen. But there was a tiny notice in the foyer, such as you sometimes find in this part of the city, that later in the day there would be an adult limited performance of an older print, one of the man – woman versions over a hundred years old.

I watched the two straight films. Then I bought a ticket for the freak-show.

The audience laughed a lot, some of it hysterical embarrassed guffaws, and some frank laughter, genuinely helplessly tickled at the spectacle.

There was even a moment when he is in bed with her and they are naked. He kisses her breasts, he does it with excitement and with ecstatic love, and she responds to him. At this moment, even the laughter fell silent. From disgust or astonishment, or, as in my own case, out of a sort of *dread*?

I came from the View and immediately called Marco, and lied. Then I called Jenny, and I lied. I called my mother last, and went over, and sat in her bedroom because she had a cold. She's got a girlfriend now who even looks slightly like Eleanor, and the girlfriend, who wants me not to mind her, was extra tactful and left us alone.

But I couldn't talk to Lin. And indeed, what was there now to say?

About midnight, I reached home, and Jenny.

She said, "Druse called me today."

"It's all right," I said. "I know. I know it wasn't anything."

"I was only," she said, "so sorry for him." She came to me, and held me in her arms. And I held Jenny and kissed her hair. No one would have laughed to see me do it, or recoiled in revulsion. But my heart was cold. And cold it has remained.

The leaves fell, and the days fell, and winter came, and I worked hard at C-E, and Jenny worked hard. We're saving up now, since more and more Lin keeps hinting about granddaughters. And I believe Jenny believes it will heal our marriage, this peculiar stillness which has settled over it, like snow.

Druse, I heard, went north, and is working for a branch of C-E near the ocean.

Darling Jenny, if only I could tell you. If only I could trust you, the way Druse trusted you, with the secret of difference. This bruises you, you think it's your fault. That I don't love you now because I think you're a traitor, or a tease.

Jenny, I'll always love you. But not the way I did. I can't. I wasn't waiting for you, after all. No. I was waiting for him. And he – *he* was waiting for you.

It'll be spring soon. The bare trees on the Avenue will spin green floss about themselves, and the grey river brighten. Everything is always changing. Seasons, weather, time. So why not the climate of love? Why not?

Oh, Jenny, why not?

Biographical Notes

Editor

Born in Dublin in 1969, **Emma Donoghue** is an Irish writer who after eight years in England has moved to Canada. Though she is best known for her contemporary Dublin novels *Stir-fry* and *Hood* (which won the American Library Association's Gay, Lesbian and Bisexual Book Award) she has also published a sequence of rewritten fairy tales (*Kissing the Witch*), and is now exploring historical fiction. Her novels have been translated into Dutch, German, Swedish and Hebrew.

Her plays include *I Know My Own Heart* (based on Anne Lister's Regency diaries), *Ladies and Gentlemen* (about a male impersonator in 1880s vaudeville, published by New Island Press in 1998), and *Trespasses* (based on an Irish witch trial of the 1660s). Donoghue followed up *Passions Between Women: British Lesbian Culture 1668–1801* with an anthology of four centuries of poetry, *What Sappho Would Have Said* (published in the US as *Poems Between Women*). In 1998 she produced a biography of an extraordinary Victorian lesbian partnership, entitled *We Are Michael Field*.

"The Tale of the Kiss" first appeared in *Kissing the Witch* (London: Hamish Hamilton and New York: Joanna Cotler Books, 1997).

Emma Donoghue says: "The first twelve stories in *Kissing the Witch* are all rethinkings of classic European fairy tales. But the thirteenth and last, 'The Tale of the Kiss', is my own, though it draws on folk motifs about consulting witches for help. (Marina Warner's *From the Beast to the Blonde* was a stimulating source.)

Its narrator features in the previous story as the witch to whom the 'Little Mermaid' character goes for help. I really wrote this story so that a witch would get kissed, in order for the title of the collection to fit ..."

Authors

Dorothy Allison was born in Greenville, South Carolina. She is the author of *Trash* (a book of short stories which won two Lambda Literary Awards), and a book of poetry, *The Women Who Hate Me*. Her non-fiction includes a collection of essays and autobiographical narratives called *Skin: Talking about Sex, Class and Literature* (which won a Lambda Literary Award) and a short memoir, *Two or Three Things I Know for Sure*. Allison has served as editor of *Conditions* and taught at institutions such as Vassar College, Wesleyan, Florida State University and George Washington University.

Her 1992 novel *Bastard Out of Carolina* was a National Book Award Finalist; a film version was directed by Anjelica Huston and shown on Showtime in 1996. Her most recent novel is *Cavedweller*.

"River of Names" first appeared in Elly Bulkin's anthology *Lesbian Fiction* (1981) and was collected in Allison's *Trash* (1988).

Madelyn Arnold was born in Kentucky in 1948 during the beginning of the post-war baby boom, the eldest of a working-class family of nine. Her German – Jewish mother was a musician and artist; her mixed-race father was a part-time labour organizer. She gained a BA in Microbiology from Indiana University, joining the first Gay Liberation Chapter there in 1969, the very first week of its existence. After college she found an English major's entire library at a garage sale, bought it and read it, starting at Z; soon she started to write.

Arnold studied portrait painting at art school, sang profes-
sionally for a while, and has worked as a laboratory technician,
a racing driver, a mental hospital assistant, a printer, a cab driver
and a truck driver. She took an MA in Writing, and has taught
college classes in composition, creative writing and literature.
Her life has been marked by chronic poverty and she has multiple disabilities, including severe asthma with an allergy to book
dust.

Her novel, *Bird-Eyes* (Seal, 1988), won the Lambda Literary
Award for Best Lesbian First Novel. She followed it up with a
collection of stories, *On Ships at Sea* (St Martin's Press, 1992).

"See You in the Movies" first appeared in Arnold's *On Ships
at Sea* (1992).

Rebecca Brown's works of fiction include *The Haunted House,
The Children's Crusade, The Evolution of Darkness, The Terrible
Girls, Annie Oakley's Girl, The Gifts of the Body* (which won a
Lambda Literary Award, among others), *What Keeps Me Here,*
and *The Dogs: A Modern Bestiary*. Her work has been widely
anthologized and translated into German, Dutch, Norwegian
and Japanese. She lives in Seattle.

"The Dark House" first appeared as a "story / chapter" in
Brown's *The Terrible Girls* (1990).

Rebecca Brown says: "*The Terrible Girls* was several years in
the writing. Like almost all of my work, 'The Dark House' is
emotionally autobiographical. Like much of my work, it makes
use of employment humiliations suffered by writers who live in
the USA. That is to say, I once worked as a coffee-cart girl,
though I did not wear the uniform."

Born in Nanaimo, Vancouver Island, in 1938, the daughter of a
coal miner, **Anne Cameron** learned the art of storytelling from
Scottish, English, Native and Chinese storytellers. Supporting
herself with a series of "mind-numbing jobs", including telephone operator and medical assistant, she began writing poetry,
fiction, collections of Native myths for children and adults
(including the famous *Daughters of Copper Woman*), and plays
for stage and radio. She has published contemporary and

historical novels (*Kick the Can, Escape to Beulah, South of an Unnamed Creek*) as well as several collections of stories that mix realistic and fantastic themes.

Her 1979 film *Dreamspeaker* won seven Canadian Film Awards, and as a novel it won the Gibson Award for Literature. Her subsequent films include *Ticket to Heaven, Bomb Squad, The Tin Flute, A Matter of Choice, Homecoming*, and *Drying Up the Streets*. Her poetry collections are *Earth Witch* and *The Anne Poems*.

Anne Cameron lives on a 30-acre farm near Powell River, BC, with 153 rabbits, 103 chickens, 16 turkeys, 9 cows, 7 ducks, 5 geese, 2 cats, 2 turtles, a horse, a donkey, a dog, 5,000,000 mosquitoes and a variable combination of children and grandchildren.

"Did'ja Ever Hear of a Goolieguy?" was first published in Cameron's 1989 collection, *Women, Kids & Huckleberry Wine*.

Christine Crow studied in Cambridge and Paris before going to lecture in Scotland in 1965. In 1979, after publishing several books about the poetry and thought of Paul Valéry, she was promoted to a Readership in French Literature at the University of St Andrews, but in 1986 she gave up teaching in order to write full-time. Her novel *Miss X, or the Wolf Woman* appeared in 1990.

She has contributed pieces to *Taking Reality by Surprise, Lines Review* and *Tea and Leg-Irons*, and has published poetry for children in the USA. She lives by the sea in Anstruther (a Scottish village), where she paints as well as working on two more novels and her first collection of poetry.

"If Pigs Could Fly" is published here for the first time.

Christine Crow says: "This story reflects my usual interest in questions of identity and the mixed blessing of labels, 'lesbian' included. Perhaps it was also an experiment in writing a story which invites psychoanalysis of itself (instead of psychoanalysis of the writer). There are some playfully obvious smokescreens about giving birth, literary procreation included. I don't think I like this story very much, but am glad if it can give rise to any thoughts on the nature of imaginative literary 'exorcism'."

Jane DeLynn is the author of the widely acclaimed novels *Don Juan in the Village, Real Estate, In Thrall* and *Some Do*, and the recent collection *Bad Sex is Good*. She has been published widely in anthologies in the US, Great Britain and Japan, and has written articles and essays for a number of magazines including the *New York Times, Mademoiselle, Glamour, Harpers Bazaar*, the *New York Observer*, the *Advocate* and *Tikkun*. She lived in Dhahran, Saudi Arabia for two months during the Gulf War as a correspondent for *Mirabella* and *Rolling Stone*.

"Puerto Rico" is a story from *Don Juan in the Village*.

Jane DeLynn says: "I find women confusing, even more so than men, and I often write to try to make sense of something. The characters (the pilot and the two women – including what they said about horrific acts by their fathers) are based upon real people I met in that little island off Puerto Rico, and so are some of the events in the story, though I took them farther than they occurred in real life. I'm not sure the story helped me 'make sense' of anything, but at least I was able to express in a story that was satisfactory to me my inability (yet once again) to make sense of the world."

Elise D'Haene's novel, *Licking Our Wounds* (Permanent Press, 1997), was the winner of the Best Gay and Lesbian Fiction at the Book Expo's 1998 Small Press Awards. An excerpt will be featured in Susie Bright's *1998 Best American Erotica* (Harper Collins). Her short fiction, "Married", was published by *Modern Words* (1996) and won a Hemingway Award for Best Short Fiction. "Breasts", another short fiction, was published in *Hers 2* (Faber & Faber, 1997).

Elise D'Haene currently writes for film and television and says that if she doesn't sit down soon and write prose, her mental health will be seriously compromised. She lives with her lover, Celeste, and their dog, Alfie, both constantly reminding her "what's it all about".

"Self-Deliverance" first appeared in *Hers*, edited by Terry Wolverton with Robert Drake (Faber and Faber, 1995).

Elise D'Haene says: " 'Self-Deliverance' was one of those stories that wouldn't let me go. As a native Michigander, I felt I had left these characters behind and, despite my best efforts, I couldn't wrestle them away from my dreams. They yapped at me endlessly until I sat my butt down and wrote the story. I miss them."

The award-winning short story writer, poet and novelist **Mary Dorcey** was born in County Dublin, Ireland. In 1990 she won the Rooney Prize for Literature for her short story collection *A Noise from the Woodshed*. Her novel *Biography of Desire* was published in 1997 to critical acclaim and reprinted three months later.

She has published three volumes of poetry: *Kindling* (1982), *Moving Into the Space Cleared by Our Mothers* (1991), and *The River that Carries Me* (1995). Her stories and poems have been collected in more than fifty anthologies and her work is now taught on Irish Studies and Women's Studies courses in universities throughout Ireland, Britain, Europe and the United States. Mary Dorcey is a Research Associate at Trinity College, Dublin. She has lived in the United States, England, France, Spain and Japan.

"A Country Dance" first appeared in *Girls Next Door: Lesbian Feminist Stories*, ed. by Jen Bradshaw and Marg Hemming (London: Women's Press, 1985).

Marion Douglas lives in Calgary in Alberta, Canada, where she works as a school psychologist and a writer. She has had stories published in several literary journals. Her first novel, *The Doubtful Guests*, was published in 1993. *Bending at the Bow*, her second, published in 1995, won the Alberta Book Award. She is now working on a third novel.

"Magic Eight Ball" is published here for the first time.

Marion Douglas says: "This is the first chapter of a novel about two kinds of pleasure – the pleasure of aloneness and the pleasure of intimacy – and the anxiety that their endless jostling seems to create."

Patricia Duncker was born in Jamaica in 1951, and now teaches writing in the Department of English at the University of Wales, Aberystwyth. She published a study of contemporary feminist fiction called *Sisters and Strangers*. Her first novel, *Hallucinating Foucault* (Serpent's Tail, 1996), won the Dillons First Fiction Award and the McKitterick Prize, and has been translated into seven languages. Her collection of short fiction, *Monsieur Shoushana's Lemon Trees*, followed in 1997. A novel about the nineteenth-century colonial doctor, *James Miranda Barry*, who was amongst other things a transvestite and a crack shot, is forthcoming from Serpent's Tail in 1999.

"Aria Nova" was first published in *Monsieur Shoushana's Lemon Trees* in 1997.

Patricia Duncker says: " 'Aria Nova' is an autobiographical short story, and the orchestra was really there."

Dale Gunthorp was born in South Africa in 1941, and has lived in England since the mid-sixties – first in London, currently in Stratford. She wrote "for the Commonwealth for many years, and now for whatever demon it is that makes it the only absolutely necessary thing to do." Her published titles are: *The Flying Hart* (short stories, Sheba, 1991) and *Looking for Ammu* (thriller, Virago, 1992), both under the pseudonym of Claire Macquet (her grandmother's name), and under her own name a novel called *Georgiana's Angels* (Virago, 1999). She has also contributed to *Cancer through the Eyes of Ten Women* (Pandora, 1996) on behalf of the artist Catherine Arthur, and has stories in two Onlywomen anthologies as well as *Brought to Book* and *Worlds Unspoken*.

"Kermit's Room" is published here for the first time.

Dale Gunthorp says: " 'Kermit's Room' started life as a bit of nonsense for my then new lover, Julie Millard, who is impossibly untidy. I am fanatically tidy – at least I think I would be, if I didn't always live with untidy people. The story grew into an exploration of the desire for apartness, while everything in nature is tangled up with everything else and no one thing can exist otherwise. I didn't intend it then to turn into a metaphysical definition of love – as the perception of the pattern in that apparently chaotic tangle – but I hope that's what it did. I use comedy in part to disarm, in part for its conciseness, and also because that's the way the world seems to be."

Susan Hampton was born in New South Wales in 1949. A poet and prose writer, she co-edited *The Penguin Book of Australian Women Poets* (1984). Her collection *Surly Girls* won the Steele Rudd Award in 1990. She has worked as a Writer in Residence at many Australian universities, and currently teaches writing at the University of Canberra.

"The Lobster Queen" first appeared in Hampton's collection *Surly Girls* (1990).

Jane Harris writes short stories. She also writes for the screen and in 1998 was short-listed for the BBC's Dennis Potter Award.

"Monopoly" first appeared in *The Crazy Jig* (Edinburgh: Polygon, 1992).

Born in Ashburton, New Zealand, in 1965, **Annamarie Jagose** is a senior lecturer in English at the University of Melbourne. She is the author of *Lesbian Utopics* and *Queer Theory*. Her short stories have appeared in anthologies including *New Women's Fiction 3* and *The Exploding Frangipani: Lesbian Writing from Australia and New Zealand*. Her first novel, *In Translation* (1994), won the PEN Prize for Best First Novel; her second, *Lulu:A Romance*, followed in 1998.

"Milk and Money" was first published in *The Exploding Frangipani*, edited by Cathie Dunsford and Susan Hawthorne (Auckland: New Women's Press, 1990).

Aileen La Tourette writes radio drama; her last play was *My Darling, My Darling, My Life and My Bride*, reconstructing the mysterious death of Edgar Allen Poe. She is presently working on a play about the little-known Irish poet Thomas Dermody, whose grave lies near her home in South East London. In 1984 she and Sara Maitland co-published a book of short stories, *Weddings and Funerals*.

La Tourette is writing a collection of poems called *Downward Mobility* and a new novel about ageing, death, and the impossibility of defining sexuality. She earned an MA in Poetry from the University of Huddersfield and now (among other things) lectures part-time in Imaginative Writing at Liverpool John Moores University.

"The Triangular Eye: 1, 2, 3" first appeared in *Weddings and Funerals*, by Aileen La Tourette and Sara Maitland (Brilliance Books, 1984).

Aileen La Tourette says: "I divide my time, as they say, between Liverpool and London. Division of one sort or another seems to be a theme of my life."

Born in London in 1947, after secondary school **Tanith Lee** worked as a library assistant, a shop assistant, a filing clerk and a waitress, as well as spending a year at art college. In 1970-71 she published three children's books. In 1975 Daw Books USA published Lee's *The Birthgrave*, and twenty-six of her books thereafter, enabling her to become a full-time writer.

To date she has written fifty-eight novels and nine collections of novellas and short stories. Four of her radio plays have been broadcast by the BBC and she has written two episodes of the cult BBC TV series *Blake's Seven*. Lee has twice won the World Fantasy Award for Short Fiction, as well the August Derleth Award in 1980 for her novel *Death's Master*. She lives in southeast England with her husband the writer John Kaiine, one black-and-white and one Siamese cat.

"Love Alters" was first published in *Despatches from the Frontiers of the Female Mind*. There Tanith Lee wrote of it: "Like a lot of the speculative science fiction I've written, it pivots on the principle of a reverse image. It isn't only the future that's on trial here, but the present. After all, yesterday, today was tomorrow."

Jenifer Levin's novels are *Water Dancer* (nominated for the PEN/Hemingway Award), *Snow, Shimoni's Lover* and *The Sea of Light* (nominated for a Lambda Literary Award). She has taught fiction writing and literature at the University of Michigan, and written for *The New York Times*, *The Washington Post*, *Rolling Stone*, *Mademoiselle*, *Ms*, *The Advocate*, and many other publications. Her short stories are collected in *Love and Death & Other Disasters: Stories 1977–1995*. Levin has studied, lived and worked in Europe, the Middle East, South America and Southeast Asia, and now lives in New York City.

Anna Livia was born in Dublin in 1955, grew up in Africa (Zambia and Swaziland), went to university in England and now lives in Berkeley, California. She is the author of four novels: *Relatively Norma*, *Accommodation Offered*, *Bulldozer Rising* and *Minimax*, as well as two collections of short stories: *Incidents Involving Warmth and Incidents Involving Mirth* (formerly *Saccharin Cyanide*). Her new novel, *Bruised Fruit*, is forthcoming in 1999 from Firebrand. Anna Livia is also co-editor of *Queerly Phrased*, an anthology about language, gender and sexuality.

"Pamelump" was written in December 1984 and first published in *Incidents Involving Warmth*.

Anna Livia says: "I wrote 'Pamelump' when my lover was critically ill with a mysterious illness (it turned out to be multiple sclerosis). At one point, she was so sick she could not eat unaided or lift her head from the pillow. She told me if this was how she had to live, she would rather die, and she asked me to help her. I refused. We got locked into one of the strangest and most terrifying arguments I've ever had. After a while, I could no longer think about the situation as an adult. By simplifying my intellectual processes to those of an eleven-year-old girl, and by setting the story back in my African childhood, I found I could create the distance I needed to understand my lover's point of view. I'm happy to report that she survived the crisis.

"When 'Pamelump' was first published in 1984, it was criticised by activists for the disabled as unnecessarily negative because the disabled character kills herself. This was considered a cop-out: all kinds of body, and all levels of ability were to be celebrated and cherished. While I commend these sentiments, they did not correspond to the world-view of the character in question. I wrote the story in part as a challenge to us all to make the world the kind of place we all want to live in."

Born in New York, **Elizabeth A. Lynn** received an MA from the University of Chicago in 1968, and moved to California in 1972; she now lives in the San Francisco Bay area. Her first short story was published in 1977. Her first two novels were *A Different Light* (1978) and *Watchtower* (1979), which won that year's World Fantasy Award for Best Novel. Lynn's latest novel, *Dragon's Winter*, was published by Macmillan in 1998; she is working on a sequel. Apart from writing, she also teaches martial arts.

"The Woman Who Loved the Moon" was first published in *Amazons!* (1979), and won the 1980 World Fantasy Award for Short Fiction.

Elizabeth A. Lynn says: "The setting for this story, the imaginary country of Ryoka, has remained in my imagination for nearly twenty years, and is the setting for *Dragon's Winter*."

Ingrid MacDonald was born in southern Ontario in 1960 of a German mother and Cape Breton father. She took a degree in religion and literary studies at the University of Toronto. A writer, broadcaster and visual artist, she is the author of *Catherine, Catherine* (Toronto: Women's Press, 1991) and a play, *The Catherine Wheel*. Her short story "Travelling West" was a winner in the 1990 *Prism International* Fiction Contest. Ingrid teaches creative writing in Toronto where she lives with her family.

"The Catherine Trilogy" first appeared in MacDonald's 1991 collection, *Catherine, Catherine*.

Ingrid MacDonald says: "The story of Catherine Linck and her wife, Catherine Muhlhahn, comes to us through a court record from Halberstadt, Prussia (now Germany). Translated into English by an American, Brigitte Eriksson, 'A Lesbian Execution in Germany 1721, The Trial Records' is published in the *Journal of Homosexuality* (Vol 6, Fall/Winter 1980/81).

"I first read the account there and the life of Catherine Linck electrified my imagination with significance for lesbian existence. I was drawn to this heroic anti-hero, a woman of impulse, flaws and passion. I wrote the story in fictional biographic form as 'The Catherine Trilogy'; a stage adaptation followed, entitled *The Catherine Wheel*. The Canadian premiere of the play in 1994 coincided with the 300th anniversary of Catherine Linck's birth. It has taken three centuries for us to be able to understand the complexities found in such a woman's life: the fluidity of gender and identity, her love of and yet conflict with women, and her struggle to be fully human against the constraints of her time."

Sara Maitland was born in London in 1950 and brought up in Scotland. With Zoe Fairbairns, Valerie Miner, Michele Roberts and Michelene Wandor she was in the *Tales I Tell My Mother* group which published its first collection in 1978, and has been a professional writer since then. Although she has published novels (most recently *Brittle Joy* – Virago, 1999), theology, non-fiction books and journalism, and has written for radio and TV, short stories are her favourite form.

"The Burning Times" first appeared in Maitland's collection *Telling Tales* (1983).

Sara Maitland says: "Witches (in various forms) have always been an important metaphor, partly because they can fly and partly because they have both a historical and a mythic reality. It is this meeting place between social and imaginary realities within the context of the liberation of women that I continuously seek to explore in my writing. (Recently with Paul Magrs I have described this fictional space as Queer Realism.) 'The Burning Times' was a response to some remarks of Mary Daly's in *Gynophobia* about the betrayal of women by women during the witch-trial era – an attempt to explore how/why women might do this, without representing them as either totally innocent victims or damned sex traitors."

Born in Ireland in 1957 and raised in Trinidad, **Shani Mootoo** is an Indo-Trinidadian-Canadian writer. *Out on Main Street* is her first book of short fiction; her first novel, *Cereus Blooms at Night*, was a finalist for Canada's Giller Prize and the Chapters / Books in Canada First Novel Award. She is also a visual artist (participating in many solo and group shows) and video-maker; her videos include "English Lesson" (1991) and "Wild Women in the Woods" (1993), which have been shown at international festivals. She divides her time between Vancouver and New York.

"Out on Main Street" first appeared in Mootoo's 1993 collection of the same name.

Sigrid Nielsen grew up in rural California, lived in Santa Fe and New Mexico, then moved to Scotland in 1979. She co-founded Lavender Menace (later West and Wilde) lesbian and gay community bookshop in Edinburgh. She has also worked as a bus driver, hotel auditor, and ghostwriter. As well as publishing short stories, she has edited, with Gail Chester, *In Other Words: Writing as a Feminist* (Hutchinson Education, 1987).

"The Woman She Came to Seek" was first published in *And Thus Will I Freely Sing: An Anthology of Gay and Lesbian Writing from Scotland*, ed. by Tony Davidson (Edinburgh: Polygon, 1989).

There Nielsen described this story as "a collision between two novels, *The Sorceress Graeylaw*, about Catriona and Anne, and *Liberties*, a novel about Jean, Céline and three other gay characters in the French Revolution."

Jane Rule was born in Plainfield, New Jersey, in 1931. She grew up in the American West and California, and moved to Canada in 1956. She is probably best known for her 1964 novel, *Desert of the Heart*, which inspired the film by Donna Deitch, *Desert Hearts*. Her fiction is particularly noteworthy for its portrayal of varied communities; her books include *This Is Not For You, Theme for Diverse Instruments, Contract with the World, Outlander, A Hot-Eyed Moderate, Inland Passage, Against the Season, Memory Board*, and *After the Fire*. Her *Lesbian Images* (1975) was a groundbreaking study of lesbian themes in modern literature.

In 1976, Rule settled on Galiano Island off the coast of British Columbia. She involved herself in the defence of the Toronto gay magazine *Body Politic* during censorship attacks by the Canadian Government in the 1970s and 80s.

"Middle Children" was first published in the *Ladder* magazine; it was first collected in Rule's *Theme for Diverse Instruments* (1975).

Born in Inverness in Scotland, 1962, **Ali Smith** now lives in Cambridge, England. She has worked as a sandwich packer, cinema usher and university lecturer. After writing poetry and several plays (produced in London and Edinburgh), she won the Macallan *Scotland on Sunday* Short Story competition in 1994, and published her first collection of short stories, *Free Love*, a year later. Her first novel, *Like*, appeared in 1997.

"Free Love" is the title story of Smith's 1995 collection.

Ali Smith says: "It took two days – one to write it and one to hone it, and I wish all stories were as accommodating."

Born in 1940 to Russian Jewish emigrés in London, **Michelene Wandor** was involved with the Women's Liberation movement from 1969 and edited its first English essay collection, *The Body Politic*, in 1972. She was a member of the *Tales I Tell My Mother* group along with Sara Maitland, Zoe Fairbairns, Valerie Miner and Michèle Roberts. Wandor is known for her journalism, poetry (*Gardens of Eden* and *Touch Papers*), stage plays, dramatizations of fiction for radio and television, studies of theatre (*Look Back in Gender, Understudies*, and *Drama Today: A Critical Guide to British Drama 1970–90*) and anthologies of plays (*Plays by Women*, Methuen). Her short stories are collected in *Guests in the Body* (1986).

"Some of My Best Friends" first appeared in *Passion Fruit*, edited by Jeanette Winterson (Pandora, 1986).

Marnie Woodrow is a 30-year-old writer living in Toronto, Canada. Having worked as a dishwasher, bartender, book-store slave, amusement park moose and house-cleaner, she describes herself as "a university drop-out with very few regrets". She is the author of two short fiction collections, *Why We Close Our Eyes When We Kiss* (1991) and *In the Spice House* (1996). Her forthcoming novel is called *Dragging the River for Angels*, and she is currently working on a third collection of short fiction. Woodrow can be reached through her website at www.pneumatic.com/spicehouse.

"In the Spice House" is the title story of Woodrow's 1996 collection.

Marnie Woodrow says: "This story was first composed at high speed on the back of sheets of scrap paper. I wrote it before going to work, a Sunday morning. It was the first rough draft I ever let anyone read in longhand, right away, and the person I showed it to still acts as my literary eyes and ears."

Shay Youngblood was born in Columbus, Georgia to a family of loving, old black women, and "raised as an only child by seven mothers". Her poetry and short stories appeared in magazines including *Essence, Catalyst* and *Conditions*. Her 1989 collection, *The Big Mama Stories*, was adapted into a full-length play called *Shakin' the Mess Outta Misery*. Youngblood's highly acclaimed first novel, *Soul Kiss* (1998), was a finalist in the Ferro-Grumly Awards.

"Funny Women" is taken from *The Big Mama Stories* (1989).